Readers love *Dare to Love Forever*
by JAKE C. WALLACE

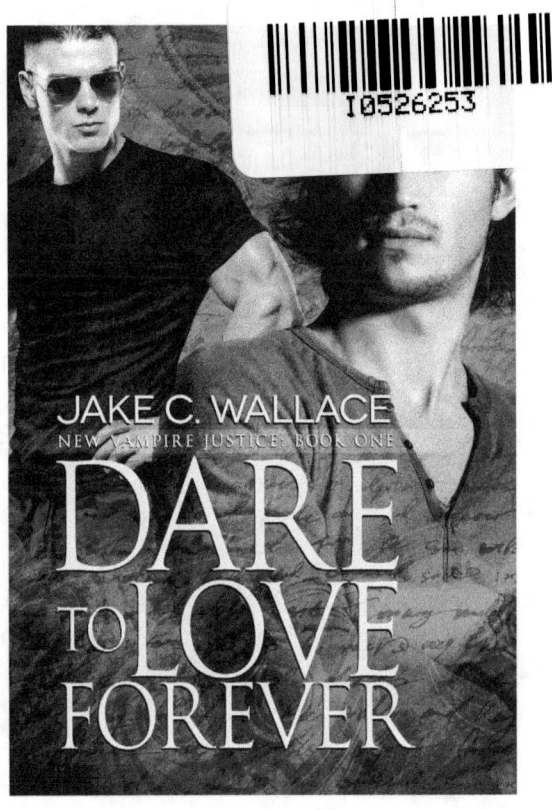

I0526253

JAKE C. WALLACE
NEW VAMPIRE JUSTICE: BOOK ONE
DARE TO LOVE FOREVER

By Jake C. Wallace

Soul Seekers

NEW VAMPIRE JUSTICE
Dare to Love Forever
A Chance for Us

Published by Dreamspinner Press
www.dreamspinnerpress.com

A CHANCE FOR US

JAKE C. WALLACE

DREAMSPINNER
PRESS

Published by
DREAMSPINNER PRESS

5032 Capital Circle SW, Suite 2, PMB# 279, Tallahassee, FL 32305-7886 USA
www.dreamspinnerpress.com

A Chance for Us
© 2016 Jake C. Wallace.

Cover Art
© 2016 Reese Dante.
http://www.reesedante.com
Cover content is for illustrative purposes only and any person depicted on the cover is a model.

ISBN: 978-1-63477-721-6
Digital ISBN: 978-1-63477-722-3
Library of Congress Control Number: 2016913067
Published November 2016
v. 1.0

Printed in the United States of America
∞
This paper meets the requirements of
ANSI/NISO Z39.48-1992 (Permanence of Paper).

For my sister, who's always been there, even during the tough times, and accepts me for who I really am. She has no idea how much that means to me. Love you, sis.

CHAPTER 1

JUSTIN MASTERS needed something to clear his spinning head. He was having another bad day, one of the worst he'd had in weeks. He clutched his knees to his chest, squeezing as tight as he could, the pressure making it hard to breathe. His fingers were knotted together and ached. His need to feel anchored, tethered to the earth, was like a hard lump rising in his throat. He bit the inside of his cheek, the pain cathartic. Any moment, he was sure he'd be stuffed back into his head, trapped and helpless as he had been for over seven years.

That period of time held only memories of fear and anxiety and pain. If someone were to ask him where he'd been and what he'd done, he couldn't answer, but ask him how he'd felt and the words would be incongruous with one another. While he recalled fear and pain, he also recalled warmth and safety. Now he struggled every day to keep from returning to that vaguely remembered version of hell.

Until five months ago, he'd been nearly catatonic, a prisoner in his own mind, drifting, fearful, mindless, knowing he was alive in some reality, but not having a coherent thought to make sense of anything around him. Then he woke up. Slowly, painfully, he came back to reality in a body seven years older than he remembered, to the fact that his mother died while he was away, and to Max, a vampire.

Like a newborn babe opening his eyes, Justin recalled his first clear vision of Max, the New Vampire Justice Lieutenant, with the kind blue-green eyes, round wire-framed glasses, wavy, shoulder-length blond hair tied messily in a ponytail, and a smile that immediately warmed the coldness of Justin's last seven hellish years. The man Justin currently awaited to enter the room where he spent every day, useless and cast aside. Justin wasn't on top of anyone's list. Just a collateral human the vampires had rescued in their battle with the evil Jameson Merrick, the man who'd tried to use Justin's former boyfriend, Carson Locke, to gain the power to rule the vampire world.

Just Carson's name sent a shiver of fear and confusion through Justin. At sixteen, he'd fallen in love with the reclusive, beautiful Carson, the Tabula Rasa vampire whose bite could turn a person into a mindless, reprogrammable husk. But six short months later, they were both kidnapped. Justin could still recall the moment when Carson was forced to bite him, which sent him into those seven years trapped in purgatory.

Shit, speak of the devil. Carson stood in the doorway with an NVJ officer, no doubt coming to save the day. He owed Justin much more than that. Justin glared at his former boyfriend as he rubbed his palms over his thighs. The constant, dull ache in his thigh bones was a relentless reminder of the gunshot wounds from their kidnappers when Carson had refused to bite Justin. Justin closed his eyes as visual memories of the searing agony and terror of knowing he was going to die ramped up his anxiety. He'd loved Carson, and had felt responsible for their situation. The pain in Carson's eyes, his tears as their kidnapper commanded he bite Justin or allow him to die, still haunted him daily.

"I-it's okay, C-Carson," Justin whispered. *"G-gonna ki-kill me anyway."*

He'd given Carson, a Tabula Rasa vampire, permission to bite him, had known that acquiescence meant death. The pain of two gunshots in his thighs assured that he was ready. But Justin hadn't died that day when Carson sank his teeth into his neck. What had happened was worse than any death he could have imagined. With one bite, Carson had killed Justin while his body lived on.

And then he'd woken up to no memories and Max. Seven years after Carson bit him. A miracle, he'd been told. Why had he woken? No one could explain past the fact that Carson, with some scary, ancient thing inside of him, had entered the building where Jameson Merrick had held Justin and an NVJ team, including Max. Carson had pulled Justin from one hell to live another.

Justin gasped in a breath. Fuck, he'd done it again. Max would be pissed when he got there. And he'd come because he was the only one who could help. Then he'd see that Justin had gotten lost in his head again, lost in the nightmares of his past. Max would want to know why he hadn't used the techniques from his therapist, Walt. Justin grunted. They never worked. But it didn't matter. He was too far gone to get back on his own. At that point, only physical pain or being wrapped up, practically restrained until he couldn't move, would center him and bring him back to reality.

Great, there was Doc talking with Carson. Doc's solutions always came in the form of a needle. Drug him. Justin banged his forehead against his knees. Maybe he could bang hard enough to knock himself out, maybe have a stroke, become a vegetable like Tommy Dennison upstairs. Then Max wouldn't be burdened with a dependent head case. Max was always pushing Justin to be more independent, rely on himself more. Max, who'd rescued Justin, taken him in, held him whenever he thought he'd shake apart, helped as Justin relearned to take care of himself, his cooking, his laundry, and, hell, even to go outside without falling to pieces. Max's bid to stop Justin from relying on him was like a knife to his chest.

Justin had fallen in love with Max. Max who was caring, attentive, unflappable. Justin had fallen in love with his crooked grin, his wavy blond hair with the sides that always escaped his ponytail, the way his glasses were always askew, his quiet and contemplative demeanor. Justin believed Max didn't see a potential lover in him, but a needy little brother. Despite being only two years younger than Max, Justin was still that sixteen-year-old, but now in a man's body. He couldn't make it through a day without somehow clinging to Max. What kind of life was that for a straight man who wasn't even related to Justin?

His chest tightened and pushed his rate of breathing higher. Something horrible was going to happen, and it wouldn't be his own death as he hoped. He couldn't breathe, couldn't think, and was going to lose it big-time. Again.

MAX KINCAID shuffled through the papers on his desk, searching for the report on a missing human. He was dead tired. Sleep had become a commodity during the last five months. His usual good mood was in the crapper, and he needed a vacation. Fat chance of that. His team had been appointed by the director of New Vampire Justice, Carina Williams, also a member of the president's cabinet, to clean up the corruption left behind by the former Director for the Advancement of Vampires, Jameson Merrick. Everyone on Max's team, which included a half-dozen NVJ officers, had moved their lives to Washington DC, a place Max hated with a passion. He was knee-deep in political bullshit and people—fucking people everywhere crammed into a sixty-three-mile area. He'd grown up outside of Utica, NY, which could be considered large for a city, but Washington was just too much. And if it was too much for him, he knew it had to be terrifying for Justin.

Director Lincoln Samuels—Max still laughed at the title his best friend had acquired—had moved New Vampire Justice Headquarters from the center of the city to southwest DC on the Anacostia River. Taking his entire task force to DC was dependent on stipulations agreed to by the entire team. In the end, the NVJ headquarters housed several DC NVJ teams, the new Center for the Advancement of Vampires, and a state-of-the-art clinic headed by Simon "Doc" Reynolds, separate apartments for the task force and their families, and amenities such as a gym, cafeteria, and an Internet café. Max and Justin had settled into the fortress, which had become a sanctuary for both of them.

Max pulled off his glasses and rubbed his eyes. If a minute went by that he didn't worry about Justin, it would be a fucking miracle. In the past five months, Justin had made incredible strides in emerging from a body on autopilot. God, it seemed like a lifetime ago Max's team had been ambushed by Jameson Merrick while on a retrieval mission for Justin. Shoved alone, or what he thought was alone, into a small cinder-block room, Max had found Justin. While he'd aged from pictures Max had seen, Max knew it was him. But he hadn't been prepared for the state Justin was in.

Justin's greenish-hazel eyes, dull and lifeless, had stared out into nothing. No emotion. No sign his mind was even in the room. If not for breathing, he could have been mistaken for a statue. A very handsome statue with his creamy skin, freckles dotting his nose and cheeks, which matched his sandy-red hair, and slim body.

Even though Justin wouldn't respond, Max had spoken about anything and everything, anything to drown out the quiet. At night when the temperature dropped, Max held Justin close to his side, sharing warmth to stop Justin from shivering. Even when night ended, Max still held him, as Justin rested his head on Max's shoulder. Eventually he had looked up at Max. That's when he'd caught the cognizance in Justin's eyes. Hearing Max say his name had brought a frown to Justin's face that quickly faded. Justin had snuggled in closer and placed his hand on Max's chest.

Max recalled how that gentle touch had caused his heart to skip a beat. Even then that memory stirred something inside. He wished he could make sense of—

The ringing of his phone saved him from his memories.

"Kincaid."

"Hey, princess, we're all in the conference room. Think you could join us?" Lincoln asked with a faux sickly sweet tone.

"Waiting for my engraved invitation, sweetheart."

Lincoln snorted. "Consider this your invitation. Drag your ass."

Max hung up the phone and rummaged through the files, finally locating the one he wanted. After grabbing a cup of synthetic blood, he sauntered down the hallway. No way was he rushing for Lincoln. He might be a director in the NVJ, but to Max, he was still the skinny kid from down the street Max could beat up. Well, until they hit puberty, when Lincoln shot up to over six feet tall in a year and a half, towering over Max. But if they tussled, Max wouldn't go down easy.

All eyes were on Max as he entered the conference room. Doc, wearing his white lab coat, smirked knowingly from his seat next to Lincoln. Max wondered if he slept in it. Next to Doc, John Dennison wore his usual scowl. The rest of the team were seated around the table: Taylor Myers, Maggie Wright, Tia Warez, Dwayne Simpson—who was the newest human member—and, shit, lab technician Casey Daley. Max hadn't expected her to be there. She smiled sweetly when he glanced her way. He nodded in greeting, maybe a little too sharply, because her smile wavered. Lately, her innuendos about resuming their former relationship had increased. He figured the excuse that he needed time to adjust to DC and Justin was wearing thin.

"Thanks for joining us." Dennison scowled deeper. "Some of us do have shit to do."

Max overcame the urge to give the uptight man the middle finger. He was a good officer, but a shitty vampire. How his wife put up with him, Max would never know.

"Yes. Try to be on time." There was a twinkle in Lincoln's eyes as he pushed a folded piece of paper down the table. Max snagged it but didn't bother to look. After Max's last late arrival, Lincoln had bet Max he'd be late again. He was now on the hook for beer and wings.

"Okay, let's get started." Lincoln opened a folder before him. "As you all know, we're getting more cases and don't have the manpower to handle them. I've brought on three new hires, vetted by Max and myself. Here's their information." He dropped a pile of papers into the center of the table, and everyone grabbed a sheet. "They all have excellent backgrounds. Two are currently NVJ, one from Buffalo, the other from Charleston. The last one is former military."

Heads went up at that last bit of info.

"You hired a human?" Tia asked, scorn visible on her face.

Leave it to her to shout out her opinion. She harbored no love for the Nons—a vampire term for humans. Seemed her entire family were anti-

Non. Not unheard of, but vampires had assimilated into human culture and most just wanted to live a peaceful and successful life. That wasn't easy given that vampires weren't afforded the same rights as humans. Banned from serving in the military, holding office, accessing human doctors and hospitals, along with dozens of other illogical discriminations, vampires weren't thought to be of the human race by some radicals. Elongated pointy canines and the need for specific proteins found in blood were the only differences between them. Seeing their "fangs" when they smiled or spoke or the fact they drank blood were the only ways to tell vampires and humans apart. Vampires relied on synthetic blood to fulfill their need. Not human blood. Biting was illegal except in a sanctioned bite club. Max shuddered at the thought of biting and sucking blood from another person.

Dwayne waving his hand at Tia caught Max's attention. "Hey, Tia, human here." Dwayne smiled wide. He loved pushing the Nons racism button with Tia. If anyone knew about racism, it was Dwayne, who was both human and black.

Tia looked him over, her scorn fading. "Yeah, well, I don't think of you as human. You're just Dwayne."

That got a tense laugh from some around the table. Apparently, Dwayne had broken through her prejudices, but only concerning him.

When Tia looked to Lincoln, he narrowed his eyes. "You got a problem with who I hired?"

Tia gritted her teeth, no doubt to keep from mouthing off to her boss. He was some scary shit when he got pissed.

"No, sir."

"Good. Keep it that way. We were brought to DC to clean up Merrick's mess and the corruption that went along with him, and to find the three hundred missing vampires. In five months we've located or confirmed the deaths of three-quarters of them, took down a dozen or so of Merrick's conspirators, which included politicians and influential leaders across the country, and we've reestablished the NVJ as a by-the-book agency."

Max snorted and there were covert laughs around the table. Not always so by the book, but close enough. Lincoln glared at them, then smirked.

"But we've still got work to do, and we need all the help we can get. We're receiving more requests from the Nons police. Three calls just today from Metropolitan PD asking for help." Lincoln pointed to Max, and everyone looked at him. "Max has a new case involving another missing human at the Mystique. Over 60 percent of our cases now involve both humans and vampires. Having human team members will be an asset when

dealing with some of those precincts that tend to be more vampi-phobic."
Lincoln ran his hand over his short hair. "We've definitely landed in Oz and
been smacked with culture shock. It's a different climate here than in Utica.
There we had a greater acceptance between vampires and humans, while
here the sides always seem to be clashing. Something's gotta give." He
sighed and leaned back in his chair, throwing down his pen.

"What is the main theory about the rise in cases?" Maggie asked. Out
of all the team members, Max found her the most personable and stable.
They all had their issues, some more than others. Out of all of the team
members, she was the officer he'd pair with when there was trouble.

Dennison grunted. "What do you think? Power. The place stinks of it,
and everyone wants in. I figure most people here would sell their mothers to
increase their cash flow. It's the culture, and now more vampires are moving
in to get their share. When they aren't getting it, they're fighting back. It's
all going to come to a head, and only one side can come out on top."

Max shot Lincoln a look of surprise and got one back. Was this increasing
violence between vampires and humans Jameson Merrick's predicted
downfall of the vampire race? Vampires fighting for equal rights caused
vampi-phobes to fight back, all fueled by inequality and fearmongering by
politicians and the media. Subjugate a group long enough and they will
inevitably fight back. Jameson Merrick had fought back, with the ultimate
plan of vampire domination—well, that and being a psychopath. Claiming
that Nons only paid lip service to equality for vampires, Jameson predicted
the destruction of the vampire race. Funny, because Merrick unleashing an
ancient power inside of Carson to strip humans of their power could have
meant death for both humans and vampires if Carson hadn't gained control.
In the end, Merrick had been killed by his own creation.

What if…. No. Merrick couldn't have known the future, even being a
shaman who possessed some powers to manipulate energy. Anyone could
proselytize the current tensions coming to a head. But total destruction?

Max looked at the folder he'd brought as Taylor reported on an
incident with the Nons police. In the folder were reports and investigation
notes from the Metropolitan PD of a missing human last seen in a bite
club. With the information about the bite club, the case immediately went
to the Metropolitan Unified Police Agency. The MUPA was formed out of
necessity when turf wars erupted between Nons police and the NVJ after
its creation in the seventies. Liaisons—just a fancy word for mediators—
reviewed all cases involving both humans and vampires and then, based on
certain criteria, assigned cases to the appropriate agency. A middleman in

law enforcement, Max hadn't experienced altercations with Nons police, but the turf wars still existed.

The case had come to the NVJ due to the bite club. Nons police had no jurisdiction over bite clubs and couldn't legally enter one for purposes of investigation. Devon Hastings was last seen at the Mystique, an exclusive bite club dead in the center of DC on 1432 Pennsylvania Ave. SE. The fifth human missing from the same club in less than a year with no solid leads.

"Max?"

Max looked up and saw Lincoln pointing to the door. A young NVJ rookie stood by the door, her eyes wide. "Lieutenant Kincaid. You're needed upstairs."

"Fuck," Max muttered as Lincoln gave him that knowing gaze.

He didn't care what Lincoln thought of Justin. He was a responsibility that Max had to see to the end.

CHAPTER 2

"GET THE fuck away from me!"

Justin couldn't let anyone touch him, didn't trust them. He felt like bugs were crawling under his skin, like he couldn't control anything, like he couldn't breathe. His thoughts raced, tumbling one over the other, and they wouldn't stop coming. This was worse than it had ever been, and he'd let it get that bad.

"Calm down, Justin. No one's going to hurt you." Walter, who happened to be on-site that day, had come running into the room like some kind of professional hero. Fuck him. Fuck them all.

Justin knew what was coming if he didn't calm down, if he didn't "self-regulate," as Walt liked to call it. How could he self-regulate when his mind was a fucking blender set on frappé? Nothing made any sense at the moment, nothing but... Max.

Why the fuck did he have to depend on the one person who didn't want him, who wanted him to get better so he could get rid of him?

Justin punched the cinder block wall, the pain rushing into his hand and arm. Maybe he broke some bones, but it didn't matter. Even if he had, they'd heal three times faster than other humans. It had been that way since he'd woken. Bruises, cuts, sprains, breaks to bones didn't matter; they all healed freakishly fast. And no one knew why, not even Doc, who was supposed to be some brilliant vampire doctor.

"Justin!"

Carson stood in the doorway, keeping his distance, as he should. This was all his fault, and Justin would have taken his anger out on him if Carson wasn't some kind of super vampire.

"Go away, Carson! This is your fucking fault! You stole my life!"

The hurt couldn't have been more apparent on Carson's face if he'd cried. Then it was gone. The stare from his brown eyes was intense. At least he didn't have the red irises and black tattooed language all over his body anymore. That had been way creepy.

A buzzing sound filled Justin's head and dizziness hit him hard. Justin staggered back. Carson frowned, and the annoying sound expanded and filled Justin's head. Carson was trying to enter his head when he wasn't supposed to be using his powers. They'd been fucked-up ever since his battle with Jameson Merrick, to the point he had nosebleeds, high blood pressure, and exaggerated weakness when he accessed them. One time, the entire right side of his body had been temporarily paralyzed as if he'd had a stroke.

"Carson, stop that crap. You're gonna hurt yourself, you idiot." The pressure in Justin's head increased, pain coating his skull. "Stop!"

Carson's body jerked, and his eyes rolled back in his head. He crumpled to the ground and wasn't moving. Fuck, what had he done?

One of the officers hanging back rushed to Carson. "Shit. Get Doc up here. And don't tell Lincoln. He'll freak." The other rookie officer in the hallway took off.

Justin's anger was replaced by fear, fear that he'd screwed up and hurt Carson. Had his anger caused Carson to pass out? Justin just wanted to feel safe and not so confused all the time. Backing into the corner, he slid down the wall, crouching on the floor. Cradling his head in his hands, he tried to catch a thought, calm his breathing, keep his mind from crumbling back into nothing.

"Justin? Hey."

Justin curled tighter into himself. So many times, he'd jumped into Max's arms when he was too far gone to get himself back. But that was before he knew Max only thought of him as a responsibility, probably a burden.

Max touched his shoulder, and warm tendrils flowed over his skin. Damn, he didn't want to like the touch, and he wanted to pull away. But already his heart was slowing and his breaths evening out. Max was there, and he would be safe.

"Talk to me." But Justin didn't know what to say.

"What happened to him?" Justin heard Doc ask, probably looking Carson over.

"He was trying to calm Justin, and then he collapsed." Of course Walt would rat him out.

"He knows he's not supposed to try to link with anyone's mind. I think he just passed out."

"What the fuck? Carson!" Lincoln roared. Justin looked up to see him kneel over the unconscious Carson. "What the hell happened?"

Well, Justin might be safe with Max there, that was, until Lincoln killed him. Justin grabbed Max's hand in desperation, the connection settling his mind.

"I didn't touch him," Justin whispered, and his body shook harder.

"I know. It's okay." Max's gentle gaze, his abject expression of concern, went straight to Justin's heart. Why couldn't Max see him, love Justin as much as Justin loved him?

Max sat behind Justin on the floor, pulling him back against his chest. Max wrapped his arms tightly around Justin's body, his grip unrelenting, near painful. Max's legs followed his arms, wrapping around his waist, hooking at the ankles. Justin focused on the Converse sneakers Max wore. The snug embrace immediately lowered his rate of breathing, and the confining immobility was like a shot of a relaxant. He shuddered from the full body contact.

Resting his chin on Justin's shoulder, Max whispered, "It's going to be okay." The soothing tone rolled over him. "I promise."

Justin knew that no one could promise him that. He needed to get back to their apartment, but there was no way he was getting away so easily. Anything he said to defend himself, Lincoln would throw back at him. Not that the director was ever really mean to him. Commanding, confident, maybe even arrogant, but generally fair. Except when it came to Carson. No one fucked with Carson.

IT HAD taken a while for the drama to calm down, but Justin was finally in his bed at the apartment he shared with Max. To Justin's relief, Carson woke and confessed that he'd tried to enter Justin's mind before he passed out, clearing Justin of any wrongdoing—well, not all of it. He'd freaked out and pulled most of the building into the uproar, if you went by John Dennison's side of the story. At least this time Doc didn't need to drug him.

Max, in his usual caring and helpful manner, led him back to the apartment, never once raising his voice or chastising him. He never pushed, never questioned Justin, never tried to force him into talking, explaining, into doing anything. Sometimes that calm demeanor made Justin want to scream, get him to react. Say anything, something.

His head was partially clear. Settled was all he could call it, but it wouldn't last. His meltdowns would get old fast. Sooner rather than later, Max would pawn Justin off on someone else. He had to get his shit together, but he didn't know how.

MAX LEANED against the kitchen counter, arms crossed, staring at the floor. Lincoln and Carson sat at the table. Doc rested his hip against the center island. The situation felt like an intervention.

"His episodes are getting worse," Doc said, breaking the silence. "While they aren't as often, they're increasing in magnitude. And his last brain scan was off. I didn't like the look of it."

"What do you mean?" Carson was pale, with large, dark circles under his eyes. He looked as if he were sick with something. He never should have tried to intervene with Justin.

Doc sighed. "I'm not sure. Since he woke up, the scans have always had anomalies, but lately there are more."

Carson rubbed his head. "Maybe that's why I couldn't get into his mind. I wanted to calm him, but when I tried, it was like something shot into my head, and I was out."

Lincoln scowled at Carson in a loving manner. How he managed that, Max had no clue. "You shouldn't have been trying to do anything, baby. You could have caused permanent damage. We don't know why you're having these serious reactions when using your powers, but why risk it?"

"Because I can't not help. I can't not try." Carson looked down. "If I have to live with the crap Jameson shoved into me, I should be able to use it for some good."

Lincoln's face softened, and there was that guilt again. Guilt for feeling what Carson was going through was his fault. Lincoln put his arm around Carson's shoulders and drew him close, kissing him on the temple.

Lincoln was a Sanatore vampire, one of six known species of vampires with some kind of special ability. For Lincoln, his blood could heal other vampires, but with a price. Healing Carson had bonded them, but no one could have predicted Carson would be the reincarnation of a vampire never seen before. A Salutem, as Jameson had called him.

"Are you okay, Carson?" Max hated to see Carson so drained. He'd lost his ability to affect objects with his energy after defeating Jameson. Entering the minds of others, sensing their thoughts, moods, and intentions was still possible, but to the detriment of his health.

"I'm good," Carson said a little too quickly.

"No, you're not. You need to stay out of Justin's head." Lincoln looked to Doc.

"Is Justin dangerous?"

Max shot him a look. "He's not dangerous. He's more scared than anything." And who could blame him? There were times Max just wanted to wrap him up tight and keep him safe, but that wouldn't help him become an independent human.

"I can't answer that. The instability of his thought processes is certainly affecting his recovery. But why they're unstable is unclear to me. I don't know anything about individuals who've suffered the effects of a Tabula Rasa bite. We all know how rare they are, and their bites are even rarer. There's no record of anyone ever recovering. Maybe having been under those effects for so long is having a negative impact. Or...."

"Or?" Max prodded Doc to continue.

"Something could be keeping him from healing on an emotional level. Thoughts and feelings and emotions can affect brain waves, can keep someone stuck where they are."

"But he's seeing a counselor, right?" Carson asked.

Max ran his hand through his hair, pulling a large chunk from the ponytail. He yanked the elastic band out in frustration and threw it onto the counter. "I've attended some of his counseling sessions lately, and they've been rough. His emotions and moods are all over the map. One second he's laughing, then yelling, then crying. His reliance on me for keeping an even keel is... problematic."

Doc raised a questioning eyebrow. He did that often instead of asking for clarification.

Lincoln had no issue asking. "Problematic?"

"I've been there from the beginning, from the moment he started becoming cognizant of the world. He feels safe with me because he's latched onto me like I'm a mother duck."

Lincoln laughed. Max bristled, causing Lincoln to raise his hands in supplication. "If you think he sees you as a mother, then you're sorely—owww!"

Carson gave Lincoln a death glare. And for several moments, they stared at each other.

Max rolled his eyes. "It's not polite to speak telepathically to each other when others are in the room."

"I concur. If you have something to say, spit it out," Doc said.

Carson's face reddened while Lincoln held his usual stoic expression. Neither budged. Then Carson spoke. "Let me talk to him."

Max choked on a laugh. "I don't think that's such a good idea. He was pretty pissed off at you today."

Lincoln turned to Carson. "No way. You aren't going near him."

Carson glanced sideways at Lincoln and then waved Max's concerns off. "He needs someone to blame. We've had a few civil moments in the past few weeks. Besides, if he's angry at me, I might actually get something out of him. I knew him before all of this happened to him."

Loved him, Max thought, then shook off the odd thought.

"Just let me try. What could it harm?"

"I don't want you to get hurt, baby." Lincoln rested his forehead against Carson's and cupped his cheek. Max pursed his lips at their show of affection. They loved each other deeply. Max feared he'd never have that again. He'd already lost the love of his life to cancer. He hadn't found anyone special since Grace.

"I have to try to help him, and I promise, just talking, no use of my powers. Justin's right. I did this to him."

"Forced to do it," Lincoln added.

"Still. I have to try." Carson put on that pathetic, mushy, pleading expression that Lincoln fell for every time.

Lincoln nodded. "I'm going to be right here, though."

"No, you're not. He won't hurt me or anyone else. So you're going back to work." He pointed to Lincoln and then looked to Max and Doc. "And so are the rest of you. I can take care of myself." Carson stood and ended the conversation.

Max coughed out the word, "Whipped."

Lincoln growled and stood with a menacing glare. "Fuck you, Kincaid."

Doc and Max both laughed heartily and followed Lincoln from the apartment. Before he closed the door behind him, Max looked back at Carson, who was waiting quietly in the living room. Max debated what to say, but in the end just closed the door.

JUSTIN HEARD the front door shut and shot out of bed. Max never left without telling him he was leaving. When he pulled his bedroom door open, he gasped, seeing Carson standing there.

"Oh shit."

"Sorry. I didn't mean to scare you. Can we talk for a minute?"

Justin wasn't sure how to answer. He'd seen Carson dozens of times around the NVJ. They'd even exchanged a few words once Justin overcame the panic attacks caused by seeing his former boyfriend. But now they were alone.

"Where's Max?" Justin looked past Carson but didn't see anyone. Why would Max leave him alone with Carson? If that wasn't a kick in the teeth.

"He had to go back to work—you know, save the vampire world and everything."

Carson's quip fell flat with Justin. "I'm tired. Maybe we can talk tomorrow." *Please leave.* Justin could already feel his skin starting to crawl, a precursor to losing his shit. Twice in one day might get him shoved into a bed in Medical with a Thorazine drip.

Carson cocked his head. "I won't hurt you, Justin. I just want to talk."

Carson stepped away and moved to the couch. Justin, knowing he didn't have a choice, carefully tread across the blue area rug, soft beneath his bare feet. He sat in the chair farthest from Carson. It wasn't that he was afraid Carson would hurt him. Logically, he knew that he wouldn't. The illogical, primal part of his brain was what was on alert. There was no arguing once it targeted a possible threat. Walt told Justin he had an overexcited fight-or-flight reflex due to the traumatic events of his past with Carson. When he asked Walt how to fix that, he said something about restructuring thought processes, but Justin had been only partially available that day for conversation so he couldn't recall much. With Carson there, Justin was on high alert and focused.

Carson wore his usual jeans, T-shirt, and runners. Carson worked in some capacity for the NVJ, but didn't wear the NVJ uniform—black T-shirt with NVJ in white letters across the chest and black cargo pants tucked into military-style black boots. Maybe, Carson thought, along with his dark hair, it was too much black, or maybe he was bucking the system.

"How're you doing?" Carson leaned back against the couch, no doubt to appear less threatening. He and Justin were about the same height, but seeing Carson so tall, filled out, and matured as a man was still startling. They'd been intimate, short of intercourse, at sixteen, but Justin felt he didn't know the man before him anymore. His love for Carson was in the past with that boy he'd met jumping a fence.

"Good," Justin blurted out, almost forgetting to answer.

Carson studied Justin silently. That caused the bugs under his skin to scurry. He eyed his bedroom door and the sanctuary behind the wood with longing.

"You wanted to talk?"

Carson merely nodded and continued staring. Justin flicked his thumbnail to center himself. Jesus, why was Carson staring?

"I can't read you."

"You're trying right now? Isn't that kind of rude?" Just because Justin wasn't as together as the rest of them didn't mean he didn't have a right to privacy.

Carson looked embarrassed. "I'm sorry. You're right. I'm not trying to read your mind or anything, because we know how well that goes for me. Just trying to get a general sense of how you're feeling."

"You sure you should be doing that? You tried to get into my mind earlier and look what happened." That had been annoying, and Justin didn't want him to try again.

Carson leaned forward and rested his elbows on his knees. "I did because I wanted to help you to calm down, that's all. Even though I can influence the thoughts of others, I would never do that without permission unless it's an emergency or, well, if the job requires I do so. Or if I want my head to explode. I just wanted to send you calming thoughts, and I was afraid you were going to hurt yourself."

Probably more like he thought Justin might hurt others, but he kept his mouth shut. If he ever hurt anyone, Max would surely toss his ass to the curb.

"It didn't work." Nothing worked. Maybe heavy-duty medications would, which scared him to death. They'd doped him up once, and the effects had come too close to how he'd felt when he first woke. Foggy, spacey, confused. He didn't need any reminders.

"No, it didn't. I was blocked from going in too far. I'm not sure why, but it could have had something to do with the state you were in." Carson chewed on his bottom lip, and Justin knew exactly what that meant.

Justin grunted. "You don't believe that."

Carson looked surprised. "How did you know—"

"You chewed on your lip. You always did that whenever... well, you know."

A grin split Carson's face. "You remember that, huh?"

Justin remembered his life before being bitten, the memories clear. But there were times when fractured memories flooded his mind. Their familiarity was fleeting and hadn't come from his precatatonic state. Were memories surfacing from the black pit hiding those seven years? Had Carson seen any of them? There were some things about him no one should ever know.

"Yeah, but that doesn't mean I want to stroll down memory lane." Because that would just be hellish.

Carson grimaced. "Right. Well, I'm not sure why I was blocked, but when I tried to push against the resistance, what I got in return was like… feedback, you know, like from a sound system."

"To me it sounded like a buzzing sound. Made me dizzy."

"You can't stop what's happening, I mean, the panic and fear, can you?"

Justin frowned. "Of course I can't. Do you think I would run around acting like that if I could help it?"

"Sorry, that sounded like a question but was really meant as a confirmation. Your lack of control overwhelmed me. When I tried to find a source, I couldn't pinpoint any." Carson wrinkled his brow, as if he felt sorry for Justin.

"You felt that?" Justin had lost count of how many times he'd failed to convey that state of chaos in his head, and here Carson had experienced it firsthand.

"Yeah, I did, and I have to say I don't know how you handle it. I mean, it's what I imagine having a tornado in my head would feel like."

Justin sank back against the chair. He was so tired, and speaking with Carson only added to his fatigue. His life was fucked-up, he was sure, beyond any means on earth to repair it.

"I also learned something else that has me worried for you."

Of course there had to be more. "Don't tell me, I have a tumor or mad cow disease or something equally fatal." Morbid jokes were all he had at that point.

"No. But I know how you feel about Max."

CHAPTER 3

JUSTIN'S HEART seized, and he jumped from the chair without thought. "I don't know what you're talking about."

Carson stood as well, probably sensing Justin's plans to run. Had he told everyone about his feelings for Max? Had he told *Max*? He'd be mortified.

"Don't freak out, okay? I just want to talk."

"There's nothing to talk about. Max took me in and helped me. That's it."

Carson's face showed he was calling bullshit, but Justin didn't care. It was none of Carson's business.

"Okay, I can see how freaked you are about this, so I'll just say one thing. Be careful. Max is…." Carson's gaze flitted across the room, stopping on the top of the bookcase by the chair. The picture of Max's dead wife Grace was the only item of any interest among the books.

Grace. That was all Justin knew of her. Her name, what she looked like, and that she'd died. Max never spoke of her… ever.

Carson leaned forward and rested his elbows on his knees. "He's confused. Grace was sick for a long time, and he took care of her. He's only dated a few other *women* since then."

No lack of innuendo in that statement. Did Carson think Max had taken Justin in to atone for being unable to save his wife? A second chance? "I know he likes women, and it doesn't matter why he took me in. I don't expect anything from him." Justin pushed out Carson's suspicions trying to take root in his head. He did love Max, and he thought that someday the man could love him back. He believed Max interacted with him, talked to him, and touched him in a way that differed from the others in his life. He needed to be right about what he felt from Max.

"I didn't mean to upset you. I just don't want you to expect too much of Max and get hurt."

"I won't. I'm sorry, I really need to go. Thanks for your concern."

Justin rushed to get to his room before he lost it in front of Carson.

"Justin. Stop."

Why he obeyed that command, he had no clue.

"I want you to know how sorry I am for what I did to you. I know it doesn't mean much, but…." Carson's lip quivered.

Justin looked hard at Carson, trying to see the boy he once loved, but he'd changed so much. Maybe if he still had that boyish look, that thin frame, Justin could see him. Maybe it would be easier for him to connect the two.

"I…." Justin frowned. Why let Carson suffer any more because he couldn't sort his own thoughts? "Listen, you were forced to do what you did. Monrovia had already shot me twice in the legs and was about to shoot me in the face right in front of you. You saved me from that, and…." He couldn't say he was glad he hadn't died, because that was a lie. "You're feeling guilty for something you couldn't prevent. I don't blame you, Carson." That part was true, but when he had to blame someone, Carson was the logical person.

Justin stepped into his bedroom and shut the door before Carson could say anything more. He leaned against the wood, creating a barricade in case Carson tried to enter, but he heard the front door shut. Justin could finally breathe again. He focused on a single photo of him and Max pinned to his wall. Justin didn't own many things. Not much to own when you had only just returned to the land of the living, but of all of his meager possessions, that photo was what he cherished most. That photo, with Max's arm around his shoulders, both of them smiling, was a snapshot of what Justin wanted to be with Max. A happy, smiling normal couple in love.

How he would get there when he was a broken-down mess was beyond him.

MAX STOOD before the doors to the medical wing. What Doc said about Justin's brain waves and their irregularities had niggled at Max and blossomed into fear. Justin had already been through hell and back and didn't need anything else messing with his head.

He pushed through the doors into the quiet unit. Mostly the medical wing was for treating the NVJ officers and their families. But given that there were far fewer options for medical care for vampires than for humans, the unit was open for acute care, and from time to time, a civilian vampire with serious issues received treatment since Doc was a specialist in such things. Today, there was only one patient, and since it was lunchtime, Max knew where to find Doc.

Max made his way to the farthest room down the hallway. He stopped before the observation area's windows and looked in. Doc sat on a stool next to the bed, his lunch laid out beside the patient. As he ate, he talked to Tommy Dennison, who remained motionless, eyes closed as if he were asleep. But he wasn't merely sleeping. He'd been shot in the chest when everything with Jameson had come to blows. In the following days, he'd suffered a stroke and a severe infection and hadn't woken since. Doc and Tommy had something in the past between them, a serious kind of something with love, and had just reconnected when, *bam*, Tommy was shot.

Max knocked on the window. Doc turned, smiled, and then waved him in. Max entered and stepped up to the bed.

"Hey, Max. I was just regaling Tommy Boy here with tales of the world as we know it. Wasn't I?"

Doc patted Tommy on the shoulder, and his eyes opened.

Max jumped in surprise and pointed to the vampire who was supposedly in a coma. "He opened his eyes!"

Doc nodded with a somber expression. "Yeah, Tommy Boy can open his eyes."

As Max looked closer, he noticed the vacant look in Tommy's eyes as he stared at the ceiling.

"But… how can he open his eyes when he's in a coma?" Max couldn't believe Tommy opened his eyes.

Doc sat back on his stool. "Minimally conscious state. There are many stages of coma. He opens his eyes, and there are times he can even track people and objects. He makes facial expressions. His favorite lately is frowning. He can even answer yes and no questions occasionally, though without much reliability, but he's not what we consider awake." Doc rested his hand on top of Tommy's. "Sometimes he'll even hold my hand."

Man, that had to be rough, to get a response from someone you love, knowing they aren't aware you're there. "Will he eventually wake up?" Max recalled Grace's last days in her fight with cancer. She was in and out of a coma due to brain swelling. Worst time of his life. Max had done exactly what Doc did. He talked to her, touched her, because that's all he could do. He'd never felt so helpless, and there had been no hope because Grace was dying, but maybe it was different with Tommy.

Doc got off the stool and gathered the remnants of his lunch. He patted Tommy on the shoulder. "See you in a bit, Tommy Boy." He motioned for Max to follow him.

On the way down the hall, Hilary, one of the nurses, stopped them. She smiled wide, and Max returned the smile.

Doc tossed his lunch in the garbage can. "We need to turn Mr. Dennison in a half hour. I'll be back then. I left a list of labs, so please draw those now and get them to Casey."

"You got it," she said. "Max, you going out on Friday? A bunch of us are going into the city for drinks. Want to join us?"

Max had only been half listening. "I'm sorry. What?"

"Drinks Friday night in the city. Come along." She leaned closer, and Max could smell her perfume.

Justin wouldn't be able to handle a bar filled with noise and people. "I can't, but thanks for the invite."

When she pouted, Max crinkled his brow and wondered what was up. "If you change your mind, let me know. Bye, Max."

"Yeah, see ya, Hilary."

When they arrived at the main reception area, Doc leaned against the front counter. "Seems like someone's got a crush."

Max sucked in a breath and shook his head. "What? No… I don't, I—"

"Calm down, Romeo. I wasn't talking about you."

Max shoved his hands into his pockets, unsure what to say to that.

"Hilary was flirting with you, in case you didn't notice."

"I didn't."

Doc cocked his head, his gaze on Max, but he didn't speak.

Max cleared his throat, feeling as if he were under a microscope. "I wanted to talk to you about Justin. What you said earlier about his brain waves being off. Is that bad? I mean, he's not going to go back to the way he was, right?" Max wasn't sure he could handle seeing Justin like that again.

Doc crossed his arms. "I don't think he will. What I said this morning was the truth. I don't think this is an indication that his recovery is reversing. But what is happening, I haven't been able to pinpoint."

Max nodded and chewed on his lip.

Doc leaned closer. "Listen, if it would be easier on you, I could move him here. We have the rooms in the other wing that are set up like regular bedrooms. He'd be comfortable, and you wouldn't have to deal with the disruption to your life."

Max's mind reeled at the thought of not having Justin in his apartment. It wasn't right. It just wasn't. "No. He's mine."

Doc's eyes widened.

Jesus, what was he saying? "What I mean is he's mine to take care of. I can't just abandon him. He trusts me and I'm…." Fuck, what was he?

"You're what, Max?"

Yeah, what, Max? What the hell are you to Justin? Damned if he knew, so he came up with the best thing he could think of. "I'm like his big brother… family. He doesn't have anyone."

Doc narrowed his eyes. "A big brother, I see. Okay, big brother, just be careful with him. His reality may be different than yours."

Max frowned. "I don't know what that means."

"Hey, Max."

Max turned to see Lincoln waving him out of Medical. "Got your new recruit here. Let the good times roll." He grinned wide, exposing his fangs. Max rolled his eyes.

"Be right there. See ya later, Doc. Thanks."

"Later."

Max joined Lincoln in the hallway along with the tank standing beside him. The human was large, and his muscles bulged everywhere. He had to have at least a forty-five-inch chest. And his neck was as thick as a tree trunk. This guy was a serious gym rat. His hair wasn't more than light bristle on his head. On the side of his face was a jagged scar reaching from his temple over his cheek and jaw, ending at his collarbone. The scar pulled down one side of his mouth in a permanent frown. He wondered if it was a combat wound.

"Lieutenant Max Kincaid. Wesley Reiser."

"Welcome aboard." Max shook the large man's hand. He was average height, but what he lacked in height he made up for in width.

"Call me Wes."

"All right, ladies, you both get the pleasure of heading down to the Mystique." Lincoln handed a file folder to Wes. "Read up on the way."

Max grunted. The Mystique was high-end, for the wealthy and influential. "Aren't the higher dregs of society your domain?"

Lincoln made a sour face. "Yeah, well, I'm spreading the shit around. Don't get your boots dirty. When you get back, we need to talk about a lead concerning another possible location set up by Merrick."

That snapped Max's head up. "Seriously?"

Lincoln visibly stiffened. They'd been trying to locate the last of the missing vampires, dead or alive. Max knew Lincoln wanted alive, since he'd made it his mission to find a little boy named Manuel Hernandez, one of the missing vampires. His mother had died helping Lincoln and Carson escape from the NVJ building when they'd been held captive by a corrupt director of the NVJ. Lincoln had promised her he'd find the boy.

"Yeah, but probably dead like most of the others. I don't hold much faith in the lead either. Check in when you get back." He walked away.

Max smiled at the newest team member. "Follow me. We're going to the Mystique." Max turned and headed for the elevator with access to the garage.

"The bite club?" Wes asked as he followed.

Max smirked and nodded. "Yeah, the bite club."

JUSTIN NODDED off shortly after Carson left the apartment. He slept soundly until his regular dream—or more like nightmare—started again. The same as usual, he was in a darkened room with one light shining on him. Reclined in a chair, like one you'd sit in at the dentist, but he was laid out naked and restrained, so not a dental visit. Red and black wires attached to white pads were stuck to different parts of his body. Those wires led to a machine to the left of him. Horrified, he saw those pads were also attached to his penis, his balls, and his nipples. What the hell were they there for? He didn't even want to guess.

The voices of a few people murmuring came from beyond the pool of light, the darkness masking their faces. When he tried to move, nothing happened. Nothing at all. Not a flinch or a twitch. Even his eyes were immobile, his vision limited to straight ahead and whatever he could see in his peripheral vision.

His breath caught. He tried to shout, but his mouth wouldn't move, and no sound came out, not even a squeak. Trapped in his own body. He could breathe, swallow, blink, but nothing voluntary, nothing within his control. His breaths increased, a gasping sound filling the air as the terror took over. At that point in the dream, he always woke, sweating and shaking and terrified. But this time the dream didn't stop there, and he feared he wasn't dreaming.

As his chest heaved, a beeping noise he hadn't noticed increased, keeping time with his heart rate. A vein in his neck pulsed with each pump of his taxed heart. Had he fallen back into the comatose state? Was he trapped in his head again, his ability to command his body gone? Any memories he had that he could attribute to being catatonic could only be described as trying to see underwater, the vision blurry and the sounds muffled. But right then, every one of his senses were turned up on high, and he could see clearly, smell, feel, hear as if he were there.

He needed Max, wanted to scream for him, but only harder puffs of air came out of his mouth. Movement to his side caught his attention. A large body came closer. A man. He wore a black leather mask that covered his entire head and face. His T-shirt and jeans seemed out of place in what Justin believed to be a hospital.

"Hey. Welcome back," the man said in a deep voice. So familiar that he started to relax. "Just calm down. I've got what you need right here."

Welcome back? What the hell did that mean? Where was he? What he needed was to get out of there, but he couldn't do anything to help himself or even plead for mercy.

The man disappeared and then reappeared to his left. He flicked a switch on a large black box and fiddled with the knobs and buttons. Some of the wires attached to Justin's body were plugged into the machine. An overwhelming mix of emotions ran through him—anticipation, relief, dread, elation. Somehow, he knew what was coming, as if it had happened before.

"Now I know this isn't your favorite, but last time you took some major voltage. Even I was amazed at the pain you endured." The man leaned close to Justin's face, his breath hot and stinking of something spicy. He instantly knew that he hated the man and needed him at the same time. "It was beautiful how you suffered for me last time. I do enjoy these times when you're awake and in pain. A shame you won't remember it."

Justin wanted to scream, but he knew he wanted the pain more, needed the agony, and had no fucking clue why. He just needed it badly.

The man grinned. "Pain is the key."

He flipped the switch on the machine. Not just pain. Searing agony, like hundreds of needles, plunging into his cock, his balls and, *ohhh*, his fucking ass. His hole was stretched wide by something large, jolts of electricity attacking him from the inside. He couldn't move away from the source, couldn't scream. The pain was relentless, and his mind scrambled to make sense of the overload. His head spun as the pain intensified, radiating from his groin, tingling, clenching muscles, pulling skin tighter. His cock wasn't just in pain. It was on fire. A cold sweat broke out across his skin. His legs shook. His nut sac spasmed.

The pain pushed him further into his head. His thoughts jumbled, and his hyperventilating pushed his dizziness.

In the midst of the attack, his limbs lightened, feeling as if they were lifting away from his body. He was hard, throbbing, blood pumping into his engorged cock, the head deep red, precum pouring from his piss hole and pooling on his abdomen. Gods, how he needed to come. Would have done anything to get there. A wave of pleasure rushed over him, a ball of energy expanding so massively in his groin that he was sure he'd explode.

The man chuckled and ran his fingertips lightly along the oversensitized skin of Justin's cock. His shaft spasmed and bounced under his tormentor's touch. A vision of Max, naked and hard, flashed into Justin's mind for a split second. A roaring sound filled his ears, white light flashed before his eyes, and his balls pulled tighter. The pressure in his head grew and expanded, and he was blown out of his mind.

Bolting upright in bed, Justin gasped and doubled over as his cock erupted in his underwear. Spasms in his groin and clenching muscles in his stomach kept him bent over, unable to straighten. His mouth opened in a silent scream. The orgasm was relentless, his cock and balls throbbing long after his cum had ceased pumping. Sweat dripped from his face. He panted and flipped onto his stomach, humping the mattress in hopes the friction would cease the orgasm, which had become too much. His hips slowed, then he lay motionless. His heart raced as he tried to catch his breath.

Slowly, he settled back into his head, his overworked muscles unknotting. Drained and exhausted both physically and mentally, he stared blankly at the wall. A dream that had been filled with pain and a waking orgasm, equivalent to the magnitude of an earthquake, should have left his mind reeling and his body wired. He should have been terrified. Instead, his body was liquid, practically floating, sated, and replete with post-orgasmic bliss.

All because of the pain. What kind of sick shit was his brain manufacturing? Fucked-up mind meant fucked-up output, right? What the hell else would he dream? But for once his thoughts were quiet, the anxiety absent, the confusion cleared. He almost felt… normal, yet a tear rolled from his eye, because he knew it wouldn't last. How could it?

Pain is the key.

CHAPTER 4

MAX AND Wes's trip to the Mystique had been waylaid by a call to a disturbance at a local restaurant. The NVJ had been called for assistance with a vampire locked in a bathroom, claiming to have a bomb. Half the team had shown up, and after four hours of waiting, the bomb squad finally broke in and found the son of a bitch sitting on the toilet, stoned out of his mind, burning his skin with a lit joint. No bomb to be found. He was now in the segregated vampire psych ward of George Washington University Hospital.

Max entered the apartment and dropped his jacket onto the hall table. As he unlaced his boots, he drew in a deep breath. Damn, that smelled good. Justin was cooking. He'd taught himself over the last several months and cooked better than Max ever hoped to. If his nose wasn't failing him, that smell was his melt-in-your-mouth pot roast.

Before entering the kitchen, Max paused and peered inside. After the incident that morning, he was unsure what mood he'd find Justin in. Just because he was cooking didn't mean he wasn't struggling or pissed off or depressed. He cooked dinner for Max no matter how he felt, and that was something Max appreciated, but it caused him guilt as well.

Justin stirred something on the stove. As usual, the counters were covered with bowls and food and other cooking implements. Justin was an "active cooker" as Max liked to call him. He could tell the level of disorganization in Justin's brain by how large the mess was. This wasn't too bad. Possibly the episode from that morning had been a fluke, though Max knew that was wishful thinking. Justin's change in behavior recently unnerved Max. Right then, though, Justin appeared calm, even relaxed, as he cooked. That gave Max the courage to enter.

"Hey."

Justin whirled around, and a large grin split his face. Max's heart skipped a beat seeing the brightness in Justin's eyes and light in his expression. Damn, he actually looked happy.

"You're just in time. Dinner's ready. Wanna set the table?"

Max nodded and went to the cupboard, pulling out plates and glasses. "It smells so good."

Justin opened the oven, and more scrumptious goodness poured into the air. "I hope it's okay. This cut of meat appeared a little tough, so I added some broth to the pan."

Max's stomach growled. "Your meals are always the best. Better than a cold sandwich from the commissary."

Justin snorted. "Dog food would be better than one of those sandwiches. I had the tuna salad. I think they mistook cat food for the tuna."

Max laughed. "Yeah, don't touch the tuna."

"Wash your hands, and then we can eat."

Once his hands were washed, they both sat at the table. Max dug into the meat, which was so moist it could be cut with a fork. "Oh, my gods, I think I love you."

Justin flinched. Max immediately regretted his declaration since it seemed to make Justin uncomfortable. "I mean, this meat is to die for." He stuffed a large piece into his mouth immediately followed by one of the small, red potatoes to keep himself from going on.

Justin poked at his meat with his fork. "Thanks."

The brightness in his eyes had faded. Max could have kicked himself hard for messing up. He had to do something to salvage the mood. "So, I'm free for the evening."

That brought a hint of a smile to Justin's face. It was a running joke between them since Max was free every evening. He rarely went out, rarely did anything but work since they'd moved to DC. "I was thinking maybe a movie and some popcorn, or we could play some Monopoly, or...."

Justin dropped his fork, his eyebrow raised. "Can we go down by the river again?" His excitement was palpable, and Max couldn't say no.

"Sure, let me grab a shower after we eat, and we'll head out."

After dinner, Max showered quickly and pulled on a pair of cargo shorts and a T-shirt. He also grabbed some bug spray since the mosquitos would be out to dine once the sun set. He contemplated his gun resting on his dresser. They'd be leaving the secure property, but they weren't going far. The river ran right behind their building. No reason he'd need it, so he left it behind.

In the living room, Max found Justin pacing. Not frantically as he tended to do, so maybe this was more from nervousness over going out. He had on a pair of aqua board shorts, a dark blue T-shirt, and his hiking sandals. His hair, which he hadn't cut since they'd come to DC, was a mess of sandy curls. He looked like a surfer boy, except missing the tan. Max imagined him glowing with a tan from the sun and then wondered why he'd thought that.

Justin practically jumped a mile when Max asked if he was ready. Within minutes, they were at the back gate. The sun was low in the western sky, but it was only seven o'clock and it wouldn't be dark until almost nine. The sweltering heat of the day waned, but the air was still thick and humid. When Max swiped his key card and input the code, the gate swung open, and they walked out onto Half Street.

Justin was quiet, hands stuffed in his pockets. There wasn't much traffic in this area, which Max liked. They were close to some interesting places like Nationals Stadium, the grounds of the War College, and the Riverwalk. It didn't take much to entertain Max, and Justin seemed similar in his need for the simple things. He'd probably had enough excitement to last a lifetime, even if he couldn't remember most of it.

As they came to the Environmental Conservation Corps building, they walked onto the property and headed for the riverbank behind the building. They passed under the trees and onto the familiar rocky path. In the small glade, one could pretend they weren't in a city at all. As they approached the water, the birds sounded in the trees and gulls flew by, water lapped at the shoreline, and boats passed on the river. As they exited the underbrush, they came to the rocky shore. The air smelled fishy and a bit musty, but the breeze helped. Justin made his way to his usual big rock and sat down. He was quiet and still. Max wasn't sure what that meant, so he made his way to a rock nearby and sat as well.

The sun danced across the ripples of the river, creating pops of light on the water. Despite the occasional sound of a motor in the distance, the area was quiet, peaceful. Max picked up some pebbles and tossed them one after another into the water. Justin wasn't usually a word-a-minute guy, but he generally wasn't that quiet.

"Since the last time we were down here, I've been thinking maybe we should get some poles and do some fishing," Max said, hoping to start a conversation.

Justin grunted but kept his gaze on the water. "If you fish this river, don't eat your catch."

"Why not?"

"It's one of the dirtiest rivers in America, along with the Potomac. Apparently politicians aren't the only dirty things in Washington." Justin had said it without so much as a chuckle.

Max laughed out loud, and Justin gave him a sideways glance. "Duly noted. No fishing in the dirty river."

Justin shrugged. "You can fish, just don't eat them."

"Well, what's the fun in that? Do you fish?" Max asked, which was stupid because he knew exactly what Justin did and didn't do.

"I did when I lived with my grand—in Gifford. I was probably around fifteen the last time I went."

Silence reigned. Max knew about Justin's grandfather. The man had sold Carson out to a vampire hunter, and his grandson as well. Had to hurt when your own family turned on you.

Justin sighed. "I used to have an uncle who took me as well, but he moved to Utah." He frowned. "Who moves to Utah besides Mormons?"

Max shrugged. "What about your father?"

"Never knew him, and my mom never talked about him."

Max's grandmother had raised him after his mother split when he was about two months old. Her addiction to crack was more important than raising her kid. He learned from Lincoln that she had OD'd before Max turned ten. The police had contacted his grandmother with the news. She buried her only daughter in the family cemetery without any services. And Max knew she'd done it for him. So he didn't have to deal with that burden at such a young age. He did learn who his father was, and that was the only regret he had, not knowing his mother. Really didn't matter. His life had been good, though. Still was.

Not wanting to bring the mood down or ruin their fun, Max steered away from the parent subject. "Tell me what else you know about the Anacostia River."

Justin seemed unsure but then let his knowledge loose. "Well, it's also known as the 'forgotten' river, because of the pollution and lack of development in the area."

Justin's knowledge of the area mesmerized Max. Justin confessed to spending hours on the Internet out of boredom. Since he had a view of the river from his bedroom window, he'd searched for information on the Anacostia and then for history about DC.

"I always loved history class in school. Even thought about majoring in history in college. I loved to read about the history of war, the politics surrounding wartime, and the resulting social ramifications. I also thought about teaching history at one time. But… you know." Justin shrugged.

He rarely opened up about anything from his past before Carson. Talking about the ordeal of being bitten and the results of that event seemed easier for him than his life prebite.

"Well, you're in the right area for learning about politics and its history. You're really smart, Justin. You could do anything you want, anything you put your mind to. Look how far you've come in just five months. I mean, seven years of nothing, and then you're here today. You amaze me."

Justin looked to him. His face didn't give anything away, didn't betray him, but his eyes told Max he liked the praise.

"Nah. I screwed up again this morning. Can't go to college when I might freak out in the middle of class. I'd be out on my ass in a second."

"Today was a minor setback. You can do it. It might take some time, but we'll get you where you want to go." God, Max hoped he could.

Justin looked out over the river, seemingly lost in thought. When he didn't answer, Max assumed Justin was finished with the topic. Max leaned back and lifted his face to the waning sun. Being surrounded by trees on three sides, the setting sun, the muffled noises of the city, all increased the intimacy of their spot. Max had to admit he liked Justin, liked spending time with him, and Justin seemed just as content with Max's company. They fit together effortlessly, easily. He imagined under different circumstances they could be friends, hiking, exploring the city, hitting the bars. When Max thought of picking up women, he had to stop there, and not because he knew Justin was exclusively into men. No, it was something deeper that unsettled Max. He quickly pushed that thought aside. He sighed. Once Justin was further in his recovery, Max was sure Justin would move on with his life and no longer need Max. *No longer need him.* At least Justin needed him for the short term. No one had since Grace. It was good to be needed.

"Hey, look what I found."

Max hadn't seen Justin move from the rock. He stood farther down the shore, holding something round and covered with leaves and dirt. Maybe at one time it had been bright green.

"Is that a Frisbee?"

Justin smiled wide. "Yeah. It must have washed up on the shore. Man, I haven't played with one of these since I was a kid." He squatted and swished the disc in the water, washing away some of the debris and dirt from the toy.

A surge of warmth filled Max's chest, seeing Justin's glee from something as simple as finding a Frisbee. "Hey, why don't we go throw it around?"

"Really?" Justin's beaming smile was just too much.

"Sure."

"Okay. We can go up to the front of the Environmental building."

Justin bounded over the rocks toward Max. As they walked up the bank, Justin chattered about memories from his childhood, which seemed to be idyllic once upon a time. Tree-lined street, tons of kids close to his age, hidden forts, cops and robbers, football, baseball, and a swimming hole. For that moment, Justin was a normal guy, a friend with no issues, no concerns, no horrific past.

"Heads up," Justin shouted, and the Frisbee wafted on the air. Max snatched the disc.

"Okay, who was the first girl you ever kissed?" Justin smiled coyly.

The question hadn't been expected. "That would be Tammy Larson, first grade."

Justin raised an eyebrow. "Started young, I see. I bet the girls were all over you."

Max let out a cackle. "I wasn't what you would call prime material when I was younger. Acne, skinny, no muscles, glasses. My head was too large for my body. I was the opposite of attractive."

Justin shook his head as if he didn't believe Max.

"It's true." Max caught the Frisbee and threw it back. "Just ask Lincoln. He'll gladly announce all of my teenage shortcomings. Of course, Lincoln was one of those teens who went from a skinny runt to a six-foot-tall, zitless babe magnet once we hit puberty. I didn't grow much at all past the age of fourteen, so I was still the target of the jocks who had to prove their manliness by beating down a geek. They'd wait until Lincoln wasn't around and jump me. But I wasn't going to be anyone's doormat. I learned to fight back physically and mentally. Most of them left me alone, but there were always those few who had to try more than once." Max shook his head. "Any popularity I enjoyed was by association with Lincoln."

Justin shrugged. "Popularity's a double-edged sword. I mean, people are friends with you just because you're popular, which is so subjective anyway. Just because you can throw a ball straight and hit a target doesn't mean you're more special than anyone else." He returned the disc, and Max caught it but paused.

"Says only those who were wildly popular. Let me guess, quarterback, adorable, all-American boy type. Girls falling all over you even though they knew you were gay. Yeah, I know the type. Let me play my violin for you."

Justin smirked. "Said like the loser you thought you were. I bet you were a little hottie." Justin cleared his throat. "I mean, to the girls, that is."

"I had some dates. Nothing serious. I was into school, loved it all, especially science. Now your turn. Your first kiss."

"Tenth grade. Henry Desmond. Tight end." That had them clutching their sides and gasping for air. Once they were composed enough, they continued leisurely passing the Frisbee, sharing more information about their respective pasts, staying away from anything too serious such as Justin's kidnapping and Max's dead wife.

Despite the darkness, the overhead lights in the stone-covered parking lot were bright, casting that bluish tint on everything, especially Justin's pale skin. They both got a good laugh out of that.

As he threw the Frisbee to Justin, a sound in the trees behind Max caught his attention. The disc took a wild turn to the right, and Justin raced after it. Rustling leaves indicated possibly a squirrel or another city-dwelling animal scurrying around in the darkness. Justin hadn't noticed anything and continued to search for the disc beneath a dense bush. When the loud crack of a stick rent through the air, Max knew that was no squirrel. Something— or someone—heavy had stepped on that stick. There weren't any animals large enough around the area, leaving only one possibility: someone. The hair on Max's arms stood on end, and a cold chill raced down his spine. He jumped a mile when the Frisbee smacked him in the arm.

Justin laughed until he saw Max's face. "What's wrong?"

Max shook off his apprehension and smiled. "Nothing. Mosquitos are getting thick. Let's head inside for that movie."

Justin nodded, jogged to Max, and then picked up the disc. As they started off on the short walk to the gate to enter the NVJ building, Max knew he wasn't overreacting. Next time they left the building, he'd bring his gun.

CHAPTER 5

THE CALMING effect Justin achieved from the dream earlier had dissipated. He paced around his room in the darkness. He'd yet to fall asleep, and it was 3:00 a.m. His evening with Max had been fantastic, ending with movies and popcorn. They'd laughed, and in that bubble of time, Justin had felt like his old self again. He hadn't laughed so much since, well, he had no clue. But since the movie ended and Max had gone to bed, that creeping foreboding had slowly filled Justin's mind, running hot under his skin. Something lurked beneath that feeling, which notched up his fear and need for something he couldn't name. Since his awakening, he hadn't been able to examine the etiology of his fear, his uneasiness, his panic. The melee generally engulfed him whole, sudden, and hard. This was different. The buildup was slow, almost methodical, giving him time to examine the stages. What had changed that dynamic?

The dream had occurred.

The pain.

Because Max slept in the other room, Justin couldn't make any noise. If he were to hurt himself, even for good reason, and Max heard, he'd check on Justin. Max couldn't know, and the thought of his disapproving face chastising Justin flooded him with dread. What if he couldn't do what he needed to get relief because others were around? What if the last time had been a fluke and never worked again? Shit, he was heading for another panic attack.

He pinched the skin of his inner thigh hard, biting on his wrist to muffle the groan. The short burst of pain swiftly released endorphins, but they weren't strong enough to compete with the irrational fear. His frustration grew. If only he could find a way to be quiet and do…. Do what? What had happened in his dream wasn't anything he could do to himself. Would he even want to?

Yes. Gods, yes, he needed something, anything. But he couldn't. His dread of Max finding out was stronger than subduing the fear. He stripped down to his underwear and settled into the corner of his room farthest from the door. He focused on breathing. Tried to only pay attention to each breath… in… out… in… out… in. His heart beat so hard his breath hitched with each beat. Could someone die from fearing nothing? But calling it fear wasn't right. There was more to it than that. Loss of control, an unraveling of his ability to keep himself together, a great need as if something was missing. One piece of a larger mechanism that would keep him on an even course. One unknown piece. Some days, he wished to be catatonic. Seemed so much easier.

Gasping with that thought, he pinched both thighs until he wanted to scream from the pain. He sucked air in between his gritted teeth. He didn't want to be nothing again. Didn't even know what he'd been doing every day for seven years. He moved his hands farther up his thigh, seeking more sensitive areas. Whatever cliff he was about to fall over, the searing burn in his skin held him on the edge. Crazily enough, the pain meant safety.

When the back of his hand swiped his balls through his underwear, he froze. Visions of someone manipulating his sac, pinching and squeezing his balls, inundated him. Visceral. He could almost feel the pain and the surge of relief, hear his voice begging, pleading with some faceless person to squeeze harder, harder, the agony seizing his breath and within seconds, pleasure filling every fiber of his body and cum spurting from his cock.

Justin bolted upright. He clutched at the dresser beside him with one hand and the windowsill with the other, holding on for dear life. His pleading voice ran circles around his head. Had he begged for the pain in that fucked-up fantasy, tied to that chair? Or worse, had he done so in an actual event from his past? No. Nothing like that had ever happened to him. His mind was cracked, his sanity dissolving. That had to be the reason, but if so, why was his mind going to pain and pleasure?

He chuckled morosely. Maybe his yearning for Max got mixed up with a need to harm himself. He'd heard of people who hurt themselves intentionally, using pain as a cathartic release. But he thought about his need for the pain, its continued growth, unstoppable. But why? The pain helped to settle his mind, but it wasn't for his emotional distress—he craved it like a drug. There was something else, some unknown explanation he couldn't put his finger on.

Justin eyed the computer on his desk. Max had put the computer in Justin's room to allow him to catch up on the world he'd missed while basically sleeping. And he'd missed a shitload. After he'd caught up on all he wanted, the computer filled time, curing endless hours of boredom. Now that gateway could possibly provide answers he didn't have.

Sitting at the desk, Justin powered up the desktop. His leg bounced as he waited, wondering just what he was searching for. Those bugs were back, crawling beneath his skin, his mind frantic for something, but he ignored the need.

"Just open the browser and search for information. Information never hurt anyone." Over and over, he repeated the words until the computer booted. Clicking on the browser link, he thought of exactly what it was that he was looking for.

Stick to the basics.

In the search box, he typed, "Why do some people like pain?"

The first search result: "The Pleasure of Pain." Pleasure from pain? Why he questioned the title, he was unsure, but he clicked on the link. The article started with a description of a person tied down, immobile despite their struggle, forced to submit, to endure whatever the captor wished. Justin barely breathed, his attention rapt on that description. An itch to be tied up, even tortured as in his dream, expanded, filling him. But it couldn't be called torture, could it, if he wanted the pain, if the end result was pleasure?

Torture? God, he didn't even know himself anymore. His dissonance intensified, knowing what he wanted and who he believed himself to be were two different things. But still he read on.

Farther down the page, a word caught his eye: sadomasochism… S&M. Even he knew S&M meant something bizarre, and people had to be sick to want such things, right? Or maybe not if he was lucky. He definitely wasn't a sadist. The thought of doing to someone what he'd dreamt wasn't even fathomable. But a masochist—he read further—a person deriving pleasure from pain or humiliation? Different from those who used pain for catharsis, or a coping mechanism. He shook his head and wondered just how much weirder and screwed up in the head he could get.

Pleasure from pain.

What scared him the most? Having such vivid visions of being hurt, of the precise methods used, when he'd never even seen such a thing. He balled his fist as the familiar anxiety pushed through and filled his head. He clutched at his hair. What was happening to him? He squeezed his eyes tight and wished for the calm he'd experienced that morning. He thought of playing Frisbee with Max, how Justin had just been himself, the person he remembered. Why couldn't that last?

His breaths increased, and his thoughts fled to that state of chaos that would break him and send him spinning with no way to stop. Banging his fists on his thighs, he said, "Stop!"

Grabbing the mouse, he clicked on the search box and typed "masochism videos." Thumbnails of videos showing women bound or enduring beatings filled the screen, some downright graphic and gory. A woman bound in ropes, contorting her body, her legs spread wide as a man whipped her. A woman with the largest dildo Justin had ever seen stretching her ass wide. Another showed a woman whose breasts had been nailed to a table. Fuck. He shuddered with revulsion. No, that was too much. And none of them showed men. He needed something closer to what he'd dreamt. Back at the search box, he typed "gay masochism videos" and clicked on the first link.

His breath caught when he saw dozens of thumbnails of bound men at the whim of their captors. Justin opened a video of a naked man tied to a chair with red rope while another man stroked his hard cock. Justin leaned closer as the video filled the screen. Bound tight, without a millimeter of wiggle room, a blindfold covering his eyes, the tied man panted and groaned. His tormentor knelt before him and kneaded his pecs roughly and pinched his nipples hard. The bound man whined and writhed as his tits were twisted until he shouted. When released, his nipples were bright red, as if they could lactate blood.

The man grasped the bound man's shaft slowly, turning his pained expression into one of pleasure. Justin could tell the man was ready to come, needed to come, but his tormentor released his cock. The bound man whined pitifully. Hard and leaking, his cock bobbed in the air. The man grabbed a large black vibrator, turned the base until it hummed, then touched the tip to the end of his captive's shaft. He bucked and pleaded that it was too much, but the torture continued. The twisted pleasure on the bound man's face was exhilarating. Justin's heart raced, but he didn't get hard, even imaging what the tied-up man was feeling.

The bound man stiffened. "Gonna come." Moaning loudly, believing he'd be allowed to come, so ready for release… so ready….

The man let him go with a maniacal grin.

"Nononononono! You bastard! Let me come, please!"

The man laughed and attached a metal clip to each of his nipples. The tortured man's head dropped down, and he groaned. When the clips were twisted and pulled, his shouts filled the air. His hips bucked minutely, his cock never losing its hardness despite the apparent pain.

If Justin was a masochist, then why wasn't he hard watching the torture of this man, believing that he knew exactly what the captive man was experiencing?

The vibrator was placed under the tied-up man's large balls, pushed against his taint. His legs tensed, his muscles contracted and relaxed, his whimpers were audible, his need to come communicated with his entire body. As his balls were massaged, his high-pitched whines thrilled Justin, but still, he wasn't hard. He found himself wishing the tormentor would squeeze the man's balls, pinch them, slap them, attach those metal clips to their skin. Shoving his hands into his underwear, Justin cupped his balls, rolled them as his attention remained on the screen. His testicles felt heavy. Since his return to consciousness, he hadn't come much, rarely getting hard except from fantasies of Max (which he wouldn't allow too often) or with that dream where he'd lost his shit over being subjected to pure torture.

Unconsciously, he pinched the skin of his sac. That was enough to get the blood rushing into his groin and a rise out of his cock. He flicked his nipple, tentatively at first, but then pinched hard enough to rival a metal clip. He gasped, bucked, and whimpered, the pain intoxicating.

On the screen, the shouts and pleas of the bound man to make him come were juxtaposed with his screams and attempts to move from the pain. Still his dripping cock remained hard, his will gone, reduced to a baseless, mindless need. Anything, Justin imagined. The man would do anything. Promise anything. Give anything. Believe anything. Want anything. Just to come.

Want *anything*.

Justin jumped up and nearly tipped the chair over. He ripped the power cord from the wall, the dark screen ending the torturous scene. He didn't want any of this! Fueled with anger and humiliation and downright disgust, he used his arm to swipe the top of his dresser clean. His books, his collection of smooth rocks he'd collected at the river, practically everything he owned, hit the floor in a loud crash, despite the carpet. His chest heaved, his anger spiked, and when the door flew open, he whirled around.

Max, disheveled hair flying around his head, no glasses, pajama pants and shirtless, rushed into the room. "Are you okay? What was that noise?"

If Justin had just been up pacing, unable to sleep, he wouldn't have cared if Max had come in. But Justin was in his underwear and…. He looked down, the light from the living room hitting his thighs perfectly, exposing dozens of purple and red bruises. Anger smashed into his chest. He rushed at Max, arm cocked to throw a punch, but Max was trained and his reaction fast. He quickly had Justin laid out on the floor with his body plastered on top of Justin. His weight, the iron grip on Justin's wrists pinned to the floor, soothed him. He hated it and loved it at the same time. Mostly he hated himself, loathed the messed-up excuse of a person he was, because why else would he desire things so disgusting, so depraved? Tears stung his eyes, and he bit the inside of his cheek to get control.

Don't ever cry ever again, he told himself.

Their heaving breaths filled the air, intimate in the darkened portion of the room. Max lifted his head, their bodies lined up perfectly, his face inches from Justin's, his lips so close. Justin had to resist lifting his head and running his tongue over them.

"What do you need right now?" Max asked.

Fucking loaded question.

Max's eyes were dark and his lips pale, and for a moment Justin allowed himself to believe they were lovers. Max pinning him down, between Justin's legs, thrusting slowly, lovingly. How he wanted to tell Max that what he needed, who he loved, was him. But Justin couldn't handle the rejection, the pitiful look Max would give him.

"Nothing. I'm okay now." *Says the shaking in my voice.*

Max didn't move, speak, or even blink. His weighted gaze was uncomfortable, yet Justin refused to look away.

Kiss me please.

Max finally moved his arm, but he didn't get off of Justin as he thought he would. Instead Max ran his hand over Justin's forehead, into his hair, then down over his cheek. Justin shivered, his skin tingling from the gentle touch.

"Are you sure?" Max whispered.

With his hand free, Justin reached for Max's face, his fingers shaking, ready for Max to rear back and ask him what Justin thought he was doing. But Max stayed still, his eyes never wavering from Justin's. When his fingertips ran across Max's jaw, Justin swore Max shuddered. Wishful thinking for sure. Justin traced circles with his fingertips over Max's cheek, mesmerized, so lost in the intimacy of the moment.

"You're so handsome," he whispered, ignoring the inappropriate nature of the statement.

Max's smile caught him off guard. "Ummm, thanks."

Justin realized what he'd said. His stomach flipped as he felt his arousal in his groin, his cock filling, and wasn't that just a good way to get a punch in the face.

He squirmed. "Let me up, please. Let me up." Justin's struggling and his panicked tone widened Max's eyes, but he complied.

Justin scurried to his dresser, grabbed sweatpants, and pulled them on. He was semihard and prayed Max hadn't noticed the bruises. "I'm sorry I woke you up. I couldn't sleep, and I started to think too hard, and then I...." Justin looked at the items littering the floor. "Maybe I shouldn't stay here."

Justin kept his back to Max, willing his erection down.

He'd gotten hard.

Without pain.

Because of Max.

He heard Max come closer and tensed. Max rested his hands on Justin's shoulders and then ran his hands down over Justin's arms, no doubt meant to be comforting, but truthfully, it felt like thousands of erotic fingers. Justin blew out a breath.

"I like you, Justin. I like having you here. I've lived alone for over two years, and since having you here, I've realized I don't like it. You don't have to stay if you don't want to. But know that I don't want you to go."

Max's declaration brought Justin a modicum of relief. He hadn't screwed everything up—yet. Maybe he could stop that from ever happening. Maybe what had just happened between them, Max allowing Justin to touch him without punching him, was a step forward. Maybe Max could come to love him. That was the hope Justin needed.

CHAPTER 6

RESTLESS ALL morning at work, Max jumped from one task to another, never settling for long. After an hour of that, he went to the gym and ran on the treadmill. The exercise helped settle him, but back at work it wasn't long before the fidgeting started putting him on edge.

Max had left for work while Justin was still asleep, which Max was grateful for. Something about the night before, the closeness they'd shared on the floor, was twisting up his gut, which was ridiculous. He'd merely attempted to soothe Justin as a parent might do for an upset child. And it had worked. When he'd left Justin's room, he appeared calmer, less agitated, and crawled back into bed.

And if Max wanted to get any work done, he'd have to focus.

"Hey." Wes stood in the doorway. Max couldn't get over the width of the officer's shoulders. "Wanna head down to the Mystique and then grab some lunch?"

Max dropped the paper he'd been trying to read and stood. "Yeah, let's go." He grabbed his jacket. It was the perfect distraction.

The Mystique wasn't far from the Capitol building, making it the playground for some of the richest, most influential, and most powerful people in the country. The bite club was members only, with private entrances, vetted staff, and complete anonymity for all members. Word was the nonrefundable application fee alone was ten thousand dollars and that only bought an interview and a background check. No guarantees of being accepted. The other rumor? Members forked over anywhere from twenty- to fifty-thousand dollars a year for the privilege of either being a vampire's pain slut or being allowed to drink human blood. Max had never tasted the real stuff and definitely never sunk his fangs into a vein. No desire for either.

As Max drove, Wes spoke as he perused the file. "Devon Hastings, eighteen-year-old human, last seen at the club on the night of June the twenty-sixth." Wes set the file down. "How in the hell does an eighteen-year-old afford a club like the Mystique?"

Traffic slowed as the midday rush hour was upon them. Max sighed and looked to Wes. "How do you know what the Mystique costs?" Maybe Wes was into the bite scene, but then again, Max hadn't seen the telltale marks on his neck. But that didn't mean anything. There were other places that were popular for biting, namely the groin area.

"I have a few buddies I served with in the area who go to the clubs. One of them does it for the pain and the other for the BDSM and pain part. Of course, they don't have the kind of dough or power needed to get into the Mystique. Everyone talks about the place like it's the ultimate fantasy club."

Wes didn't mention if he went to the clubs himself, but Max figured it was none of his business. "You from this area?"

"No. Highgate, Vermont. A small town in the Northeast Kingdom surrounded by farmland. Lived about ten minutes from the Canadian border. I just recently moved to DC."

"Sounds cold. Is that how you got those muscles, lifting cows?"

Wes snorted. "Not cows. Weights. I got into lifting after I got out of the Army. It's a healthier way of handling the crap that tries to fuck with my head after being stationed in Afghanistan."

"That bad?"

Wes shrugged. "Buddies died in front me, civilians, and it didn't matter how young. Playing in the sandbox changes a person. Some come back, can't handle it, and get into drugs, alcohol, gambling, some become assholes, some sluts, and some, like my buddies that I mentioned, find the something they need in pain. Trauma and PTSD do crazy shit to a person's head."

Max couldn't imagine witnessing that horror. "What about you?" Max immediately regretted asking. None of his business.

"Me? I shoved it all way down inside and went the asshole route. When I found that I was hurting good people, I decided the only way I was going to change was to get back into the closest thing I could find to being in the military."

Max raised a brow. "You think the NVJ is like the military?"

Wes chuckled. "Closer than regular police and less stringent than getting into the FBI. Plus, I've dealt with some shit that you wouldn't believe. Kind of up your alley from what I hear."

Max was the one to chuckle now. "Stranger than a crazy man trying to use an ancient prophecy to dominate the vampire world by turning a vampire into a super vamp with powers to influence thoughts, communicate telepathically, and destroy entire buildings with his mind?"

"Incubus."

Max huffed. "Excuse me? Did you say incubus?"

Wes nodded and smirked. "Possesses bodies, strong as fuck, takes over their minds, uses them to suck sexual energy from its victims. Pretty much it's a sexapalooza until the body wears out, then it impregnates a woman and reincarnates itself into that kid and thus it goes for centuries."

"And you met one of these? For real?" Max wasn't sure if Wes was pulling his leg.

"Oh yeah. The guy possessed by one and the Hunter, a guy whose job it is to kill them. Trick is you have to figure out who they are because they wear human suits."

Max wiped his mouth. "Fuck. Seems we've both seen some shit."

"And then some."

Max decided he should ask Wes about his experience with bite clubs after all. The information could be helpful. "So have you tried a bite club yourself?"

"Not me, no. I'm not into being bit. Sounds painful."

So much for intel. "You know, I don't get it, but to each his own." Max finally pulled into a no-parking zone near the club. The NVJ logo on the side of their SUV would give them a free pass for parking there.

"So what's the plan?" Wes asked.

Max put the vehicle into park and shut off the engine, eying the entrance to the club. "We go in and try to get some information about this kid. I'm thinking it's going to be a bust since the staff won't want to lose their jobs and the members have too much money to care about one missing kid. Devon was sponsored by a member, which means he was probably someone to be used and then discarded when the man got bored. Reports from a couple of Devon's friends said he's into the BDSM scene. Over the last year, four other humans have disappeared after visiting the Mystique. Not a trace."

"Damn. You'd think that news would get the place shut down."

Max snorted. "Yeah, not with the money in this place."

They exited the vehicle and pulled on their NVJ windbreakers. Max adjusted his gun holster as they approached the front door. They were met by a large vampire in a suit and tie. He and Wes were matched for size.

Bouncers in a suit and tie only spoke to the obscene high-end nature of the establishment.

Max yanked out his ID, as did Wes. "Lieutenant Max Kincaid and Officer Wes Reiser. We're here about a missing man, Devon Hastings, who was last seen here on June the twenty-sixth."

The vampire frowned as he surveyed their IDs. "The NVJ has already been here and questioned everyone."

The man turned to head back inside, but Max beat him to the door. Fucking dickhead wasn't going to dismiss him.

The man growled.

"What's your name?" When he didn't answer, Max said, "We could bring you in for questioning as well as obstructing an NVJ investigation."

The vampire looked like he was chewing nails. "Jeffrey Smyth."

"Mr. Smyth, the NVJ has jurisdiction over all certified bite clubs and, pursuant to NVJ statute 341, can enter any establishment at any time without notice if there is just cause. I'd say five missing humans last seen at this club is just cause. Now, you can either let us in, or I can call Director Samuels, and he can order this club shut down until our investigation is concluded. Care to explain to your boss why that happened?"

"Fuck you," the vampire said and opened the door, allowing them to enter.

"Thank you. We'll start with you. Follow me." Max entered the darkened entryway, followed by Wes, who chuckled.

"You're some badass SOB for such a little guy."

Max shook his head. His day just kept heading south.

JUSTIN WANDERED the apartment, wondering when Max would return. He tried TV, music, his computer, but nothing kept his attention. Still wound up from the night before, he needed something to distract himself before he ended up in the same boat as yesterday morning. He eyed his cell phone—which Max had given him—on the coffee table. The phone held only a few numbers. Max's of course, as well as Lincoln's, Doc's, and Walt's. Often he called Max, and just the sound of his voice would help. But he couldn't call him after all of the shit he'd pulled the night before.

"If you don't knock it off, he'll kick you out." He spoke out loud as a reminder of the consequences of losing control again.

That was enough to kick his heart rate higher. He couldn't understand why he'd been so unsettled for the past few days. He'd believed that he was finally starting to move in the right direction, toward some normalcy, but then the dreams started. Constant unease settled into his bones, and without any provocation, he went from calm to freaked out at the snap of a finger. Walt told him it was common for people who'd survived a trauma, some PTSD reaction, but Justin barely had any clear memories of being catatonic. His issues had to come from being shot and bitten. But if that were the reason, why hadn't he been freaking out since he'd woken up? Why had the last two months been so harsh? Didn't make any sense.

He wandered into the kitchen and perused the fridge. He wasn't hungry. He wasn't anything but wired. His thoughts started to race one after the other. He pressed his fingertips into his thighs, and pain from the bruises there caught his breath. He'd been careful to keep the bruises up high on his thighs so his clothes would cover them. He gathered the skin beneath his sweats between his finger and thumb and pinched, increasing the pressure until he dropped to his knees from the sharp pain. He panted through the stinging ache. Blood rushed to his head, and his cock stirred. Why the hell that worked was beyond him.

Visions of being bound to that chair flashed into his head, the helplessness of being tied, of being forced to take the pain, sent a shudder through him. Gods, he was a sick fuck, but that pain, those restraints, were like a balm on his frazzled nerves. Pinching his thighs wasn't enough anymore, though, and he wondered what else could mimic the experience in his dreams. If he could administer his own controlled sessions, he might be able to use them to keep his cool. Anything to allow him to stay levelheaded and not drive Max away.

He searched the kitchen drawers. Anything he did to his body would have to be easily hidden from Max and Walt. Any visible marks would bring questions, and his answers would convince them he was certifiable. As he searched, his hands shook with the thought of using some of the items he found. A roll of cotton string caught his eye, and a small bag of wooden clothespins. He envisioned his balls trussed up, bound and squeezed tight, the pins pinching his ball sac, his nipples, his cock.

He grabbed the string and pins and raced to his room, locking the door behind him. Max wouldn't bother him if the door was locked. It was an understanding they had. A locked door meant Justin needed time to himself.

He couldn't comprehend what he was about to do except to say he was doing what he needed. Stripping off his clothes, he ran his fingertips over the mottled bruises on his thighs, turning to the mirror to appreciate their deep color. His cock stood out from his body but wasn't as hard as it could be. The ultimate goal wasn't to come—well, not yet. The deep calm, the clearing of his head, the state of mindless bliss. Why he needed the harsh input to quiet his body and head wasn't forefront in his mind.

Grabbing the string, he widened his stance, grasped his balls in one hand, and pulled them away from his body. Wrapping the string loosely around the top of his sac didn't feel right. He tightened the restraint until he felt the edge of pain. He continued to wrap the skin between his balls and body until the oval testicles were shoved tight into the bottom of the sac, the skin taut, shiny, and turning purple. The throb increased in time with his heart, the pain spiking as he pinched at the skin on his balls. Each nip raced a tingle up his spine, and he sighed as the pain faded into a contented ache.

He took the clothespins to his bed and lay on top of the covers. For several minutes, he rubbed at the sensitive skin of his balls, lulling himself into a semihypnotic state. The irritation was enough that he had to refrain from closing his legs, but his thoughts quieted, his nerve impulses slowed. He still had a way to go. He grabbed a clothespin and twirled the wooden clip with his fingers. Anticipating the pain was a heady rush. He envisioned colorful clothespins covering his body, pinching the skin, creating a red and angry hue. The pleasure beneath the pain convinced him that he'd recalled a memory, and not something his mind had created.

Focused back on the clothespin, he pinched it open. With his other hand, he pulled his nipple to a hard peak, tugging it away from his body. Going in horizontal, he clamped the pin between his fingertips and his chest. He hissed, arched his back, and then settled. The initial excruciating pinch dulled into a pulsing agony. Without hesitation he repeated this on his other nipple, the twin channels of pain infiltrating his mind and flaring pleasure in his groin.

His cock rolled as the shaft filled, lifting upward, pulsating deep inside. Closing his eyes, he breathed in through his nose and out through his mouth, his jaw shaking minutely, his toes clenching and then unclenching. Lifting his hand, he flicked the pin on his right tit. Sharp tendrils of pain filled his chest. He flicked harder until a cold sweat broke out on his skin and his teeth clenched. Warmth suffused his groin, his bound balls aching and balancing the pain in his chest.

Opening his eyes, Justin stared at the ceiling, taking in steady breaths, which was something he knew to do but couldn't recall how. More pins were clamped next to the first ones. When he could endure the stinging ache, he moved lower. Grasping the taut skin of his balls and pulling outward, he panted hard in preparation and then added the pin. A strangled cry erupted from his throat, and he bucked up from the bed as searing pain pierced his sac.

Quickly, he added another and then another, panting and sweating, and more focused than he could remember being since waking. A massive ball of agony encompassed his groin and chest, expanding with each pin. Picking up his last pin, he lamented having no more and had to make that one count. Clutching his hard dick with his hand, he stroked lightly, gasping as the pleasure pushed the pain higher. A bead of sweat rolled off his forehead and into his hair. His legs and arms shook. He could barely pinch the wooden pin open. His hand made it nearly impossible to control the pin. Finally, he centered one of the ends of the pin over his piss hole. Opening the jaws wide, he rested the other on the side of the mushroom-shaped head. In one motion, he stuffed the end into his urethra and released the pin.

He jackknifed on the bed, moaning and bucking and digging his nails into his thighs. The pain washed through him, seizing his chest. He gritted his teeth and extended his neck, blood pulsing into his head. His stomach roiled with nausea. More sweat tickled his scalp as it ran through his hair. The initial onslaught receded. His cock and balls and tits beat with an angry pulse. Muscles slowly unknotted, his jaw unclenched, his stomach settled. A wash of relaxation, as if shot up with a drug, soothed his battered nerves. The familiarity of the state wasn't as distressing as it should have been. He'd been there before, floating in warmth, safe and suspended in pleasure that dulled his pain receptors.

A voice spoke in his ear. "That's it, float and enjoy, baby."

The man from his dream. Had he fallen asleep again, or were his dream world and reality merging?

Justin opened his eyes to the same tiled ceiling, bound to the same chair. Shit. Before he could check his surroundings, something was placed over his eyes and ears, obstructing his vision and muffling his hearing. Before his eyes, images flashed that didn't make sense. A low drone of words, barely audible, started. Floaty and tingly as he was, the input entered easily. His thoughts were tamed and ordered as if being reprogrammed. Nothing mattered but being there in that moment, not the future, not the past. Only that second, in that state, which he never wanted to end.

Blissfully floating, he should have been bound and immobile. He spread his legs to each corner of the bed, raised his arms over his head, and clasped his hands together. He imagined Max strapping each ankle and then binding his wrists with a leather strap. Max, fully clothed, gazed down upon him laid out naked, the only person Justin would trust to place him in such a vulnerable situation. Max would never harm him… well, except to give Justin what he needed.

Pain and pleasure.

That thought raised flags in his brain. When he met Carson, he'd been a virgin, never moving past giving each other blowjobs. Pure pleasure. When had he started needing the pain? Was he even a virgin anymore? The black hole of the last seven years held the answers. And he knew the truth was more terrifying than not remembering.

"Calm down." It was Max's voice, not the man from his dreams. A pin twisted and he felt another fresh wave of pain. He choked out a gasp, his eyes watering. "There you go. I'll take care of you."

Justin's breaths evened out, and pleasure ruled again. The flashing images returned as he floated higher and higher, unsure if he was even in his own head anymore. His cock ached with need.

"Max, touch me," he whispered.

Fingertips ran over Justin's engorged shaft. He raised his hips, chasing the touch. His breaths increased as fingers curled around his cock, the pleasure instantaneous as his shaft pulsed and shot. Justin squirmed and moaned as cum covered his stomach, a never-ending orgasm that enveloped his entire body, shaking him to the core.

When he opened his eyes, he was alone.

CHAPTER 7

MAX GRUNTED in frustration as the sixth staff person they'd questioned walked away, and they had nothing. Only the bartender, a burly Russian vampire with a thick accent, had any recollection of the kid. And he'd only noticed the human when the man he'd accompanied ordered a drink of top-shelf rum and Coke. According to the bartender, Devon had gazed about wide-eyed like a kid at an amusement park. Unfortunately, the rides in that place weren't what most would call fun. In that dark establishment with the plush regal carpets, carved wood, and fine furnishings, they were costly and, for some, the ultimate thrill ride.

The large room he and Wes sat in was empty, but one staff member had mentioned there were rooms in use twenty-four hours a day on the premises.

Wes frowned as he looked around. "Reminds me of a brothel, a very expensive one. Same vibes, same result. Get your rocks off."

Max had to agree. He rubbed his eyes. Three hours. He was exhausted and starving, having only had a cup of blood that morning. He hadn't slept much after Justin woke him the night before. Max pulled out his phone and hit the screen. No calls or texts. He'd hoped Justin would check in as he usually did, but even that had changed recently. Everything had changed, and some of it not just on Justin's end. What he thought he understood until recently, now confused the hell out of him.

"Lady troubles?"

Max hadn't been paying attention. "What?"

"I asked if you had lady troubles. You seem very distracted."

"Not a woman. A guy."

Wes didn't even flinch. "Got you by the balls, eh?"

"What?" The word came our harsher than Max liked.

Wes raised his hands. "Sorry, man. Didn't mean to pry. Hey, I'm into guys, girls, vampires, humans. No judgment here."

Max huffed. "It's not like that. Justin's just a kid we rescued when we went after Jameson. I found him, and he kind of latched onto me. It's a long story, but in essence, he lost his memory for seven years. He's been having a rough time lately."

Wes nodded. "Sounds rough. How old is he?"

"Twenty-four."

Wes frowned, his scar stretching and pulling down his cheek. Max again wondered the story of such a wound but didn't ask.

"That's far from being a kid."

"The last memory he has is of being sixteen, so he really didn't grow up. I guess I just think of him as a kid since at times that's his maturity level."

"What do you mean?"

Max sat back in the chair, wishing the owner would appear so he wouldn't have to continue with this line of questioning. For some reason, he thought his life with Justin should be kept private, but apparently Wes thought different.

"He can't handle his emotions. He has outbursts of anger. He'll be laughing one moment and crying the next. He has no idea how everyday life works. He isn't motivated by anything, doesn't seem focused. He argues with his therapist and tells him that he doesn't know how to help him. He's just very unstable."

Wes furrowed his brow. "I thought you were going to tell me he stays out all night partying or does drugs, refuses to get a job, plays video games all day, and won't do anything to help out. Teenage shit."

Despite his issues, Justin always helped out around the apartment. Cooking dinner, laundry, dishes, vacuuming, even cleaning the bathrooms. Max was a self-proclaimed slob. Being a widower and alone, he had quit caring. Their apartment was clean because of Justin. And before he'd started having issues again, he'd been helping out around the offices, running errands between departments, cleaning, filing. And as for trying to get better, while he argued with his counselor, it was because what he'd suggested wasn't working for him.

"From your silence I'm guessing that's not the case."

Max shook his head.

Wes leaned forward. "What you described sounds like someone coming back from a war zone to civilian life, in a manner of speaking."

Max didn't know how or why he'd allowed himself to think of Justin as a kid. Maybe at first he'd been closer to a kid, but now he was a man dealing with a shitload of crap.

"Gentlemen."

Max looked up to see a tall, attractive woman in a red wrap dress, tied at the waist. Her dark brown hair spilled around her shoulders in waves. Her emerald eyes were striking.

Max and Wes stood.

"I'm Marshall Stone."

Max and Wes gave each other a sideways glance.

"You thought I'd be a man. Well, dear old dad wanted a boy." She cocked her head, her eyes on Max.

Max cleared his throat. "Sorry." He'd heard stories of Marshall Stone having balls of steel. Apparently they weren't referring to ones between her legs. "Lieutenant—"

"Maxwell Kincaid." She offered her hand, and he took it. "Yes, I know who you are."

"You do?"

She smiled coyly. "I keep up on the vampire as well as the human world. Everyone knows about your team taking down Jameson Merrick. News like that may fade, but the effects create long-lasting ripples in the community."

Max frowned but didn't ask what that meant.

She turned to Wes, and he introduced himself. "Quite the big guy, aren't you? Have you ever been to a bite club, Officer Reiser?"

Wes's cheeks reddened, and he shook his head. He was being professional, but Max could tell he was taken with the lovely Marshall Stone. Max found that he wasn't affected by the stunning woman.

"I apologize, gentlemen, for Shane, who met you at the door. He told me what happened, and I assure you he will be… reprimanded appropriately. We cooperate with the NVJ and follow all laws, I can assure you, to keep our clients safe."

"He told you what happened?"

Ms. Stone raised her brow. "My employees are very loyal to me and tell me everything."

"Really. Did any of them tell you about Devon Hastings?" Max asked.

She smirked as if his question amused her. "Of course. But I imagine it's nothing more than what they've already told you. Mr. Hastings was a guest of Gale Nelson, CEO of Nelson Technologies. Gale has been a member here for four years."

Max knew of the human entrepreneur who was in his forties. He'd created a lucrative operating system for cell phones, many wildly successful apps, and also created security software. His products sold around the globe, and he was one of the richest men in the country. From seeing him in the news, Max knew he was married and had a family. What was he doing in a bite club with a barely legal human boy?

"I know who he is. Do your clients make it a habit of bringing children into the club?"

Devon was eighteen and legal to enter a bite club, but the thought of this creep playing with kids half his age disgusted Max.

Ms. Stone retained her neutral expression as if she dealt with those questioning her club and the morality and ethics of her clients on a regular basis. "He's of age, Lieutenant. I assure you we work within the law here. As for your opinions about Mr. Nelson, what you think about the lifestyles others choose isn't up for judgment here. I created this club as a place for those who enjoy an alternative lifestyle of play without the condescension of others. Just because you don't approve doesn't mean it's wrong."

She stepped closer to Max, her eyes playful but still carrying an authoritative air about her. Max imagined she led in the bedroom as well as the boardroom.

"I know that you've never been in a bite club before, Lieutenant Kincaid. You shouldn't judge that which you don't understand."

Max shifted, uncomfortable. "I'm here investigating a missing person, Ms. Stone. I don't need to understand what goes on here." Which he knew wasn't the case, but he felt she was trying to manipulate him.

"Now, now. We both know that isn't true. How about a tour?" She threaded her arm into Max's. That close, he noticed how much taller she was than him, especially in the red high heels. Her grip was tight, as if to say she wouldn't take no for an answer. Max glanced at Wes, who shrugged. It would get them a look around.

"Lead on," Max said.

They entered a hallway as plush as the room they'd left. Ornate sconces and paintings in gilded frames hung on the wall. Closed doors didn't allow them to see what was hidden behind them. Each door had signs with different names that Max recognized as suburbs of Washington and the surrounding area.

At the end of the hallway, they entered what looked to be another lounge with a long wooden bar. At the far end of the room was a vacant stage. Men and women—human and vampires—sat at tables surrounded by deep-cushioned chairs, drinking and eating. The men and women around the tables were fashionably dressed with expensive haircuts and fine jewelry. Beside the tables were low stools where men and women of a variety of ages sat. Many were scantily dressed, some very scantily. Some wore what looked to be collars around their necks. Some were naked. Max assumed they were a mix of vampires and humans.

"We offer many types of play here besides biting, which as you know can be very erotic for the biter and the bitee. Of course, you wouldn't know personally, since you've never bitten a human, but I'm sure as an NVJ officer you were aware of that fact."

"How would you know if I've bitten anyone or not?" Her assumptions annoyed him.

She laughed almost musically. "It's my job to know." She raised her arm. "This room is for dining, as well as shows and exhibitions. Biting and sexual acts aren't allowed in here. For that we have rooms. Let me show you one."

As they left, a young man turned his head and smiled in their direction from his low seat. A vampire. His wide eyes were all over Wes, and Max could swear they were filled with hunger and lust.

"Do many of your members sponsor guests?" Max asked as they walked into the hallway.

"Oh yes. It allows them to bring in their own entertainment without the cost of membership for their guest."

"Do you provide entertainment?" Because that would be considered prostitution, Max thought, even if only for biting.

Ms. Stone narrowed her eyes, then smiled. "Members may choose to bite or play with one another. Also, the staff are free to play when they aren't on the clock, with my permission. But, no, Lieutenant, we don't provide our members with entertainment for their personal use. As I said, we do provide live entertainment, which includes demonstrations of biting and BDSM, as well as other forms of artistic sexual expression, short of intercourse. All following the laws."

She paused at an ornate wooden door. "This is one of our private playrooms. Nothing happens in a room without supervision of a staff person with specific knowledge of the biting laws. As for whatever else happens, that's between two consenting adults."

She pulled a band holding a key from her wrist and opened the door. Max was shocked to see two men in an adjoining room, separated from them by a glass window similar to what they had in their interrogation rooms.

"Two-way mirror?" Wes asked.

"Yes, it is. This gives staff the ability to watch without being an intrusion."

Wes chuckled. "That must be some job."

The room was as opulent as the rest of the place. In the center was a large bed. Overall it resembled a bedroom, but with some added bonuses. A wooden contraption resembling a large X stood before the window with a young man strapped by the ankles and waist to the wood.

"How old is that kid?" Max demanded.

"Eighteen. But don't take my word for it." Ms. Stone pulled a file from a pocket on the wall and handed it over. Top and center was a copy of a District of Columbia driver's license confirming that Michael King was in fact eighteen. Max handed it back.

She returned the folder. "Now that you're satisfied all is legal, it appears they are ready to proceed." She pressed a button on the wall. "Whenever you're ready, Antoine." The man grinned, and Max caught sight of his elongated, pointed canines. Another vampire.

Max sputtered. "What? We don't need to see this."

He'd watched enough porn to know that someone strapped to that contraption was in for some harsh treatment. He wanted to back away but was caught by the similarities between the boy and Justin. Same pale complexion, same freckles, same lean body. Max had only ever seen Justin totally naked by accident and ignored the funny stirring in his gut at the time.

That stirring returned.

Antoine tightened the straps on the human boy's wrists, secured to the tops of the X.

"I want you to see how beautiful this can be; how pleasurable the acts are for both participants. We aren't here to hurt anyone—unless they ask for it—or take advantage of them. I assure you that Antoine and Michael have played together many times and each partner is getting exactly what he wants."

Max swallowed hard. Wes's gaze was glued to the men before them, and he shifted nervously. First day on the job and he was watching a sex act. Max thought that had to top the list of best or worst first days ever. Were they really going to watch such an intimate act?

Antoine stepped up before Michael and lifted a red ball with straps to his mouth. Michael opened and accepted the ball. Antoine secured the strap behind his head, then ran his hands over Michael's creamy skin. Chest, stomach, arms, legs. Max's stomach reared into his throat as Antoine stopped to stroke Michael's stiff penis. A moan escaped the boy's lips, and Max jerked. When Antoine took both nipples between his fingers and twisted painfully, it was all Max could do not to cover his own. Michael howled, eyes shut tight. Ugly red marks marred his nipples and surrounding flesh.

"This is a sadist and masochist pairing," Ms. Stone said. "Michael takes pain beautifully. And Antoine is a master at bringing a person to a state of bliss from pain alone. We do have some sadists who enjoy giving pain for the sake of that pain only, however Antoine enjoys using pain to produce an orgasm in another person."

"What do you mean by 'pain for the sake of pain'?" Max asked.

"Not all sadism revolves around sexual behavior. As an officer of the law, I'm quite sure you've seen the products of many sadists. Some sadists get satisfaction from humiliation, mental anguish, fear, torture. Think of this as a more palatable and legal way to practice the art of giving pain to another."

Antoine repeated the nipple torture several times until tears formed in Michael's eyes. Max had his gun, and if he thought for one moment the boy was being hurt without consent, he'd smash the window and arrest Antoine.

"They do use safewords, Lieutenant, in case you felt Michael was in danger." It was as if she read his mind. "Michael's safeword is daffodil."

"And how is he supposed to speak with that ball in his mouth?" Wes asked before Max got the words out.

Ms. Stone pressed the intercom button again. "Michael, dear, please say daffodil."

Michael looked into the mirror and said the word, which was muffled but clear enough. If Max heard that word and the fucker didn't stop, then he'd kick his ass. For some reason, he felt a protective streak for the kid.

Antoine picked up a pair of silver clamps from the table. He murmured something to Michael that Max couldn't hear, then proceeded to tease his nipples to stiff peaks. He opened a clamp and caught one of Michael's nipples in the jaws. Michael groaned as he looked at the shiny clamp, his breaths fast and uneven. A red flush crawled up his chest and into his face. Max couldn't see his eyes because his head was lowered.

Antoine clamped his other nipple and fastened a chain between them. What looked to be weights hung from the center, pulling the clamps downward.

Max had seen some light BDSM—spanking, plugs, vibrators—online, but those had been with women and weren't about pain. He looked to the table filled with implements sure to cause pain. He had expected Antoine to return to the table, but he didn't. He stood beside Michael, continuing to stroke his skin, every few seconds batting the clamps, lightly and then hard. Michael bucked and writhed as far as the restraints allowed.

Antoine licked the boy's chest, swirling his tongue as he covered every inch. Michael was still, as if the touch wasn't painful enough. When Antoine latched onto his skin with his teeth, Michael bellowed behind the ball and threw his head back against the wood. The torturous licking and biting continued, Michael's chest littered with deep red impressions of Antoine's teeth. *A forensic investigator's dream.* He had to remind himself that what he was watching wasn't a crime, wasn't coercion. This was wanted, desired, and one look at Michael's erect penis, the purple-red color of the head, the precum dripping down his shaft, off his balls and onto the floor confirmed that reality.

As Antoine continued biting, he grasped Michael's balls and squeezed. With a flick of his wrist, he twisted, and Michael stiffened and screamed. Tears spilled from his eyes and down his cheeks, wetting his mottled chest. He huffed frantically when Antoine released him and went to the table. Max couldn't take his eyes from Michael. The boy's chest heaved and his legs shook, but he was quiet.

Antoine returned holding black Velcro strips with wires connected to them, and wrapped one around the base of Michael's cock and another to the tip. Wires could only mean one thing: electricity. Antoine ran a hand over the smooth skin of Michael's thighs. Soothing strokes. Max focused on what looked to be older bruises on the skin. Small round purple bruises.

Antoine pinched the skin on Michael's thighs, and he screeched. Antoine pinched his way up to Michael's balls. Max heard muffled cries of "stop" said over and over by Michael, but still Antoine continued pinching and slapping. Nothing Michael tried freed him from the endless pain. When Antoine finally ceased, Michael's chin fell to his chest. He sucked in air around the ball as drool dripped from his mouth and ran down his chest.

Max had seen those round purple marks before on Justin's thighs. He had wanted to demand that Justin tell him how the bruises had gotten there but resisted at the time, having had a good idea. Seeing this show, he'd been correct about the pinching.

Antoine picked up a butt plug with wires attached, added some lube, and knelt behind Michael. Max couldn't see. Michael jerked, grimaced, and shuddered as Antoine worked the plug into his ass. When he stood, Antoine went to the black box to which the wires were attached. With a flick of the switch, Michael grunted and his entire body, including his penis, jolted. His hands fisted, his toes curled, and then he relaxed. Antoine returned to Michael, who jolted again, and this time his groan was louder and longer. Max wanted to stop the torture of the boy who looked so much like Justin. It was when Michael raised his head and seemed to look straight at Max that his heart skipped a beat. Michael's pupils ate up most of the brown of his irises, and his focus was far off, almost drugged, and definitely not that of a person in immense pain.

Another jolt and Michael screamed loud and long, and instead of tensing with disgust, Max found himself reacting to the disturbing scene. His groin warmed from the rush of blood, his uniform pants tightened, and his breaths were short and shallow. Antoine stepped before Michael, whose head lolled to the side. He ran a gentle hand over the boy's face, petting his hair and murmuring in a soothing tone. Michael nodded minutely, and Max wondered if he even comprehended what was being said to him.

Antoine turned off the machine and removed the attachments and plugs. He undid the straps on Michael's legs and then his arms, which fell and dangled at his sides. The strap around his waist was the only thing holding him upright. Antoine stepped before him and released the strap, and the shaking Michael fell against him.

Antoine turned the floppy Michael and pulled him against his chest. Michael faced the mirror as his head rested back on Antoine's shoulder. His legs shook and his cock, still leaking and hard, jerked. It looked painful. How he was still hard after that torture, Max wasn't sure. Who knew pain could be arousing? When he looked at the welts on his chest and thighs, Max's mind flashed to Justin, and his stomach jumped as he recalled Wes's words.

...some... need pain. Trauma and PTSD do crazy things to a person's head.

Max focused on Michael's eyes. The hooded gaze was distant yet cognizant. Antoine reached around and grasped Michael's hard dick, stroking in long, steady motions. Whimpers emerged from Michael, increasing in intensity. That noise went right to Max's already hard cock. He was so focused on Michael that when Antoine plunged his fangs into Michael's shoulder, Max jumped.

Michael didn't scream. Maybe he didn't have anything left in him, or maybe he was beyond the pain. His chest heaved, and Max swore his own rose and fell in the same rhythm. Antoine sucked Michael's skin and jacked the human faster. Michael jolted, his legs shook, and his eyes never wavered from their vacant stare. He grunted, guttural and rising in pitch. His hips thrust forward several times into Antoine's fist, and then he came in a long continuous series of spurts. Max stepped back upon seeing the pleasurable expression, the sated and serene bliss. He envisioned Justin, pinching his own thighs, causing himself pain in an attempt to what, get off? And why did Max have that odd feeling in his stomach again?

He looked to Wes, who stared at him with an odd expression. Ms. Stone merely smiled, something between innocence and satisfaction. Max felt as if he'd been manipulated and played and fucked with. He didn't like it.

"We're done here, Ms. Stone." Max tried to regain his cool. He was sure his hard-on was outlined visibly in his pants. "The NVJ will be in touch when we need something else. If you hear anything more about Devon Hastings, please call the office."

Ms. Stone stepped forward, and Max focused on her face and not on anything in the room behind the glass. "Come back anytime, Lieutenant Maxwell Kincaid, as my guest." With what appeared to be a second thought, she turned to Wes. "You as well, Officer Reiser."

Wes nodded politely.

Max wasn't up for pleasantries but said, "Thanks for your… help. Let's go, Wes."

Max fled the building, wondering what the fuck had happened.

CHAPTER 8

AFTER SHOWERING, Justin took his newfound quiet and calm and left the apartment. He'd tried to call Max, but he didn't answer. He got off the elevator at the main level and wandered into the office area where the desks of those on Lincoln's team were located. To the left was Max's office. The door was open and the room empty. He entered to the mess that was Max's workspace. Justin shook his head at the chaos, which Max claimed was organized. Justin had spent so much time in that office in his hours of needing to be close to Max, and in his boredom as well. He'd been over every inch of the place and didn't feel he'd find anything to occupy him.

John walked in and gave Justin a hard stare. "Where's Max?"

"Umm, out somewhere."

A longer stare and Justin wanted to bolt from the room. When John held out his hand with a small black box, Justin wasn't sure what to do.

"Give this to Max."

"What is it?" Justin took the small box. On the bottom was a magnet. On the side a switch.

"GPS tracker for a vehicle."

Justin frowned.

"We put them on vehicles and track them through Comms." John blew out an annoyed breath, and Justin wondered what he expected him to say. "Jesus, just put it in his desk and don't play with it." He left, and Justin stuck his tongue out at the cranky vampire.

After slipping the GPS into the desk, he exited the office and nearly ran into Casey. "Sorry." He backed away quickly. Even if he felt calm, he still didn't want to be touched.

"Hey, Justin. No worries. Is Max around?" She peered into the office. Her blonde ponytail flipped over her shoulder with the movement. She wore her lab coat over a plain T-shirt and jeans.

Was everyone looking for Max? "No. I don't know where he is."

Her bright expression faded. "Oh. I was hoping to talk to him about something. I'll leave him a note. Thanks."

She entered Max's office, and Justin took the opportunity to slip away. As he walked down the hallway, officers passed by, most giving him a wide berth, having experienced one of Justin's many meltdowns. Yup, ticking time bomb. Stay back....

No. That wasn't true anymore. If he could use the pain whenever he needed, he'd be okay. And then he could impress Max, show him he wasn't as damaged as he appeared. That he could be normal.

Justin stopped before the open door to one of the large meeting areas where teams discussed open cases. No one was in the room, so he wandered in. On every available space was what looked to be thousands of pages of reports, information, research, maps on the missing vampires. Pictures with names, personal information, and dates when they'd gone missing covered the walls. Some—more than half—were marked deceased. Many of those vampires Jameson Merrick had used for their powers, then killed.

He walked slowly around the room, as picture after picture of victims left no visible wall space. Coming to a photo of a man who looked a lot like Carson, Justin paused. *Carl Winters. Deceased. Cause of death: Car Accident. Homicide. Suspect: Jameson Merrick.*

Carl Winters. Carson's father. And shit, Jameson was suspect in his death. Jesus. Apparently, it wasn't an accident if Jameson had something to do with his death.

The door opened, and Justin whirled around. Caden Locke, Carson's little brother, stood in the doorway, smiling a mile wide. His black hair flopped in his eyes. He wore flip-flops, neon yellow board shorts, and a white tank top. On the front of the shirt, a donkey had what looked like a lightning bolt pointing to his backside. What did that...?

Oh. Justin rolled his eyes. Pain in the ass. So Caden.

The little miscreant rushed to Justin and slapped him on the shoulder. "Hey, Justin, how's it hanging?"

Justin took a step back from the boisterous poster boy for getting into trouble. To say Caden had become a little wild since moving to DC was an understatement. He went to college in DC and lived with his uncle in one of the apartments in the building. He was rarely there. Justin tried to avoid him when he was around since Caden was a little too intense for him. And Caden was forever trying to get Justin out of headquarters and into one of the bars. The kid was only eighteen and constantly getting himself into shit. Drove his brother and uncle and Lincoln nuts.

"I'm okay. What're you doing?"

Caden pushed his too-long bangs away from his face. "Not much. Classes are out for the summer, and I've been hanging at the ocean with some friends. Just got back into town. You seen Carson?" He looked over Justin's shoulder, as if Carson would pop out at any moment.

"No, I haven't."

Caden's smile widened. "Thank the gods. I don't need a lecture about getting a job for the summer for the six-thousandth time. I'm young. I should be living the high life, right?"

Fuck if Justin knew. He was just trying to live. Period. "I guess."

Caden shook his head once again as if he didn't understand Justin. Not many did.

"Hey, I'm sorry about your father."

It was shitty that Caden and Carson had lost their mother a few months ago as well. Jameson had sent some ape to take Carson, and he'd stabbed Carmen. Justin had always liked her, even though he'd never met her. Justin had been Carson's secret, since being a Tabula Rasa put friends in the no column. Dangerous vampire and all.

Caden frowned and then caught sight of the picture. "Oh no. He was Carson's father. My dad still lives in Gifford."

"Oh, that's good." Justin stuffed his hands into his pocket as Caden surveyed the room.

"Looks like they've found out what happened to a bunch of those vampires. Still a lot missing, though."

The door opened, and Caden, upon seeing Carson enter, sighed. "Hey, big brother, how's it hanging?"

Lincoln followed a visibly pissed-off Carson in. The room got more crowded by the minute. Justin shrunk back toward a corner.

The twist of Carson's mouth showed his anger, but in his eyes Justin thought he saw relief. "Don't 'big brother' me, Caden. Where in the hell have you been? Uncle Graham has been worried and so have I."

Caden's smile didn't fade. He lifted his hands. "Chill, Carson. I told Uncle Graham I was going to the beach to visit some friends."

Lincoln pointed a finger at Caden. Even Lincoln's finger intimidated Justin. "That was over two weeks ago, and no one's heard a word from you. You're only eighteen."

His smile gone, Caden crossed his arms. "I don't need a father, Lincoln. Got one of those already."

Was Caden trying to end his life prematurely? The director was three times his size.

"You're here under the care of your uncle and brother, not your father. If you want to live by his rules, then go back and live with him. Here, you're under my command."

Caden's pouts negated the anger he tried to show. "I'm not one of your officers that you can boss around."

Lincoln took a menacing step forward, and Justin sucked in a breath. "You want to test that theory?"

Carson put his hands on Lincoln's chest. "Whoa there, big guy. Let me handle this? Please?"

Lincoln frowned and stepped back. Caden smirked as if he'd won some victory.

Carson's eyes narrowed. "You might want to dial down the attitude a few notches, little brother. You can't just take off like that. You know there are people out there looking to get even with us, with me, after what happened with Merrick. A lot of powerful people went down with him, and others lost shitloads of money. They aren't going down easy. And don't forget the others who would do anything to get their hands on me and my powers, including kidnapping my irresponsible little brother."

Caden's smirk faded, and his expression lost some cockiness. "I just wanted to have some fun. I'm sorry."

Don't fall for it, Justin thought.

Carson pinched the bridge of his nose and sighed. "I know it sucks being stuck here. I've been there, but it could all go to shit if you aren't careful."

Caden appeared remorseful. *Appeared* being the operative word. "I'm sorry. I won't take off again, promise."

Carson smiled and ruffled Caden's hair. "Let's go see Uncle Graham so he can stop worrying. I'll meet you at home."

Lincoln nodded and raised an eyebrow as they left the room.

"How long do you think it will take before his remorse wears off?"

Lincoln looked to Justin, surprised either because he didn't know Justin was there or because he'd actually spoken. "Two hours, tops."

Justin chuckled. "I'd give him an hour on a good day. When I knew him… before, that kid always acted without thinking. Hasn't changed a bit."

Lincoln sighed, nodding his agreement. "If that's what it's like having kids, I think I'll pass."

But Justin knew that wasn't true. Lincoln talked incessantly about adopting kids when their lives weren't in constant danger. Justin thought he'd like a family and let that dream go as he always did. If Grace hadn't died, Max would probably have at least one kid by now. Probably be cute too.

Justin looked at the other pics on the wall and felt Lincoln's gaze follow him. The vampire made him nervous. What he'd heard about the director, how he'd almost gone crazy after his first bonded mate rejected him, made Justin wary. Although they did have that "nearly crazy" thing in common.

"You're looking good."

That caught Justin's attention. "I'm doing okay."

More silence, and then Lincoln came closer. "Max is really worried about you. About what's going on with you." Fuck, here it came. The warning from the best friend. Don't fuck up Max's life. Maybe even move out and go away. Carson had certainly blabbed to Lincoln.

"I'm not going to mess up Max's life. I really want to get better, and I'm trying. I don't know what else to do."

Lincoln crossed his arms, surveying Justin. There was that underlying connection between them. Justin had been in love with Carson in the past. Lincoln loved him now. Couldn't they just like the same baseball team or something? Somehow Justin knew that connection was something that Lincoln held against him. Justin didn't love Carson anymore. He loved….

Best not to even think it.

"I know you're trying. I don't blame you for what's happening."

That was news to Justin. "Really?"

"I have to say when I first heard about you from Carson, I wasn't thrilled, probably even jealous of your history. But it didn't change my decision to have Max and his team go to retrieve you and bring you back to Utica."

"You sent them to get me?" No one had ever mentioned that before. "Why?"

"Because you were important to Carson and we learned your mother had died. We feared if anyone found out about you, they could use you. Since you had your mind wiped, anyone could try to exploit you, try to reprogram you, use you against Carson. I wanted you where you were safe.

The safest place was at the NVJ. As part of the NVJ, I swore to uphold the law and protect those who couldn't protect themselves. That includes ex-boyfriends." Lincoln smirked.

Justin raised his brow. That information changed his prior belief that Lincoln only cared for Carson. Maybe under that tough exterior was a kind heart. Go figure.

"So how's the search going?" Justin went back to looking at the photos.

Max spoke often about the investigation and endless search, but Justin had never seen the photos. Actually, he'd never ventured into that room before. The building was huge, with tons of offices and conference rooms, and there were several he'd never seen.

"Slow. After the initial influx of info from Jameson's records and those linked to him, all we have are dead ends."

Justin knew the NVJ had found several of Jameson's labs around DC where he'd lived part of the time under another name as the Director of the Center for Vampire Advancement. More labs had been located around Utica, New York. Jameson came from a small town south of the city. He'd started the labs with the main purpose of holding those vampires he'd kidnapped for their powers. He spread the large number of vampires he'd taken between dozens of labs. To run the labs and keep an eye on his possessions, he partnered with other vampires with the promise to fund any venture they had an interest in. A perk to running the labs was access to the kidnapped vampires once Jameson had finished with them—dead or alive.

What those vampires had done in the name of science, or for their own sadistic pleasure, wasn't anything Max would share with Justin. Many had survived Jameson only to become victims of those placed in charge.

He shuddered. "Do you think you'll ever find the rest of them?" And would they still be alive?

Lincoln went to a photo on the wall a few feet from where Justin stood but remained silent. Was he afraid to say what he truly thought? Justin looked at the picture and made out an image of a boy, but he couldn't see the image clearly. The expression on Lincoln's face was one of loss. Had he lost someone to Jameson?

"Who's that?"

Lincoln reached up and ran a finger over the picture. "Manuel Henderson. He's eleven now. Eight when this picture was taken. He's a

Sanatore like me. Jameson took him for his powers, just as he took Manuel's father a few years earlier. His mother was Officer Maria Henderson. If it wasn't for her, Carson and I never would have escaped the NVJ building where we were being held by one of Jameson's partners. She was shot and killed. Earlier she'd given me this picture and asked me to find him if something ever happened to her." Lincoln swallowed hard. "I owe her my life, and I promised her I'd find him."

Justin hoped he did. "How many are still missing?"

"Out of the original three hundred and six, less than a hundred. The more time that passes, the less likely they are still alive. They were all on Merrick's list of those he'd kidnapped, but that's the last time many of them were mentioned in any records. Who knows? Maybe some were offloaded to someone else."

"Like who?"

Lincoln shrugged. "Just a theory that hasn't materialized. What happened to them might never be known."

And Justin could tell that ate at Lincoln's gut, as if he felt personally responsible for them. Justin approached the photo of Manuel. As the boy's face came into focus, a jolt ran through Justin. Visions of the terrified boy, crying for his mother, locked in a cage, tied to a table, screaming, fueled livid helplessness. Someone yelled Justin's name, pushing into his head, but he ignored the voice, trying to sort through the vague memories that held a strange familiarity. Over and over the same visions came with nothing more to show him where he'd seen the boy.

"Justin!"

Justin's eyes popped open. Max stood before him, eyes wide. His hands clutched Justin's biceps. Apparently he'd been shaking him.

"Thank the gods." Max wrapped Justin in his arms.

Justin peered over his shoulder to see Lincoln and some huge NVJ officer he'd never seen before staring at him. He looked at Lincoln. "I remember that boy."

Max let Justin go and stepped back. The confusion on his face mirrored Justin's own. "You remember who?"

"Do you mean Manuel?" Lincoln pointed to the kid's picture.

Justin nodded.

"Why do you think that?" Lincoln frowned, and Justin knew he didn't believe him.

Max stepped in between Justin and Lincoln. "What happened just now? Your eyes were open, but you were just staring...." Max's voice caught, and Justin saw a shake in his jaw. Max took in a deep breath. "I thought something had happened to you."

Max seemed freaked.

Doc rushed into the room, stopping when he saw Justin. "What's wrong? I was told you were unresponsive." Doc surveyed Justin and furrowed his brow.

Probably sick of running for another thing wrong with Justin.

"We were looking at this picture." Lincoln gestured to the photo. "And then he just went blank. No movement, nothing. His eyes were open, but he didn't move when we touched him or said his name. He just wasn't there."

Just wasn't there.

How many times had Justin heard that to describe how he was before waking to Max? Max who appeared upset, or maybe just sick of Justin's issues? But then why the relieved hug? Max confused him to no end.

Doc pulled out one of those annoying penlights and shined it into Justin's eyes. The pain caused him to jerk. "Could have been some kind of a seizure."

Justin pulled away from Doc. "No. I remembered something. That boy. I've seen him before."

"That's not possible," Lincoln said. "He's been missing for almost three years, taken by the NVJ. Most likely he was shipped off to one of Merrick's remote locations we haven't located yet. His mother knew who had Manuel and what was happening in the NVJ. Director Feith, who aided Merrick, used Manuel's safety to keep her from telling others what she knew."

Justin looked at the group of men staring at him with their doubt. He wasn't sure of a lot of things, but he'd seen that kid before. "I know it sounds crazy, but when I saw that picture, I had memories of him. He was in a cage and crying for his mom. And… he was on a table and screaming. They called him Manny."

Max gave Lincoln a sideways glance and then looked back to Justin. Max wasn't going to believe him and that plunged a knife into his chest.

"Experiencing memories imprinted when he was catatonic isn't out of the realm of possibility," Doc said. "Just because a person appears unresponsive doesn't mean they can't create memories of what's around them."

Max rested a hand on Justin's shoulder. "You were at the Oneida Commons for two years before Jameson had you. It's a long-term care facility for those who can't care for themselves for any number of reasons. I checked the place out, and it's legit, but...." He lowered his head. "Fuck."

"What?" Lincoln asked.

Looking up, Max said, "The only information we had for Oneida Commons was obtained when we hacked into the facility's computer records. We only looked at Justin's records. No one else's. We never even made it into the building before we were ambushed by Merrick's men."

Lincoln's mouth dropped open. "And we never checked the place out after everything went down." He turned to Wes. "Go find Wright. Have her get everyone into conference room B in twenty minutes. Justin, join us, please."

They all filed out except for Max and Doc.

Doc gave Justin a poignant look. "Once you're done playing with the big boys, come and see me." He left Justin alone with Max.

Justin wasn't sure what to say, so he stayed quiet. Max didn't come closer, didn't speak. Justin couldn't help but peruse Max from head to toe. He loved seeing Lieutenant Kincaid in his uniform, loved when he pulled his hair back into that messy ponytail resting on the nape of his neck. Couldn't help but stare at his pink lips, the perfect bow shape, and wonder how they'd feel against his. He also couldn't ignore the uncomfortable air that had grown between them recently. He feared it expanding until they were practically strangers.

Max's behavior around him vacillated from his relaxed, easygoing demeanor to one that was distant, hesitant, maybe even aloof. Justin lived on borrowed time with Max, and his heart was breaking.

He decided to speak. "Were you out?"

Max seemed to break away from his thoughts and nodded. "Wes—he's the big guy who was just here—we had to check out a bite club up by the Capitol building."

"Bite club?"

Max's eyes widened, fear ruling his expression. "Shit. Sorry, I didn't mean to say... shit."

Justin's irritation rose. Max was trying to protect him again. "Why would you be sorry?" he asked, even though he didn't want an answer. "What's a bite club?"

Max's expression turned into one of concern. "Nothing you need to worry about."

"Stop trying to protect me. Just tell me what it is." Max, in his self-appointed big brother role, gave Justin a condescending look, which didn't do much to soothe Justin's ire. "I can take care of myself. If you haven't noticed, I'm perfectly fine right now, and I did that myself. I don't need a big brother."

He needed a lover.

Max crossed his arms over his chest and surveyed Justin. Possibly he found what he was looking for, because he said, "A bite club is an NVJ-sanctioned club where vampires can bite others who want to be bitten."

Justin swallowed hard because he knew firsthand a vampire's bite hurt like a bitch. Painful. Pain. The thought of Max sinking his fangs into his neck caused him to jerk slightly. Arousal hit him hard, and his cheeks heated.

"I didn't want to tell you because I thought it might trigger something or make you remember something that you didn't want to."

Justin guessed that was a good reason and showed Max was thinking about his well-being. "I'm sorry. I get why you didn't want me to know, but I won't be able to live in the real world if I can't handle things like that. Just… just don't keep things from me, please." What a hypocrite he was, asking Max for his openness when Justin himself kept secrets.

Max's eyes narrowed for a moment, and then his face relaxed. "Okay. No more keeping things from you just because I think they'll upset you."

Justin smiled but had a premonition that eventually he'd regret asking.

CHAPTER 9

MAX SAT next to Justin in the conference room, Justin's presence undeniable, as if he had some invisible pull on Max. He wished the kid—not a kid, a man—was safe in their apartment. While Max had agreed he wouldn't keep things from Justin, he wasn't so sure he could stick to that promise. His fierce need to protect Justin was bone deep. He wouldn't, couldn't, put his recovery, his safety, in jeopardy. Justin caught Max staring and smiled. Max smiled back and felt the heat creeping into his cheeks. His body was becoming foreign to him. Blushing wasn't something he remembered doing for a long time.

His focus was needed on work, not his body's fucked-up reactions. He picked up his pen, intent on scribbling some notes, but ended up clutching the plastic implement in frustration. His entire had world flipped around, and he was helpless to stop the disturbing motion. He'd never felt so unsettled.

Lincoln entered the room with Carson, but Max was distracted by thoughts he had no right thinking. Visions of a human bound to a cross, writhing in agony and pleasure, marks covering his creamy skin, bright red mixed with fading purple and yellow. Marks like those he'd seen on Justin's thighs. He shuddered as he recalled Michael's lust-filled, vacant stare, driven further into his head in reaction to the pain. Max's cock rose to memories of the moans and groans, the beautiful submission of the man who looked so much like Justin.

"Max."

Max jerked in his chair. The pen he held flipped into the air and almost hit Dennison. "Jesus, Kincaid. Get a grip."

"W-what?"

Justin touched Max's arm, and he pulled back involuntarily. He hadn't meant to do that. Everyone stared at him. And there was Casey practically sitting across from him. When had she shown up?

"I asked about the info you have about Oneida Commons." Lincoln's brow lowered, and Max knew that look. He would be interrogated later about what the fuck was up with him.

Max cleared his throat and opened the folder of information compiled by one of the rookie officers. "Oneida Commons is a long-term medical care facility with doctors, skilled nurses, a psychiatrist, mental health counseling, and physical and occupational therapy on staff. The average age of residents is...." *Really?* "Twenty-five. Ah, it says here the facility specializes in young adults with severe organic mental disorders including those with nonorganic etiologies. This includes but is not limited to traumatic brain injuries, physical disease, severe psychological trauma, abuse and neglect, chemical and toxic exposure, overdose, and other cognitive impairments not due to genetic disorders or psychiatric illness. State-of-the-art diagnostic and rehabilitation services are provided. Time in residence varies per individual since all treatments are tailored to the individual."

Max flipped the page. "Looks like they have a sliding scale fee and don't turn anyone away because they can't pay. Applicants must meet strict admission criteria before even being considered for acceptance." What Max read next raised alarm bells in his head.

"What is it?" Warez asked, no doubt seeing his surprise.

"They don't accept any kind of insurance, no private insurance, Medicaid, Medicare, nothing."

"That's impossible," Dennison said.

"How can a specialized facility fund care like that without insurance?" Dwayne asked. "I had to put my grandmother into an assisted care facility, and it was a minimum of three thousand dollars a month. This place offers skilled care and rehabilitation services, which can double the price. My grandmother's facility was county-owned, a nonprofit, and even they didn't have a sliding scale. Sounds fishy to me."

"I have to agree." Lincoln pulled out a piece of paper, jotted something down, and pushed it to Wright. "Here's an order to secure their bank records."

She eyed the paper. "I know you're all-powerful and everything in this new position, but don't we need an order from a Nons court for this?"

Lincoln grinned. "Through NVJ's newest agreement with Congress, negotiated by Director Williams, NVJ doesn't need a court order to obtain information required to clean up Merrick's mess as long it pertains to corporations, businesses, etc. It didn't hurt that several senators and congressmen were part of his scheme. Politicians are bending over backward at this point in time so work your magic and find out where their money comes from. They could be a nonprofit and have a funding source through private or corporate donations, but I highly doubt it."

"Dennison, you and Myers hack into their system and get me a list of residents, past and present. Any patient who's ever set foot in the door."

"Can't you just sign us a magic paper?" Taylor chuckled. "Pretty please, oh supreme leader?"

Max smirked. Taylor always could lighten the mood.

"Unfortunately, buttercup, this is personal health information, and even the NVJ can't get that without a court order."

"I love when we get to break the rules." Dennison rubbed his hands together.

"And it never happened, so keep it between those of us in this room. It could take months to get a court order, and we don't have that kind of time. If what Justin remembers is true...." Lincoln balled his fists on the table, and Max knew he feared for Manuel. "Let's just say what little he remembered wasn't pleasant."

All eyes turned to Justin, and Max watched him shrink down into the chair. What if he was wrong? What if it wasn't a memory at all but a fabrication he thought was real? What would that mean for his mind, which seemed to be strung together by fragile threads? What if he only got worse? Max couldn't lose another person, especially with the way he felt about Justin.

He closed his eyes and corrected his thought. The way he felt for Justin, like a brother, because anything else was impossible. He'd always been attracted to women without a doubt. Soft skin, long flowing hair, hourglass shape, breasts and clits.... And when Michael's naked form—no not Michael's, Justin's—popped back into his mind, he stood so rapidly that his chair flew backward and banged into the wall.

"Where's the fire?" Wes chuckled while all eyes studied Max.

Max scrambled to say anything. "We have some leads to follow up on with the human missing from the Mystique. He was a guest of Gale Nelson."

"CEO of Nelson Technologies, Gale Nelson?" Carson asked.

"That's the one. Wes and I will hunt him down and set up a time to meet. Let's go, Wes."

Carson turned to Lincoln, and they were at it again with that creepy, staring, telepathic communication thing. Lincoln nodded, and before Max could escape, he said, "Kincaid. Wait for me in the hall."

Could this get any more annoying?

Max nodded and avoided looking at Justin. "Doc wants to see you." And he practically bolted from the room.

In the hall, he asked Wes to meet him in his office. Saluting, Wes sauntered off with Maggie and Tia. Maggie was definitely flirting with Wes. Casey exited the room and drew his attention. She looked good. Soft waves around her face, released from the usual ponytail worn in the lab. Her lab coat was absent. Her blue button-up shirt matched her eyes perfectly. Max wondered why he'd been putting her off for so long. He wasn't lonely, but apparently he was sexually frustrated, as evidenced by his getting hard by the unsolicited show at the Mystique and sitting next to Justin.

"Hi, Casey."

Hearing Max, she immediately stopped and smiled.

His chest warmed. The attraction was definitely there, so what was he waiting for? "I got your note on my desk that you wanted to see me."

Casey nodded but hesitated, smile waning.

"I wanted to see you too." He ignored the clench in his gut with his words.

His confession widened her smile.

Without hesitation—which would allow him to second-guess his decision—he asked her out. "How about drinks sometime?"

The shocked then pleased expression on her face caused him to laugh. He so needed to get out and do something that didn't have to do with work or Justin.

"Of course. I mean, yes. I would love to have drinks with you... sometime. When would you like to go?"

Max's phone buzzed in his pocket. He raised his finger for Casey to wait and pulled it out. When he swiped the screen, a text from Justin popped up. He looked into the conference room, but Justin was gone. Max hadn't even seen him slip out. He opened the message.

Invite Wes to dinner tonight. I'll cook some steaks.

Max raised an eyebrow.

"What is it?" Casey asked.

Max slipped the phone back into his pocket. "Nothing. How about seven thirty for drinks? I've been wanting to go to the Bluejacket. It's a microbrewery, and I heard their craft beers are good."

"That's sounds great. Meet you at seven fifteen in the garage?"

Max smiled coyly. "See you then."

He'd done it. A date. He could start moving forward toward... something.

Lincoln waited a few feet down the hall, his face expressionless, and Max wasn't sure what that meant.

Max held his smile and slapped his hands together. He forced happiness to show, and not his underlying disappointment... or maybe sadness. He attributed his reaction to the fact he was truly moving forward after Grace.

"Made a date with Casey."

Lincoln cocked his head and pursed his lips. "I heard." Nothing more. Max wanted to ask him what his problem was when Lincoln said, "What spurred that on?"

Max wasn't sure what he meant. "Things are settled. She's been waiting."

Lincoln nodded slowly. Max hated when he did that. It meant he wasn't buying what the other person was selling.

Max didn't have time for downer Lincoln. "I've gotta find Wes to follow up on the Mystique lead."

As he went to walk away, Lincoln grasped his arm. "That's what I wanted to talk to you about. The security footage from the Mystique shows Devon Hastings exiting the building at 2:00 a.m. Alone."

Max sighed and wiped his hand over his jaw. "Any idea where he went after that?"

"I have the tech team checking local businesses for access to any exterior camera footage. It's going to take a while."

"Still, I want to talk with Nelson. He was one of the last people to see Devon, and he sponsored the kid."

"I agree." Lincoln dropped his hand. "Listen, you want to get a beer after work? You do owe me."

"I'll have to take a rain check. Justin invited Wes over for dinner. Then Casey and I are going for drinks. If it wasn't a date, I'd invite you and Carson, you know."

"Justin's cooking you dinner and then you're going out with Casey?"

Was he being sarcastic? "Yeaaah." Max drew the word out, unsure what Lincoln's point was.

Lincoln patted him on the shoulder. "Be careful, my friend. Let me know when you want that rain check."

Max let Lincoln walk away without questioning his cautionary statement. Ironically, Max already had that warning in his head, and he wasn't sure why. For once he thought clearly. Casey was a great person, and they'd had fun in the past. Maybe she was the one.

JUSTIN WHIPPED the potatoes and hummed some song, the name of which escaped him. Cooking relaxed him. Cooking for Max more than relaxed him. The look of delight, of gratitude, of euphoria on Max's face tripled Justin's love for him. Max's praise validated that Justin still had some worth in a world where he was useless. And Max was always home for dinner, which meant he wanted to eat with Justin. Spend time together. Justin wasn't sure why he'd panicked when he saw Max speaking with Casey. They'd dated in the past. Lincoln had mentioned that fact before, but it didn't mean anything. He was coming home for dinner. Justin might have baited him a bit by inviting Wes, but really he did want to know the people Max worked with. His interest would show Max he was invested in everything he did.

The perfect partner.

Earlier, he'd returned to his room for a session with the clothespins and rope. He'd taken his time during that session, wrapping both his balls and the base of his dick tight. While searching for more clothespins, he'd come across a stash of bulldog clips, their searing pinch greater than the wooden clothespins. Using the holes at the ends, Justin had strung them together, giving him the ability to yank on several of them at a time. The second session had been no less fantastic and sating than the first. He was flying on pleasure and pain by the time he'd come. Now that satiation had crossed over, and the high had translated into happiness. If he could stay calm, could control his anxiety, his restlessness, his fear, he could focus on Max, on building a life with him. Eventually, he knew Max would see him differently. He lived for the day Max would gaze at him as he did that picture of Grace. Full of love and longing.

"Hey, we're here."

Justin's stomach jumped with anticipation when he heard Max enter their apartment. Justin quickly wiped his hands and grabbed two beers from the fridge. In the living room, Wes's mass took up a large portion of the space. Justin swallowed, unexpected fear rising upon seeing him. Justin had met many people since coming to the DC headquarters, but they hadn't been in his private safe space. If he was going to change, then his fear of people he didn't know was going to have to cease.

Max smiled upon seeing him, and Justin grinned back to hide his uneasiness.

"Dinner's almost ready." Justin handed a beer to Max, moving closer to him and farther from Wes. Justin had to work hard to avoid staring at the nasty scar on his face. That wound had to have hurt like a fucker.

"Wes Reiser, this is Justin Masters. My roommate."

That was a kick in the stomach, but what else could he have said? Friend might have been better... partner.... Justin forced his smile to remain. "Nice to meet you." Justin stuck out his hand, and Wes wrapped his huge paw around it. *Jesus, don't cringe, you coward.*

"Thanks for the invite. Damn, you're a handsome one, aren't ya?"

Justin's cheeks heated. He looked to Max for his reaction to Wes's comment, but he didn't appear to be affected. Justin's mood was heading south fast.

"Thanks." Justin fumbled the sweat-covered beer but managed to hand it over. "Just let me check on dinner. Relax."

He rushed into the kitchen, drawing in deep breaths as he checked on the steak under the broiler. Satisfied, he pulled the pan out and then plated the meat. Anything to distract himself. Of course Max would call him his roommate. They hadn't moved past that stage yet.

"Stop overreacting," Justin mumbled, chastising himself. Add that to the list of things to fix about himself.

"Need some help?"

Justin whirled around to see Wes in the doorway. The feeling of being a rat trapped by a very large cat came to mind.

"Umm... I... ummm.... Where's Max?"

Wes motioned with his beer bottle over his shoulder. "He jumped into the shower quick. Just wondered if I could help. I'm pretty handy in a kitchen."

Justin froze, his mind ready to flee as if he were in danger. Ridiculous, right?

"Y-you can take the food to the table." Justin pointed to the dishes on the island.

Wes nodded and grabbed the potatoes and green beans. Justin followed behind with the steak. He'd set the table earlier. He just needed to heat the blood in the microwave for Max.

"So where're you from, Justin?"

He closed his eyes and then hit the reheat button on the microwave. "Gifford, New York."

"I'm from Vermont, near Lake Champlain. Been to the New York side many times. Is that anywhere near Utica? Max said he comes from near there."

"About an hour north." Justin wondered what Max had told Wes about his past. Some people asked Justin some annoying questions even if they were only curious. Except some were just nasty—like whether anyone tried to fuck him when he was catatonic. Who would even think to ask that? But leave it to John to come up with something so sick and perverted.

"How did you meet?"

Justin's tongue felt as if it had doubled in size. What the heck was he supposed to say?

"Case I was working on." Max entered the kitchen freshly showered, shaved, his hair pulled neatly into a ponytail. He wore that blue button-up shirt and the tight jeans that had Justin nearly drooling every time. His glasses were missing. "Wow, that looks and smells amazing. Let's eat."

"Heck, Kincaid. You don't clean up half bad. I might even take a stab at you myself." Wes waggled his eyebrows.

Justin knew he was joking, but the hint of lust in his eyes proved to Justin that Wes was into men. Justin had seen that look enough in his life—what parts he was awake for—even in so-called straight men.

"Keep your gun in your holster." Max chuckled and sat.

Wes followed. Justin grabbed the blood from the microwave and set it next to Max.

He smiled as he picked up the cup and took a drink. "Good as always."

Wes set his beer down. "Never get used to seeing that."

"It's just food."

"I'll stick with steak." Wes grabbed the plate, and now Justin wasn't sure he'd made enough food. He could see Wes eating everything he'd made and still being hungry. The huge man could have Justin's portion since he was too ramped up to eat. He focused on being alone with Max after dinner. A romantic movie, dim lights, moving closer on the couch. Just enough to set a mood that might lure Max in. It wouldn't be the first time Justin sat close to Max on the couch, except then, the closeness Justin had initiated was needed for him to feel safe. Now he had a different goal. *Just go slow*, he reminded himself.

Wes and Max filled their plates. Justin took much less, but Max didn't say anything about his need to eat as he usually did. Taking a bite of steak, Wes moaned, and Max nodded. "Told you. The man can cook."

"Oh, you're one lucky vampire." Wes closed his eyes, his expression bordering on ecstasy as he chewed the seasoned meat. When Max smiled at Justin and winked, he knew he had to be glowing.

"So, what're your thoughts on the Mystique?" Wes asked, raising a knowing eyebrow.

Max's fork stopped midway to his mouth. He looked to Justin nervously and then to his food. "I think they know more than they're saying. Although Lincoln told me earlier that Devon Hastings was seen in security footage leaving the building alone at 2:00 a.m. Doesn't mean someone there didn't have something to do with it."

Justin poked at his food with his fork. "Is that the bite club you went to?"

Max nodded and from his expression didn't appear to want to talk about it, but Wes did. "Yeah. It was quite the experience."

"Did you see anyone get bit?" Justin shuddered when Max's hand rested on his arm. Again with the protective stuff. Justin looked to Wes, who eyed Max. "Wes?"

Wes shifted his large frame in the small chair. "Umm, yeah. We were invited to a show."

Justin tried to imagine a room full of people gawking at a vampire biting a human. Should have been repulsive, but that wasn't how he felt. "Like a stage show?" He wanted, needed, to know more.

Wes was clearly uncomfortable and looked unsure what he should say.

Max sat back in his chair and picked up his beer. "More like a private show."

Private? Justin's jealousy and anger ramped up when he thought of Max watching someone bite a woman. Was it just a bite, or was it a bite with sex? "Was it a woman?"

Max drained his beer and stood, heading to the fridge. Justin turned, his gaze following Max. When Max turned around, he said, "It was two men. And it wasn't just a bite."

Wes chuckled. "A sadist masochist pairing the owner called it."

Justin glanced away from Max to see Wes grinning. Justin's gut clenched, hearing his words. Was this some kind of joke? Had Max figured out Justin's secret and they were both playing him?

"Hey, are you okay?" Max sat in his chair, definite concern on his face, but….

Justin blinked and nodded but waited for the punch line, which was him. "You really saw someone who was…. What did they do?"

Now Wes looked to Justin with an expression of concern. "It was just two guys. One who likes to give pain and the other who gets off on it. Some people who like to bite or be bitten have those tendencies. I mean, it hurts to get bitten, and you have to like causing pain to bite, right?"

Justin felt as if he'd fallen into that rabbit hole and was spinning. But neither Max nor Wes acted as if they were only trying to yank Justin's chain, for which he was grateful. He looked up at Max, who raised his brow in question.

"Sounds different," Justin said and popped a piece of steak into his mouth.

Everyone at the table seemed relieved that the strange conversation had ended. Justin thought he would try to get more information from Max later. Maybe he could get Max to talk about what he'd seen and how it had affected him. Right then, Max wasn't letting anything show.

Max asked Wes about Vermont, then the conversation turned to sports, and that remained the topic for the rest of the meal. After dessert, Wes and Max helped clean up. When Max looked to his watch and swore, Justin hoped he'd seen how late it was and that it was time for Wes to leave.

Instead, he dropped his towel and said, "I'm sorry. I have to go."

"Go where?" Had Justin forgotten something?

"Oh, right, you've got a hot date." Wes winked. "Don't leave the lady waiting."

CHAPTER 10

JUSTIN COULDN'T breathe, as if he'd been smacked in the gut by a two-by-four. He clenched his teeth and fought to stop the horrified look that wanted to surface. His mind raced over the words. A date. Max had a date with someone else. Casey. It had to be Casey. While Justin had been foolish enough to think they were headed somewhere, Max had been making a date with Casey. Justin's legs shook, his gut roiled, and a high-pitched noise buzzed in his ears. Any effects he'd gained from his session earlier were quickly dissipating. Why did he have to be so fucking fragile, even if he was watching the person he loved heading out on a date with someone else?

Max patted his pocket, then twisted around, picking up the wallet he'd dropped on the counter. Justin had to say something, anything, but the only thing that came out was, "Your glasses."

Max smiled nervously. "Got my contacts in. Okay. I've got my keys and wallet. Now, if I can calm my nerves, I'll be good."

Justin swallowed repeatedly. Shattered was all he could feel.

"I believe it's kinda like riding a horse, they say." Wes winked.

"I've never ridden a horse." Max looked to Justin. "Not sure when I'll be home. Lock the door, okay? I have my key. Wes, I'll see you tomorrow."

"Have a good night, Lieutenant. Don't do anything I wouldn't do."

Max snorted. "I'm sure that's a short list." He stopped by Justin and ruffled his hair, just like a kid. "Thanks for another delicious dinner."

Justin watched him leave the kitchen. The door closed, and Max was gone. Justin turned to the sink and the pan he'd been washing. Mechanically, he scrubbed in mindless circles, staring into the greasy water. He thought he'd been in the race to win Max's love, but in reality he hadn't even been invited to compete. The bugs were back, and he wasn't putting up with that shit anymore. He rinsed the pan and turned to see Wes still standing there. Justin had forgotten about him.

"Uh, thanks for helping to clean up. It looks good."

Wes nodded and appeared to contemplate something. "You didn't know he had a date, did you?"

Strange question.

Justin shrugged and folded the towel in his hand, avoiding Wes's gaze. "He's an adult. He doesn't need my permission to go out. I'll just watch a movie."

Wes leaned forward and rested his elbows on the counter. "How come a good-looking guy like you doesn't have a girl?"

Even stranger question, and pretty personal. He should've refused to answer, but what the hell. "Don't like girls. I'm gay."

"I know."

Justin frowned. "I'm sure Max told you."

"No. I'm pretty good at reading people. The way you look at him, it's not hard to see."

That brought a bark of laughter from Justin. "Apparently to everyone but the person I want to see it. But he's straight and I know that. No changing that." No matter how hard Justin tried. The truth finally seeped like a cold rain into his heart.

Wes fiddled with a pen on the counter, his lips pursed. When he straightened, he appeared pensive. "Max is really confused right now."

Jeez, did everyone know Max but Justin? Wes had just met him. "How can you—"

"I know I just met him, but like I said, I can read people pretty well. Comes with some expensive government training. I don't know what he's thinking, so I can't say. Give him some time. He might surprise you in the end."

Justin's anger rose with this stranger's supposed knowledge of something that was none of his business.

Wes must have sensed that because he said, "Sorry for making you mad, and it's none of my business. Again, dinner was magnificent. And if you ever just want to talk, come and find me. I'm staying in apartment three, downstairs." Wes tapped his knuckles on the counter and left.

After he closed the door, Justin dropped to his knees and pounded his fists on his thighs.

"You won't fucking fall apart. Never again. No one is ever going to mess with you again." He was done being a victim.

He left the kitchen, grabbed his cell and his jacket, and left the apartment. Down the hall, he knocked on apartment ten. He tapped his foot as he waited, every ounce of mental energy spent holding back the ten-ton boulder of emotions and fear threatening to roll over him. Just give him a little time, and he'd do something about that.

The door opened, and Caden's Uncle Graham smiled at him. "Justin. How're you?"

"I'm good." His voice was choppy and higher in pitch. He coughed and pinched the skin on the side of his leg through his jeans. "Is Caden here?"

"Oh, no. I just got home from work. Late night. He left a note saying he was going out but didn't say where. At least he left a note." Graham chuckled, but Justin could see Caden's antics wore on him. Unfortunately, Justin was about to add to that list of unsanctioned, unapproved activities.

"Okay, I can call his cell."

"Is everything okay?"

Justin forced a smile. "Max had a date, and I was bored."

"Good for him," Graham said, and Justin knew he hadn't said it to be malicious, but the words stabbed just the same.

"Thanks." Justin walked away, pulling his cell from his pocket.

"Hey, if you talk to Caden, tell him to be home early."

Justin nodded to Graham over his shoulder as he opened the contacts on his phone.

Within seconds, Caden answered and loud music spilled out through the phone. "Hello?"

"Caden, it's Justin."

The music and voices were really loud. "Who?" Caden shouted.

"Justin!" His voice echoed through the hallway, and he looked around. He pushed open the door to the stairs next to him where he couldn't be heard.

"Hold on a minute."

Justin heard rustling and some muffled sounds, and then it was eerily quiet.

"Okay. Had to get outside. Who is this?"

"It's Justin."

"Hey, man! What's up?"

Justin rested his head back against the concrete wall. "I need you to take me to a bite club."

Silence, then, "I'm sorry. Did you say a bite club?"

"Yes. You've been to one." Justin knew he had been—he'd overheard Carson reaming him out for his visit.

"Yeah, but you know what goes on there, right?"

Justin hoped he knew exactly what went on there. "Yes."

More silence. "Listen, bite clubs can be… rough. I mean a piece of meat like you will have the vamps fighting to get a bite."

"Good. The rougher the better." No point in beating around the bush.

"Whoa, dude! Seriously! I have a club for you then." The excitement in Caden's voice was a tad scary.

"As long as there's biting and… other stuff, and you don't tell anyone. Not even Carson."

"Why in the hell would I tell Carson? He acts like he's eighty years old. I'm not too far away from you. Meet me at the back gate in fifteen minutes and get ready to have the time of your life."

Justin counted on it.

"Max?"

Casey leaned forward, her eyebrows raised. Her aqua eyes sparkled in the low lights of the bar, which backlit her in a way that gave her an ethereal, angelic glow, and still Max's mind was on Justin. The pained look he'd tried to hide when hearing about Max's date had been burned into his retinas.

"Sorry. I was just thinking about the missing human at the Mystique." A flat-out lie. Great way to start a date.

Casey cocked her head and frowned, and he figured he'd been caught in the act. "Isn't he like the third or fourth one from there?"

Max sipped his beer, a hearty hoppy ale. "Fifth." He shook his head. "Sorry. No work talk. It's hard for me to shut it off. Been a long time since I did much else but work and sit in front of the TV."

Casey laughed, and he focused on the lovely sound. *Justin has a great laugh too.*

Max scooted closer to the bar-height table where they sat and leaned forward to show his interest. "So how're you enjoying DC?"

She ran her finger around the rim of her glass. "It's way different than Utica, as you know. It's nice to get out, but the number of people is just amazing. And overwhelming."

"Don't I know it. Takes twice as long to get anywhere. Justin and I got out yesterday and went down by the river. It was nice and peaceful." He chuckled. "Justin found this old Frisbee, and he was so excited. You would have thought he'd found some rare treasure. I haven't thrown a Frisbee since college, and it took a while to get back into the swing of it."

"How's Justin doing? I see him around the office." She looked down. "I've heard some of his outbursts."

Max wasn't sure what to say. He didn't want to violate Justin's privacy. "He's okay. Some days are better than most."

She nodded and sipped her beer. He was bombing their date big-time. It was as if he'd never been on one before. Five years ago. The day of his first date with Grace and his last. From that moment, they'd been together. That was a long time ago.

Jeez, focus on your hot date.

"Anyway, what've you done in this great capital of ours besides work?" Max asked.

She pushed the hair from her eyes, her fingers delicate and thin. Justin's were long and thin as well, almost feminine, but he was far from girly.

"Let's see, I went to a Nationals game with Tia and Maggie. That was fun, but baseball is one of the most boring sports. We also went to the Museum of Natural History, which was a-ma-zing. I could spend days in there."

"I've wanted to go there since we moved."

She smiled gently. "We should go sometime." The coy, flirty glance she sent his way unsettled him. Another date? They hadn't even finished this one. He needed another drink.

"I should take Justin there too. He loves history. He was going to major in history in college."

As a different waitress walked by, Max called to her. When she turned, he asked for two more beers and flashed her a wide smile.

Any pleasantness she'd shown faded, and she crinkled her nose. "Sure."

Casey watched as she walked away. "Rude or what?"

Max leaned back in his chair. "Lover of vampires, I guess. Seems to be a theme in this city with certain people. Mainly white urbanites who grew up with too much money."

"Utica wasn't like that?"

"For the most part, but there were groups who didn't like vampires. Racism is everywhere, and vampires top the list right now."

She gave him a sour face. "Don't you mean *speciesism*. As if we're an entirely different form of organism. I mean, vampires are the result of an evolutionary process. We come from the same line as humans. Vampires have just evolved to need certain properties in blood for nourishment. No different than vampire finches."

Max guffawed. "Vampire finches?"

"Yeah, on the Galapagos Islands. The finches actually drink the blood of birds they clean of parasites. The blood drinking evolved from their pecking behavior used to remove the parasites that they eat. Pecking can draw blood, which they seemed to find tastier than parasites."

Max made a sour face. "I'd choose blood over parasites."

"Evolution creates a myriad of adaptive behaviors, like people indigenous to hot climates have extra melanin in their skin theorized as a protection against skin cancer. Jury's still out on that one for some in the scientific community. Anyway, people should be amazed by our differences and stop treating us, and anyone different than them, like lepers."

Max drained his beer. "Well, Africans were seen as savages and, even though slavery was abolished in the late eighteen hundreds, racism against blacks still exists today. We vampires are in the same boat. Could take another couple hundred years before anything changes."

"Maybe we should file our fangs like they used to do." She hissed at him, mocking the depictions of vampires in mainstream media. "And if I read one more article claiming we drink the blood of rats, I might scream."

He chuckled, but truly their third-class citizenship could keep a vampire from gaining any success in the country. While they were considered legal citizens, they were different. Their ancestors had migrated north from Central and South America. History told of vampires originating in Europe and fleeing to the New World to avoid persecution, landing in South America. Max still had some distant relatives in Peru and Brazil, but most of his ancestors had migrated into Mexico and the United States, seeking better lives. Like they had for the past century, vampires fought to gain acceptance and the same rights afforded most humans. Still, there were those who believed vampires didn't belong in their country, even on the planet.

"Rat blood. Yuck." He shuddered.

Casey waved her hand. "Let's forget that waitress and get out of the politics of everything else and have a good time."

Their original waitress eventually returned with their beers, a large smile, and no attitude.

"Thanks," Max said, needing the drink. Maybe if he drank more, he'd loosen up. He noticed Casey hadn't finished her first beer but didn't say anything. She seemed to like the pale ale she'd chosen.

"So, you said you watch a lot of TV. Watch anything good lately?"

Now that was something Max could talk about. "Watched *The Hangover* the other night."

Casey lit up. "I loved that movie. Remember the part where Stu's complaining that the woman is wearing his grandmother's holocaust ring, and Alan says, 'I didn't know they gave out rings at the Holocaust.'"

Max joined in. "How about when Alan dresses as Rain Man and counts cards?"

"Yes!" Her eyes widened, and she pointed at him across the table. "The tiger song!"

Max tipped his head back and roared. "Justin laughed so hard his face turned beet red and he almost peed his pants when he heard that. Damn, he must have laughed for five minutes straight, which was so awesome because he never really laughs, I mean, not like that. And I was laughing because he was laughing so hard. It just went on and on, and it was one of the best nights ever. Justin has the greatest laugh!"

Max wiped the tears from his eyes with his napkin, a few chuckles still escaping. When he looked to Casey, her smile appeared strained, her expression odd. "What about you, Max?"

"What do you mean?" He had a feeling he'd said or done something wrong.

Her expression softened. She reached across the table and rested her hand on the back of his, her soft skin so different from Justin's. "What do *you* like? I know what Justin likes. You've talked about him all evening. How about telling me what you like."

Like a bolt of lightning, one thought hit hard. *I like Justin.* He gaped, trying to think past that single life-altering thought. No, it just meant he liked Justin. Just as a friend. Right?

"You look confused."

Confused was an understatement. He stared into the depths of his empty glass, seeking some kind of answer as unease settled into his skin, his muscles, his bones. The disquiet he denied originated from the dissonance of knowing he was a straight man who *liked* a guy.

What did *like* mean in terms of Justin? To Max it meant that he wanted to see Justin's smiling face when he came into his office, watch him cooking the meal they'd share, playing Frisbee or catch or, God help them, fishing the Anacostia, to be the one to hold him close and chase his demons away... to be in his life forever.

Max raised his head and met Casey's gaze, which was like a solid slap, because Max wanted Justin to be the one sharing a beer with him. He wanted it to be Justin and no one else.

Casey sighed and pushed her extra beer across the table. "You look like you could use this."

Max picked up the glass of warm beer and took a large gulp. And then another. He set the glass down, again avoiding Casey's eyes. "I'm sorry. This is the worst date ever."

"Believe it or not, I've had worse."

"Ouch," Max muttered.

What was wrong with him? Beautiful, successful, down-to-earth Casey sat across from him. Any man would be lucky to have her. Men around the bar had been checking her out all night. So perfect, but not what he wanted. She wasn't the scrawny kid, lost and alone, that Max had rescued, cared for, who became stronger by the day, the beautiful man who had stolen his heart. The previous night, when he'd lain on top of Justin, his hard body, flat chest, cock and balls against him, Max had gotten hard. He'd been inches away from kissing him, wanted to kiss him so badly, his body reacting to not a man or woman but who Justin was. He'd fallen for the person. But when he'd jumped up and fled to his own room, the distance allowed him to dismiss his desire away as something else. Just as he'd been dismissing every sign that he was falling for the human.

"Want to talk about it, or should we fall into a drunken state of ignorance?" Casey's smirk was endearing and annoying at once.

"While I'd love to sink into a night of utter drunkenness and blissful ignorance, I'm thinking that would only complicate things."

"I concur."

"I also don't believe I should say anything to the contrary since I brought you here for a date. Wouldn't that be tacky? Me talking about someone else while...." He shook his head, remorseful. "I'm afraid I've already hurt you enough." He was a heel.

A flash of something akin to sadness crossed her face, but she quickly pulled the emotion back. "Max, we're friends. I won't lie and say I didn't want something more because I did. But sometimes these things don't work out. It's not as if we're in a relationship. We've only been out a few times, and that was over six months ago."

"You're being a better sport about this than most women would."

"Pfft. Those women are insecure and need a relationship to fulfill them. Me, I'm made of tougher stuff. I don't need a man to keep me happy. Although it'd be nice to get laid once in a while."

Max laughed heartily and actually blushed.

"Besides…." She leaned over the table and whispered, "That new guy, Wes, is quite the gorgeous package of man. And that scar makes him look badass. Maybe…."

Max put his hand over his heart. "Jeesh, you've moved on already? I'm crushed." Max feigned sadness.

She straightened. "No, you're not." Casey threw her napkin at him.

"Hey! No throwing stuff."

"Oh, I'll kick your ass, Kincaid."

He didn't doubt that for a moment. "Well, Wes thinks you're quite the hottie yourself. Maybe there's a chance."

She smiled wanly. "Maybe. Once my heart mends."

"I am sorry, Casey. Really sorry."

She was silent for a moment, and Max knew she wanted to say something that would challenge him. It was how Casey was. "You want to know how you can show me that you're sorry, really sorry?"

Max nodded.

"By not wasting this opportunity, no matter how much it defies who you think you are. Finding someone special who makes you laugh, makes you want to spend time with them, makes you love life, even when it's crap, hold on to it, tight, and never let go." She paused and looked away for a moment. When she faced Max again, she appeared vulnerable. "Just so you know, I didn't come on this date blind. I've seen the way Justin looks at you. Everyone has. And none of us have been able to ignore the way you look at him as well."

Max's eyes widened. They'd all noticed when he hadn't even known. All of Lincoln's—make that the entire team's—comments hadn't made a bit of sense, but now they did. He took in a deep shuddering breath, and then downed the rest of Casey's warm beer.

She waved her hand at him. "Don't freak out. At first we all kind of thought it was hero worship on Justin's part, and a brotherly kind of love on yours, but as time has gone by… well, it was harder to deny."

"Then why go out with me?"

"To see which was true. And after hearing you talk about him, well, you're as bad as my little sister going on about her fiancé. I swear to the heavens, every sentence she utters starts with 'Mark this' and 'Mark that.' But you know what? I can't deny I'm a little jealous that you found that person."

"Someday soon you'll meet someone who sweeps you off your feet. You're a wonderful person, Casey, and any guy would be lucky to have you." Max was still unsure if the same thing had happened for him.

The silence filled the area around them. Max was lost with no clue how to move forward.

"You could start by telling me."

"Huh?" Max was confused.

"You said that you had no clue how to move forward. Start by telling me."

He huffed. Now, he was speaking his thoughts. "Jeez, could you have given me something easier?"

She shrugged her shoulder. "Once you say it, then it'll be out there, and from there it'll only get easier."

As Max tried to put words in order before he spoke, his phone rang. "Do you mind?"

"Ugh, if you must." Casey rolled her eyes dramatically.

He smiled at her, but also because he thought Justin was calling. Swiping his phone screen, Lincoln's name popped up.

"It's Lincoln," he told Casey, then answered. "Hey, loser. Checking up on me?"

"Max, our surveillance team covering the Mystique reported seeing Caden and Justin entering the building."

Dumbfounded for a second, Max wasn't sure he'd heard right. "Justin and Caden… at the Mystique?"

"Yes."

"Tha—That's impossible. Justin doesn't leave the building. He's—"

"Max, it's them. I'm headed there now."

Max jumped from his seat. "Get the team in there to get them!"

Casey's eyes grew wide, and she stood as well.

"They've been in but couldn't find them anywhere."

Oh fuck. Justin was missing. No, it wasn't even possible. "I'm on my way. Call everyone."

Pocketing his phone, Max pulled out his wallet and threw down enough for the drinks and a hefty tip. His head spun. Shit, he'd drunk quite a bit.

"What's wrong?" Casey grabbed her sweater and purse.

"I need you to drive me to the Mystique."

CHAPTER 11

JUSTIN GROANED. His eyes were heavy and refused to open. When he tried to move, nothing happened. The same fucking dream with his body frozen. Relief. He needed to hurt, needed to be knocked out of his head, needed the physical pain to soothe the sadness of… of…. He wasn't sure, but the bugs under his skin had tripled in size.

"Hey, baby. You finally coming around? I have to confess, I may have given you a wee bit too much this time. But that's okay, we have time. No one knows where we are."

The words jammed together in Justin's head, but the voice of his nocturnal torturer soothed his nerves.

"You have no idea how much I've missed our playtime. You were my favorite. You know that, right? And then he took you away from me." Hot breath caressed Justin's ear. "I bet you've been going out-of-your-mind crazy without our sessions. Don't you worry. We're going to have one right now and set you back on your intended path."

Warning bells went off in Justin's head. The man had missed him? This wasn't right. The dream had never gone that way. Everything was wrong. The man moved away, and Justin fought hard to force his eyes to open, panic raining down on him.

I bet you've been going out of your mind without our sessions.

His breaths increased, and then he heard an incessant beeping noise. He was close to hyperventilating. He couldn't breathe.

Hands ran soothing circles over his chest. "Hey, hey. It's okay. You're safe. I'm going to give you what you need. Don't you worry." Something touched his left nipple, gentle, too gentle. When it ran over the nub, the short burst of pleasure caused him to catch his breath.

Without warning, fingers twisted his nipple. Pain ripped straight into his chest. He gasped and choked, and his eyes popped open. His vision was blurry. He couldn't move against the pain, couldn't pull away. The initial spike of agony faded to an angry throb. A wash of calm filtered through, but still, he feared what would come next. He blinked, trying to focus his vision. Movement caught his attention to his right. A large figure dressed in black stood beside him. His face looked like a black blob, but Justin knew it had to be the mask he'd seen in his dream.

"There's those beautiful eyes. I must say that I don't know how you woke up while you were gone. When I found you, saw you conscious, walking around talking…." A tight pinch to his right nipple and the clip bit hard. He panted through the pain, waiting for the rush of endorphins, which broke through after the agony subsided. Pain and pleasure in the same breath. "You were a sight to see. Surprising since we were the ones in control of your waking. We're going to fix that right now, though, and then you can go back to training. You were so close to finishing. My star pupil."

Training? Star pupil?

Justin blinked rapidly as he fought for control over his body. The man moved lower and rubbed his fingers over the sensitive scarred flesh left by the gunshots to Justin's thighs.

"I see that you've been trying to get what you need, haven't you?" He chuckled. "Oh, yes, look at these bruises on your thighs… your balls"—he cradled them in his hand—"your cock. Torture on your cock and balls has always been your favorite. You make me proud, baby."

He grasped Justin's burgeoning cock, and despite wishing to the contrary, the slide over his skin felt good. His cock started to respond. Flashes of pain ran through his balls as they were pinched over and over until Justin gasped for air. Tears flowed down his cheeks. He hated the pain and needed it at the same time.

"Beautiful."

"How're you progressing?" The woman's voice came from the right of Justin.

Justin strained to see who was there, but she was beyond his line of sight.

"Oh, our newly returned student is coming along nicely. His body hasn't forgotten how to respond. And our little man here has been carrying on without us. Bruises everywhere."

"Do you think someone helped him?"

The man surveyed Justin, who could now see his captor clearly. Yeah, it was the same man in his dream, and realizing this wasn't a dream terrified him. He needed…. Needed what? It was as if he couldn't access part of his brain. Where had he been when he'd been dreaming? It was right there, just out of reach.

"Not sure, but I have a feeling he was doing what he needed to keep sane all by himself. You've seen what happens when our trainees don't get the input on a regular basis. I'm sure he's been trying to maintain the status quo."

He'd been trained to take pain? What the fuck? How did he not remember something like that? It couldn't be true. His mind shadowed with fear, his heart once against racing.

"His reaction says different," she said. "He's near panic."

The man stepped up to Justin. "Look at me, boy." The tone was commanding, firm.

Justin immediately looked into his eyes, and their familiarity hit him hard.

"Calm down."

As if his will was not his own, Justin stared into those dark eyes, unable to look away. His breaths slowed, his heart rate lowered. Pain throbbed in his chest, in his groin.

"His mind's fighting to make sense of all of this because he's been away and had other experiences. Without maintaining controlled environments before the training is complete, you know this happens. Give me an hour to reintroduce the program, and it'll be as if he was never gone."

"That's all you have. After that we have to move. We were just lucky he left without any officers, but they're going to know he's missing soon enough. I want him long gone before that happens. His absence has put me way behind in my research."

"You got it."

"One thing we need to know is how he was pulled out of the resting state. Without the proper sequence, that's impossible. We can't allow that to happen again."

"Let me get him back onto the program, and it's possible he can answer that question, but don't get your hopes up. He might not know."

He didn't know but thought he should. A large store of information in his head was unattainable.

"Now let's get down to business." The man grasped Justin's nipple and twisted hard. A scream pushed out of Justin's throat, along with more tears. He was sure his nipple had been ripped off. The other nipple was given the same treatment. A pair of nipple clamps was put into place. When the man twisted them, another scream pushed from his throat.

When Justin looked down, his dick had softened. Despite the agony, he felt triumphant.

His triumph was short lived. Something cold touched his bound nipple, and he smelled alcohol. More pulling of his nipple and a short groan escaped. A searing pain shot through his chest. He couldn't move against the pain, couldn't pull away. The initial spike of agony faded into an angry throb. Calm filtered through him. He blinked, trying to focus on what had caused him such pain. A needle with a light blue tip had been pushed through his areola just beneath the clamp. The man moved around the bed to the right side. His gloved fingers held another needle. He pinched and pulled Justin's nipple and closed the clamp around the middle. Justin whimpered. The man merely grinned, grabbed the clip and pulled up. Justin's heart rate shot through the roof as the needle was lined up. He tried to shout, but nothing came out but grunting. The needle plunged through his skin, and his grunt became high-pitched squeals.

"That wasn't so bad, was it?" Justin looked into the man's dark eyes. His irises appeared black, creating two orbs floating in a sea of white. "Quite the rush of pain, huh? Needles pack a large amount of pain in a tiny package. I can tell you still don't like them that much, so let's move on to something you really enjoy suffering through."

The man moved about picking up items and placing them onto a tray beside him. "I'm not sure if you remember how these sessions go, so I'll give you a reminder. First, I'm going to overload your body with pain until your mind can't take another ounce and you're sure you'll go insane from the relentless assault. That'll open up the part of your mind we need to access with the program. Luckily for us, you're a natural pain slut. Others would have had to go at it a different way with mind-altering drugs and some extra programming. Have to say, I like you naturals the best."

The fucking man had explained Justin's torture as if he were explaining how he was going to fix a faucet. Fucking sadist.

And you're his masochist.

But Justin didn't want the overload of pain. He just needed that cathartic release, like he'd experienced in the dream, and in his room. Anything to erase the overall sadness.

All of that was quickly forgotten when something put pressure against his hole. He jerked and hissed and looked at the man standing between his legs. He held a thick metal rod, which he slowly pushed into Justin's ass.

He groaned, being stretched until he thought he'd rip wide open. Panting, he tried to push the intruder out, but those muscles wouldn't respond. He was thoroughly being violated by proxy of a huge dildo. His dream had focused only on the pain and pleasure and had left out the humiliation, the vulnerability, and the fear.

Justin blinked several tears from his eyes. Pain like that was too much.

The dildo began to vibrate, filling Justin's rectum and groin. He didn't have a choice but to react.

"Feels good, right? Just give it a minute."

Justin's shaft filled, despite his reluctance. The man snapped a leather strap around the base of his cock and under his balls. The restraint was tight. Another strap with two wires attached was wrapped just under the crown of his cock. Now this was what Justin had seen in his dream. Maybe what the man considered pain wasn't Justin's definition. Except for the dildo. That was agony.

The man reached over and pushed something on top of a rectangular black box, about the size of a brick. The tip of his cock tingled. The foreign sensation was odd and unsettling. His attention was drawn to the man who had grasped a nipple clamp in each hand. Justin hadn't even thought of them since his tits merely throbbed. He caught something on the man's face—

No! Don't!

Both clamps were ripped off his nipples at once. Justin howled as the man pinched his nipples so fucking hard, the fiery hell pain clutched Justin's chest.

Fuckfuckfuckfuck! Stop! Please, stop!

The pulsing agony clouded Justin's head, blocking out any pleasure in his groin. The man released Justin. His chest heaved, trying to catch his breath. When he could think again, the dildo still vibrated in his ass. A stinging jolt hit his cock. Another squeeze of his tits. Over and over the process repeated until he couldn't breathe, couldn't string together a coherent thought, drooling and sobbing, his voice failed from his screams.

His vision blacked, and when his eyes focused, the man was in his face. "*Shh, shhh, shhh.* You did good, baby." The man stroked Justin's forehead, his cheeks, his hair. "Such a good boy."

The torturous hands were being gentle, and Justin wished he could lean into them. The stinging jolts to his cock were barely felt. The vibrating dildo continued, competing with the pulsing pain in his chest. He needed pleasure. Why wasn't he getting any?

"You need to be able to endure longer sessions because some sadists are real bastards and will probably want to hurt you for a long time. And they might not care about your pleasure. You might never orgasm again once you're delivered. But during training, I promise in the end there will always be release."

If Justin could've begged, he would have. Anything for release. Anything. No more physical pain. No more emotional pain. Just no more pain.

"Now we use those channels in your mind, opened by the pain, to restart your training, and then you will get to come. You want that, don't you, baby? Blink once for yes."

Justin blinked once, pleading with his eyes. Despite the pain, his cock was hard and dripping precum on his stomach, the head a deep red color.

The man grinned wide like a proud papa. "You always do, but first I have a video for you to watch. Get through this, and you'll get your reward and a nice rest."

Yes. An explosive, blissful orgasm.

Goggles were placed over his eyes and headphones over his ears as in his dream. The screen inside the goggles flickered, and a video of a screaming man hanging upside down while another man shoved a huge dildo in his ass played. Another clip of a man bound to a table, hot wax dripped on his nipples and genitals. Words flashed too quickly to read in between the clips. The vibration in his ass increased again, and he groaned. A pinch in his arm startled him. His arm became cold. More clips. More words. Slowly his body came back under his control again. But being bound, he still couldn't move.

He gasped as an unexpected jolt ran through him.

He panted as the vibrations filled his groin.

More words.

Slave.

Obey.

Increased vibration.

Pain.

A jolt to his cock.

Rewards.

An intensifying, moan-producing vibration pushed him higher.

Pain.

A pinch to his balls.

Rewards.

Vibrations covered his shaft, running from tip to end.

The muscles in his stomach and thighs spasmed as he mewled, the pain followed so quickly by the pleasure that they melded. He gasped as a volley of stinging slaps hit his chest. The pain in his nipples was tremendous. Tremors shook his entire body. He stretched his neck. Panting. Gasping. Sobbing. Grunting. Spasms never reaching their peak.

The headphones were removed. His sounds filled the air. He wanted more. Needed more.

So close.

So close.

The words came faster with their corresponding sensation.

His world was a pinpoint of need.

Only one goal.

"You want to come, don't you, baby?"

"Y-yes. Pl—oh gods—p-please!"

"You've done so good, so good for me. We'll play again soon."

The leather strap was ripped from his cock and the command "come" was all it took. His mouth opened in a silent scream. His balls tightened as if gripped in a vise. Air was trapped in his lungs, his stomach a hard rock of muscles. Eyes wide, he watched clip after clip of torture scenes. His voice broke through with an inhuman sound as his entire body pulsed and cum shot over his chest and his face. His muscles shook uncontrollably.

On and on the orgasm roared. His vision blackened, the image of a man's balls, needles pushed into the loose skin, faded. Seizure-like jerks invaded his body. The restraints dug into his skin, but he could barely feel them. The bliss encompassing, invading, and canceling out any pain until he floated. The black diminished, and there was a blue screen, the clips gone.

Words in white crossed the blue. *Sleep, Justin.*

The man whispered, "Sierra, lima, echo, echo, papa, Justin," into his ear.

His reality faded into nothingness.

MAX CLUTCHED his phone in his fist, wishing the traffic would disappear. The Nationals game had ended about a half hour earlier, but the traffic was still a fucking nightmare. He waited for any news of Justin, praying they found him safe, hoping they'd missed something at the Mystique.

The Mystique. What in the hell had Justin been thinking? Why would he want to go there? Why—?

Max's date with Casey.

But why the bite club? Max's grip tightened, his other hand curled into a fist on his thigh. The bruises on Justin's thighs reared up from his memory.

Fear unlike he'd ever felt mixed with jealousy. Justin was so innocent. So naïve, and he'd gone to that place where people like Antoine were doing.... Justin wouldn't... couldn't....

"Stop the car!"

Casey hit the brakes. "What's wrong?"

Max yanked the handle and pushed the door open.

"Max, what're you doing?"

He jumped out of his seat and slammed the door. He shouted through the window, "Meet me there!"

Running past car after car, he wove through traffic, his legs pumping faster, pushing harder to cover the distance to the Mystique with only one thought: Justin and what he'd chosen to do by going there. As he crossed the first lanes of Pennsylvania, he barely missed being clipped by a truck with its horn blaring. The next set of lanes, he had to stop for a group of cars.

"Let's go!" he shouted as cars passed. Seeing an opening, he tore across the three lanes and then down the sidewalk.

Images of Justin bruised and battered pushed him harder. What if Justin really was hurt? What if he was missing? What if...?

No.

The Mystique was in his sights. He plowed through crowds of people.

"NVJ! Move aside!"

He had to elbow his way through the thick crowd. At the door, another burly man stood guard.

Max's chest heaved as he demanded, "NVJ. Let me in."

The man scowled. "Show me some ID."

"How's this?" Max reared back and let loose, his fist connecting with the man's jaw. Before the guard could react, Max rushed through the door. He found Lincoln in his NVJ uniform with a cadre of NVJ officers inside.

He bent over and braced his hands on his thighs, practically hyperventilating. "Where… is he?" More breaths. "Tell me… you found him."

Lincoln shook his head, and Max was sure he'd pass out right there.

CHAPTER 12

MAX TOOK a moment to catch his breath. He wiped the sweat from his forehead and face with his hand. "Where the fuck is he?" Heads turned, but he didn't care. Max straightened.

"Calm down," Lincoln commanded and moved Max away from the crowd.

"What're you doing out here standing around? We need to be in there looking for him!"

The man Max had hit outside rushed at him. Lincoln practically clotheslined him.

"That fucker hit me!"

Max stood his ground as the overgrown vampire tried to push past Lincoln. Nice try.

"Myers! Wright! Get this asshole out of here!"

"NVJ, asshole. Bye-bye." Max grinned as the man shouted obscenities while being dragged away.

Lincoln stepped close to Max, so close he had to look up. What he saw was Lincoln in full-on scary director mode.

"Listen. I know you're freaked out. I've been there. But if you don't pipe down and get into officer mode ASAP, I'm going to have your ass hauled out of here. Capiche?"

Max continued the stare-down. Right then, he could treat Lincoln as his superior or get thrown out. He gave Lincoln a tight nod.

"Good. Now, Myers and the new hire, Jordan Turner, were watching the club when they caught sight of Caden and Justin going through the front door with a woman. Taylor knew enough to come inside immediately and grab them. They searched the place and didn't find them. Right now we're waiting for permission to review their security tapes. As you know, unless there's sufficient evidence of a crime, we can't order an establishment to provide us with anything."

"But we can search a bite club without cause."

"And we did that and found nothing. Their argument is that people come and go all of the time. There's more than one exit."

"Where's Marshall Stone? Get her out here."

"She's not on the premises. Her staff have called and left a message for her to come in." Lincoln looked behind him and then leaned closer. "We're also waiting for the arrival of a specialist." He raised his eyebrows.

Max copied Lincoln's expression, surprised he'd allow Carson anywhere, much less give him the okay to use his power, despite Caden being his brother.

"What about his issues?" While Max wanted to do everything to find Justin, hurting Carson wasn't one of them.

Lincoln wiped at his mouth, and Max saw the frustration on his face. "He wants to try. He's...."

Max smirked. "He's coming whether you want him to or not."

"Yes." Lincoln didn't hide his exasperation. "I swear that man is going to age me before my time."

"But you loooove him," Max teased. Truthfully that was an understatement. Their love superseded everything, even Carson's stubbornness and Lincoln's overbearing protectiveness.

Lincoln snorted. "Not like it's a secret."

Max lowered his head and stuffed his hands into his pockets. Casey's words filled his head. Maybe she was right. Once he told someone about Justin, it would become easier. Did he need easy? What he really needed was to be sure. Was he?

Yeah, he was.

When he raised his head, Lincoln appeared to study him. Max's hands shook, and his stomach pushed up into his throat. If he couldn't say the words, then maybe it wasn't real. But it was real. And every moment since he'd finally reached that stage of clarity only solidified his surety.

"I like Justin."

Lincoln didn't move, no expression, not a twitch, no indication he intended to react. Max felt like a bug in a jar.

"You mean, you like, *like* him?" Lincoln's lips twitched.

Max couldn't help but smile. "You're an ass."

Lincoln chuckled, but his eyes said he felt for Max. "I know, my friend."

Max frowned, wishing he could kick himself in the ass. "I screwed up, and he took off with Caden to this place where people come to…. You know what." Max rubbed his hands over his eyes.

"Carson's here." Lincoln waved him over. He'd come with Dennison. Max bet that had been an awesome ride.

Carson wore an NVJ uniform. "Anything?" he asked. He looked better than the last time Max had seen him, but still….

Lincoln touched Carson's arm covertly. "No." Then they stared at each other, and Carson nodded, then cocked his head and gave Lincoln that "stop worrying" expression. When Carson smiled warmly, Max couldn't help but wonder what Lincoln had said to elicit such a reaction. Would he ever see that expression from Justin? Fuck, would he ever see him again?

Lincoln smacked Carson's arm, exuberant joy all over his face. "Oh, by the way, Max likes *likes* Justin."

Carson let out a deep breath. "Thank the gods. If not, I thought things were going to get messy real soon."

"Seems like they're pretty messed up now." That was an understatement.

"Let me see what I can do."

Lincoln cleared the way for Carson and led him to a man in a brown suit with slicked-back gray hair who stood sentinel at the hallway entering the main building. He looked seasoned, not someone who'd cave quickly. When Carson approached, the vampire sneered.

"Officer Locke, NVJ."

"You got that warrant?"

Carson shook his head and smiled, oozing charm. Did he think this guy would care?

"Then back off." The man looked away.

"I think you meant to say, you'd like to show us where the two young men, who we're looking for, went when they came in here earlier."

Silence reigned, and the man appeared to be thinking. Lincoln watched Carson closely.

"Yeah, I can show you where they went."

Max had only seen Carson practice using his influence in controlled environments, but never on someone in the public. He appeared fine for now, but he had to keep implanting that suggestion if the man's mind overrode the idea. That's where the major issues had arisen previously.

"Okay, Dennison, you come with us. Wright and Turner, guard the door. No one in or out. Relay that to the officers stationed at the exits. If anyone tries to leave without permission, arrest them. Let's go."

The influenced guard smiled pleasantly at their group. "Right this way, officers."

As they followed the vampire, Max muttered, "What the fuck?"

Carson smirked and gave him a sideways glance. "I may have suggested he be polite as well." Dennison sniggered behind them. Maybe Carson could implant that suggestion into the surly vampire as well.

As they followed their escort, women and men stepped back to allow them to pass, many wide-eyed upon seeing the troop of NVJ officers invading their sacred playground. If anything happened to Justin, Max would burn the place to the ground.

Another corner and there were two more guards standing at the end of the hallway in front of a door.

"Gene, what the hell are you doing?" The woman to the left, in a white blouse and black skirt and heels, squared off with their cadre. Carson sped up, keeping in step with the man leading them.

"I'm showing these officers to the young men downstairs."

"Have you lost your mind?" The man next to the woman reached into his suit jacket. Shit! Lincoln and Dennison both whipped out their guns, training them on the man.

"Freeze!" Lincoln's command echoed down the hall.

The man appeared confused and then nodded. "Yes. Go right ahead."

The woman gave her colleague an outright glare. "No! We weren't advised of any warrant."

Carson looked to Lincoln, and Max noticed his face had paled significantly. "She's human."

"Then she's not an employee and has no authority to stop us." Dennison rounded the group with his gun aimed at her. "On your stomach, hands behind your back."

The woman looked as if kicking Dennison in the balls was an option, but she complied. Dennison zip-tied her wrists and then moved her away from the door, searching her for weapons. Her partner willingly unlocked the door and waved them through. Lincoln moved cautiously to the young guard, relieving him of his weapon and patting him down.

"He needs to come with us." Carson lifted his chin toward the younger guard. His voice wavered slightly. When he faltered on his feet, both Max and Lincoln were at his side steadying him.

"You're stopping right now. I'll cuff them both." Lincoln's voice was a growl, but he gently cupped Carson's cheek.

Carson shook his head. "We can't. What if we can't find them down there? What if they're somewhere that's not easily accessible? We need to keep going. I'm good."

Even Max knew that was a lie. Lincoln tried to speak, but Carson raised his hand in protest. "Dammit. If I can't use this power to find my brother and Justin, what good is it?"

Lincoln pursed his lips, and his shoulders dropped. "Okay. But if it gets worse, we stop immediately. Got it?"

"Yeah." Carson exhaled. Max knew he couldn't keep this up much longer.

"Lead the way." Lincoln turned to Dennison. "Bring her along. If she makes a noise, gag her."

They herded into the stairway to the lower level, which curved to the left. At the bottom was a large area that looked to be a lounge in the same tacky brothel-like décor. It was empty. Closed doors lined the walls. The vampire led them through a door to the left into a small area with paneled walls and nothing more.

"Through there." The gray-haired guard pointed to the wall. He flicked open a panel to reveal a keypad.

"Through where?" Max asked. It was a wall.

"The middle panel opens." The man stared at them blankly.

Max scowled. "Open it! Now!" How much longer was this going to take? He was about to lose it.

The man jerked his eyebrows high on his forehead. "We don't know the code."

Max grabbed the man's lapels and slammed him into the wall. "Don't fuck with me!"

Hands grabbed Max's arms, and he struggled against them.

"He's telling the truth, Max," Carson said. "These two don't know it. No clue about her."

The woman tried to step away, but Dennison held her firm. "Only the boss knows the code. I swear. No one is allowed in there without her permission."

Lincoln pulled out his radio. "Wright?"

"Yes, Director?"

"Has Marshall Stone arrived yet?"

The woman in Dennison's custody snickered.

"Negative."

"ETA?"

After a few seconds, Maggie said, "None. She remains unreachable, I'm told."

Lincoln snorted and holstered his radio. "Right."

"How the fuck do we get in?" Max paced before the panel. "How thick is this?"

No answer from any of them. Carson looked to the younger guard, who readily answered.

"It's a veneered panel, I believe."

Lincoln grasped Carson by the biceps and scowled. "Fuck, your nose is bleeding. That's it." Lincoln pulled out a bunch of zip ties from his pocket and spun the older man around, securing his wrists together. Dennison followed suit with the younger man. Carson wiped at his nose, looking in disgust at the blood on his fingers.

"Break the connection now." Lincoln moved Carson back to the wall and sat him on the floor, wiping at his face.

Max couldn't wait. "Dennison, give me a hand here. We can probably break through this."

The two guards shouted to be released, no longer under Carson's influence. Using their shoulders, Dennison and Max battered the fake wall. Wood cracked and plaster rained from above. Over and over, Max slammed his shoulder into the cracking panel, ignoring the pain. He'd get to Justin no matter what. He blocked out thoughts he was injured, or worse, not there.

One last effort and they busted through.

"Fuck! Justin!" Max rushed to the table where Justin was bound, his legs secured in stirrups. Except for Justin, the room was empty. Dennison ran through an open door across from them, and his pounding footsteps echoed into the room.

"Justin? Look at me." Max's voice cracked as he looked over Justin's battered and naked body. Wires were attached to his penis, his nipples were a bloodied and bruised mess, and red marks littered his chest, as if he'd been whipped repeatedly. Max gently cupped Justin's cheeks and turned his head. Justin's eyes were open, and Max gasped. He swore his heart stopped.

"No. No. Justin, look at me. It's Max. I'm here. I'm here." Justin was breathing, so that was good. When Max tapped his cheek, there was no reaction. *This can't be happening.* Justin had to be in shock or something.

Lincoln rounded the table, assisting Carson to a chair. His nose had ceased bleeding. His face and shirt were covered with blood.

Max turned his focus back to Justin. "He's in shock. Look what they fucking did to him! Justin, come on. Talk to me… please."

"Max," Carson said softly.

Max shook his head. He ran his palm over Justin's forehead, his cheeks. His beautiful man. Justin's eyes remained unfocused, appearing to see nothing. Tears stung Max's eyes. What had he done?

"Max, he's… he's back in the catatonic state."

Max's head snapped around. He narrowed his eyes at Carson as if he were the one responsible. "How could that happen?" He searched Justin's neck, his body, but there were no bites. There were only two other registered Tabula Rasa vampires in the country capable of placing him back into that state. "How the fuck did this happen?" Max stood and pushed a black box from the table. "Why the fuck did I have to go out on a fucking date? This is my fault!" His heart was crumbling. He'd had Justin right there and treated him as if he didn't matter. He did matter. More than he'd ever know.

Leaning over Justin again, Max pushed his hair from his forehead, stroking lovingly. "I'm so sorry. You mean so much to me. I'm sorry I didn't know. Sorry I didn't tell you. Please wake up. Please." Max's throat closed painfully around his words.

Officers began entering the room. Lincoln removed his shirt and covered Justin's groin, and Max was grateful. He hadn't even thought of that. He'd fallen apart in front of his fellow officers, but he didn't give a fuck.

Lincoln radioed for Doc, and NVJ officers conducted a search of the remaining rooms for Caden. Max stayed next to Justin, talking to him, soothing him, watching for any sign he was coming around. Max squeezed his eyes tight as they continued to tear. He'd give anything, do anything to bring Justin back.

And whoever did this to him would pay.

Max stopped Taylor, who looked away. "I'm sorry, Max. We came right in."

"I know, man. Can I have your jacket? To cover Justin."

Taylor nodded enthusiastically. "Yeah sure." He removed his windbreaker and handed the jacket to Max.

"Thanks." The jacket covered Justin's chest and stomach, giving him a bit more privacy.

"Is he okay?" Taylor asked. His attention was on Carson.

He'd slumped over, elbows braced on his knees, hands holding his head.

Shit. Max searched the room but couldn't see Lincoln.

"Taylor, could you just stay with Justin for a moment? I'll check on Carson."

With Taylor's affirmation, Max crossed the room and went down on one knee. "Hey, Carson, we'll find your brother, I promise. I'm going to get whoever did this."

When Carson lifted his head, his black hair hung over his eyes. He pushed the hair behind his ears and swiped at his tears. "I'm supposed to take care of him, and I didn't. I can't lose him too."

Max snorted softly. "He didn't let you take care of him. Since we came to DC.... Well, it doesn't matter. Wherever he is, we will get him back."

Fresh tears spilled down Carson's cheeks. "I promised Mom he'd be safe. He's my little brother."

"Listen, I don't know what happened here." Anger surged as Max glanced at Justin. "They hurt Justin and took Caden and messed with my family. They're going to wish they hadn't." He just needed the right leads. No one was escaping his wrath.

Carson took in a deep breath. "Sorry for crying."

Max shook his head. If he weren't so angry, he'd probably be crying as well.

Carson wiped at the drying blood on his face with a shaky hand. "I might be able to get him back, like last time. He might know where Caden is. Maybe he heard something or saw something. I just need some time to recover. I'll do whatever I have to do to bring Caden back and help Justin."

Max nodded. "Why did this happen again?" he asked, more to himself than Carson.

"I don't know. Maybe the torture he endured here...."

Max didn't ask for more. Did it matter? All that mattered was Justin coming back to him. He patted Carson's knee, returned to Justin's side, and thanked Taylor, who left to do his job. Max placed a gentle kiss on Justin's lips. "I'm here, Justin. And I'm not going anywhere."

MAX WATCHED Justin being carried out on a gurney. Max followed Doc, who had no info to give. He needed to run tests, but Max knew what they'd say. Catatonic. Maybe this had been inevitable given the issues Justin had been having and the odd results of his last brain scan. Or maybe he'd been hurt by Max. He needed to stop wallowing. None of that would bring Justin back to him. As he was heading out of the room, he spotted Casey, who looked down at Justin's vacant face with a horrified expression. When she noticed Max, she rushed to him.

"What happened to Justin? Who did that to him?"

He wasn't sure he could answer or lose the tentative hold he had on his anger and pain. He blew out a breath, keeping control. "We don't know. We found him here like that." He rubbed at his sore shoulder, lost about what to do next. He needed to find whoever did this, but he wanted to be with Justin as well.

"I'm so sorry, Max. Did they find Caden?"

"Not yet."

When Max saw Marshall Stone enter the room, he turned on her. "What did you do to Justin? He's been tortured, and the guy who came in with him is missing!"

"Max." Lincoln's warning was ignored.

"You want to show us around again? Because that did a hell of a lot of good last time!"

The club owner's mouth gaped, eyes wide, hand clutching at her throat. "I didn't, they weren't…. No one was even scheduled to be down here."

"What's with the hidden door? Did any of the other humans missing from this club end up down here?"

Lincoln eyed Max but was silent.

"What? No. This space is a rental for those who want a special experience."

"And what experience is that?"

She hesitated and looked into the room where Justin had been beaten. "Role play, kidnapping… torture. Some of the other rooms are themed. Basements, warehouses, rooms in run-down houses."

"You mean, rooms with no escape."

She narrowed her eyes at Lincoln. "The play is consensual. Contracts are completed and signed. Each party knows exactly what will happen.

Safety measures are in place. We have cameras where someone is assigned to watch."

Max's heart leapt. "You have video of this room? I want to see it!"

"No, Lieutenant Kincaid. We only have a camera feed for monitoring. We only video tape if the room is booked. When no one is scheduled, the cameras are off. Even if there was a tape, I couldn't—"

Lincoln narrowed his eyes, his expression far more foreboding than Ms. Stone's. "There're now a total of six people missing, Ms. Stone, five humans and my brother-in-law, a vampire, all last seen at your club. Lieutenant Kincaid's partner was tortured right in that room and is now unresponsive."

Her mouth snapped shut. Her gaze went to Max, who only stared back without reaction, but inside, the pride of hearing Justin referred to as his partner was unfathomable.

"You and your club could be held liable for each of these crimes without your complete cooperation. You will grant us complete access to your security tapes and staff. We will comb through every inch of this building with your help. And you will hand over a complete list of your members."

Max believed the vampire had been ready to agree to everything Lincoln demanded until that last one.

"I can't do that!" She appeared thoroughly mortified. "My members count on the Mystique to keep their membership status private. Many influential and important people join this club because I can guarantee their privacy. My business has been built on that promise, and I don't intend to compromise my reputation. The only way I'll turn over that list is through a court order."

Lincoln pulled out his phone and swiped the screen. A few taps, then he lifted the phone to his ear, his eyes never wavering from Ms. Stone. She fidgeted with the gold links of her necklace, her nervousness not going unnoticed. Max was sure many of those on that list preferred to remain anonymous.

"Sorry to call so late, Director." Lincoln smiled as he listened, then laughed out loud. "So you liked that one, did you? Well, now it's your turn. Hit me with your best shot, Carina." Max heard a delighted laugh come through Lincoln's phone. Ms. Stone's face blanched with her realization of exactly who Lincoln spoke with. Director Williams was very well known in the vampire world. Lincoln covered the receiver and whispered, "The director and I have been exchanging jokes by e-mail, a contest to see who can find the best ones. I think I'm winning."

Her face paled further. Max wondered if any members of her club were higher up than a presidential cabinet member.

Lincoln continued his conversation, conveying to the director what had occurred. Max enjoyed every single moment of watching Ms. Stone squirm, realizing she'd already lost.

"I'll keep you updated on Justin and Caden…. Yes. Thank you for your concern, and I look forward to seeing you…. Good night." He pocketed his phone. "A courier will have the warrant here within an hour."

Ms. Stone stiffened. Max bet she hadn't counted on Lincoln obtaining a warrant this late on a Friday night. "You see, Ms. Stone, Justin and Caden are under the protection of the NVJ due to the trauma they suffered at the hands of Jameson Merrick. After that, Director Williams took a special interest in their well-being and keeps close tabs on them."

Jameson Merrick was another name nearly every vampire recognized.

"She's very upset over the events of this evening." Lincoln looked across the room and then waved Maggie over.

Marshall Stone's discomfort and fear satisfied Max. If she hadn't ignored the seriousness of humans missing from her club, things might be different. Her blasé attitude during Max's last visit did little to convince him she had no knowledge of incidents in her own club.

Maggie stopped next to them and glanced at Max, her expression filled with concern and sadness. "Yes, Director?"

"Take Murphy and Myers. Gather all of the staff on the premises and get a list of those not working tonight. Put the staff in separate rooms upstairs and let them know they aren't allowed to leave, vampire or human. When I'm done with Ms. Stone, we'll start questioning everyone. Contact those who aren't working and order them to appear at headquarters for questioning tomorrow. Anyone who isn't readily available for questioning because their whereabouts are unknown, red flag them."

"You got it." She squeezed Max's arm before she walked away—her silent show of support, no doubt.

Max closed his eyes. The sadness and gestures of comfort were reminiscent of the period before and after Grace had passed. He didn't want to be in that position ever again.

CHAPTER 13

MAX FORCED his mind back into officer mode. "Ms. Stone, one of your guards mentioned that you were the only one who has the codes to unlock these rooms. If that's so, then how would a person exit once inside? Are you always on the premises when these rooms are in use?"

She frowned, no doubt with disbelief that her guard would spill such information. "No, of course not. Mr. Franks was mistaken. There's a code for each door, but a unique one is created each time a member pays for use of a room. Those codes are delivered in an encrypted file only accessible through one of the computers available on location. The member logs into their account to access the code with their private password. Once their paid time is up, the code is replaced with a generic one prechosen by me."

"And are you the person who creates and erases the codes?"

"No, I have software that generates a code when payment is confirmed. Start and end times assure the code is activated for the client's arrival and will no longer work once that time ends. In between clients, my code is the only one that allows access. If anyone has to come into this room for any reason, such as the cleaning crew or repairs, it's under my direct supervision. This is to ensure that no one can place listening or covert recording devices within."

Max looked to Lincoln. "The system could have been hacked."

Ms. Stone shook her head. "That's not possible. The system isn't connected to the Internet or any network outside of the building. It's self-contained, as are our membership records. The only access to the system is within the building. We have top-of-the-line software to encrypt the data so even if someone gains unauthorized access to the records, they can't read them without the software. That's how Mr. Nelson designed the software."

"Gale Nelson created your software?"

"Yes."

Max pursed his lips. "He sponsored Devon Hastings and would know how to access information in his own software."

She scoffed. "You can't think that someone with the reputation and money of Gale Nelson would be involved in any of this. It's preposterous." She waved her hand in the air and actually looked amused.

"You'd be surprised by the number of people with reputations that we've found to be involved in 'something like this.'" Max copied her gesture and waved his hand. "Again, Jameson Merrick."

Her expression changed from concerned and distressed to defensive. Her earlier display of shock and distress might have been an overexaggeration. Hang around a person long enough and their facades slip sooner or later.

"If we're done here, I have things to attend to. I'll have my lawyer here to review the warrant when it arrives. Gentlemen." She nodded to them and left without waiting to be dismissed.

Yeah, Max had had enough as well.

Lincoln pulled Max away from the other officers and forensic team buzzing around. "How you doing?"

He couldn't answer that question if he tried. He shrugged his shoulder. Lincoln touched Max's arm, shifting into friend mode. "You don't need to be here. Go and be with Justin."

Be with Justin, comatose once again. Max tried to see the smiling and laughing man he cared for so much, but all he could see was his battered body on that table. He balled his fists at his sides.

Lincoln squeezed his shoulder. "Hey, this isn't your fault."

Max didn't want pity or sympathy. Not from Lincoln.

"Look at me, Max."

Max pursed his lips but lifted his chin defiantly.

Lincoln snorted. "Yeah, that look isn't getting you out of this. I'm not some pansy ass who will back down."

That only raised Max's ire. "I don't need your lecture about whose fault this is and who to blame. Talk to me when you stop feeling guilty for bonding with Carson and feeling responsible for all of the issues he's having with his powers."

Lincoln's eyes darkened instantly. Max didn't falter, because he knew Lincoln carried a dump truck full of guilt even though his blood had saved Carson's life. The chance of bonding with Carson by Lincoln sharing his blood, practically nil. No one could have predicted any of the fucked-up events that had occurred after that.

Lincoln nodded sharply. "Sure. Blame yourself all you want. But don't let it get in the way of what you feel for Justin. We've all seen it, felt it, even if you're late to the party. I won't blame you for that, because I have a pretty good idea why."

Max crossed his arms, his body tense. "Oh really? And what's that, Lincoln? And don't give me any of that crap about my not being over Grace. I'll never be over losing her, but I've moved on." His tone dripped with challenge. Butting heads with Lincoln was nothing new.

Lincoln crossed his arms as well and exhaled. "No, I won't tell you that. I think your confusion comes from your relationship with Justin and how you initially viewed your role with him. He latched onto you, and you took care of him, got close, and when your feelings for him crossed that line from what you called being the 'big brother' to, well, whatever you feel about him now, you freaked."

Max ran his fingers through his hair. He blinked repeatedly, trying to soothe his irritated eyes. He hadn't worn contacts in over a year, yet he'd put them in for his date. Maybe subconsciously, since Justin always said that he liked Max in his glasses. Max huffed to himself. Max had missed—or ignored—every signal Justin had given.

"I feel…." Shit, why was this so hard?

Lincoln smirked. "A guy once gave me some good advice when I questioned everything with Carson. Speak with your heart and not your head."

Max guffawed. "That sounds so cheesy. I can't believe I said that."

Lincoln raised an eyebrow. "Best advice I ever got."

Advice was something Max didn't want but needed. His tipping point had arrived. Lean the wrong way, do the wrong thing, and everything he believed he wanted might vanish. Maybe already had.

"I don't want to live without him. I want…." He couldn't help but smile. "I want everything with him."

Lincoln's smugness caused Max's jaw to clench.

"Arrogant prick," Max muttered. "I'm going back to headquarters. Probably get some sleep. Looks like you're going to be here all night long." Max became the smug one right then.

Despite the jab, Lincoln chuckled as Max walked away. An icy grip clenched Max's chest with the thought of returning to Justin. What if Justin never came back?

MAX ENTERED the medical wing, rolling his shoulder, the ache growing as time progressed. He immediately spotted Hilary. She smiled wide. Max thought of her flirting and remained apathetic. He didn't want her to believe he was interested.

"Where's Doc?"

Hilary's smile faltered, most likely because he wasn't being his charming self. "In with a patient." Her hand went to her mouth. "Oh crap, he's with Justin. I'm so sorry, I didn't even think. I'll show you where they are."

Max followed closely, wanting to run, but he kept his cool. Stuffing his hands into his pockets helped him keep from pulling his hair out. As they passed Tommy's room, he noticed an attractive, black-haired woman sitting next to his bed.

"Who's that?"

Hilary looked through the observation window. "Someone named Olivia from Rochester. She came in looking for Tommy. I brought her to Doc, and then he let her in. I think she's a relative."

Max shrugged. He thought he'd met all of Tommy's relatives as they'd come to visit him. But he'd hadn't seen her before. He'd have to ask Dennison who she was.

Justin was in the room next to Tommy's. Inhaling and releasing the air slowly, Max fought off hope he'd find Justin awake and lucid. He prepared for reality and entered the room.

Doc stood before a side table, perusing an assortment of papers. "Hey, Max. Come in." Max thought it was funny that Doc's white coat and dress clothes had been shucked for a pair of green scrubs.

Justin lay on his right side, knees bent, a pillow under his head, a sheet drawn up over his waist. He was topless, and bandages covered what Max could see of his chest. His eyes were closed, which relieved him. Miriam, another of the nurses, fiddled with Justin's IV. She smiled when she saw Max and then went back to her work. She was in her early forties and always had a nice manner about her when she was with Tommy.

Max approached the bed, unsure what to do. Justin's chest rose and fell rhythmically. His hand curled under his chin as usual when he slept. Right then, Max would have believed it was any other day and Justin would smile wide, seeing Max. Just another reaction Max had dismissed as part of a platonic relationship.

He touched Justin's arm but pulled away quickly. He didn't know if he should, now that he knew his own true feelings.

"Talk to him." Doc stepped up to the other side of the bed.

Max didn't answer.

"You're standing there like you don't know what the heck to do."

"I-I don't. He's back to… to this again. How did this happen?" Anger smacked him in the chest, threatening to wash away his calm. "He wasn't bitten, so was this going to happen anyways? Or is it because of what was done to him in that room? Maybe it pushed him back into his mind. I can't… I need… I need him." Max wanted to kill whoever hurt Justin.

Doc cocked his head. "I heard you finally got your head out of your ass. I'm guessing from where Justin was tonight, you hadn't told him about that extraction yet."

"Christ, Doc." Max groaned. "Yeah, I was a blind idiot. I freely admit it. And no, I haven't told him because that realization smacked me right in the middle of my date with Casey."

Doc narrowed his eyes at Max. "Casey told me about you finally admitting to having feelings for Justin, but not that you were out on a date when you did. You better not have hurt her." Doc had a protective father-figure streak when it came to Casey, and Max could see the challenge in his eyes.

Max sighed and wiped at his mouth. "I don't know if I hurt her. But she did agree to go out with me even though she already suspected my feelings. She's the one who pointed it out to me…. Or, I should say, hit me over the head with it. I didn't mean to hurt anyone." Especially Justin. This time he didn't hesitate to touch him, running his palm over Justin's arm, the contact calming and right.

Doc appeared to back down. "Yeah, well, okay. And to answer your questions, I don't know why this happened again. I don't think the events at the Mystique were the main cause. I have a dozen theories but none concrete or provable at this time." Doc paused, his eyes narrowed as he gazed down at Justin, as if thinking something over. The hesitation was telling. He didn't want to tell Max something.

"You know something."

Sighing, Doc rubbed the back of his neck. "When I examined Justin, I found bruises. Older ones that look to be in various stages of healing on several parts of his body. With his accelerated rate of healing, my guess is some are days old while others are newer."

Max squinted. "What do you mean on several parts of his body?"

"His chest, around his nipples, his thighs… his penis and testicles."

Doc's gaze was too intense. Max looked away. "I saw the ones on his thighs recently. I didn't know…. I thought he was hurting himself, but I didn't say anything. I didn't want to freak him out or push him away. I was going to bring it up at our next appointment with Walt."

Doc peeled back the bandages covering Justin's chest. Even in the short amount of time since he'd seen him at the Mystique, his bruises had visibly healed. His nipples were bright red, with specks of dried blood. The angry purplish color of his skin was darker than earlier. The long marks where he'd been whipped had deepened.

"Here are some pinch marks." Doc pointed to smaller, narrow bruises, about a half inch long, that were almost invisible. "See how there's yellowing around the edges? That means they're in a later stage of healing. If I have to guess, I'd say they were caused by some kind of clamp. The same bruises are on his balls and penis. The ones on his thighs, those look like he pinched himself. They're more round." Max was unsure what to say, so Doc went ahead. "They're most likely self-inflicted."

Of course they were. Max had known. Seeing the bruises on Michael at the club, the same shapes…. How else could they have happened? No one was hurting Justin at headquarters, and he didn't leave the property without Max—until that night.

"What's your opinion on why?"

Doc rocked back on his heels, arms crossed tightly, eyes on Justin's mangled chest. "There're many reasons people hurt themselves. Some suffer severe depression or PTSD caused by past trauma, abuse, mental illness, body dysphoria. That distress builds and builds over time. Most people find healthy or socially acceptable ways to relieve that distress. Some people don't, or try but nothing works. They want to feel something different and search for some kind of release. Some find endorphins, released by pain, to be cathartic. But the release is short-lived. Over time they need more pain to achieve the same results. Some become addicted to the pain, and I have to tell you, self-harm can become quite severe. I've treated the wounds of some vampires compelled to mutilate parts of their bodies. One vampire cut off one of his own testicles because his dysphoria toward them was so severe."

"He cut one off, like with a knife? Was he drunk or high?" Max squeezed his legs together.

"No drugs. No alcohol. Just took a knife and a pair of kitchen scissors to his balls. Videotaped himself doing it as well. He got one out before he started to hemorrhage. Came into the ER where I was doing my residency. Passed out on the floor in the waiting room. When he came to, he begged me to remove the other one."

"Damn. That's fucked-up."

"But not as uncommon as you think. There are unlicensed people who will castrate a man for the right price and those willing and desperate enough to seek them out. They'll do anything to relieve their suffering."

You'll do anything.

Is that what Justin had done?

"And then there are the masochists who like pain, in much the same way most of us like pleasure. People want to be hurt for different reasons. Some want pain for the sake of pain, and for others, they need it for the sexual release."

"That's what Marshall Stone said when she gave us a private viewing of a masochist and sadist pair at the Mystique yesterday."

Doc's eyes widened in surprise and question.

"Yeah, I know. It was disturbing to say the least." And arousing. And mind opening. "Justin wasn't there for that, he wasn't. He wouldn't...." Justin, appearing so innocent in sleep. The thought he wanted anyone else raised jealousy in Max.

"Liking pain or needing pain isn't a horrible thing, Max. There's a whole culture around the masochist and sadist part of the BDSM world."

Max frowned. "He wants to be part of the BDSM world?"

"You're not hearing me. It's possible Justin went to the Mystique in search of someone who could fulfill that need and got in with the wrong person. It doesn't mean he wants the pain every day or that he needs someone labeled a sadist to do it for him. What he needs most is trust in whoever helps him to meet his need. I can't say what Justin was doing, but the marks on his body point to more than a passing fancy."

God, did Justin need Max to be that person? Need Max to hurt him? How could he physically hurt Justin? Fuck, if he needed that level of sadism, Max couldn't do it. He just couldn't.

"The person who did this got off, physically or mentally, causing Justin pain, hearing him cry and scream, seeing his reactions, maybe even smelling his blood."

"Damn, Doc, you make this person sound like a demon."

He shook his head. "Not a demon. Probably a sociopath. They lack empathy. As a cop you've most likely dealt with a sociopath. Narcissistic, self-centered, lacks emotion, manipulative."

"Are you saying what happened to him wasn't what Justin went to the Mystique for?"

"Exactly. You won't know what he needs until you talk to him, so don't run away from something good, because you'll be able to find ways to help him."

Max shuddered with thoughts of what might have happened if they hadn't found Justin. If this guy had Caden....

Max rubbed his face. He had to admit he was terrified if Justin needed pain from others. He didn't know if he could do that for him. "This is so beyond me."

Doc circled around the bed. "What's important here is that you have some understanding of what's happening with him. When he wakes up—"

Doc raised a hand to stop Max from making assumptions. "When he wakes, he's going to need support and help figuring out why he's hurting himself, and you're the person he trusts most. If you allow your judgments and feelings about this to get in the way, he'll probably turn that need inward and suffer even more. Can you put aside your feelings to help him?"

What choice did he have? Because it was Justin, even if it made Max uncomfortable, he would. "Yeah. I just want him to be happy, no matter how that happens." And what Max had seen at the Mystique, he couldn't get that out of his head. "Right now, I wish he'd just wake up."

"I'm waiting for the results of the MRI. Carson will see what he can do after he's rested. Whatever occurred the first time Justin was pulled from his catatonia wasn't in play this time, since Carson's proximity to Justin didn't have the same effect. That could be because of Carson's issues since he fought Merrick." Doc snorted. "Of course, Carson wanted to try the minute I had Justin settled, but I put the guy in one of the rooms down the hall and gave him something to help him sleep. He looked like hell." Max had to agree with that. "Lincoln has called and harassed my staff every thirty minutes on the dot. I took his last call. He said there's no word on Caden."

"Nothing. No one claims to have seen him. Just like every other human who has gone missing from there." If anything happened to Caden, Max feared for the person or persons responsible. Carson wouldn't stop until they were dead. Last time someone had tried to hurt Carson's family and Lincoln, it had ended with Carson taking down an entire building with his mind.

"Do you think he'll forgive me?" Max focused on Justin's face. "I mean, if I hadn't gone on that date, he never would have gone to that club." Then he thought about it. "Doesn't matter. I'll wait no matter what."

"Good answer." Then Max remembered Doc was an expert at waiting for the person he loved to wake up.

"How's Tommy?"

Doc flinched, puzzling Max. "He's the same. I have some other things I need to check on and then maybe get some sleep. You should do the same. If you want, I can have a cot set up in here."

Max thought about the offer, then nodded. He probably wouldn't get much sleep anyway, sleeping in the apartment without Justin in the next room. That thought dropped his heart into his stomach. He'd come to count on Justin being there to such a degree that without him life wouldn't be the same, and that thought made Max smile.

"I'll get that cot." Doc left the room, closing the door.

Max leaned over Justin, resting his cheek against Justin's. Max closed his eyes and breathed in Justin's scent. He felt Justin's stubble, but Max continued to rub their faces together as he held Justin's hand.

"I'm here and waiting for you to open those beautiful eyes. When you do, I have something I need to tell you, so come back to me, please, as soon as you can."

CHAPTER 14

MAX PEELED himself off the hard cot after a crappy night of sleep. He stretched his sore shoulder and worked the kinks out of his body. Justin's eyes were open again. Did he even know it was morning, or that the sun shined in the room? Maybe it was best if he didn't.

Max kissed him on the cheek and told him he'd be back later. After showering in his apartment, he dressed in his uniform. Headed back to Medical before going down to work, needing to check on Justin once more. That hadn't been the plan, but his heart had something else in mind.

Entering Medical, he found the reception area buzzing with more staff than he'd ever seen at one time there. It appeared that most of the nurses and other Medical employees were there, which was strange. Unless something had happened. That flipped Max's stomach.

Was Justin okay?

Max found Doc speaking with the dark-haired woman who'd been sitting with Tommy the night before. Since she was now standing, he couldn't miss that she was very pregnant. The pinched and guarded expression on Doc's face, and something about his stance, threw Max off. Despite the woman speaking pleasantly, calmly, Doc appeared pissed off.

When Doc noticed Max, he raised a finger, then continued his conversation with the woman for a few seconds. He watched her waddle off down the hall toward Tommy's room. Doc crossed the room and rubbed his forehead. He looked dead tired.

Max frowned. "Did you get any sleep?"

"A few hours."

"What's going on around here? Looks like everyone who works here is, well, here."

"Lincoln didn't call you?"

Dread clutched at Max's chest. "I don't know. I left my phone in Casey's car. What's wrong? Not Justin, please."

"Justin's fine, just to ease your mind. Come to my office."

Max's hands shook, thinking about Justin.... *He's fine. Get a grip.*

Max followed and shut the door behind him.

Doc sank into one of the chairs in front of his desk. "Tara Collette has been found. She's pretty beat up, possibly been tortured. She was brought in about a half hour ago."

The first human to disappear from the Mystique. "She's here? But it's illegal for you to treat her. She's not a vampire."

Doc looked Max directly in the eyes. "She is now."

Max gaped and then closed his mouth. Doc had to be trying to get one up on him. "Yeah, right. Nice one, Doc."

Doc didn't smile or lose that fucking hard expression.

"That's impossible. Vampires are born. You can't make someone into a vampire any more than you can turn someone who's Caucasian into an Asian. Do you mean she had work done to get fangs? I've seen those people with the cosmetic teeth who claim to be vampires."

"I tested her blood. She has vampire markers. And she's been drinking synthetic blood."

Humans couldn't drink synthetic blood. Certain components messed with blood cell production in humans and could cause a myriad of other health issues. Not that some Nons who wanted to be vampires hadn't tried to drink the stuff and suffered the consequences.

"Again, not possible."

"You're not telling me anything I don't know." Doc rubbed at the nape of his neck. "I've sent the test results to a vampire genetic specialist from New York City. Maybe he can help me find something. I've limited access to Tara's room to only my most trusted staff. I told everyone else that she came here first and has an unidentified illness that could be contagious so I can't transport her to a Nons hospital. I placed her in the quarantine room. This information needs to stay between as few people as possible. Can you imagine the panic that news like this would cause?"

"A human turned into a vampire. Yeah, it'd be hunting season on vampires, an all-out war." Could things get any worse? "Where was she found?"

"Dumped right on our doorstep."

"Seriously?"

"Seriously."

A human turned into a vampire and the evidence is dumped right on NVJ's doorstep. Maybe that infectious disease thing wasn't too far off. "That seems too convenient, a way to get her in the door. Are you sure she doesn't have some kind of contagious disease, or is she going to wake up and try to kill us all?"

"That's the other reason she's quarantined. I've had her restrained until she wakes and we can talk with her. There's an officer posted outside of her room. No one gets in, and she doesn't get out."

"Damn," Max muttered. He turned when the door opened.

Lincoln entered, his face a steely mask of determination. The door slammed behind him. "What'd you find, Doc?"

"She's a vampire all right, as impossible as that sounds. Someone out there is experimenting on humans, and what they can do…. Fuck, it's scary." Doc's eyes were wide, his face ashen, and his gaze far off as if he were running scenarios through his mind.

That look on Doc tended to send Max into high alert. "What's wrong?"

Doc's eyes focused, and he rubbed his chin. "Do you remember the Human Genome Project back in 2003?"

"Yeah. They found all of the human genes and made a map or something? What about it?" Lincoln asked.

"What no one knew at the time was that a map of the vampire genome was created as well. The information was and remains top secret."

Lincoln grimaced. "If it's so top secret, then how do you know about it?"

"Because I was on the team that mapped the vampire genome based on the human genome."

"That's amazing." Damn, Max knew Doc was smart, but wow. "Why the big secret, though?"

Doc leaned heavily on his desk. He was a good-looking man for being in his fifties and generally looked forty at the oldest. Right then he looked older.

"Not to get too complicated, the Human Genome Project only sequenced the euchromatic regions of the genome. In the nucleus, these are the most active portions of the DNA, and that comprises around 90 to 92 percent of the entire human genome."

"What's the other 8 to 10 percent?"

"Heterochromatin DNA. These tend to control gene expression by either making a gene inactive or influencing expression through repetition, or allowing or disallowing chromosomes to fuse."

Max blinked rapidly. So much for not getting complicated. "Okay, how about you tell me why this has you freaked out."

"Because we found that the genomes of humans and vampires are identical."

Max and Lincoln both looked at each other, then back to Doc.

"What?" Humans and vampires genetically identical? Max thought of the implications.

"How is that possible?" Lincoln asked.

"The variation between humans and vampires lies in the expression of the genes. In vampires, the heterochromatin DNA is responsible for activating the genes that make vampires into vampires."

"But wouldn't that mean the Human Genome Project would have found the vampire genes in humans?"

Doc raised his brow. "They did."

Lincoln's expression was incredulous. "Excuse me? The government's main reason for not including vampires in that project is that according to law, vampires aren't considered human. We aren't important enough even though we pay taxes, same as humans. What you're saying is that vampires have the same exact genome as humans, and no one said anything about that?"

Doc nodded, his features hard. "When results were brought to the National Institute of Health, who contributed to funding the human project, the research was deemed flawed by half a dozen of the top geneticists in the world. It's not."

Max furrowed his brow. "Why would they accept it? Then the government would have to admit vampires are the same as humans, and they couldn't discriminate against us anymore. They'd have to give vampires equal rights. We're tied to a legend of evil predators that attack at night and drain people of blood. In the past twenty years, there's only been a handful of attacks where a vampire actually bit a human without provocation, not in self-defense. Those attacks outweigh the thousands of vampires who've been the victims of hate crimes and discrimination. The politicians need something to strike fear into the hearts of Americans. You've heard them. We're a silent threat, ready to strike. If something goes wrong, the economy tanks, violence increases, people struggle to survive, blame the rise of the vampire population. We're the reason humans' lives are miserable."

Max sighed heavily. While many other industrialized countries had passed laws protecting vampires, accepting them as equals to humans, the US was far behind the times. Politics was mainly to blame, some fearmongering. Money wins, and the racist rich and powerful donated millions to the campaigns of vampi-phobic politicians. To hear some speak, allowing bloodsucking demon vampires to have any rights would lead to the religious and moral destruction of the country. Fucking drama queens. What they really feared had nothing to do with saving the country from dangerous vampires or religion but losing privilege and power over others.

Lincoln, who'd gone uncharacteristically quiet, finally spoke. "You and whoever else did this vampire project are just sitting on information that could change the lives of millions of vampires, get them better jobs, better healthcare, equal rights? Why would you do that just because the NIH didn't approve? They aren't the end all and be all of the government." Max was angry, but Lincoln was pissed.

"No, but the FBI is."

"The FBI? Why would they care?" Max asked.

Doc stood and opened the bottom drawer of the file cabinet next to his desk. He pulled out a thick manila envelope and then offered it up for one of them to take, which Lincoln did. On the front was the Department of Justice seal for the FBI. Lincoln opened the flap and then looked to Doc, who nodded him on.

Lincoln pulled the pile of papers from the envelope and frowned. "What's all this?"

"Results of an investigation the FBI conducted on me containing half-truths, lies, and manufactured evidence for charges of conspiring to overthrow the government of the United States. Every member of the vampire project got the same prize. What you hold is enough evidence to get me thrown into a federal prison and never see the light of day again if I don't follow the stipulations of the plea agreement."

"Jesus, Doc, you pled guilty? What the fuck were you thinking?" Lincoln's voice boomed across the room.

Doc's demeanor, his posture, hardened. "I was thinking that I didn't want to disappear from the face of the earth for revealing my research to the world. The FBI, politicians, the president didn't give a shit about the rights of a vampire scientist who had enough information to throw the current societal order into chaos. We were all screwed with a capital S. Fifteen months we were held in a federal prison while our lawyers filed motion after motion only to be shot down. They were harassed, their families threatened. These were good people trying to make the world better. None of us deserved to be treated like that. The only ticket to freedom came from playing their game. Turn over all of our research, notes, hard drives, everything, and never reveal what we discovered to anyone. To do so would negate the plea agreement, and we'd be thrown back into prison for life."

Lincoln was silent, as was Max. Blown away and pissed off topped the list of how he felt, knowing what the US government had done and continued to do, racial discrimination and hate of vampires. "So there's no proof the research existed."

"Nothing in print, vocal, or digital media, per the plea agreement." Doc's brow raised, and his lips thinned. His smug expression told them proof still existed in some form somewhere. "We may be free from confinement, but we will never be free of FBI scrutiny. I am required to turn over anything they ask for without argument. And they check in periodically when work is slow."

"I'm sorry, Doc. I jumped to conclusions," Lincoln said.

Doc waved him off. "We could spend all day talking about the inequality of vampires and humans, and the ethical flexibility of the US government, but vampires will be in grave danger if humans find out about Tara. I mean danger equal to or greater than the early twenties when vampires were nearly slaughtered out of existence in the US."

"Fuck," Max whispered.

"When can we talk with her?" Max knew Lincoln was chomping at the bit to question the newly made vampire. Max understood. She could have information on who did this to her and the whereabouts of the other missing humans along with Caden.

"I have her heavily sedated. She was frantic when she woke, babbling and screaming, disoriented. She has extensive scarring on her body, fresh bruises and open wounds."

Max heard the door open behind them. Both he and Lincoln turned to see Carson standing in the doorway. He looked as if he'd just woken, his hair mussed, eyes puffy. He wore a gray T-shirt and black sleep pants. His face no longer held the pallor from the night before. Max hated that his first thought upon seeing Carson was if he could try to help Justin right then.

In the blink of an eye, Lincoln had Carson wrapped in his arms. He seemed to melt into the large man. "I missed you." Lincoln placed a kiss on Carson's lips.

Carson chuckled. "I just spoke to you like twenty minutes ago."

"Exactly."

Max shook his head at the lovebirds and turned back to Doc. "You think she was tortured?"

"Are you talking about the human turned into a vampire?"

"Yeah, we are."

Carson nodded and looked up at Lincoln. "We need to find Caden." The "I can't lose another family member" was the underlying message Max heard loud and clear.

"We're tracking down some leads. The more we hear, the more I'm convinced what happened to Justin and Caden has to be connected to the missing humans. Once we talk to Tara Collette, we'll hopefully have more to go on."

Carson looked to Doc. "I still can't believe she's been turned into a vampire. I mean, that's fiction crap."

Doc only shrugged.

"When do you think Tara will be awake?" Max asked.

"Maybe after lunch. I want to wake her slowly, give her time to process where she is."

"Hey, Doc. Got those test results." Hilary stood at the desk, holding up a paper.

"Excuse me."

When he walked away, Carson turned to Max. "Have you seen Justin?"

"I slept in a cot in his room. He's still the same."

Max didn't want to ask and thought if he pushed Carson to act, Lincoln would get angry, but then Carson spoke up.

"Let me grab some breakfast, and then I'll see what I can do to help." Carson shot Lincoln a warning glance.

Lincoln raised his eyebrows but only said, "Come on, we'll get some breakfast."

Max shoved his hands into his pockets. "Thanks. See you in a bit." After taking a minute to breathe, Max headed to Justin's room.

As he walked away, Max heard his name called. Casey held up his phone. "You left his in my car. How's Justin?"

"Thanks." Max took the phone and pushed it into his pocket. "The same. I was just heading in to see him before I went to work." Max chewed on his lip. "How are you?"

She frowned, then snorted. "I told you I'm good. I'm happy for you and Justin. And after last night, seeing how… seeing you at the Mystique and how wrecked you were, I knew that you belong together. I can see you really love him."

That took Max by surprise. He didn't know about love, as in true love, but he couldn't deny he loved Justin. What exactly that meant, he didn't know.

"Thanks, Casey, for everything. I'm a little lost right now, and you've helped. Really. You're a good friend."

She smiled, her eyes so kind, so giving. He would have been lucky to have her, but Justin had his heart. "I have to get to work. See you later."

Max waved and continued to Justin's room. Inside, he halted when he saw Miriam leaning over Justin's bed, her face really close to his.

"Excuse me."

Miriam jumped and spun around. "Oh, Lieutenant, you scared me. I was just talking to Justin. You know, they say it's important to talk to them, because they can hear you."

Max moved to the bed. Justin's eyes were open, vacant, unchanged.

"I'll let you two have some time alone." She practically fluttered from the room. Too damned cheerful, though Max figured being glum and down didn't help patients, even if they were catatonic.

Max took Justin's hand in his. The deep red on his chest not covered by bandages had faded, and in some areas the skin had returned to its normal color. The visible bruises were a muted shade of purple. Justin's accelerated healing was still functioning.

"Hi, Justin. I have to go to work for a while. Carson's going to come in and see if he can wake you up. I'll be here when he does, and can't wait to see you."

No reply, no physical indication he'd heard Max. Just the blinking of his eyes. Max kissed Justin on his forehead, then left his room and headed for his office. He had to find the person who'd shoved Justin back into his head.

ENTERING THE office area, Wes cornered Max and patted him on his sore shoulder. Max flinched slightly.

"Damn, I heard what happened. How's Justin?"

Max gritted his teeth, knowing he'd be hearing that question dozens of times and the answer would be the same. "He's okay physically. He's still not awake."

Wes leaned closer. He was one large man and caused Max to feel a tad claustrophobic. "I heard what happened to him before, about being unresponsive for so many years, and… I just wanted to say I'm sorry this happened to him again. I'm here to help you get the person who did this to him, no matter what."

Out of everyone who'd asked about Justin, Wes had been the first to offer Max the help he needed to distract himself. "I appreciate that, Wes. I need to focus on something else for a few hours."

Wes nodded and straightened. He glanced away and looked pensive.

"Something wrong?"

"I don't want to pry." He blew out a breath. "I'm not sure if I should tell this, but I hung around and spoke to Justin last night after you left."

Max stiffened. "You did?" Wes might know how Justin felt about Max's date. Did he want to know?

"Yeah. He was pretty upset because…. Shit, I don't think I can tell you this."

"Because he has feelings for me?"

"Uh, yeah. You know about that?"

"I did as of last night on my date. Casey clued me in to some facts I'd chosen to overlook."

Wes shook his head slowly. "Ouch. Not exactly date conversation. So are you going on another date with Casey?"

Max snorted. "It would have to be a threesome if I did."

Wes grinned maniacally. "Got you by the balls, heh?"

Max smiled as his face heated. "Okay, yeah, by the balls. Think he owns them, in fact."

Wes's grin faded a bit. "Good for you. He's a great guy, and he's got it bad for you."

Max rubbed at his temples, afraid to ask, but he had to know. "What did he say about my date?"

Wes leaned against the doorjamb. "He thinks you're straight and that everyone knows he's got feelings for you but you. I'm guessing until your date, he thought, possibly, you might feel the same, if not now, one day."

"I am straight. Or I was… until Justin. I mean, I've never had a problem with men being with men, or even with jacking off with a bunch of guys, but my attraction has always been to women so it's confusing—and not, at the same time, if you can understand that." He was attracted to Justin, all of him, but his first thoughts of the man weren't to fuck him. He wanted to love him, care for him, be with him, share his life with him. What if the sex part never came? Was that even possible, especially if Justin needed something most people didn't?

"Sometimes it takes the right person to get us to look past gender and beyond their parts. Love their mind, their soul…." Wes sounded choked, and his eyes showed a vulnerability that looked odd on such a strong man. Had the same happened to him? Although he'd said he was attracted to both men and women, maybe he hadn't always known that to be true.

Max bit the inside of his cheek. "Yeah, you're right."

"Of course I am. Now let's take a look at what the team found last night. Hopefully we'll find something about Caden. Carson and Lincoln must be going crazy not knowing where he is."

Max nodded, and they headed to the conference room to sift through mountains of information. He had to work, or he'd go out of his mind thinking about Justin.

CHAPTER 15

THEY ENTERED the conference room and found the information piled on the table. Tia, Dwayne, and Dennison were already sifting through reports. Wes headed for the coffeepot on the side table.

Dennison threw down the paper in his hand. "You know what fucking cracks my ass? How the only person who saw Caden and Justin was the guy manning the door. He doesn't remember seeing them enter with the woman that Myers and Turner spotted. Says he let them in but can't remember with who. And then poof! Caden just disappears." He furrowed his brow. "That punk is always in trouble. I told Lincoln he should have pinned his ass down long ago, but what the hell do I know?"

"Absolutely nothing." Max picked up an interview report. Dennison scowled deeply, but Max ignored him. "Any information from the surveillance tapes?"

Tia gave him a wide-eyed look. "Oh, funny you should ask. The system failed practically at the exact moment the boys entered the building. Can you imagine that?"

"Go fucking figure." Max scanned page after page of the Mystique staff interviews without a single lead. The longer Caden was missing, the less likely he'd be found.

"Is there any connection between those missing and Caden and Justin?" Dwayne asked, finally looking up from the folder he'd been reading. He looked dog-tired.

Tia reached for a folder and pulled out a piece of paper. Scanning, she pursed her lips. "Nothing came out of our analysis. Nothing matched. Except for Caden and Justin, none of the missing humans knew each other, had mutual friends or family. All had different jobs, schools, neighborhoods. Only thing they have in common is they're human and went missing from the Mystique. None of them were even sponsored by the same members. The sponsors have no priors, nothing to indicate they were responsible for those missing. All of them have been interviewed except for Gale Nelson."

"Reportedly, he's out of the country and isn't returning until the beginning of next week. Lincoln's working on speeding that up," Dennison said.

"Do you think these people know who Caden and Justin were and targeted them? This mysterious woman gets them in without question. She had to have been a member, or at least a staff member. Did we get a good description?" Wes stirred his coffee and sat next to Dwayne.

Dwayne reached out and snagged a sheet. "Here's Taylor's report. Woman was average height, appeared to have reddish hair to her shoulders. Wearing a bright green minidress and white knee-high boots. Seriously?" Dwayne shook his head. "They were unable to get a look at her face."

"In other words, nothing." Leave it to John to point out the negative.

"And Tara Collette was found outside of our building?" Max couldn't comprehend why they'd dump her there. What was their motive? What was that supposed to say besides "Look, we made a vampire?"

"Dumped out of a black van without plates at the back gate." Tia sat back. "Myers found her this morning on his way in. He's stuck in quarantine."

"Whoa, why?" Wes sat forward.

Tia shrugged. "Doc thinks she's sick with something and doesn't want to chance it since he doesn't know what."

"She's probably got something that's meant to kill all of us. Frickin' germ warfare," Dennison said.

Everyone looked to him with wide eyes. If Max hadn't known the real reason for the quarantine, he would've been pissing himself like the rest seemed to be.

"I was just up in Medical, and Doc has ruled out anything deadly. He's just going to keep her isolated for a while longer to make sure he hasn't missed anything." Max watched them all visibly relax.

Dwayne lifted the corner of his lips. "Doc doesn't miss anything."

Dennison stood and stretched. That jogged Max's memory. "Hey Dennison, who's the woman up with Tommy?"

He dropped his arms and stared blankly at Max.

Max shifted his gaze. "Woman about this tall." He held his hand at shoulder height. "Short, black hair, very pregnant."

Every muscle in John's body jerked at once, his jaw dropping open. "You saw her?"

"Yeah, a little while ago talking to Doc."

"Fuck me." With that, he was gone from the room.

"What the hell was that about?" Wes asked.

Max had no clue. "Family issues, I think. So, do we have the list of members yet?" Max sifted through the mess on the table.

"Lincoln has it," Dwayne said. "From what I heard, once Director Williams saw who's on the list, she cut off access to everyone but Lincoln. There's some big names on it."

"I'd love to get a look at that list." Tia's expression was mischievous as usual.

"Bet it could ruin some lives if that info got out," Wes added.

Max waved his hand in a gesture of annoyance. "How about we focus on finding Caden and the rest of these missing people? Their chances of being alive increased when Tara was dumped on our doorstep. She's been missing longest, almost a year."

The door opened, and Carson and Lincoln entered. Max swallowed hard, wondering if it was time to see what Carson could do for Justin.

"A friend of Caden's just came in. She claims she was with them last night before they went to the Mystique. Tia, I want you to interview her with me." Lincoln scanned the documents on the table.

"I want to be there." Max needed to be there.

"I need a female officer with me for the interview. She's scared, and too many people will freak her out. If you want, you can watch from the observation area. We're in interview room A."

"What about Justin?" Carson asked, his attention on Lincoln.

Lincoln gazed softly down at him. "Let me interview Caden's friend, and then we'll head up to Medical."

Max thought Lincoln probably wasn't eager for Carson to put his health in danger. Understandable, but what choice did he have? Justin wasn't a priority. Caden was.

"Okay. I'm going to check on Uncle Graham first."

"I'll let you know when I'm done." Lincoln kissed Carson on the forehead.

Max and Tia followed Lincoln from the room, leaving the others behind. They were all silent until they reached the interview room. Lincoln opened the door and stepped into the observation room. Sarina Jenkens sat at the table, facing the two-way mirror. She screamed rich kid. Her styled hair, trendy clothes, gold watch, diamond earrings. She came from money.

Lincoln pulled a folded sheet of paper from his pocket. "Sarina Jenkens, twenty, student at American University with Caden. Been friends for over a year. Those few weeks he disappeared, he was at her parents' vacation house in Virginia Beach. Last night, Sarina says they were at a friend's house, Winn Bryant, when Caden received a call from Justin." Lincoln's eyes flicked to Max and then back to the paper. "Justin asked Caden to take him to a bite club. Justin was picked up outside of the back gate, and they went to the B&D Club."

That place was a disease-infested dive. Drinking blood had the same drawbacks as unprotected sex. Diseases like hepatitis and HIV could be passed. Clubs were supposed to test members. It was time-consuming and often impossible to monitor if test results were manipulated. Max knew some of the cheaper clubs cut corners, especially the B&D.

"Why'd she come in?" Tia asked. "We haven't released information that Caden's missing."

"She doesn't know that. She got worried when she couldn't reach him this morning. Says she and Caden picked up Justin here last night and drove to the B&D. Before Caden and Justin left for the Mystique, she says she tried to talk them out of going, but they went anyway. She refused to go. She called the main switchboard looking for Graham to see if Caden made it home. I had all calls concerning Caden routed to me. She's freaked because I brought her in and haven't given her any information. Tia, you go in first, warm her up to you. I'll come in shortly. I'll do most of the questioning. You'll be her protector in there, get her to where we need her so she'll answer everything."

Tia nodded and entered the room. The girl started when the door opened, then relaxed slightly but was still visibly revved up. The speaker wasn't on so they couldn't hear what was being said. Max went to hit the button, but Lincoln stopped him.

"What?" Max's nerves were on edge, and his stomach was knotted and nothing was moving fast enough.

"I have the members list for the Mystique."

"I heard. Some big names on it?"

"And then some. I just wanted you to know I can't let anyone see who's on it."

"I get it."

"Okay. Hang tight. I'll be out in a few."

Lincoln went into the room and sat across from Sarina. Max turned on the speaker and crossed his arms, hoping this girl had info about Caden for them.

Lincoln had no sooner sat when he began. "You said that you know Caden from college?" He wasn't modifying his deep voice, and Max could tell he intimidated her. She might have tried to play Tia if they'd been alone, but not with Lincoln there.

"Where's Caden? Is he okay?"

"Just answer the question, Ms. Jenkens."

She looked to the left. "We had the same Intro to Psych class and became friends."

"And he was with you at your parents' beach house in Virginia Beach the last couple of weeks?"

"Yes," she answered meekly.

"Were any other friends there with you and Caden?"

"Winn Bryant and Skylar Young were there for a while. Do you want—?"

"Were your parents there with you?"

"No."

"Who are your parents?"

"Gale and Yvonne Nelson."

Max closed down his reaction. Lincoln's jaw twitched but otherwise remained nonreactive. "You said your last name is Jenkens."

She nodded a little too hard. "I use my stepmother's maiden name. My father's afraid if people know who I am, I could be in danger."

"Your father is Gale Nelson, of Nelson Technologies?"

"Yes. But I don't know what this has to do with Caden. Please, I'm really worried."

How could that be a coincidence? That name had been popping up a lot lately.

"Where are your parents right now?" Lincoln's tone became terser, more commanding, and Sarina shrunk back into her chair.

"Why? I didn't do anything wrong!"

Tia reached across the table and touched her hand. "We aren't saying you did, okay?" Tia turned to Lincoln and frowned. "Commander?"

He sneered at Tia, his expression hard, eyes dark. "I'm in charge here, and she needs to answer the questions unless she has something to hide."

"I'm sure she doesn't. She's just scared."

The corner of Max's lips lifted. They were good at the nice cop/mean cop routine. Lincoln could rattle the person while Tia kept them feeling safe enough to break down and tell what they didn't want to tell.

Lincoln sighed heavily. "Sarina, you said you last saw Caden at the B&D. Is that correct?" Lincoln's tone softened, as if he'd listened to Tia's suggestion.

She nodded, confusion on her face. "Yes. Is he here? Is he in trouble?"

Lincoln ignored her. "We know you picked up Justin Masters at 8:15 p.m. at the back gate of this building. Caden used his key card. Had you ever met Justin before?"

"No, but Caden's talked about him a few times. He said he didn't go out much because of something that happened to him when he was a teenager. He wanted to get him out, help him have some fun. Are they okay?"

"Was anyone else with you?"

Her mouth opened and closed. "Yeah. Skylar and Greg Mendelson."

"Are these friends of yours or Caden?"

She frowned. "Both."

"And did they go to the B&D with you?"

She fidgeted, running her fingers, tipped with a french manicure, through her silky blonde hair. "No. I dropped them off at Ultra Bar. They didn't want to go to the bite club."

"And you did?" Tia asked.

Sarina nodded.

"Have you been there before, Sarina?" Tia used her sweet, I'm-your-best-friend voice.

Sarina hesitated and bit her lip. "Yes, but my stepmother doesn't know. I would be in so much trouble." Her voice shook. Max could tell she'd finally realized this wasn't just a friendly chat.

"Just answer our questions, okay?" Tia remained calm and reassuring.

Sarina nodded. "Okay."

Again it was Lincoln's turn. "So you got to the B&D at what time?"

"Around eight forty-five, I think. I can't be sure."

"It was just you and Caden and Justin?"

Another nod.

"Answer verbally please."

"Yes."

"Did you go inside?"

"No. We were waiting in line outside, and this woman came up to us and offered to get us into the Mystique."

"And then what happened?"

She let out a breath. "I told her no, but Justin, he got really excited and said yes. Caden wasn't sure, I mean he tried to talk Justin out of it, but Justin was going with or without him. Caden wasn't going to let him go alone. So they left."

Max's chest clenched painfully, hearing that Justin had wanted to go. That gave possible credence to what Doc had said earlier about Justin seeking a place where he could get what he needed. He'd sat right at their kitchen table and heard Wes and Max talk about what they'd seen there.

"What did this woman look like?"

Sarina looked up. "Taller than me, but not much. Horrendous red wig, brown eyes with too much black eyeliner, her two front teeth overlapped slightly. Her red lipstick was stuck to her teeth, that's how I noticed her teeth. She wore some horrific lime-green dress with white knee-high boots. She was a train wreck."

"Did she tell you her name?"

Sarina rolled her eyes. "Spice. You know that's fake."

"No last name?"

"No."

"Have you ever seen her before?"

She shook her head, then remembered to answer. "No. I don't think so. I mean, she was wearing a wig. She didn't sound familiar."

"Was she alone? Did you see anyone else who appeared to be waiting for her?"

Her eyes were shinier, and her lip quivered. "No."

"Okay. They left with her on foot or by car?"

When she didn't answer, Lincoln raised his voice. "Answer the question, Ms. Jenkens."

She jerked. When she blinked, a tear escaped down her cheek, and Max had to wonder why she was crying. "Th-they walked down the street, and at the corner, they got into a limo. I don't know who was in it."

Max closed his eyes. Some fucking rich son of a bitch with too much money was responsible for all of this crap. Someone like Gale Nelson. Had he lured Justin and Caden away when his daughter was right down the street?

"And you didn't happen to see the license plates to that limo, did you?"

"No." She sniffled, and Tia handed her a tissue from a box on a side table. She wiped her face.

"Any distinguishing emblems, signs?"

"No."

Lincoln leaned forward, his eyes pinpointed on the girl. "Did you have anything to do with Caden and Justin being invited to the Mystique?"

She took in a shuddering breath. "No."

Lincoln was silent, his eyes never wavering from the crying girl. Something wasn't adding up, but Max had no clue what. That her father was Gale Nelson couldn't be a coincidence. Could it?

"Where're your parents now, Ms. Jenkens?"

"Why? Am I in trouble?"

Lincoln didn't even direct her to answer the question. Just waited.

"My stepmother is at the condo in Georgetown, or she was this morning. My father's away on business."

"Where?"

She closed her eyes. "Umm, this time he went...." She frowned.

"Now, Ms. Jenkens!"

Even Max jumped at that.

"New York. He went to New York."

"Where in New York?"

"He was flying into Syracuse. That's all I know."

Syracuse was close to Oneida. Max had a feeling this girl knew more than she was saying. But what?

"Stay here," Lincoln said, and he exited with Tia.

"Max, come with me." They walked back toward the conference room. "Out of the country, huh?"

"Doesn't know his geography, maybe? Thinks New York is another country? Could be a legitimate mistake." Max shrugged. He got more wound up by the minute. Nothing was making sense. There were too many pieces and no vision of what the larger puzzle would be. "Either his daughter is lying or his staff is. Seems a little too much like a coincidence that his name keeps coming up, doesn't it?"

"Certainly got my Spidey senses tingly. I'll call Carina once we're done upstairs and get her to use her influence to get the man back here."

In the conference room, the other officers were there except Dennison. That piqued Max's interest, but he couldn't focus on anything but Justin.

"Okay, listen up." All eyes were on Lincoln instantly. "I just interviewed Caden's friend, Sarina Jenkens. Her father happens to be Gale Nelson. That name keeps popping up a little too often for my liking. A couple of you head down to his offices and then his home. Someone is lying about his whereabouts. Check the airport for flight records. A man that rich must have a plane, I imagine. I want to know where he actually landed. I need someone to head down to the B&D and ask around about the woman seen entering the Mystique with Caden and Justin. Tia has a description. Also a limo picked them up near that location. Ask around. I'm thinking there aren't too many limos parking down there. The rest of you handle the remaining interviews of the Mystique staff. I've got the DC police watching the Mystique. Do we have the bank records for the Oneida Commons?"

"Came in today, boss." Maggie smiled.

"Then tell me where their funding comes from. Tia, get Casey down here to watch Ms. Jenkens. We'll keep her here until she starts to protest. Casey can take her and get her something to eat or drink at the commissary. Tell her we might need her. Not a word about Caden missing or about Justin. She's not to leave or call anyone. They took her cell when she came in, but don't allow her have access to any phone or computer."

Tia crossed her arms. "I'm not a rookie."

Lincoln didn't remark, and Max preceded him out of the room. As they made their way to the elevator, Lincoln pulled out his phone. "Let me get Carson to meet us in Medical." As he waited for Carson to answer, he frowned. Hanging up, he said, "Probably set it down at Graham's. I'll shoot him a text."

Max's head was spinning from all that had happened. His shoulder ached like a bitch. He looked at his watch. Two in the afternoon and he hadn't eaten since breakfast. He would grab some blood when they were finished. Hopefully things would start looking better once Justin woke up. Max believed he could give them information that would bring them closer to finding Caden. Max didn't even want to imagine what Caden was enduring after seeing Justin and Tara.

The elevator door opened, and they both stepped in. The doors closed, but Lincoln didn't swipe his card for access to the medical wing.

"You doing okay?" Lincoln asked.

Max gave Lincoln a sideways glance, knowing the more he complained the longer they'd be stuck in that box. "Yeah. I'm good."

Lincoln nodded, rocking slightly, his eyes on the ceiling.

"Christ, just say it."

Lincoln turned a surprised gaze on Max.

Max rolled his eyes. "Jesus, I don't need Carson's abilities to know you want to say something, so just say it."

"Okay, sure. You need to know that I want Carson to be able to help Justin as much as you. I'm hoping he can wake him up. Shit, not just for him and you but for Caden." Lincoln's lips thinned.

"But?"

"But I won't let him hurt himself. I can't let that happen. If I think he's heading that way, I'll stop everything."

Max gritted his teeth and counted to five. He swiped his own card and sent the elevator climbing. He was tired and hungry and fucking frustrated and overreactive. "I wouldn't let Carson harm himself. You know that."

Lincoln rubbed his forehead and sighed. "Shit, I'm going all overprotective again, huh? I thought we'd gotten past the danger, but the threats to the people I care for are back and.... When does life ever calm down?"

With his words, the elevator doors opened to chaos.

CHAPTER 16

A ROARING sound filled the air, and a wave of pressure smacked into them. A high-pitched wail, unlike anything Max had ever heard before, caused Max to cover his ears. Down the hallway near Justin's room, Carson knelt, his tattoos of the ancient writing covering his skin and glowing bright red. He held his head as he leaned over his folded knees.

"Carson!" Lincoln rushed toward his bond mate.

Max followed, terrified that Carson had tried to help and was severely hurt. Even scarier was the thought that Justin would be injured as well. The air was heavy and thick and charged with electricity. The pressure in Max's head and around his body rose. Looking to the left, Max spotted Dennison in another hallway, trying to hold his gun on the pregnant woman, bent over and clutching her stomach. What the fuck?

Pressure built in Max's head as he tried to walk, pushing against a force equivalent to hurricane winds. The pain in his head grew. Lincoln was near Carson, probably trying to reach him through their link without success. Carson had to stop whatever he was doing.

"Carson! Stop!" Max shouted, however his voice was quickly swallowed whole by the high-pitched wail. Soon Carson would annihilate them all, and once again take down the building around them. Max didn't want to die, didn't want to leave Justin when he'd just found him.

Max forced his muscles to fight the invisible pressure, push past the substantial resistance, and get to Justin. Reaching Justin's doorway, he grabbed the jamb and pulled himself into the room. The roar was deafening, and nausea roiled Max's stomach, his head ready to implode. His urgency increased as he spotted Miriam next to the head of Justin's bed. She wore an odd, shiny black helmet open in the front. Over Justin's eyes she held what looked like a shortened pair of binoculars. Justin wore only boxers. The bandages on his chest had been removed, the bruising already faded. Movement from Justin caught Max's eye. Justin's arms and legs were tied down, but he pulled against the restraints as if he were trying to get free. As if he were awake.

Max needed to get to Miriam, stop her from harming Justin. Miriam's movements were unhindered by the massive force trying to tear them all apart. Miriam grinned when she spotted Max coming toward her. Trying to get to his gun was useless. Fuck, this slow-motion shit was ridiculous.

Max reached the side of Justin's bed, opposite Miriam. His chest heaved, his muscles cramped as if he'd run a mile at full speed. If he could get his gun, Miriam was getting a bullet in her.

"Hi, Max. How nice of you to join us." That cheerful voice was grating. "I'm almost done here, and then we'll be on our way." She chuckled. "Justin's ours. Big plans for him, you know. He's quite special, and the boss is itching to get him back." She worked on a laptop on the bedside table. "Just another five minutes, and I'll have this boy back to the resting state where he should be. That silly Carson tried to wake him up. Luckily, I was able to stop him." She laughed out loud, amused by Carson's failed efforts.

Max tried to grab Miriam's arm, but his hand fell short. His body was heavier, his muscles refusing to move. He was fucking helpless, couldn't force his body to cooperate. He screamed his frustration inside of his own head.

"Once I'm done with Justin, I'll take care of your memory, and you'll forget that you ever loved him. Unfortunately for you, that means you'll be left a drooling shell, and Justin will just be another missing boy like the others, because there'll be no one who loves him or cares that he's gone. Doesn't matter how much you love him. He wasn't designed to be loved. He was designed to suffer."

Max's lips formed the word *No*, but no sound came out. He could never forget Justin, never stop loving him. Max wasn't letting the crazy fake nurse go anywhere with Justin. How? He had no clue as his body continued to fail. Another attempt to grab Miriam ended in him collapsing onto Justin. Beneath Max, Justin struggled. Max tried to climb up and look into Justin's eyes, but his head was so heavy.

A crushing counterpressure hit Max from behind. Miriam stumbled back. Her smug smile vanished. With narrowed eyes she looked past Max toward the door. Max managed to turn his head. Carson had made it to the doorway. He clutched the sides of his head, blood running from both nostrils. His eyes were mere slits, his jaw clenched tight, the red tattoos seeming to float above his skin.

Miriam moved behind Max, and he strained to see the anything-but-sweet lady. He'd fucking kill her when he got his hands on her.

She shook her head with a disapproving expression. "Oh dear, I didn't want to do this." She pushed a button on the left side of her helmet.

Max's world fell into total darkness.

JUSTIN'S EYES fluttered open, and he stared at the ceiling. He slowly worked his brain, clearing away the sleep-addled thoughts. Rising through layers of confusion filled with images, sounds, sensory overload, searing pain, agony, black masks, naked bodies, bleeding wounds, screams of pain, of pleasure….

His chest heaved, and his heart raced. He was restrained and something heavy lay on top of him. His panic rose, memories of where he was and why he was there forgotten.

Again a barrage of memories flashed through his mind, an endless assault of waking and pain and agony and release and rest and over and over. Men and women tied to tables, chained to walls, whips, needles, shocks, spanks, blood, screams…. Oh gods, he couldn't block out the visions or the desire, to be the one screaming, in agony, suffering, forced to endure the pain, rising into the pleasure, rising and rising until he was pushed from his own head.

He thrashed, needing to get free not only of his physical restraints, but of the two forces in his head. They battled, clashing, building in ferocity until he was sure he'd split in half.

"I… can't stop it!"

Hands on his face held his head from thrashing. Fighting back, Justin was helpless to stop anyone from doing whatever they wanted to him. Why did that terrify and make him feel safe simultaneously?

"Justin, calm down. I'm right here."

He had to get free. Why was he being held down?

"Justin! It's Max."

Everything would be all right if Max were there. He'd help Justin. "M-Max. I need…."

"Focus on me. Look at me. Look here…. Come on."

Justin forced his eyes to focus on Max, mere inches from his face. Beautiful green eyes.

"Thank gods you're awake. I missed you. I have so much to tell you."

Max's words didn't make sense, but Justin didn't question them, just soaked in the caring intimacy of Max.

I don't know what's wrong with me. I can't stop. My head is so full, and I don't know where it came from.

"Tell me what to do." Max ran his hand over Justin's forehead over and over, his other hand on the side of his neck. "You tell me what you need? Just tell me. Anything."

Justin wasn't sure what he wanted him to say. He tried to sit up and jerked his arms.

"I'll untie you."

Justin sucked in a breath and furrowed his brow, shaking his head.

Max paused, then smiled gently. "Okay, we can wait a minute."

Justin licked his lips and wanted to kiss Max so badly, but that couldn't happen. He knew why. Not because Max was straight. He couldn't kiss Max because he hadn't been given permission.

"I need-d-d…." He grunted when the word stuttered to a stop.

"Take your time. You can rest if you want."

But Justin knew that wasn't what he was supposed to do. He might be confused, not know what to do, but he knew that he was supposed to do what he was told.

Obey.

His will no longer his own.

"How's he doing?" Carson asked from somewhere in the room.

Justin closed his eyes, wishing the vampire away. They weren't alone, and that confused Justin further.

Max didn't look away from Justin's eyes, and that action calmed him. "How are you?"

Justin had no clue how he was.

"I'm… I'm here to do what you want me to do." Why couldn't he say anything else?

Max frowned, more in confusion than disappointment. "Just, it's okay. You don't need to do anything."

Disquiet raced through his mind. Something was wrong. Why wasn't Max telling him what to do? Images of Max commanding him to his knees, flogging his skin bright red, squeezing his balls, biting his neck…. Justin jerked.

Max's concern was nearly painful. "What's wrong?"

Justin fought his mind from speaking the same words over and over. Any attempts to say what he needed, wanted, were summarily cut off.

Never ask for anything.

His muscles flexed, and he pulled on the ropes harder. The bite around his wrists and ankles was reassuring. He searched his mind for something he could say.

"Max." Carson was still in the room.

"Hold on," Max said, continuing to gently stroke Justin's forehead. The touch, while pleasant, was too soft, too caring. Justin fought not to pull away. This was what he'd wanted from Max, right? Finally, he knew what else he could say.

Carson touched Max's arm. "I need to talk to you." He sounded panicked.

Max exhaled noisily. "Give me a minute."

The commanding tone. The forceful words. Justin stared into Max's eyes, writhed on the bed, pulling at the bonds around his ankles, pulling as hard as he could with his hands. "Max, please…."

Max smiled gently. "What do you want me to do?"

"I want you to hurt me."

Six simple words that when strung together caused Max's entire body to visibly tighten, his mouth to gape, his eyes to darken. "What?" His voice was a mere whisper. Fear clouded his eyes, but something else shadowed the fear.

Justin licked his lips. "I want you to hurt me."

"Say something else," Max commanded.

Justin couldn't stop as he said, "What do you want me to say?"

Max stood, and Justin's heart mourned the loss, but he'd been made to obey and suffer, and would gladly suffer for Max. He loved Max. Wanted to please him. Hurt for him.

Justin couldn't figure Max's expression. Justin waited to be told what to do. He yearned for the pain. The rushing high was his reward for suffering. But first he had to endure the pain. Punishment came to those who asked for their own needs to be met. His pleasure wasn't of consequence. His only tasks: suffer and obey.

His mind settled. His breaths evened out. No longer confused, no longer afraid, he waited.

Max took a step back from the bed. "Why did you ask me to hurt you?"

Justin opened his mouth, but Max raised his hand, the aggrieved expression busting through Justin's chest. Justin wanted to soothe him, offer him the only thing he had to give. When Max wanted him, Justin would be waiting.

"What's going on?" Justin hadn't seen Lincoln come into the room.

Justin looked around the room and realized he was in the medical wing. This room was similar to the training rooms he'd spent a lot of time in when he was at…. He frowned. When he was at….

Why couldn't he remember the name of the place where he'd spent many years learning and training? Those memories were sort of blurry.

Lincoln came closer and stood next to Carson. "Justin, Miriam was in here a little while ago. What did she do?"

Justin looked to Max, waiting. *Never speak without permission.* Max stared blankly at Justin. Didn't he know what to do?

"Tell him to answer," Carson said.

"What?" Max's face paled. Justin wished he'd look at him, wanted his attention again.

Max swallowed hard, his eyes rapidly going from Carson to Justin. "Umm, Justin… answer Lincoln."

Justin looked to Lincoln. "I don't know who Miriam is."

"What about going to the Mystique?"

Justin frowned. The bite club Max had talked about? He shook his head.

"What do you remember?"

Waves of memories soaked his brain, relentless, some more vivid than others, again pain that central theme.

"Holy fuck!"

When Justin opened his eyes, Carson stared down at him, mouth gaping, eyes filled with what looked to be an unfathomable horror. Justin looked to Max for what to do next.

Lincoln had Carson out the door within seconds. Justin smiled because it was just him and Max now.

MAX COULD hear the commotion Carson caused in the hallway. Max should go and find out what had caused Carson's reaction, but he couldn't pull his attention from Justin. Justin appeared calm, relaxed, sure of what he needed. Happy to see Max. Max's heart raced, and his skin tingled.

"I want you to hurt me."

For the first time, Max saw Justin as someone other than his roommate, his ward. He'd always believed the man was beautiful. Lying before him, he was sexy and desirable. Max's eyes roamed Justin's chest, the injuries to his nipples and skin nearly gone from his accelerated healing. No one could tell that less than twenty-four hours ago, his nipples had been a bloody mess, his genitals deeply bruised. Max had to do something.

"I'll be right back, okay?"

Justin appeared surprised but said, "Okay."

Max found Lincoln in the hallway with Carson cradled in his arms. The tattoos that had appeared on Carson's skin after Jameson Merrick had worked his voodoo were once again gone.

"Max. We need to talk." Lincoln ran his hands over Carson's hair and down his back. Carson stared off, an unfathomable expression on his face.

A scream filled the hallway. Max looked in the direction the noise came from.

"The pregnant woman is in labor," Lincoln said.

Max nodded. He felt disconnected and wanted to get back to Justin.

"What the hell happened here? Why were we all essentially immobile?" Max had seen some shit when Carson and Merrick had battled using their powers. What happened here was right up there with shit that was unbelievable.

Lincoln rubbed the back of his neck. "Beats the fuck out of me. Damnedest thing I ever felt. That's probably what trying to walk through a hurricane feels like, but without the wind. I've got a call out to Director Williams. We need someone to look at the surveillance tapes. Someone with some expertise who can tell us what happened."

Max looked over his shoulder at Justin's door. "I need time with him. Maybe I can get him to remember something." Lies. "Just let me talk to him."

Carson met Max's gaze. "What they did to him, Max. It all makes sense now. The way he was when he woke up. Scared, unable to regulate himself. I saw it all. Th-they tortured him, programmed him for pain, submission. Somehow that part of his mind was blocked. But his body has been trained to expect the pain. Without that programming in control, his mind has been trying to make sense of everything."

Max didn't want to believe that someone could even conceive of doing such a thing. Not to Justin.

Lincoln looked skeptical. "How do you know this?"

"I saw his memories. Not clearly, but enough to know what he's been through. And those thoughts weren't there previously."

"Baby, you can't see memories or read thoughts."

Frustration bloomed across Carson's face. "I don't know why, but I can see some of his, the ones he's thinking at that moment. I tried, but I can't access them on my own."

Max wasn't sure, but he thought that didn't sit right with Lincoln. The man could get very jealous. And he used to love Justin.

"He's acting as if he can't even think for himself. He wasn't like that when he first woke up. He wasn't the trained robot in that room." Max wasn't sure what to think.

"Something's been blocking that programming. That's what fought against me, pushing me out when I tried to see what was behind that wall. Whatever happened at the Mystique or with Miriam removed the block. He's not a robot. He's still Justin, but this training is trying to override his will."

Justin's first awakening five months earlier had taken weeks. Parts of his memories from before the bite returned. He became more cognizant, more focused, and no longer resembled the mindless human Max had found. This was different, scarier.

"What does 'programmed' mean?" Max asked.

Carson rubbed his arms as if he were cold. "His thought processes are different, more ordered, more contained. Other minds I've entered have an ordered chaos, if that makes sense. I have to work to interpret what I 'hear' in that disorder. Last time, the chaos I found in Justin's brain was immense. If I had to describe his mind now, I'd call it pinpoint focused. Single words. Obey. Serve. Pain."

"Why the hell would someone do this to him? When did this happen?" Max fisted his hands at his sides, ignoring the screaming woman, the officers gathered around them waiting for direction from their director.

Carson's face was pained. "His memories suggest he wasn't catatonic for all of those years. I got periods of memories, then periods of nothing. I don't know what it means, but from what I saw, it's like he was awake, aware, cognizant, and then he wasn't. Over and over again. Jameson was the one who took him from Oneida. Maybe he did something to place him back into that catatonic state."

"Are you saying they were controlling his catatonic state before that?"

"I think so."

Max wiped at his mouth. "So he wasn't catatonic from your bite?"

Carson shuddered. "He was when it first happened. He was in the hospital for a few weeks, and his state of awareness never changed during that time. His mother moved away shortly after to live with her sister in Massachusetts. When his mother got sick, she placed him in Oneida Commons."

Max huffed. "So these people did what? Woke him up and trained him?"

Another scream filled the hallway, a long screech, and then it ended. Within seconds, a baby cried, but Max couldn't think past the fact that someone had fucked even more with Justin's mind, had tried to change him into…. What? A pain addict? A masochist?

"Is he going to stay like this? He wasn't like this the last time he woke up."

Lincoln's eyes widened. "Oh fuck me."

Carson gazed up at Lincoln. "What, babe?"

"What if this was one of Jameson's labs? He wouldn't give a shit what was happening as long as he got what he wanted from those he'd kidnapped."

"You think whoever was running the lab had a different agenda than Merrick?"

Lincoln pursed his lips. "The others we found did, running whatever experiments they wished on Jameson's victims."

"But why Justin? He's human."

"A human bitten by a vampire. And with the Mystique involved, this could be why the humans were taken."

"Is he stuck like this forever?" Max needed answers before he went back into that room.

Max spotted Doc coming down the hallway. Doc ran his hands over his face, appearing weary. Before Max could ask again, Doc said, "From what I overheard, it sounds like you're saying he appears to have been brainwashed. His body was reconditioned and trained to respond to pain, to need it." Doc wiped his hands on a towel.

Lincoln frowned. "That type of training takes time, follows a pattern, molds the person. Basic Torture 101. And it's complicated. You have to first break the person down, make them vulnerable. Pain, stress, threats, confusion, deprivation, isolation. And only when the person stops fighting can they be shaped. That's the key. To deprogram a person, they need to be removed from that deprivation, their bodies and minds strengthened. Remind them of what their lives once were. Use techniques to counter implanted thoughts. They have clinics for those who've endured such treatment."

Love could make a person stronger, right? It was a good place to start. Max nodded. "Anything to change what they've done."

"We'll find what they've done, how their programming worked," Doc said. "That could clue us in to better ways to help him."

Max nodded.

Wes and Dennison joined them. Dennison focused intently on Doc. "How's the baby?"

"Good. Mom was close to full term. Baby's healthy. It's a boy."

"Who is she?" Wes asked.

Doc flipped the towel he held up onto his shoulder. "Tommy's wife." With that, he turned and went down the hall.

Silence reigned, and all eyes were on Dennison. He scowled and shook his head.

"His wife? Since when?" Lincoln asked.

"Long fucking story. We've got other shit to worry about right now." Dennison narrowed his eyes, as if daring anyone to mention it again.

But wow, Tommy was married and had a baby. No wonder Doc had been acting strange.

"He's right," Lincoln said. "I want everyone in the conference room downstairs in twenty minutes. Our newly made vampire vanished with Miriam. I want to know who the hell this Miriam is and why her background check didn't flag anything. And what the fuck happened up here? How'd she essentially cripple every one of us? Get me the surveillance tapes. And I want Gale Nelson here by the end of the day. I don't care if we have to bag him up and drag his ass back from Europe or New York or the North Pole. That was some high-tech shit… or something happening in here and he's our number one suspect."

Officers scrambled because Lincoln wasn't just pissed, he'd surpassed that, most likely when he'd seen Carson on the floor. Max's stomach jumped, remembering that Justin was awake. He was there, and even if he wasn't quite himself, he was alive.

"I want to spend some time with Justin. I need to try to talk to him."

Lincoln and Carson both gave him that *aww, we know what you want to talk about* look. He had no idea what he was going to say. No idea how to get past Justin's need for pain.

"You don't have to get past the pain. If pain was the way in before, it's a way in now." Carson was apparently focusing in on what Max was thinking, but he didn't care. What Carson had said punched fear and desire into Max's stomach at the same time.

Pain was the way in.

Max sighed. "I don't want to be just one of those people who hurt him for their kicks. I don't know if I can."

"Difference here is you love him." A knowing smile stretched Carson's lips. "He loves you too."

Carson's revelations should have been shocking, but they were the opposite. Relief. Happiness. And fear. What if Max failed? What if his love wasn't true love? What if he hurt Justin?

He had to stop worrying about himself and focus on what he could do, not what could happen. Max didn't want to talk about Justin or what they possibly meant to each other. He needed to change the subject.

"You okay?"

Carson frowned, possibly from the abrupt shift in the conversation. Max had been wondering why Carson didn't appear to have suffered any of the ill effects from using his abilities to stop Miriam from taking Justin.

"Yeah. Don't know why, but I am okay."

"Add it to the list of mysteries," Lincoln muttered.

Max needed to get back into the room. "Let me talk to Justin. Maybe he can remember something." Max's heart raced as he thought of Justin tied to the bed. Was he taking advantage of him? He wasn't sure what to do.

CHAPTER 17

WHEN MAX returned to the room, he pulled off his NVJ vest. Beneath he wore a white cotton T-shirt. The sight of Justin stretched out on the bed was magnificent. Max studied him closely, keeping any expression of how he felt off his face. So many conflicting emotions tumbled in his head, but one stood out from the others. If he concentrated on that one, he could stay calm and do what he needed to do.

"I want you to talk. You don't need my permission to respond. Can you do that?"

Justin nodded.

Max smiled tremulously. When Justin returned the smile, Max couldn't help grinning. "I missed you."

Justin hesitated as if he'd forgotten Max had given him permission to speak. "Was I gone?"

"Yeah. Not for long, but it was too long for me." And fucking terrifying. "Do you want me to untie you?"

Panic crossed Justin's face and then he shook his head. Max bit his lip. He trailed his fingertips over Justin's forehead, cheeks, lips. Justin drew in a shuddering breath, and Max's heart beat harder.

"You called Caden last night and asked him to take you to a bite club. Do you remember?"

Justin wrinkled his brow. "Yeah. Why did I do that?"

"I hurt you. I went out on a date."

Justin's eyes widened. "You went out with Casey."

Max nodded. "How did that make you feel?"

"Sad. Lonely. I needed something to take the pain away."

Max snorted. Pain to take away pain. Maybe he could help erase some of that pain. "I'm sorry." He hated how he'd hurt Justin.

Justin cocked his head. "For what?"

Max ran his fingertip over Justin's chin and throat. He shivered hard.

"For not knowing what I had. Not knowing that you were right there, waiting for me. And I have to say, seeing you here like this, bound to the bed, well, I shouldn't be thinking what I am right now."

His words seemed to surprise Justin, who licked his lips. A trembling need rose in Max's core. His confusion was second to his desire for Justin. Just yesterday he'd suppressed any thoughts of Justin, tried to ignore the attraction. No more.

"What're you saying?" Justin's voice was a low rumble that Max heard and felt as he traced circles on Justin's chest.

Max leaned over, his lips inches from Justin's, the lips of a man, and he wasn't freaking out, wasn't second-guessing himself. "I'm saying that I want you." Max kissed Justin's cheek. "I need you." Kissed his nose. "If you'll have me."

Max watched Justin for his reaction, any indication he understood what Max meant. Could he understand with what they'd done to him?

"Really?" Justin's voice was a mere exhale of breath.

Max nodded. He plucked Justin's nipple, and Justin's chest hitched. "Do you like that?"

Justin nodded, but pleasure mixed with confusion on his face. "The way you're touching me, I shouldn't like it. I remember something.... Someone told me I'd never want to be touched again without pain, that I wouldn't be able to stand gentle touches. Anything given with love." His eyes were glassy. "But with you right now...." His lower lip quivered.

The pained expression on Justin's face had to go. But how could Max make that happen? "What's wrong, honey?"

"It's not going to be enough."

Translation: Gentle love wasn't going to be enough. Max watched his fingers as they ran over Justin's hardened nipples, then his palm running over the silky skin of Justin's hairless chest.

"I know." Max pinched and pulled his nipple, increasing the pressure. Justin writhed and gasped. That accomplished the task of filling his cock, which tented his boxers. Doubts over being able to have sex with a man hit Max, but when he thought of sex with Justin.... "I don't want to be without you. I went on a date with Casey, and all I could talk about was you." Another pinch and Justin arched off the bed.

"Max," Justin whispered. "I want you too."

Max pinched and pulled both nipples until Justin panted and yanked on his restraints. Max leaned over again, and his lips hovered above Justin's. "I don't know how far I can go, but I'll try, okay?"

"Okay."

Max tentatively joined their lips, drawing on his love for the man tied before him. Eyes closed, Max deepened the kiss, tongue exploring the wet heat of Justin's mouth. The kiss intensified, Max giving in to the lust coating his entire body, his cock throbbing in the tight space between his groin and pants. Nothing had felt so right in such a long time.

Justin's whimpering moans were swallowed between them. Max rolled the nipple between his fingers as he plundered Justin's mouth. With swift ferocity, he clamped the nub hard, until he was sure it would pop between his fingers. Justin arched, screaming and bucking, as Max rode through the spasms of Justin's body. Releasing the nipple, Max broke the kiss. What he saw took his breath away.

Red flushed Justin's creamy skin. His chest heaved, his eyes half-open, pupils blown wide. He looked as if he'd been thoroughly fucked already.

"You like that?" Max didn't recognize his own thick voice. In the air was the musky smell of two men at the peak of arousal, their power mingling. Max was drunk on that power.

"Yes." And Justin's eyes pleaded for more. Max wanted so much more, wanted to release his cock and fuck his lover until he sprayed cum on the bed, filled him with his semen, marked Justin as his. But he didn't want their first time to be in that room, under those circumstances. But he could allow them both release.

"Do you want more?"

"Yes."

"What do you want?"

Justin writhed in his restraints, not answering.

"Answer me!"

Justin jerked. "Anything. Anything you want."

Max had no clue what happened to him. A myriad of punishments he could mete out if Justin refused to answer coursed through his mind. His hands shook, but he kept the steely expression.

"That's right. I'll do whatever I want with you." Yup, drunk with power.

Max ran his palm over Justin's stomach, a whisper of a touch. The muscles twitched, contracted, as his hand came closer to the tent of fabric. Justin was no slouch in the cock department. The hair thickened below his belly button. Max swirled his fingers through the soft, reddish hair. As he reached the waistband of Justin's boxers, Max pushed his hand under the elastic band, tangling his fingers in the mat of hair until they touched the base of Justin's cock.

Justin's breaths continued to hitch as he gasped in anticipation of the unknown. He could have no idea when and where Max's next pinch would occur. The thought fueled Max's fire. With his other hand, Max rubbed Justin's thighs, the bruises so faint they were only noticeable upon close inspection. Max drew in a shuddering breath. Could he hurt Justin enough to bruise him?

Justin watched and waited without demands, totally under Max's control. When he cupped Justin's balls through the fabric of his boxers, his eyes fluttered. Max pulled the leg of the underwear over until Justin's furred orbs were visible. They weren't any different than Max's own, and having them caressed and stroked, even a tight squeeze, was highly pleasurable to Max. But for Justin, that wouldn't be enough. Gripping both testicles, Max tugged them away from Justin's body. His eyes widened. He whimpered and fisted his hands. With a steady pressure, Max squeezed, tightening his grip, tighter… tighter. Justin grimaced, short breaths puffing out his cheeks.

"No screaming."

Justin nodded as his thighs shook, his eyes became glassy, his stomach muscles spasmed.

Tighter and tighter Max squeezed. Justin's cock twitched under the thin fabric of his boxers.

"Can you take more?"

Another sharp nod. More pressure. Justin's face was beet red. His breaths stuttered and then stopped as he grunted. More grunts. He bit his bottom lip, his teeth digging in, the skin paling. Suffering. Max felt lightheaded, his own breaths increasing.

A high-pitched whine filled the air as Justin fought to hold back his scream. His reaction, the clear distress, the pained grimace should have hit Max as wrong, should have caused him to stop or at least ease his grip, but instead he tightened his fist. Max began to doubt Justin would say if the pain was too much. If he was trained to take pain, he was no doubt trained to take torture without complaining. That fear caused Max to release Justin's balls. Instantly, Justin's body relaxed and seemed to melt into the bed, his chest heaving. His eyes never wavered from Max's, and the lust swirling in their depths stoked Max's need.

"Could you have taken more? Tell me the truth."

Without hesitation Justin gave a breathy, "Yes."

Max closed his eyes for a moment as a shiver raced over his skin, his body flushed with euphoria. Justin suffering—no, Justin suffering for him—was intoxicating, a pure adrenaline rush. Gods, what was wrong with him?

Justin's hips moved rhythmically, undulating, seeking some kind of relief. His cock stretched the front of his boxers. Max ran his fingers under the waistband and lifted it away from Justin's stomach, getting the first glance at his cock. Strings of precum flowed freely from the slit, dripping and pooling in the strawberry hairs at the base. He pulled the waistband below Justin's balls.

The vision of Justin wanting, needing, waiting, his dick hard and balls exposed, caused Max to press his cock against the side of the bed. With short pulses of his hips, he found a modicum of relief in the motion but not enough to get closer to coming. Besides, he didn't want that yet. His goal was to bring Justin as high as he could, give him some relief from whatever shit they'd programmed into his head. The difference was he would hurt Justin because he loved him.

Running his fingers over Justin's cock, Max thought back to the session at the Mystique and the blissed-out expression on Michael's face as he orgasmed. The longest orgasm Max had ever seen in any man, given his limited viewing of heterosexual porn. Would Justin experience the same?

"Fuck," he whispered.

Grasping Justin's shaft, he watched Justin's stomach muscles contract. Max puzzled over the familiarity of holding another man's cock. Against his palms and fingers, it felt no different than holding his own. The erotic thrill came from knowing Justin got pleasure from Max's hand. Blood pulsed beneath Max's palm. He squeezed the hardness and released. When he ran his fist over the head, Justin gasped. Slippery precum coated Max's palm and lubricated the shaft as he pumped, slow at first and then faster.

Justin's breaths increased, his hips rose, pushing his cock through the tight opening Max's fist created. Max thrust against the side of the bed, his eyes locked on Justin fucking his hand. Soon his fist didn't move, Justin doing the work, fucking faster and faster. Grunting and mewling and....

"So fucking hot, honey."

Max released his cock. Justin's hips still flexed and lifted, slowing, his face pained as he whined at the loss of orgasm. Fisting the throbbing shaft again, Max ran up the length at a frustratingly slow pace. Justin's moans went straight to Max's groin, practically pushing the cum from his aching balls.

"You want to come?"

A sharp nod from Justin. "Please."

Max had to suppress a cocky smirk. "Maybe I won't let you come." Another gentle caress of Justin's cock. "Maybe I'll leave you like this, hard and wanting and begging for release."

Max was surprised by his own words. Jesus, he had fallen right into the role of dominating Justin. He didn't think he was a sadist, although he couldn't deny the pleasure he derived from Justin's suffering.

More painstakingly slow strokes, and then Max increased his rhythm until Justin again fucked his fist, and when he was right there on the edge, Max released him.

A moan and Justin's head thrashed from side to side on the pillow. Sweat beaded on his skin, his hair damp. His lips slightly parted, skin flushed, a fucking beautiful sight.

Max stroked him fast. Again, Justin fucked his fist. Max furiously humped the side of the bed, and the lack of friction kept him right on the edge as well.

He stopped again.

"No! No, no, no no no no! Please... Max."

Justin yanked on the restraints. His head lifted, then dropped back. His hips rose. His cock bobbed. Max undid his belt. Ripped open the snap. Unzipped his pants and pushed his briefs down under his balls. A cold shiver raced through him as he grasped his sensitized cock.

Over and over Max teased until Justin could do nothing but sob. Max's cock throbbed in one hand while Justin's throbbed in the other. His head was light. He felt floaty, almost out of touch with the reality in the room. When they both blew, the force would be massive, possibly painful.

Max's legs shook. He had to bring them both relief before he collapsed. Leaning over, he continued the slow strokes of Justin's cock and his own.

Bringing his mouth close to Justin's ear, he whispered, "You're doing so well. I love the sounds you make." Justin gasped as his hips rocked harder into Max's fist, his cock pushing through the tight passage.

"That's it, fuck my fist. Get yourself off."

Max tightened his grip. Justin responded with a stuttered groan. His breaths were so short he practically hyperventilated. Max's balls tingled, a warm wash of pleasure radiating through his groin. What a mindfuck the entire situation was.

When short gasps turned into louder moans, Max knew Justin was close. As the volume increased, Max sealed his mouth over Justin's in a rough kiss. Justin's hips stuttered, and then he thrust hard. Another series of stutters, another thrust, and his cock bottomed out against Max's fist. Frozen, his muscles contracted, his chest still. One... two... three....

Max's hand flew over his own cock as Justin's pulsed in his fist. Justin released a scream into Max's mouth that filled his head. Justin's hips snapped violently. Cum spattered against Max. Justin's body seized, his orgasm going on and on. Max's pleasure expanded, his muscles locked, his balls drew up, and white filled the darkness behind his closed eyes. He held on as long as he could, until the muscles in his groin contracted. Pure pulsing bliss. His body convulsed as he shot cum, his spasms so violent he could feel his asshole pulsing. He broke the kiss, gasping for air.

His hands were stiff from the prolonged grip, and he had to work to open his fingers. His heart continued to thunder in his chest. Sweat soaked his hair, ran over the sides of his face and under his T-shirt. He cupped Justin's cheeks. Dazed, overwhelmed, overflowing with emotions, his connection to Justin solidified. The potential barrier of being unable to be sexually intimate with Justin had been eliminated. He rested his forehead against Justin's, and the only sound was their slowing breaths. Adrenaline high, Max was lost, so lost in Justin that he wasn't sure which way was up. He never thought someone could fill the hole in his heart left by Grace. He couldn't have fathomed the whirlwind of Justin would not only fill that hole but claim his body and soul as well.

Max moved his face a few inches from Justin, caressing his cheeks with his thumbs. Justin's eyes fluttered open, unfocused, his expression so open, so trusting.

"Hey," Max whispered.

Justin visibly swallowed. "Hey." The tone was hesitant, tentative.

Max smiled. "You're so beautiful."

Under his hands, Max felt the tremble of Justin's chin. Justin's brow pulled down in a fearful sadness as if he were about to lose something precious. Max shushed him and ran a hand over his hair.

"What's wrong?" Max thought he could fly at that moment, but Justin was on the verge of tears.

Letting out several shuddering breaths, Justin sought Max's eyes for reassurance. "There's something wrong with me."

Max smiled as gently as possible. "Hey, whatever was done, we can undo. And if you need something to get by, I'm here to give that to you. We'll work it out. There's nothing wrong with you."

Justin chewed on his bottom lip, his eyes never wavering, his body still. Max had to admit he was unnerved in the silence. Standing strong, he wouldn't let Justin down, no matter what.

"I want you to bite me."

Images of Antoine sinking fangs into Michael's corded neck stole his vision for a split second, and his body stiffened. A roar filled his ears, and the coppery scent of blood caused him to salivate with nausea—not because he'd ever drank the real stuff, but because there had been crime scenes practically bathed in the red liquid. How could he bite Justin, drink actual human blood? And why wasn't that thought as repulsive as it should be?

"Why do you want me to bite you?" Max asked.

Justin's cheeks reddened. He turned his head. Waiting for a response, Max thought how odd it was that Justin was still tied to the bed. He hadn't asked to be released, and Max hadn't thought to free him.

"I don't know."

Okay. Maybe that had been a part of whatever they'd pushed into his head. But humans who were bitten repeatedly, over time, developed puckered oval scars. Justin had nothing that resembled that type of scarring.

Max lowered the intensity of his gaze, rubbed circles over Justin's stomach. "It's okay not to know. But like I said, we'll work it out. We'll find who did this to you and how to get you back to who you are. I'll be here to help you every step of the way. I promise."

Justin's expression told Max he believed otherwise, but he nodded.

Max crouched so that his face was level with Justin's. His hand never left Justin's stomach. "How do you feel?"

"Safe." No hesitation. "With you."

"You are. Now if I don't unlock the door, someone will bust it in probably sooner than later. And while I'd love to untie you and lock ourselves in our apartment for the next week"—that brought a smirk to

Justin's face—"the people who did this are still out there, and they have Caden. I need—"

Justin's eyes opened wide, mouth dropped open. He sucked in a deep breath and thrashed in his restraints. "Oh gods, Caden! They hurt him!"

CHAPTER 18

MEMORIES OF the previous night, which had been out of reach, coalesced slowly, sharpened and flickered through his mind. How could he have forgotten?

"Hold on, let me get you untied." Max couldn't work fast enough to release Justin's ankles, then his wrists. Justin bolted upright, and Max hugged him.

Justin worked to calm down. Knowing Max would want him to help. When he spoke, he sounded less shaky. "When we got inside, two guys and the woman who got us in brought us down a hallway. Caden stopped about halfway down. He knew something was wrong. He punched the guy beside me and shouted for me to run as he tackled another guy. But more people came. Caden still fought. They just kept hitting him. And I couldn't do anything about it." He was silent for a moment. "I don't know where they took him."

Max rubbed his palm over Justin's back. "We're working on that right now. Do you remember anything else?"

Justin chuckled dryly. It was as if someone had shaken up and dumped seven years of memories into his head all at once. Overwhelmed was an understatement. He pulled away from Max. Foremost in his head was what they'd just done.

"Yeah, but right now it's kind of a mess in here." He tapped his finger against his temple. "And some of it…." He squeezed his eyes tight, frowning. "Some of it's horrible to see, but right now, they seem as if they happened to someone else. Does that make sense?"

Max nodded, and Justin couldn't help but notice Max's expression: soft, caring, but different than before. Something had changed between them, but Justin wasn't sure what, despite the mind-blowing way Max had given what he'd needed.

"But you're talking to me and not acting like some… I don't know how to describe it."

"Slave. They called me a pain slave. But I… I wasn't mindless. They made me want to follow directions, obey when I was supposed to." He shuddered as memories of some of those training points were highlighted. "What you did to me just now. Thank you. I felt as if someone had to take over and tell me what to do, or I would have lost it. I hate that someone placed that need in my head, but the fact that you gave it to me even when you're straight…." Justin looked away from Max's intense gaze, wondering what he was trying to say. "You helped. I'll try not to ask you to hurt me again."

Fuck, that was embarrassing. He couldn't believe he'd asked Max to hurt him. Justin wondered how long before he was compelled to act in ways he never remembered doing before. When he woke, his will hadn't been his own, and he'd wanted it to stay that way.

"Hey."

Justin turned back, and Max smiled slightly. "Do you think I did that just because you wanted it or needed it?"

"Well, yeah. You've always helped me to get better, and then you find out my mind's more fucked-up than we thought, and you still help me with something most guys would have said 'fuck no' to."

Max cocked his head. "I did it because I wanted to, Justin." Max ran his hand through Justin's hair, the sensation causing him to shiver. "You're perfect for me, and I didn't know it. Couldn't see past your gender. Casey helped me get my head out of my ass." Max smirked. "You should see your eyes. I don't think they get any wider."

Max took Justin's hands into his. "I was on my date with Casey. I think it was my last-ditch attempt to prove to myself that I didn't…. That I didn't feel the way my heart wanted me to."

Justin swallowed hard. His heart pounded against his ribs. "How do you feel now?"

"Like I don't want to be without you for even one minute. I want to talk to you after work, share my day with you and eat dinner with you…. Share my bed with you." Max chuckled. "After what we just did"—Max's cheeks flushed—"I want you in every way possible. You've filled my heart, and as hokey as that sounds, I can't let you go no matter what. Whatever you need or want, I'm in."

Justin's own heart sang, hearing that Max felt the same for him, didn't want to be without him.

Max chuckled. "You know, I think you stole my heart the moment you woke up and your eyes focused on mine. I remember thinking how beautiful they were… how beautiful you were. Still are."

Justin chewed on his lip. "Everyone said you were just taking care of me. That you were trying to save me because…." Shit, he shouldn't have said that. "I'm sorry." *You don't bring up a man's dead wife.*

"It's okay, because it's nothing I haven't thought myself. It's mind-blowing when you think one thing about yourself and then something challenges that belief. I've only been attracted to women. I'm not a homophobe, but men just didn't catch my eye in a sexual attraction kind of way. They still don't. But, you, you sneaky shit, you flew under my radar and got in through my heart."

Justin couldn't help but smile. "I wore you down with my charm."

Max looked thoughtful and then said, "No. You didn't have to wear me down. That's the thing. We fit, like…."

"Two pieces of a puzzle?"

Max raised an eyebrow.

"A nut to a bolt?"

Max groaned. "Stop."

Justin grinned. "A key to a lock?"

Max lunged for Justin, and he fell back onto the bed.

Justin laughed. "My yin to your yang?"

"Enough from you!"

Max trapped Justin beneath him, pinning his wrists to the mattress. Despite the fucked-up mess in his head and Caden missing, Justin couldn't help but feel good at that moment.

Max straddled Justin's hips, and their gazes locked.

"Always remember I don't want you out of some mixed-up need to make up for something in the past. Some people think I'm carrying around guilt because I couldn't save her and you come along and I see a way to relieve my guilt." Max's eyes were somber. "I loved her. And she got sick, and when it was time to let her go, I did. She didn't ask me not to mourn her. She said everyone deserved to be mourned and missed. She said she'd miss me too, but she also asked me to trust my heart again when I found someone who fit. It's easy to agree to that crap when someone's leaving, but so much harder to do."

Justin rested his palm against Max's cheek, and he turned and kissed Justin's palm. "So I fit."

"Yeah, you fit."

"What if I stop fitting? What if everything we have crashes and burns because of what's in my head? What if I do the 'tell me what to do' thing again?"

Max grimaced. "We could what-if this to death, right? We could think of everything that could go wrong, but it's a chance people take when they feel it's worth it. Will you take that chance with me?"

Justin could really hurt Max if his mind chose to totally fuck him up. Justin feared other leviathans climbing from the depths of his subconscious. Self-sacrifice—wasn't that what the hero did? Save others by denying himself? Right then, he could either hurt Max and himself by fearing the future, or he could live for the moment, love for that moment they had right then.

"A chance for us?" How could he say no? "Yes."

Max grinned and then pressed their lips together, as good as a promise, a vow, and even with the dread boiling inside, Justin was right where he wanted to be, gods help them both.

MAX LEFT Justin in the care of Doc, who had waited impatiently outside Justin's door. Max hadn't challenged his annoyance, given he'd just delivered the child of his lover's wife. A wife he had no clue existed until a few days ago. Max wondered what that conversation would sound like when, or if, Tommy woke.

Carson had joined them, and Walt had been called to come in. Justin had assured Max he'd be okay for a while. How long that would last, Max wasn't sure.

The entire building was in an uproar with the disappearance of Miriam and Tara. Monitors had been set up in one of the conference rooms. Lincoln and some of the team crowded around them, watching surveillance video from different angles and areas of the NVJ building. Max peered over Maggie's shoulder. Dennison gave him a sideways look but luckily said nothing. Max thought of him holding the gun on Tommy's pregnant wife but decided that was a conversation for later.

Melissa Halliford from the NVJ Security and Communications Division pointed to one of the screens. "Here's Miriam arriving for work last night. As with all vampire civilians, her items were scanned by security at the main entrance. She told the officer that the equipment in her bag was a gift for Justin." Max scowled. "She claimed that her brother's a software engineer and develops virtual technology for companies. Justin had mentioned an interest in trying it out. She told the officer she felt bad for Justin stuck in the building all day and wanted to cheer him up. She claims her brother donated the system."

Dennison looked to Max. "Did Justin ask to try it?"

Max shrugged. "He never said anything about it to me. They could have talked about it when he was in Medical for one of his appointments with Doc or Walt. I'd have to ask him." Max shuddered at the thought of that woman so close to Justin. What else had she tried to do to him?

"Our number one suspect is a software engineer," Maggie said. "Maybe they're related?"

"I have Tia requesting Miriam's background check right now from the Office of Personnel Management to see if anything came up. Get with Tia, Maggie. Start looking into her close relatives and friends, previous coworkers, anyone who might have a connection to Nelson Technologies or any place that could develop this type of software. Whatever she was doing to practically stop us from moving was unlike anything I've ever heard of or seen before."

"Sure, boss." She squeezed past Max, smiling and again doing the supportive arm squeeze thing. This time it wasn't as annoying as it had been previously.

"Wouldn't we have the background check on file?" John crossed his arms.

Lincoln steepled his hands. "We don't unless we have reason to. We get an all-clear from the federal personnel office or a denial for hire based on what they find. No reason."

"And why aren't we doing our own checks?" Dennison asked.

"Because in the amount of time we had to get this division up and running, using some of the systems the federal government had in place was essential. They gave her the green light, and they vet thousands of federal workers a year."

"What I don't get is this vampire's worked here for two months, right? Why didn't she try to take Justin earlier?" Wes asked from his seat next to Melissa.

Taylor rubbed at his chin. "Maybe she was approached because she worked here. Bribed."

"That's possible." Lincoln turned to Max. "Does Justin remember her?"

Max sighed. "He's a little confused right now. From what he said, the memories between the time Carson bit him until he woke up five months ago were just dumped into his head, or unblocked by whatever Miriam did to him. He needs time to sort them out, if he can."

"Carson bit Justin?" Wes's eyebrows rose high on his forehead.

"It was a long time ago, and he was forced to bite him." Lincoln's tone was harsh, giving a finality to that subject.

Max thought Wes appeared scared. Impossible. But Max continued to study Wes, and he seemed shaken and distracted.

Dennison leaned back against the table. "What exactly do you think was done to Justin?"

Max carded his fingers through his hair. "We aren't sure, but Carson says Justin's thought processes have changed. Sort of an order in the normal chaos someone should have in their head. He, umm...." Max rubbed the back of his neck. "He seems to have been trained to like pain."

That caught Wes's attention. "What do you mean?" He leaned forward, and Max knew he remembered their private show at the Mystique.

Max wasn't sure how much to reveal without invading Justin's privacy.

Lincoln saved him from answering. "I think all we need to know here is that there's someone out there who trained Justin to need pain and submission when commanded. For what fucking reason, I'm guessing...."

Max's entire body jerked as he recalled Miriam's words. "Miriam said 'Justin is ours' and they have big plans for him. She said he was 'designed to suffer.'"

"What does suffer mean?" Taylor asked.

That word made Max's stomach lurch.

"Pain slave." Wes leaned back in his chair. "Max, I told you I have some friends who turned to bite clubs and BDSM when they returned from their deployment. One of them, Rob, he wants pain, a masochist in the truest sense. He loves to be tied up, subjected to all kinds of painful torture. I mean shit you wouldn't believe if you saw it."

"A pain slut." Taylor nodded as if he finally understood.

"Pain slave or slut. Either term. My friend gets off on the pain, as in there are times he doesn't need the orgasm to get to the pleasure. Says after a while the pain gives him a high equivalent to a drug so it's not always sexual. He also says it depends on what type of play is involved. If the person causing him pain stays away from his genitals, he won't come. Sadists get their kicks from inflicting pain on others. So play without sex happens all of the time." Wes paused, and his eyes darted to Max and then away.

"What is it?" Max didn't like the pensive look on Wes's face.

"A couple of weeks ago, Rob mentioned something I didn't initially pay attention to until now. A guy he often plays with, I think his name is Toby or something, is a hardcore sadist. He belongs to several organizations for S&M and attends conferences around the country."

"Seriously, they have conferences?" Melissa's cheeks flushed. Wes smiled at her, and she returned the smile. Man, he was good with the ladies.

"They do. They have workshops on things you couldn't imagine. Rob told me about a few he's attended. One was needle play." Wes shuddered. "To each his own, I say, but count me out."

Max wondered if Justin had ever had to endure needle play. What Justin had to endure was probably a long and horrifying list.

"What did this Toby say?" Lincoln's tone was filled with the impatience he wore on his face.

"That there was a rumor someone was selling pain slaves. Twenty-four seven kind of slave."

"Is it something these slave people do? Getting sold to people?" Dennison asked. Yeah, that distaste on his face was shared by Max.

"I asked the same thing, and no, they don't. There are all kinds of slaves. Pain, sex, domestic, submissive, part-time, full-time, scene slaves—pretty much anything people want, they can usually get. They find others who want the same situation, complete contracts, but no money is supposed to exchange hands except for domestic slaves who might live with someone without paying room and board. It can get very technical. Toby seemed to get the feeling that someone was actually offering people for sale, which as we know, if it's against their will, is human trafficking. When he inquired further around the conference, no one knew anything about what he'd heard. He got the feeling he either asked the wrong questions or he'd been wrong about the chatter."

"Where was he when he heard this?"

"An event put on by the Black Rose. It's a nonprofit support organization set up for the BDSM community here in DC."

Dennison snorted. "Nonprofit for kinksters. Nice."

Max felt cold, shaken. "You think someone is selling people?" Was Justin going to be sold? What had Miriam said? Justin was "special." Was that their big plan for him?

"Tara was littered with bruises and scars," Lincoln said. "Melissa, have you analyzed the footage of the night she was dumped?"

"Yeah. Nondescript white Ford Econoline van. Model looks to be a 2014. No identifying information on the vehicle. The license plates were covered. A man or woman dressed in black, with a ski mask on, pulled Tara out of the van. But get this, first he laid a blanket on the ground, then placed her on it, making sure she was covered. I'd call him gentle."

Dennison rubbed his chin. "So he cared about her. Someone who didn't would have just dumped her on the ground."

"Maybe he knew her." Most people were abused and hurt by those closest to them.

"Could be. Or maybe someone wanted us to know what someone else had done to her, as in turned her into a vampire. This guy knows something and for some reason couldn't tell."

"So he showed," Dennison said.

Lincoln rubbed his face. "What else have we got?"

Dennison turned to the table and picked up a folder. "Here's the banking info for Oneida Commons. They aren't a nonprofit so no donations. All of their funding comes from a parent corporation called, wait for it... Jenkens Holdings."

"Sarina's last name is Jenkens. It's her stepmother's maiden name. Who's the CEO?" Max asked.

"Darin Chambers."

"Anyone on the board with the last name Jenkens?" Max knew it wasn't a coincidence.

"Yup. Chairman of the Board, Yvonne Jenkens."

"AKA Yvonne Nelson, wife of Gale Nelson." Lincoln bared his teeth.

Max shared his anger. "Shit."

"Could we get any more proof that this man's involved, maybe even his wife?" Dennison threw the folder onto the table.

"Well, if we can't get the husband, get the wife in here. If she protests, arrest her." Lincoln wasn't joking around.

"Gladly," Dennison said. "Myers, wanna come?"

He smirked. "Where're we going?"

"Georgetown."

Taylor's eyes lightened. "Can we take the Hummer with the flashy lights? I love freaking out the rich folk."

"You got it."

"Yes!"

Max shook his head as they left. "You sure you wanna send them?"

"Yeah, let 'em have some fun."

Melissa stood and stretched. "Well, if you boys don't need me anymore, I've got work to do."

"That's it for now. Thanks, Melissa."

She left, leaving only Max, Lincoln, and Wes. Max plopped into a chair, bone-tired yet revved up since his time with Justin. "Is Sarina still here?"

Lincoln leaned back in his chair. "She's with Casey. Let's see what Mrs. Nelson has to say, and then we'll lean on Sarina to see if she really does know something. That family's handprints are all over this case. I sent some guys from the Utica NVJ out to Oneida Commons to snoop around on the down low. Hopefully they can find something." He pursed his lips and glanced sideways at Max. "We need to talk to Justin."

Not a command, more of a question, Max figured, but he hesitated to agree.

Lincoln pressed further. "He could have the answers we need here. On one hand, we have Justin trained for someone's sadistic pleasure, and on the other hand, Tara, one of the missing humans who looks as if someone tortured her. Add that to a bunch of missing humans and now Caden, a vampire. And to top it off, someone turned a human into a vampire. A *human*. Does this all even fit together?"

Wes sighed. "The one thing they all have in common is the Mystique and being human, and the odds don't make that a coincidence. Caden may have just been in the way."

"Justin said he fought them when things seemed weird." Max's stomach dropped with the thought that Caden could be dead. "How's Carson doing with this?"

"A lot worse than he's letting on. Caden may be a pain in his ass, but they're close. Always have been. If he's dead, it'll kill him."

From the look on Lincoln's face, he wasn't going to be okay with that either. But Max didn't want to believe the spirited man had been killed.

Lincoln stood. "I'm heading to the commissary. I need some blood. You guys want anything?"

"I'm good," Max said.

Wes shook his head. "Definitely not blood."

"I know that. Something else, you jackass." Lincoln rolled his eyes.

Wes smirked and shook his head.

"Okay. Max, meet me in Medical in thirty minutes?"

"Sure."

With Lincoln gone, Max leaned on his elbows and rubbed his face.

"He's… intense." Wes's voice held a bit of awe.

Max barked out a laugh. "Oh, Lincoln is certainly intense. And one smart officer. He didn't get appointed as the director here by being last in line."

Wes nodded slowly, then asked, "How're you doing?" His tone was filled with concern. Max had to wonder about his earlier reaction.

"I'll be okay. Justin's back, and that's all that matters. What about you? Earlier when you heard that Carson bit Justin, you looked upset."

Wes fiddled with a paperclip on the table next to him. His brooding expression wasn't like him—well, from the limited amount of time Max had spent with him, that was.

He licked his lips, his eyes narrowing. "I know what it's like to be forced to do something against your will. When I was security in a Vermont hospital, something got into my head and influenced what I wanted, made me ask for something I didn't want. Used me, and that was the worst feeling in the world. I felt violated, dirty." He grimaced.

"What exactly tried to force you to do this?"

Wes crossed his arms. "The Incubus."

"Damn."

"Luckily it was stopped before… before the fucker raped me. Although, I was begging for it so I guess it couldn't really have been called rape."

"Jesus, Wes." Max squeezed his eyes shut. That's what had happened to Justin, and Max hadn't even…. He stood. "Fuck. These people raped Justin, used him, even if they never fucked him, they used him for whatever they wanted." They'd hurt him and then made him want the pain.

CHAPTER 19

MAX KICKED his chair, flipping it into the air and sending it crashing into another. Rage fired in his gut, his chest, painful, aching. He kicked the offending piece of furniture again and again, ignoring the sharp pain in his toes, only wanting to destroy the innocuous object as if it had been responsible for everything. When he went for the table, Wes intervened and grabbed his biceps.

"Whoa, whoa, whoa, there."

Max turned on Wes. He needed to take out his rage on someone, but he wasn't stupid enough to try anything with someone larger than him.

Wes released his arm. "I know you're pissed and need to take it out on something or someone, but if you flip this table, we're gonna have a shitload of papers to sort through." He gestured to the neatly piled papers covering half of the surface.

Max snorted, then growled deep in his throat. "How can people be so shitty to other people? What gives them a right to touch another person and try to control them? Who the fuck do they think they are?"

Why someone like Justin, who never hurt anyone?

Wes's laugh was dry, lacking any humor. "You're asking someone who's been in a war zone. I've seen the senseless slaughter of kids and women and men all sacrificed in the name of some religion or bid for power." Wes shook his head. "Suicide bombers? You think only someone who isn't right in the head or insane would do half of this shit, but no, these people were some of the sanest I've ever encountered. Some believe they're on a mission, religious or personal, or something has been ingrained in their beliefs to make them think what they're doing is right. Others are just self-centered, narcissistic fucks who think the world owes them. They are the center of their own universe. But you know what all of those evil bastards were missing?"

"What?"

"A heart. Empathy. And people who wouldn't do otherwise become sheep following them, their morals twisted around until they're doing shit they never thought possible. Only way to change anything is to take them down."

Max took in Wes's deep frown, the tightness of the skin around his scar. The man had some deep issues and seemed to have been fucked over big-time at some point in his life.

Max's anger fled as quickly as it had risen. "So in other words, don't get mad, get even."

"Oh, get mad, but focus that anger on those who deserve it. Not an innocent chair." Wes grinned wide.

Max liked the man, was glad he'd come aboard.

Max could focus his anger, and whoever waved their hand and admitted to being involved would pay.

DOC POKED and prodded and prodded some more until Justin was ready to crawl out of his skin. He knew Doc was being thorough, but the man who was usually chatty and upbeat was quiet, almost morose. He shined a light into Justin's eye, and then the other.

"Any visual disturbances?"

"Only when you shine that light in my eyes." Justin smiled, but Doc appeared distracted.

Carson, who was across the room, chuckled. At least someone was listening.

Doc put the light down and raised a finger. "Follow my finger but don't turn your head."

Justin did as he asked and sighed. "Really, Doc, I'm okay."

Except for the nagging need that he wasn't doing what he should be doing, that he should somehow be submitting, or taking directions. Max's words before he'd left had been, "You can do anything you want until I get back."

Did he really need Max's permission to make his own choices? While it was debasing and degrading to think he'd been essentially programmed to obey someone, submitting to Max piqued his arousal.

"Just want to make sure. Do you have any headaches, dizziness, nausea, anything hurt?"

Justin shook his head.

"How do you feel? Your mood."

Calm came to mind. Ever since he'd been with Max earlier. The chaos that was his mind before he'd been—What? Reprogrammed?—had disappeared. Despite fighting off memories trying to be recognized, he wasn't anxious or scared. Worried, yeah, over fear about what those memories held, but nothing close to the panic he'd been experiencing. Back to normal before the bite? No.

"I'm surprisingly calm given what I found out happened to me. My head isn't… noisy like it was."

Doc cocked his head. "You seem calmer, less tense or high-strung, more relaxed than you have been. Which, like you said, is amazing given what you've discovered about your past."

Carson sat forward. And Justin could tell he wanted to ask something. Carson gestured toward Justin's head. "May I?"

Why not? He'd been violated six ways to Sunday already. "Sure."

Carson's gaze was intense, and the feeling of being invaded made him want to squirm in his seat. When Carson's eyes narrowed, Justin's stomach flipped.

"What?" Justin asked.

Doc looked between them with a curious expression.

"It's amazing. Even now your thoughts, their order, is different than when you woke up this last time. Your thoughts were simple, focused around obeying, serving, and need. Almost a mindless state driven by those thoughts. They're closer to resembling what I might find in others with normal thought patterns, but…."

Carson's frown never meant anything good.

"But?" Doc asked.

Carson rubbed his palms on his thighs and seemed to be speculating. "But there's something on the edge of your mind, almost waiting? I know that sounds weird, but I can't describe it in any other way. Can't feel what that is."

That sounded more ominous than Justin liked. He hated to admit it, but if he had a choice to return to how he was just a few days ago, or how he was now, he'd choose now, just because of how he felt right at that moment. But was this the proverbial calm before the typhoon scenario? Was that "thing" at the edges of his mind really a dark, churning tempest gaining power that would eventually blow in and wreck him?

Doc rubbed his chin. "You said before that there was something blocking you when you tried to read Justin. That's gone?"

Carson sat back. "It is. That was like an actual wall blocking what was behind it. I'm guessing memories and probably the conditioning they put you through. I can also tell you're blocking those memories from being seen."

Rubbing his temple, Justin quickly thought of Max, of being happy, before the mention of those past events could fill his head.

"And you're doing a pretty good job at it. Most people get distracted, and bam, they can't help but remember."

Doc leaned forward. "His conditioning is sophisticated, highly detailed. Could be that ability was part of the training. Subconscious, like someone who blocks out something horrible that happened to them. It's possible."

Justin swallowed hard. "I'm afraid if I remember, if I see what they did to me and it becomes real, then I'll fall apart and be weak again. I don't want that." A spark of anger lit in his gut. "For months, I've felt vulnerable and scared and just plain messed up." His voice rose. "I'm not going back there again. I almost lost everything because of what's in my head and how I acted." He clenched his fists. "I'm just lucky Max didn't turn tail and run, despite how he feels about me. Still, I'm going to try my hardest to keep it from happening again. I gave up struggling and started drowning." Because that's what the past five months had felt like, drowning slowly. Now he held control for the first time since their kidnapping seven years ago, even if that control was an illusion. "If I sit and feel sorry for myself, I will get lost again. I'm stronger than that. I love Max, and no one is going to take that from me. Especially not some messed-up memories. I won't let them beat me."

Doc and Carson stared at him as he jutted out his jaw. Justin was certain defiance was foremost in his expression.

The corner of Carson's lips lifted. "You sound like the Justin I used to know. The one I fell—" Carson shifted nervously and cleared his throat. "I mean, the person you were back then, who didn't stop even when the odds were against you. Remember that game you played against Hammond High?"

Stunned, Justin nodded. "I showed you the video of that game, right? I can't believe you remember that."

Carson's tone was soft. "I do because you were amazing in that game. Those guys from Hammond were huge and fast, and they were obliterating your team. Even to the end, you were pushing everyone to fight, to keep going."

"Of course you'd remember the game that we lost."

"By three points, after being down sixteen at the half. And the local paper wasn't about the loss the next day. They were about you and your grit and determination against great odds. But that's how you were about everything, and those qualities are still in you."

Justin felt his cheeks redden. "Thanks. I forgot about how I used to be. It seems like a million years ago. There are times you just have to take the ball and run even if you get crushed. It's so worth it."

He glanced at Doc, who'd lost the severe edge to his expression. He was actually smiling slightly.

"Yeah, I know what you mean," Carson said.

For a moment their gazes met, and Justin remembered his time with Carson, falling in love with him, the excitement. He'd felt like a hero to Carson, someone who could make his life better. But now that feeling was muted, a good memory that warmed his chest, but nothing else. He was more like….

"Friends?" Justin asked.

"Definitely," Carson said.

Doc frowned in confusion. "Okay, I'm guessing that's something only you two would get, so moving on, I don't think there's much more I can do at this point. Physically you're healthy. Even mentally you're more stable than you were." He stood. "I've got people who really need me. But if anything comes up, I want you in here ASAP."

"You got it." Justin saluted.

"Bye, Doc," Carson called after him. Doc waved halfheartedly and was gone. The concern for Doc on Carson's face confirmed Justin's suspicions.

"Is he okay?"

Carson chewed on his lower lip, his eyes still on the doorway. "I don't think so, but he wouldn't admit it." Carson looked to Justin. "I don't know if you saw the very pregnant lady here the past couple of days. Well, that was Tommy's wife. She actually went into labor and delivered the kid here. It's a boy."

Justin had never met Tommy before he went into the coma. He'd gone into his room a few times with Max and hung out. Max would talk to him, read the paper to him, watch movies. Seeing Tommy often put Justin's situation into perspective. He wasn't catatonic any longer and should be more grateful.

"But aren't Doc and Tommy in love?"

Carson slumped in his chair. "They were sometime in the past. During the Jameson fiasco, they reunited. That was right after I got those powers and couldn't control them, so I could feel their attraction and love. It was quite… large and complicated even back then. Tommy didn't mention a wife, so Doc was blindsided."

Justin rubbed his hands together. "Must really suck that he can't go and demand answers or at least punch Tommy in the face for not telling."

"I get the feeling Doc would punch first and ask later, but…."

Justin knew the "but." Tommy might never come out of that coma, and Doc might never get the chance. Damn, that was harsh. Justin really liked Doc. The doctor had worked relentlessly to find a way to help him.

They left the conversation about Doc at that. Justin wasn't sure what he should do right then. Max had left him in that room and had said do anything he wanted until he got back. Should he leave or wait?

When he looked to Carson, his expression had changed. The sadness was front and center. Carson had to be freaking out. He was hiding those feelings well.

"I'm sorry about Caden. If I hadn't called him to take me to the bite club, he'd still be here." He was rolling in the guilt.

Carson's eyes focused on Justin. "Caden could find his own trouble without your help. I told him that he just couldn't go running around without being careful, but he didn't listen."

"Still…."

Carson narrowed his eyes. "We'll find him."

A statement. No ifs. A promise. But what shape would he be in? A flash of memory and Justin gasped, the answer in his own mind. If they did half of what they'd probably done to Justin, that shape might be bad.

"You okay?"

Justin rubbed his forehead. He didn't want to remember, wanted to stay as he was right then, but what if the answer to where Caden was rested in those memories? If he ignored them, he could be sacrificing Caden. Shit.

"I may be able to help."

Carson frowned. "How?"

"By remembering what happened. I could know something that could help find him."

Carson was silent. Justin knew he was thinking which way to go. Martyr self-sacrifice direction to keep Justin from having to relive the unknown, or selfish direction and agree to let him find his little brother. Justin's guilt would decide for him.

"I don't need your agreement."

Carson's eyebrow raised, and his hands were clasped before him. "What if Max doesn't want you to?"

Translation: What if he said no and Justin had to obey? "We don't tell him?"

Carson barked out a laugh. "Yeah, I like my balls, thank you very much."

If Max said no, Justin knew that the inflexible, neurological nightmare in his head would no doubt force him to obey.

"I can probably help you, guide you through. I mean, in theory. Like I said earlier, I never see images or memories the person has. My information comes from feelings, or the result of thoughts. I can't read minds, although sometimes it's not hard to put enough information together to make a good guess."

Justin had kept his distance from Carson since he'd come back from la-la land, so he wasn't exactly sure what else he could do. "What else can you do?"

"I can influence a vampire's mind. Plant thoughts and get them to act how I want. Doesn't work on humans for some reason. Probably some weird effect of whatever Jameson filled me with. I don't do that much."

"But you've done it?"

"I used it at the Mystique to get them to lead us to you."

"Do you use it to help catch people for the NVJ? Get them to tell the truth?"

"No." His tone was adamant. "Like I said, I rarely use it. That was a special circumstance. Could you imagine if the world found out what I could do? There's enough suspicion where we're concerned. Plus, it's cheating? I don't know. Feels wrong to me."

"Could you do that to me? I mean, help me to not automatically obey Max when he says no to what I want to do."

Carson jumped from the chair and paced. "No. That's a violation of a person's mind, an intimate act, and it's dishonest. Getting into someone's head and messing with their will isn't something you just do. Look at you. Someone messed with your head without permission, and I'm sure it's pretty shitty."

A shiver raced through Justin. Shit, he had been more than violated. He'd been pretty much mindfucked. "You're right. We have to convince him. You may have to do most of the convincing since I'll be overruled by my head. But I have to do this."

The guilt was just too heavy, too suffocating. He had to help find Caden.

MAX WAS taking a break from the chaos. They were waiting for Yvonne Nelson to be brought in. Apparently she hadn't been home, but Dennison and Taylor had tracked her down to some high-end spa. When Taylor had called to say they had the lively package and were returning to the Batcave, Max hadn't been able to catch his breath. When he mentioned something about inappropriate groping, he prayed that meant Mrs. Nelson.

After eating a sandwich, Max heated a cup of blood and then sat in a chair in the lounge that overlooked the river. He thought fondly back to the many times he and Justin had gone down to the river. Those memories and the tons of other good memories far outweighed those not so pleasant. The fact that Justin had to once again rely on Max to keep him safe wasn't as terrifying as it once had been. Without knowing exactly how far the training to obey others went, Justin could be vulnerable and unable to advocate for himself. From what Max had seen, he hadn't turned into a mindless robot. And Max seemed to be the only one he felt compelled to obey. No one had rushed to him to say Justin was in trouble, so he had to be doing well with Carson and Doc.

What unsettled him was the question mark in Justin's future. A future that was irrevocably tied to Max's. He loved the man, wanted him in his life, and, daring to hope, maybe someday a family. He and Grace had envisioned their future would include children. Why not with Justin?

"Hey."

Wes hovered nearby.

"Hey. Something up?" Gods, that wouldn't be surprising.

Wes shrugged. "Nothing. Everything."

Max snorted. "I know the feeling. You picked a nice time to join the team, that's for sure."

Wes seemed to hesitate.

"You just stopping by, or you looking for a place to hide for a while?"

"I could use a break. Am I interrupting your quiet?"

"Nah. I've been here for a while. Have a seat." Max gestured to the seat next to him.

Wes collapsed into the upholstered chair, and the wood beneath the fabric groaned in protest.

"Ahhh, so good to sit. Feels like we've been going for days." Wes kicked his booted feet up onto the windowsill.

"Amen," Max muttered, sipped his blood, and frowned. Cold already. He chugged the rest and grimaced as he set the cup down. "Anything new while I've been hiding?"

Wes gazed out the window and rested his head back on the chair, appearing to truly appreciate the comfort. "Colmar-Houssen Airport confirmed Gale Nelson's plane landed on July nineteenth. The plane is still sitting in the airport. What they can't confirm is that Nelson was a passenger. The hotel is refusing to confirm he is staying there, and it would probably take an act of Congress to get them to confirm if he is or isn't."

"So his plane's in France, but we can't confirm if he is or not. He could be anywhere, including New York like his daughter said. He was contacted by the NVJ and required to return. According to initial contact with his office, he was to be back by now."

"You think he's staying gone for a reason?"

"He's the suspect of the hour. Staying away only increases his guilt. His wife is on the way in with Dennison and Taylor, gods help us with that."

Wes rubbed at the seam on the outside of his thigh. "What's Myers's story?"

Max furrowed his brow. "Umm, he was at the NVJ in Utica when I joined. Definitely a class clown, he's always pranking someone. Although since we came here, he's toned it way down. Now it's more like fake spiders in desk drawers and rubber snakes in toilets. For being over thirty, he's got the sense of humor of a kid."

Wes appeared fidgety, and then he got it.

"Oh. You mean story as in his *story*. I have no clue really. I can't say he's ever mentioned dating or even having a girlfriend or boyfriend." And wasn't that odd, now that Max thought of it. He couldn't say that about anyone else on the team. "Can't help you there."

Wes gave a halfhearted nod. "Just curious. I'm not looking to date at the office. I may kid around about it, but it's best not to get involved with a team member because it's way awkward when it ends badly."

Max's phone vibrated. A text from Lincoln told him Mrs. Nelson had arrived. He stood. "Duty calls."

Wes stood as well and stretched his back.

"So what if it doesn't end badly?" Max challenged.

Wes patted Max's shoulder. What was probably meant as a gentle gesture felt like a brick. "With my track record, it's a given. I'll check in later." And he left.

Max entered the viewing area of the interrogation room and cursed that he hadn't checked in with Justin. Hopefully this wouldn't take long. Lincoln was gazing through the two-way mirror with an assessing frown. Max stepped up beside him and looked into the room.

CHAPTER 20

"WHOA, THAT'S Mrs. Nelson?"

The woman sitting at the table reminded him of a rich socialite. She wore large, rose-tinted glasses. Her brown hair was swept up in a flattering style. Her makeup had that flawless look, smooth, which gave her the appearance of wearing none. Her neck was long and lean. He imagined that she was tall. Diamond earrings, gray top, gold and diamonds around her neck and on her fingers. The rock on her left hand was disproportionate to her slim fingers.

Myers sat across from her as the woman giggled and gave him coy looks, her flirting blatant. Myers seemed unaffected yet amused.

"She's exactly the type of person I expected to be married to Gale Nelson." Lincoln crossed his arms and glowered.

"Are you stereotyping, Director?"

Lincoln glanced over at Max. "Tell me you didn't."

"Plead the fifth."

Maggie walked into the room. "I hear I have some babysitting to do?"

Max smirked. Lincoln pointed through the glass. "I'd like you to sit in the room while we interrogate her."

Maggie peered in, and her eyes rounded. "Who's that?"

"Yvonne Nelson. I don't want you involved in the interview. From what I've observed, she has a fondness for men."

"Really? I wouldn't have noticed. If you wait long enough, she'll probably be sitting in Myers's lap."

Max and Lincoln looked at each other. A silent *should we?* passed between them.

Maggie giggled. "Myers is so uncomfortable. Look at him."

Max hadn't noticed, but even though he was smiling, the gesture was forced, his posture stiff. Under the table his thumb and forefinger were rubbing together rapidly. "Is he nervous?"

Lincoln narrowed his eyes, and his mouth dropped open. "You think she intimidates him? I mean, she is a beautiful woman."

"Don't let Carson hear you say that." Maggie's tone warned but was tinged with humor. "Yeah, she's way out of his league. Not to mention married to that arrogant ass."

That caught Max's attention. "What makes you say that?"

"That she's out of his league or her husband's an arrogant ass?"

Lincoln's jaw ticked. "The latter."

Maggie's cheeks reddened slightly. "She's always in the gossip magazines. They like to show her alone on vacation in some exotic location or at social functions. He's always off working somewhere. They say when the two of them are together, he's aloof, pays her no attention, rarely talks to her. She was photographed once with a bruise on her cheek, you know, with one of those telephoto lenses. There was speculation over if he'd hit her. She gave the door excuse. At least that's what I've seen in the line at the grocery store."

Max stared at Maggie, unsure how to respond to that.

"All that from standing in line, huh?" Lincoln's tone was deadpan, and Maggie appeared mortified.

"Relax, Wright. Jeesh, you're too easy." Lincoln went to the door, apparently having decided to rescue Taylor.

Taylor couldn't have looked more relieved if he'd been pulled out of an interrogation himself.

"So long, Officer Myers. It was nice to meet you."

Taylor nodded on the way out, and his expression was inscrutable as he passed by Max. Had he met his match?

They settled around the table, and Lincoln introduced himself.

"Oh, Director Samuels. We both attended the reception for Senator Brooks. I've been hoping to get to meet you and your lovely partner, but you left before I could make my way to you. You know how those events are."

Lincoln nodded but didn't indulge her further. "This is Lieutenant Kincaid."

Her face lightened, and she extended her hand. "Lieutenant, the pleasure is mine." Her hand was slim and soft and lingered a bit too long.

"This is Officer Wright."

She gave Maggie a smile filled with dazzling white teeth. "Officer Wright. Let me be the first to commend you. I have long been a supporter of women in nontraditional roles. I support you. In fact, I'm a huge supporter of the vampire community. If we can't all live on this earth together with equal rights for everyone, then we are no better than animals."

What was she? A politician? Max bit his lip.

Lincoln cleared his throat. "Thank you, Mrs. Nelson, for your support. And thank you for coming in to speak with us."

"Anything to help the vampire community. What can I do for you, Director?"

Lincoln set the paper in front of her, and she scanned the document. "You're listed as chairman of the board of Jenkens Holdings."

Her breath seemed to catch in her throat. "Yes, I am. Why do you ask?" Some of her composure appeared to return.

"What exactly is Jenkens Holdings?"

She shook her head, chin higher. "The corporation is a subsidiary of Nelson Technologies, set up as a property holding company. I'm not sure of the specifics, but there's some tax benefit for Gale to rent properties that Jenkens own. Seriously, I don't get it. They're all the same company." She waved her red-painted nails in the air.

"And you're the chairman of the board?" Max thought the chairman should have a greater understanding than that.

She sighed. "In name only."

"But you use your maiden name as a board member." There was something fishy there.

She leaned forward. "You see, Gale didn't want his name associated with Jenkens Holdings but wanted control. Gale is really the one who runs Jenkens. I just do what he tells me." Her eyes widened, and her mouth formed a red *O*.

Maggie snorted and then coughed.

"Certainly." Lincoln wrote down more on his pad.

"I wasn't supposed to tell you that. Please keep that between us."

While Max couldn't see her eyes clearly, the way she rubbed at the base of her throat, continually licking her lips and fidgeting with the ring on her left hand, showed a certain level of distress or nervousness.

Maybe if he could shake her up further, she'd spill something.

"Jenkens is your maiden name, correct?"

"It is."

"And you set up this corporation?"

She actually laughed. "Me? Oh no. I don't know the first thing about business."

"Then who?"

"Why, my husband, of course." Her voice was shakier, her composure once again faltering. "He told me to sign the papers. I sign whatever he puts in front of me."

Interesting. Maybe the gossip rags weren't that far off.

Maggie leaned forward and touched Mrs. Nelson's arm. "Would you like a glass of water, Yvonne?"

Max lowered his eyes. Maggie always knew when to step in with empathy.

"Thank you. No."

"Mrs. Nelson, have you spoken with your husband lately?"

Her eyes widened. "Has something happened to him?"

Lincoln leaned back in his chair. "No, which is why we've asked you his current location."

Her smile faded. "Is he in trouble?"

Lincoln continued with his charming expression. "Please let us know the last time you spoke with him?"

She wrung her hands on the table before her. "I spoke with my husband last night after I returned from dinner with friends at Marcel's."

"And where was he when you spoke to him?" Max wondered what was with her sudden nervousness.

"Colmar, France. He's been there since the nineteenth."

"And the reason for his trip?"

"International technology conference."

"What conference was he attending?"

"I don't know what it's called. He's always at some conference or meeting or merger. He doesn't share his calendar with me. You'll have to call his secretary to find out what it was."

Lincoln wrote on the pad before him. "When do you expect him to return?"

She hesitated. "He said he was going to be there for a few more days. Something about a lucrative deal with some businesspeople he met there. He said he'd call me when he knew when he was landing."

So he wasn't on his way to the US as the NVJ had been informed by his office.

"You have a daughter, Mrs. Nelson?" Max asked.

"No."

Max raised a brow.

"Sarina is my stepdaughter."

"Do you know where she is?"

Her lips thinned. "Is that what this is about? What has she done now?"

"Have you seen her?"

She slumped in her chair. "This morning at breakfast when she finally came home after being out all night. That girl is so ungrateful and wild. She's constantly causing me to worry. I think she resents me for her mother leaving. I wasn't even around then."

"You don't have a good relationship with your stepdaughter?"

"Believe me, I have tried from day one to be someone she could count on, someone who would help her grow into a confident young woman. But she does whatever she pleases and her father indulges her at every turn." Max thought she actually appeared sad. "I've always wanted a daughter, but Sarina is spoiled and I've caught her stealing from us, once right from her father's wallet. She's a liar and a manipulator. She's been arrested many times." Max had read her record. Minor teenage stuff. Mrs. Nelson leaned forward, clearly distressed. "She goes to those bite clubs. Can you imagine? Those places are filled with diseases and sex."

"So you're saying Mr. Nelson lets Sarina do what she wants and covers for her?"

Max watched Lincoln's jaw tick. Was he wondering if Sarina knew more than she let on?

She nodded. "When I try to intervene and talk to him about how she's living her life, he gets angry." Her chin quivered. Max and Lincoln both looked to Maggie, helpless. Max could tell she wanted to roll her eyes.

Maggie leaned forward and touched her arm again. "What happens when he's angry?"

More hand twisting. "I can't."

"Mrs. Nelson, we can't help if we don't know what's happening." Max felt for the woman now that she'd dropped the flirty, flamboyant facade.

"No, Officer Wright, you don't understand. If he even knew I was here, that I said anything…. Oh, why did I come here?" She shook in her chair.

Maggie patted her arm. "We won't tell him anything, but if your husband hurts you, it's not okay." Maggie's voice was soothing and comforting. "Please."

Mrs. Nelson lifted a shaky hand and removed her large colored glasses. Despite her eye makeup, Max could make out the fading bruise beneath her eye.

"What happened, Mrs. Nelson?" Max tried to be soothing like Maggie, but his anger bled into his tone.

"It was my fault. He warned me to stop talking, but I was trying to get him to send Sarina somewhere for help. I begged him before... before she ended up addicted to drugs or sick or dead." A tear escaped her eye and ran over her cheek.

"And what was his response?" Lincoln asked.

The quivering increased. "He hit me." She sobbed heart-wrenchingly.

"And has he hurt you before?"

She nodded. "But I shouldn't have pushed him. It was totally my fault."

"Has Sarina ever seen your husband's violence toward you?"

"Yes." Her voice was small, meek. So far from the coiffed and confident woman they'd first met.

Max sat back and sighed, more convinced that Gale Nelson was the devil.

"Mrs. Nelson, you can press charges against your husband for hitting you and any past abuse."

Her eyes flashed with fear. "I couldn't. He'd be furious, and he knows people who will take his side. Very important people. Why do you think Sarina gets away with so much and hasn't been in jail?"

"Is there at least someone close to you who you can stay with until you can figure out what you want to do?" Max didn't want to tell her the possible trouble her husband was in and that when they caught him, he'd be going to jail for a long time.

She chewed on her red lip. "I can stay with my friend. She lives in Capitol Hill."

Maggie stood. "Come with me, Mrs. Nelson, and we'll take you there."

"Home will be fine. My driver can take me once I pack."

Max shook her hand, as did Lincoln. "Mrs. Nelson, we need to be able to contact you. Please don't leave DC without telling us."

She sighed. "Gale did something, didn't he?"

"We need to question your husband in conjunction with an ongoing investigation. If you speak with him, let him know that it will be better for him if he comes in soon to speak with us."

She nodded and bit her lip, as if thinking of something, and then turned and left with Maggie.

"Jesus," Max muttered when they were out of earshot. "Money doesn't make you immune, does it?"

Lincoln guffawed. "Money makes it more likely to happen. He's probably been getting away with illegal activities for years."

They left the room and found Dennison leaning against the wall, his face absent of his usual scowl. He didn't appear to notice them. "Dennison?"

That shook him out of his funk. "Sorry."

"About?"

He shook his head. "Nothing. I just came from Medical. Olivia's gone." The scowl returned, tinged with anger.

Max knew that name, right? "That's...."

"Tommy's so-called wife."

Max was confused. "They aren't married?"

"They are, but she scammed him. Got him drunk, had sex with him, and then came back three months later and says she's pregnant. He marries her out of some screwed-up chivalry, then she claims to have lost the kid. Tommy was devastated. I figured that was the end of her, right? Wrong. She hangs around for about a month after that, tells him that she's pregnant again, making me think she lied the first time. A month later she disappears with around five thousand dollars of his money. And then she shows up here, with her sob story that she didn't know anything about Tommy being shot and that she loves him."

Lincoln raised his hand. "Hold on. She left as in left with the baby?"

"As in she left *without* the baby. I don't even know if the kid is Tommy's. I told Doc to do a paternity test. He was already on it. She needs to be arrested for abandoning her kid and for stealing from Tommy."

"Without Tommy to say he didn't give her the money, there's nothing we can do. They're legally married. If she's gone longer than twenty-four hours without contacting us, we'll track her down." Lincoln grunted. "Can anything else go fucking wrong?"

Lincoln stomped off, leaving Max with Dennison. "What if she doesn't come back and it's his?"

Dennison wiped his chin. "Damned if I know. I mean if it's Tommy's, the kid should be raised by family, but me and Deana… I don't know how we can with four of our own. I mean we would if we had to, but man, I've already lost most of my hair from having four kids under eight in the house. Now a baby?"

Dennison's wife Deana was as patient as a saint. Max wondered how she could handle Dennison and their four rambunctious kids.

"Any other family?"

"My dad's in his sixties. I have some aunts, some cousins. Once we know for sure if he's Tommy's, then we'll decide what to do." He scrubbed at his face. "If it's his, we'll make sure the kid gets what he needs."

Only a few times had Max ever seen Dennison let down his defenses and actually appear to be a decent vampire. Once had been when Max had walked in on him when he was sitting with Tommy. Emotions weren't Dennison's thing, but his defenses had been down as he'd talked to his kid brother. Max had actually felt something, seeing the pained expression on his face.

"If you need any help, Dennison, except for diaper changes of course, let me know."

"Sure." He walked away without another word. Max wondered if it was happy hour yet.

Lincoln appeared in the hallway. "Kincaid, I need you with me. I want to talk to Sarina again."

"Fuck my life," Max muttered and headed down the hall.

JUSTIN WASN'T sure he could get any more bored than he was. Max was still working. They'd finally declared they cared for each other, even though no one had admitted aloud to the L-word yet. He missed Max and had contemplated heading down there, but he was sure he'd only be in the way. He wandered down the hallway of Medical. With the human-turned-vampire Tara and Miriam gone, the place was eerily quiet. The room where Tommy's wife had been was empty, the bed stripped. He wondered where she went. Farther down the hall, he stopped before Tommy's room. Doc was rocking in a chair next to Tommy's bed, holding a blue bundle.

Tommy's baby.

"He's quite the handsome kid you've got here, Tommy Boy. But of course he'd be beautiful like his dad. I think he's got your nose. There's a shock of black hair on his head, almost like a Mohawk." Doc chuckled as he gazed down on his former lover's baby. "Set of lungs that could wake the dead. Also like his father."

The melancholy smile wasn't what Justin would have expected. Shouldn't Doc be pissed off?

"This little guy is innocent. He didn't choose his parents." He looked at the baby. "No you didn't, did you? Oh, what a big yawn." Doc's baby talk amused Justin, and he chuckled. Doc looked up and scowled. "What, an old hardened man like me can't soften up to a baby?"

Justin gaped for a moment, unsure what to say. Had he pissed Doc off?

"Jesus, I'm just messing with you. Come in."

"Can I?" Justin pointed to the baby as he came closer.

"Sure. Come and take a peek."

Justin stood next to Doc and gazed down on the small… vampire? He couldn't remember if the mother was a vampire. What happened when a human and a vampire mated?

"What is he? Vampire?"

Doc lifted the side of the baby's tiny, bowed upper lip. He had the tiniest, cutest fangs. Justin had to stop himself from turning to baby talk. "Vampire. His mother's human."

"So a human and a vampire can make a vampire."

"Could go either way, but vampires with one human parent tend to have less pronounced fangs and may not need blood. A blood test at birth tells if they'll need blood in their diet."

Justin reached over and touched the baby's hand. His skin was so soft. The baby snuffled and stretched, then his mouth made sucking motions.

Again, Justin wondered if he and Max could ever be parents. That was way in the future, of course, when their lives and Justin himself weren't so screwed up.

"What do you need, Doc?" John stepped into the room, nodded to Justin, and immediately stepped up to Tommy's bed, squeezing his brother's hand. His gaze bordered on loving as he looked down on his brother. "Do you need help turning him?"

Doc stopped rocking for a moment, but then started again. Justin wasn't sure what he should do, so he stayed put.

"No. I called you up here because I have the results of the paternity test."

John stilled, and his eyes were back on his brother.

"Congratulations, Uncle John."

Justin swore he could hear John's teeth clenching. He ran a hand over his bristle cut. "Tommy, you stupid son of a bitch. How could you get her pregnant after what she did?"

Justin wondered what she'd done.

"I spoke with Deana. Things are crowded in our apartment here in the building. We would have to move into a bigger place. I can't imagine five-bedroom houses are cheap in DC."

"Do you want him?" Doc was once again gazing down on Tommy's son.

John walked around the bed and stood before Doc, his eyes on his nephew. He squatted, and Justin moved back. John ran his finger over the back of the baby's hand just as Justin had.

"Fuck, a baby. My gods, we just got the twins out of diapers. And with four kids, we're strapped as it is. But he's family, and you don't turn your back on family." He stood and paced away.

"I want him."

Justin looked to Doc, probably wondering if he'd heard right.

CHAPTER 21

JOHN WHIRLED, and his face scrunched up even more than usual. "What?"

"I said I want the baby. I want Tommy's baby. I want to raise him."

The silence reigned until John raised a hand toward his brother. "You want the baby he had with someone else? Did he even bother to tell you he was married and his wife was pregnant?"

Doc's expression hardened. "It's not like we had the time with what was happening. And you said she'd disappeared. Maybe he thought she wouldn't come back."

"Let's call bullshit and stop trying to make Tommy smell like roses. He didn't tell you because he's a selfish bastard, said with love for my brother. One thing our father taught us was how to be selfish assholes. Tommy wouldn't have told you until she showed up. And she'll be back for money."

"I know. We have an understanding."

John gaped. "Tell me you didn't give her money."

Doc was silent.

"Fuck a duck, Doc. She's never going to go away. She'll use you until you have nothing left."

"I caught her leaving. When we cut through the bullshit, she said she never wanted a kid and couldn't be a parent. I said I could. She said she wanted money. We came to an agreement. She can't come back for a year."

John wiped at his mouth. "How much?"

"That's between her—"

"How much?"

"Ten thousand."

Justin gulped.

John raised and then dropped his hands in a hopeless gesture. "And what if she decides a year isn't long enough and comes back next week and wants more or she'll take the baby?"

"If she does, she'll go to jail."

"Why?"

"Doesn't matter. I have the power here. Ten thousand is nothing if I get to be a father even for a while. Tommy could get better some day and want to raise him. Either way this child will be with his father."

"It can't be that easy."

"It is, and all I need is your blessing because you're his family, his blood, and I won't stand in your way if you want to raise your nephew. We're all like a big family already. He'll be where he belongs."

John dropped his shoulders. "If I never change another diaper, it would be too soon. Seriously, Deana and I just got the boys sleeping in their own rooms. I'd really like to sleep alone with my wife without a kid, or kids, between us."

Doc pursed his lips. His brow pulled together, and Justin thought he even saw Doc's chin quiver. That look…. Justin felt Doc's joy even though he tried to hide his reaction.

"Thank you," Doc whispered.

"Congratulations, Dad, it's a boy. Welcome to the family." John grinned.

Justin couldn't believe what he'd just witnessed. When he looked to Doc, he was smiling wide at the baby that for all intents and purposes was now his son. Just wow.

"Since you're Tommy's power of attorney, you would have to sign guardianship over to me legally. Are you sure that's something you want to do?"

John heaved out a breath. "Yeah. I just… I want to help. I mean, I don't have much money, but—"

Doc waved him off. "I'm a fifty-year-old bachelor. Money is not a concern for me. But I want him to know his family, you and Deana and the kids, even his grandfather."

John smiled. "Again, anything but the diapers and you got a deal. What's his name? My first choice would be John, but I've already got a son with that name. Could go with your name."

Justin snorted. "Doc?"

Doc gave him a sideways glare. "No, you knucklehead. Simon."

Well, Justin felt like an ass. Of course Doc was a nickname.

"My dad, he died when I was a kid. I always said if I had a son I'd name him after my dad."

"He's technically yours, Doc. Whatever you want as long as his last name is Dennison."

Doc nodded. His gaze softened as he looked down on the baby. "What do you think, Ryan Thomas Reynolds Dennison? You like that name? Yeah, me too."

John chuckled. "That's a mouthful." He looked down on his nephew. "Welcome to the world, Ryan Dennison. If you need anything, let me know. I'm going to head back to the apartment and let the kids know they have a new cousin and let Deana know that we're off the hook for anything other than babysitting duty." John looked abashed. "But, again, we're here whenever you need us. You, Tommy, Ryan."

Doc waved him off. "I get it, John. Believe me. That brood of yours is big enough. Have a good night."

"See you tomorrow, Doc. Justin."

That was a first. Justin had often wondered if John even remembered his name. The man had definitely never addressed him directly before.

Doc continued to coo at his son.

"Congratulations." Justin felt like an intruder, so he headed for the door. Besides, he wanted to be home when Max finished work, which hopefully would be soon.

"Thanks, Justin, for helping me to decide to do this."

That stopped Justin in his tracks. "Me?"

Doc smiled. "Yeah. When you were talking with me and Carson, you said, 'If I sit and feel sorry for myself, I will get lost again. I'm stronger than that.' And then that you loved Max and that 'no one is going to take that from me.' You were right. We can fight for what we are or get lost in the fear and anger. Thanks for reminding me what's important."

Huh, something Justin said had changed the course of someone else's life. That made him feel good. "You're welcome. See you later."

But Doc had already returned to speaking to Ryan. He was going to be a great dad.

ONCE AGAIN Max was with Lincoln and Maggie, this time in the interrogation room speaking with Sarina.

"Your stepmother just left." Lincoln loved to deliver good news.

Sarina appeared to try to mitigate her response, but her shock was apparent.

"Why was she here?"

"Your stepmother said you're a troublemaker."

This time, Sarina didn't even flinch. "And a pathological liar, right? Said I'm spoiled, out of control, need to be reined in?"

Max leaned forward. "Yes."

Sarina shrugged. "I freely admit that I went through a rebellious time. Skipping school, shoplifting, sneaking out at night, going to parties, some drugs, but nothing heavy-duty. No drinking because I wasn't risking getting roofied and raped. I'm sure you've seen my records even though my father had them sealed." She actually gave them a sly look. No more surprises.

"Yes, we did," Max assured her.

Sarina sat back. "I'd be lying if most of that rebellion wasn't planned."

Max rubbed at his chin. "Payback for the parents, huh?"

"Payback, bid for attention, whatever. So let me take a stab at my stepmother's visit. She sobbed all over her enormous, double-D fake tits. Gave you some story about how much my father works, ignores her, maybe even hinted to some violence. Definitely finished up with her Mother Theresa bit of taking in a troubled, spoiled stepdaughter who doesn't appreciate all she does. Probably offered to 'help' all she could because she supports vampire rights and even if her husband is involved, she would do the right thing. How did I do?" Her smug look brought a pinched expression to Lincoln's face.

After the competing stories from her and her stepmother, Max wasn't sure who to believe.

"Not bad," Lincoln said. "Has your father ever hit you, Ms. Jenkins, or hurt or threatened you in some way?"

She frowned deeply, almost appearing offended. "Never. Did she say he did?"

"Have you ever seen your father hit your stepmother or threaten her or get violent with others?"

Her eyes went comically wide. "My father?"

"I'll take that as a no. Your stepmother showed us a bruise around her eye. Are you aware of that bruise?"

"No. Unless it happened between the time I left this morning until you saw her. It wasn't there this morning."

Lincoln looked to Max. Was this a family feud they were stuck in? Max didn't give a shit. People were missing and being hurt. "Ms. Jenkens. Have you ever seen your father with men around your age?"

Her hands went up. "Whoa, whoa. Whoa. We're talking about my father, right?"

"Yes, your father Gale Nelson, labeled the 'Barracuda of the software world.'"

Her snort was loud and obnoxious. "My father is a spineless wimp. He doesn't even breathe without his wife's approval. If you're looking for the person who runs Nelson Technologies, you need to look no further than my step-monster."

Maggie, who'd been silent until then, asked, "What makes you say that?"

"Because it's true. My father's a software genius, but he probably couldn't balance a checkbook."

Max leaned forward. "Your stepmonst—m-mother. Your stepmother said different. She claimed he ran all of the businesses associated with Nelson Technologies and that's she's afraid of your father."

That brought a dry cackle of laughter from the young girl. "She's a piece of work. I'm guessing she didn't know I was here, right? That you had already talked to me? Did you mention me?"

"Why is that important?" Lincoln narrowed his eyes.

"That lady cop who has my phone found me and said Yvonne was texting and calling me like crazy. It was driving everyone nuts, and she wanted to know how to shut it off, likes it's hard." Sarina rolled her eyes with that statement. "I asked her if I could look at the texts and listen to the messages, and she let me. She sounded frantic to talk to me. What's really strange is that Yvonne never calls me herself. She always has one of her staff do it."

"She was very upset when she was here." Maggie narrowed her eyes.

"She's quite the actress, hey? Trained actually, and I have to say that she must have given one hell of a performance, because you bought the whole dog and pony show."

Lincoln stood, braced his hands on the tabletop, and leaned toward Sarina. His menacing glare wasn't anything to fool around with. She swallowed as she looked up at him, but Max caught a hint of that defiance Mrs. Nelson had spoken of in her expression.

"Listen, Ms. Jenkens. According to your mother and most everything written about your father, he's a ruthless businessman who doesn't care who he crushes on his way up. Care to tell me why we should believe you over your stepmother and most of the world?"

Damn. Whatever fear she had faded fast. Max wasn't surprised when she stood and mirrored Lincoln's position, facing off with him.

"Sit down, Ms. Jenkens."

"No. You wanted to know why you should believe me, Director Samuels. Do you want to know what happens when my father comes home from work or from a conference, or even just leaves the property?"

Lincoln gave Max a sideways glance, then looked back to Sarina.

"Go ahead," Max said.

"First, he must come through the back entrance of the house because he's never, ever, allowed to use the front entrance. At the back door, the man who owns a multibillion-dollar software empire strips out of his clothes until he's only wearing the pair of women's panties my stepmother has commanded him to wear that day." Max felt his brow rise. Beside him, Lincoln straightened and then sat. Maggie squirmed in her seat. "He then locks his leather collar around his neck with the dog tag that says 'Yvonne's Bitch,' attaches the leash to the collar, then carries the leash in his mouth as he crawls—because he's not allowed to walk upright in the house without permission—to my step-monster's office where he squats on his haunches next to her desk, waiting for her command, because he's not allowed to speak until she says. He's a frickin' *dog*."

Max had no idea how to respond to any of that.

Lincoln cleared his throat. "There are people... err... couples, who role-play."

Max had to swallow his laughter when Sarina's expression insinuated that Lincoln was stupid. "This isn't some of the time. This is twenty-four seven, every day of the year. Maybe there was a time when they did it once in a while to get their rocks off, but it's taken over his life. The weirdness never stops. I mean, who crawls around in women's underwear when their teenage daughter is home? Not to mention the crap they do in that room downstairs."

Maggie leaned forward. "So you're saying that your stepmother controls your father at home?"

"Not just home. Work, outside of work, home. E-ver-y-where. Nelson Technologies. Other companies owned by them. My father can't even pick out his own socks to wear."

Max shook his head. "The image you're painting of your father is very different than what's been portrayed in the media. He must have done something to earn the nickname Barracuda."

She sighed and seemed annoyed that he had to ask. "Using social media and small news outlets, it isn't hard to create a buzz about anything if you do it right. Tweeting, Instagram, Facebook, Reddit, LinkedIn, blogging… even posting in the comments on other articles. Anyone can publish, upload, tweet, post anything they want whether it's true or not. Post something that points to something controversial, scandalous, or suggests something that might be true, might not, then you pay people to comment on those articles and post links to more information that they've heard and read. Link them to bogus news articles that appear to be from a reputable news organization. There are tons of them out there that mimic major news networks and reputable magazines and newspapers. People these days are too lazy to even check if the web address is valid. If they share, let's say it's just a tweet—you do know what a tweet is, right?"

"Yes," Lincoln growled.

"That single tweet can reach tons of followers. Let's say only 1 percent of a group of ten thousand reads that information—that's a thousand people. If a fraction of those retweet, the number could double or triple. Throw a hashtag on and you can be trending, and then you're front and center."

She scoffed. "The minute something goes viral and enough people see the same information over and over, well, those puppets start to believe it. Even smart people, important people. Credible news networks have even started scouring social media for leads on stories and get duped all of the time. What you read about my father is a carefully orchestrated image cultivated by my step-monster. She may be the crappiest human on earth, but she knows how to manipulate people to get what she wants." She stared at them, deadpan, and asked, "Would you like to know what happens when company comes over?"

Max shook his head a little too enthusiastically. "No. Thank you. I think we have enough information."

"You're probably thinking I should be a little more fucked-up than I am." While she tried to grin, the gesture wasn't convincing. Sarina's confidence faded, and Max could see someone who appeared truly scared.

"Sarina, are you afraid of your stepmother?" Maggie asked.

She chewed on her pale lip as she looked around the room. "No. I'm afraid for my father. She's brainwashed him or something. Before my mother left, he wasn't like that. He smiled and laughed; he paid attention to us. We were a normal family. Now his entire being is wrapped up in that woman." She choked a bit. "I really miss my dad."

Max couldn't help but feel for the kid. She was right. She should be way more messed up.

Max softened his expression and lost the interrogation tone. "Do you know where your dad is?"

"He said he was going to New York, but I haven't talked with him since last week."

"Do you know why he told you New York when he told everyone else that he was going to France?" Max asked.

"No."

"When was the last time you talked with him?"

She rubbed her temple with her fingertips. "In person it was last week before he left. I keep calling him, but he doesn't answer. His last text a couple of days ago said he was okay and not to worry." She paused. "Do you think something happened to him?"

"From what it looks like, he's in France. At least that's where his plane landed."

"But he told me he was going to Syracuse."

Max shifted. Someone was lying, and he wasn't sure who. "We only know that his plane landed at Comer-Houssen Airport."

She crossed her arms. "This all has something to do with Caden and Justin, doesn't it? My father's a member of the Mystique, where they went."

The meek tone of her voice tugged at Max's heart. Caden meant more to this girl than just a friend. Max turned to Lincoln. "Lincoln?"

Lincoln collapsed in his chair. He threw down his pen. "Yes."

That brought instant tears to her eyes. "Is Caden okay?"

Maggie grabbed a tissue and handed it to her.

"Thanks."

"Listen, this news doesn't go beyond this room. Caden's been missing since he and Justin went to the Mystique."

More sobs.

"Justin was injured, but we got to him out in time. He's upstairs."

Sarina sniffed and blew her nose. "I told Caden not to go to that place. That woman was just creepy. Caden only went because he was looking out for Justin. Caden's a really good guy. I know he messes up a lot, but he's super protective of the people he cares for. He would have fought them. He would have done anything to help Justin and get them out of there."

"We know," Max said.

She wiped at her cheeks. "I know this may sound weird, but is there any way I can just hang out here tonight? I can crash on a couch somewhere. With my dad gone and everything happening, I don't want to go home."

Maggie jumped up as Lincoln was about to speak. "We can put you up in one of the rooms at the back of Medical and you'd have a bed. Come with me."

Max was expecting a scowl from their leader, but he just looked flummoxed. "That's what I was going to say."

Max rested his head on his arms. He was so tired. Their number one suspect might have bit the dust and could possibly be missing himself. And they were no closer to finding Caden or the other missing people or understanding any of the random crap that was thrown at them.

"After everything today, I could either use a stiff drink or a stiff…. Well, you know what I mean."

Max belted out a laugh. "Just because I play for your team now doesn't mean I want to be party to your innuendos."

"Get used to it. It's one of the perks of membership." Lincoln rubbed his chin. "You think Sarina's telling the truth? The stepmom was pretty convincing."

Max stood, his legs wobbly. "Luckily, we work on facts, so grab some of those rookies we love to give the grunt work to and get them checking out their stories."

"How am I supposed to prove this man likes to play doggie in women's underwear and submit to his wife?"

"That's why you're the director and get paid *mucho dinero*."

"Fuck you, Kincaid."

Max smirked. "You're not my type. Marshall Stone might know Gale Nelson's kinks since he's a member."

"Good thinking."

"I, for one, am heading home and crashing. We can pick this up in the morning because if I don't sleep, I'm gonna lose my shit sooner rather than later." The same if he didn't see Justin in about two minutes. He couldn't believe he'd ignored him most of the day.

"Sleep sounds like a great idea. Meet me here at 7:00 a.m. I have to see how Carson's doing. He was checking on Graham."

Max gave Lincoln a poignant stare. "We'll find Caden, Lincoln."

With a sharp nod, Lincoln followed him from the room. Max left the offices and returned to the apartment, dragging himself through the door.

What he saw when he entered made his jaw drop.

CHAPTER 22

JUSTIN TENSED the moment Max opened the door. He was either going to throw up or pass out. All afternoon he'd been stuck contemplating the myriad crap running through his head, steering clear of remembering anything too detailed, too harsh, or too painful. He recalled distantly the fear of being held captive by unknown people, the vulnerability and the uncertainty of his future. He focused on the moments of pleasure and, yes, of pain, like in his dream. His gut was tied in knots, his body hot then cold then hot again, his arousal running high, and his fear of rejection and being under the control of his mind were rampant. He knew he had to take control despite the training. He had free will, right? And Lincoln had stopped him on the way to his apartment and given him one important piece of information.

You were broken down and trained to act and respond in a certain way. The key is "broken down." The first step to healing for a person who's been tortured or brainwashed is to get them healthy, mind and body. Build them back up. Give them back the control. It'll be a long, hard road, but you'll get there.

So there Justin was, trying to slay the dragons and fight fire with fire. If he were to act on his terms, maybe he could grasp some of that control. In the end, he decided, he'd been a victim long enough.

Not moving, Justin watched Max's jaw twitch. Max's eyes were so dark, their intensity something Justin had never seen before. His gaze roamed over Justin's naked body, taking in the clamps on his nipples, the rope wrapped around his balls, pulling them into taut, shiny orbs, the rope he'd tied around his wrists hanging loose and pooling on the floor, his cock hard and high. Excitement built in his stomach, edging on nausea, and fear tightened his chest. Would Max reject him?

Max sauntered across the room, coming closer, and Justin swore he could feel the air shift around them as that distance diminished. His skin flushed with heat, and he shivered. Max's eyes were heavy lidded, and his breaths had increased in frequency. Beneath the black uniform pants, Justin saw the bulge in his groin. When Max stopped before Justin and ran his fingers lightly over his stomach, a shudder shook Justin's entire body.

You'll only want pain. Gentle touches, caring caresses will be aversive to you. You will wish for a heavy hand, the searing burn, the sharp pinch, the zap of electricity. That's what will satisfy you. Nothing else. You're a natural pain slut.

Those remembered words warred with his reality. If that were true, then why were Max's ministrations pleasurable? He recalled the attempts of others to caress him, and he'd begged them for the pain, struggling to get away from the gentle touches. Not with Max, though. As long as he could get the pain, the gentleness was welcome. That endeared Max to him on so many levels, right into his soul.

The tentativeness on Max's face was something Justin wanted to soothe. He couldn't recall that he'd ever cared for his trainers, couldn't recall feeling anything but fear or safety with the pleasure. He knew that when he listened to his body, ceased his struggle, focused on the pleasure that came from the pain, he could fly. But he knew that not all of his training had caused him to fly, and he clamped down on those memories.

"Look at you, sweetie."

Justin's heart skipped a beat with the endearment. Max circled around behind him, his uniformed body brushing up against his skin. Justin clutched his fists at his sides, controlled his breathing.

Stay in this moment, with Max. He'll keep you safe.

"You sure you want to do this?"

He had to do this, and yes, he wanted.

"Max," Justin whispered, needing something more, terrified because he wasn't supposed to want, much less ask. But he trusted Max, and that trust was something he was relying on to get him out of hell. He'd been at the hands of some sadistic men and women. He remembered some of their preferences, their eagerness to inflict pain, their interest in his pleasure if they had any at all. Masked faces ran through his mind, always masks, along with his training, session after session of suffering, agony, and images of others, their torment flashing before his eyes.

"What do you want?"

"Tell me wh—" Justin clamped his mouth shut. Dammit.

Max circled back around and stepped before him. "It's hard not to respond as you were trained when you're in this situation, needing the pain, or even aroused, isn't it?"

Justin nodded. He hadn't thought of that.

"Your responses are automatic, following a pattern, I imagine. You're not some trained animal who doesn't have free will. If you didn't, they wouldn't have needed to tie you up, and given your need to be bound, they must have tied you up, right?"

Justin drew in a shuddering breath. "Yes." He certainly felt calmer, even safer when bound.

Max nibbled on his bottom lip, and his brow furrowed. "I loved what we did yesterday. Loved that I could give you what you needed, but I don't know if we should…. I mean, I don't know if this is good for you. What if it ends up messing with your head more?"

Justin shared that fear. "You care about me, right?"

Max nodded. "So much."

"I don't remember feeling that anyone cared what they did to me. They took, I gave. They didn't want me; they wanted my screams and suffering. Maybe…." He swallowed hard. "Maybe we do something and I react badly, freak out, but I can't be their victim any longer. I need to change that. But right now, I don't know if I can separate that need for the pain to get to the pleasure, to feel that… bone-deep release my head will accept."

"What if it pushes you away from me?"

"I trust you, Max. I need you to trust me too. I know the fight with whatever's in my head is huge. I've already felt how massive that will be, but could you help me through some of this? I know now that you and Walt were trying to help me. I fought both of you every step of the way. I wasn't trying to, but where my mind was before whatever happened at the Mystique or with Miriam was a fucked-up mess."

"No you weren't—"

Justin's smile felt tremulous. "Yes, I was and still am. But I'm calmer now, more centered. I feel… more capable. The constant anxiety and fear that I felt when I didn't know the cause, that's missing. I thought a lot about it today, and even though the fear and anxiety are still there, I know the reason now. That's the difference. Maybe whatever Merrick did to throw me back into that catatonic state had something to do with the way I was when I first woke up. I don't know."

Max placed a hand on the side of Justin's neck, and the touch was gentle. Max's thumb ran over his jaw, the touch so soothing. "I want to do anything that'll help you, sweetie, anything you need, but I don't want this to be some way for you to prove something to yourself."

Justin grasped Max's wrist and leaned into his hand. "I want to make new memories with you, Max, before I have to remember more." Which would be sooner than Max realized. "But I won't make you do anything you don't want to do, and I won't be mad if you choose not to. I want you because... because I love you. I just don't know if I can simply make love to you. I'm afraid I can't.... That I won't be able to without some kind of pain."

You'll only want pain. Gentle touches, caring caresses will be aversive to you. Damn. Of all of the memories, he wished that was one he could un-remember.

Max looked away, and Justin thought he was angry. But when he turned back and leaned their foreheads together, Justin released the breath he'd held.

"Somehow along the way, without even knowing it, I fell in love with you too. We'll make this work. Somehow, we'll make this work."

Justin was dazed by Max's confession as the man cocked his head, placed a hand on the back of Justin's head, and guided Justin down for a kiss. Light kisses at first, then increasing pressure, tongues dueling. Wrapping arms around Justin, Max pulled their bodies together, and the friction of his clothes on Justin's cock was magnificent. Lightheaded from the demonstration of their passion, Justin grasped Max's biceps and gripped them tight. Max's fingers ran over his back, raising goose bumps over his flesh. Max's hips pushed into Justin's thigh, their difference in height noticeable as Justin's cock rubbed against the fabric on Max's stomach.

When Max broke the kiss, Justin panted, his lips pulsing with the beat of his heart. His eyelids were heavy, and he needed Max, no matter what that meant.

Max's face was flushed, his pupils wide. "I want to try something, if you'll let me."

Justin nodded without even thinking. Max's lip twitched. "You don't even know what I want to do."

"Just do it."

Max took him by the hand and led Justin into the bedroom. After closing the door, Max stood before Justin. "Undress me."

Justin didn't hesitate. He pulled Max's T-shirt over his head and tossed it to the floor. On his knees, he unlaced his sneakers, pulling them off, and then his socks, caressing the tops of his feet. Straightening up on his knees, Justin unbuckled Max's belt, opened the button, the zipper, and in one motion had Max's pants and underwear around his ankles. Before Justin's face, Max's cock bobbed, not too long but a little thicker than Justin's. His shaft curved slightly inward. His balls hung low, the skin stretched, his testicles filling the rounded bottoms. A riot of long, blondish hair surrounded his cock, sparsely covered his sac, and spread out thickly across his thighs.

"Do you want to suck it?" Max asked, his voice hoarse.

"Yes." But Justin hesitated for some reason, and that pissed him off.

Max reached out, cupped the back of his head, and gently urged him closer until Justin took over. Justin inhaled deeply the musky smell of Max, causing his own cock to twitch. The rope binding his balls made them pulse madly. He'd sucked many cocks when he was a teenager and hoped he could make this good for Max.

He opened his mouth and sucked on the head, the precum salty and tart. When Max moaned deep in his throat, Justin pushed the shaft farther into his mouth. Pulling off, he licked his lips and again took the cock in until it filled his mouth.

"Your mouth feels so good." Max didn't move, but Justin could feel minute pulses of his hips as if he were trying not to buck. Bobbing his head, Justin reveled in the easy glide of the soft skin on the underside of Max's cock against his tongue. The panting and groans from Max spurred him to move faster.

"Yesss." Max panted, and Justin bobbed faster. "D-do you want to touch my balls?"

Justin nodded, Max's cock in his mouth making a verbal response impossible. Max touched Justin's shoulder, prompting him to go ahead. In tandem, Justin gripped the base of his cock with one hand and cupped his balls with other. Max widened his legs, allowing Justin free access. Gently, Justin stroked the sac, rolling the balls in his hand, sucking on Max's cock as his lover's thighs twitched and his breath caught. Justin was making him feel good. He controlled how fast he sucked, how hard he squeezed Max's balls, controlled his pleasure. The power and control was foreign to him. He squeezed his lips and ran his mouth to the head of the shaft. Releasing, he ran his tongue around the flared head, under the ridge. Max bucked his hips, and a noticeable tremor filled his body.

Justin rubbed two fingers over Max's perineum as he sucked vigorously, pushing the shaft farther into his mouth until his throat was the only obstacle. He kept the depth and sucked harder, his tongue wriggling on the underneath. He rubbed harder, faster, as he curled his fingers around the balls and squeezed lightly.

"Ah!" Max barked the sound out, and his body jerked. His hips pushed forward. His hand tangled in Justin's hair. His stomach and chest heaved, his breath staccato and filled with sharp moans.

"J-Justin… oh, oh…. Yes! Oh, oh…. Gonna…."

Justin peered up at Max, his stomach taut, shoulders rolled over, head back, his neck stretched tight, corded, his Adam's apple bobbing furiously.

"Oh shiiiiiiit!" Max's balls pulsed in Justin's hand, the contraction felt beneath his fingers in the perineum. Max's body shook, and his thighs tensed. He moaned to the ceiling as his cock spurted over and over into Justin's mouth. Justin had to pull back slightly to keep from choking. The seminal fluid was bitter and definitely nothing Justin fancied, but he swallowed anyway. Max continued to twitch and spasm long after the cum stopped flowing. Justin licked at the cock and played with his balls until Max looked down on him.

He appeared thoroughly fucked out, his eyes in total bliss. When he fell to his knees and kissed Justin, that kiss was frantic, demanding, and totally dominant. Justin's groin pulsed, and his cock was drooling precum as he realized he'd driven Max to come, given him what he needed, without being told what to do. Even if Max had to prompt him to do what he wanted. Max had done that for him.

Max broke the kiss, caressing Justin's face, his neck, his chest. "Damn, that was hands down the best blowjob ever. You blew my mind."

"You should have seen your reaction."

"You did it to me. Made me feel so good." Max grasped Justin's shaft, and Justin gasped and groaned. "You're so hard, and you're leaking all over." Max ran a fingernail over Justin's balls, nearly a deep red-purple color and so sensitive. Hissing, he pushed into the scrape. "You like your balls tied up?"

Justin groaned in response as more scrapes of Max's fingernails caused pain through his sac.

"I do." Justin couldn't catch his breath and dug his nails into his thighs, trying to keep himself from pulling away. Pulling away wouldn't get him pleasure, only pain without release, he thought. Damn, where had that thought come from? He forced his mind back to the pain.

"Do you want me to stop?" Max asked, his voice a mere whisper.

Justin gasped and shook his head.

"Then say it. Tell me not to stop."

Through gritted teeth Justin managed to say, "Don't... stop."

Another scrape and sweat popped out on Justin's skin, cold shivers washing over him. His groin tingled, and his gut cramped. Max stopped scraping and ran his palm over the scratches, igniting a low burn.

Max continued rubbing as he ran his hand through Justin's hair. "I want to do so much with you. I want everything, but I don't know if I'm ready for you to... to fuck me."

Justin hadn't even thought that to be a possibility. The thought pulled a moan from his chest. He licked his lips, his throat dry, and he swallowed repeatedly. He blushed, thinking of the words he wanted to say. He had no clue if he'd been penetrated by a penis. Tons of other things, sure, but even if he had, he couldn't remember.

"I want you to...." Holy shit. He'd gotten that much out; he could say the rest. "Please, I want you to make love to me." Because what they'd be doing was more than fucking.

Max smiled wide, and Justin thought his reaction was a little over the top, so he chuckled. Max led him to the bed, ropes still dragging on the floor. He took off his glasses and placed them on the dresser, then opened a drawer and pulled out a bottle of lube. Justin raised a brow.

"Been me and my hand for a long time."

Max lay on top of Justin, their bodies lined up. Max wasn't as hard as Justin, but he was getting there. Kissing at first, and then Max was biting and pulling on his nipples, the action driving him insane, just the right amount of pain to keep him on the edge. Settling between Justin's legs, Max popped the top on the lube and coated his fingers.

"How much prep you want?"

Justin grinned.

"Okay, just a little." One finger was uncomfortable and then two was a burning pain. Justin wanted more. His cock bobbed as he rode Max's fingers, gasping and loving feeling full.

Max added another finger, ignoring Justin's cock and balls. When he moved and hit that spot, Justin's hips bucked off the bed. "Ohhh!"

"No coming. Not yet."

Gritting his teeth, Justin wasn't sure he could hold on as Max continued sawing into his hole, faster and faster.

The exquisite pain, the burn, didn't totally fade. His balls were on fire, trapped in the confines of the rope, his cock bouncing as he fucked Max's fingers.

"Shit, I can't wait any longer." Max removed his fingers, lubed his cock, and pushed into Justin without hesitation.

Justin's entire lower body locked up, his hole pulsed and clenched and relaxed and clenched again, confused by the large intruder. Max hadn't looked thick, but in his ass, he felt like a missile. Max stilled, leaning down and raining kisses on Justin's face, no doubt waiting for Justin to adjust to him.

"You feel so good on my cock." Max kissed him hard and deep until Justin's lungs burned. He rose onto his knees and grabbed the ropes on Justin's wrists, but he didn't tie him to the bed. He tied his wrists together. Then he pushed Justin's legs apart with his knees and hammered his hole, grasping Justin's hips. Each slam jostled his balls. He imagined the feeling of having them crushed in between them. His need to reach for Max was hindered by his bound wrists.

That was when Max leaned down. "Put your arms around my neck." His gasping words spurred Justin into action, and he lifted his hands over his head, resting them on the nape of his neck. When Max lay on him, Justin's cock rubbed between them. Max's hard stomach crushed his balls, spurring Justin to buck his hips. He panted so hard he couldn't catch his breath. He felt floaty, his vision a pinpoint focus on Max.

"Bite my shoulder, please. Just… just enough to hurt. No blood."

Max didn't stop his assault on Justin's ass. His face flushed, sweat covered his forehead and upper lip, but his gaze looked uncertain.

"I've thought about it. Jerked off to it." He needed to feel Max's teeth on his skin.

Max snapped his hips sharply, the force a searing pain in Justin's balls. "Oh gods. I'm gonna come. Please… do it now."

Max placed his mouth in the juncture between Justin's neck and shoulder. Justin felt the heat and then the pressure and a pinch and… fuck! Justin felt the moment Max's teeth punctured the skin. He pulled harder on Max's neck and bucked against him as his balls drew up.

"Harder!"

Max increased his thrusts and then sucked harder, and Justin couldn't handle that sensation. He screamed, his cock exploding between them.

When he closed his eyes, colors exploded in the blackness. He felt as if he were without a body, just a cocoon of energy, floating. Definitely flying with Max.

Grunting, Max didn't release the bite as he pushed hard into Justin, over and over. Justin clutched Max as his lover spasmed and twitched with his orgasm, his fangs still in Justin's skin. When he released the bite, Max licked at the wounds, and Justin shuddered. The bite had been as erotic as he'd imagined it would be.

"Gods, if you don't stop licking there, I'm going to get hard again." Justin chuckled, but Max was silent. Was he going to freak out? "Max?"

Max stopped licking and drew up onto his elbows. Confusion swirled in his eyes.

"You okay?" Justin knew he'd pushed him too far.

"I didn't know that biting could be so…." He shook his head. "Intimate. And I drank your blood." He sounded astonished.

"How did I taste?"

Max sucked in his bottom lip, seeming unsure. "If I said good, would that sound gross?"

That revelation spiked Justin's arousal. "No." Justin rubbed his cheek against the scruff on Max's face. "I loved it. Everything was amazing."

"More than amazing." Max lovingly brushed the hair from Justin's eyes. Without his glasses on, Justin could see the hints of yellow in his irises. While he didn't want to break the spell, he also didn't want his balls to die and fall off from the lack of blood.

Max helped him remove the ropes from his balls and wrists, and then Justin lay replete in Max's arms, curled around his man. Max drew lazy patterns on his back, and Justin couldn't believe how relaxed he was. Nothing had gone wrong, and he and Max had shared something special.

"I could lay here forever with you," Justin whispered.

Max rubbed Justin's scalp, and Justin purred from the sensation.

Max kissed his forehead. "You're mine, baby, so you aren't going anywhere."

Justin's entire body jerked involuntarily.

You're doing so good, baby.

Baby, you suffer so nicely for me.

Are you ready to fly, baby?

Take the pain, baby.

That voice, the man in the mask was all he could see. Justin gasped for air, flailing on the bed, stuck in an endless barrage of memories of that sweaty man, the stinky breath, and his hands all over him, laughing as he screamed, grinning as he begged the sadist to stop. Tied to a chair, hanging from the ceiling, from the wall, chained to the floor. Floggers, whips, electrodes, surgical steel knives gleaming under the lights, enormous dildos meant to tear him apart, the needles.

"Justin! What's wrong?"

Justin fought the hands holding him down as if his life was in danger.

"Justin!" Max grunted and tried to roll him onto his back. "You're going to hurt yourself! Come on, sweetie, please." The near sob in Max's voice broke through, and Justin choked on a gasp.

Fuck, fuck, fuck!

"What happened?"

Catching his breath, Justin focused on Max. One word and he was a freaking mess. "The man in the mask, he called me b-baby all of the time."

After that Justin couldn't speak from the wracking sobs that took over. He buried his face in his hands. Nothing could stop the tears, not even Max holding him close, crooning that everything would be okay and that he was safe. He cried for what felt like hours until he was exhausted and fell asleep.

CHAPTER 23

AFTER THE previous night, his breakdown and hours of crying, Justin woke smiling and happy, and Max was dumfounded but relieved.

"Maybe it was just something I needed to do," Justin told him when Max questioned his upbeat mood.

Max was over the moon having Justin in their apartment as his partner and his lover. As they made breakfast, there were sly glances, touching, kisses, and more touching. And laughter. As they were eating, Justin dropped a bomb on Max, and he wasn't sure how to feel given that information.

"You want to what?"

Justin took a sip of his orange juice. "I'm going to work to remember what happened to me. Maybe I can find out something that'll help find Caden."

Max sat back. After removing his glasses, he rubbed his eyes, which felt gritty from lack of sleep. Anything to give him a moment to think of a response other than "hell no."

Putting his glasses on, he saw that Justin's expression was set, determined.

"Sweetie"—he'd never use the endearment "baby" again—"after what happened last night when I called you… that word, you can't want to do this. One word and you were a mess for hours." He couldn't go through that again so soon.

"I know, but this is important. You even said yourself that the guy who was your main suspect might not be anymore, and Caden…. I can't sit around and do nothing. I may know something that can help find him."

Justin's guilt was so evident, and Max understood, but what if he went too far? What if remembering changed him?

"What if remembering goes very wrong and backfires and you get hurt even more? I mean, we don't know what they programmed into you. They had the power to put you into something resembling that catatonic state. What if that's triggered again and I can't get you back?"

He was petrified of losing Justin.

Justin covered Max's hand with his. "It's okay. I really think I can do this with Carson's help. He's going to try to guide me through my head and keep me from getting too much at once. He said he could also help protect me from getting too emotional."

Max shook his head. "Now, but later, when he's not around, you're going to have to deal with what you've seen."

Justin rubbed at his temple with short jabbing strokes. "I'm going to have to deal with it sooner or later. I'm choosing to start sooner." Justin's glare was intense as he slammed his fist against the table. Glasses and silverware jumped.

What he was trying to protect Justin from wasn't anything he could control. This was going to rear its ugly head, as he said, sooner or later. Maybe Carson could soften the blow, give Justin time to process things.

Max rubbed the back of his neck. "You're right. I'm just scared." And understandably so.

Justin's expression softened. "I am too. But maybe I can remember something that gets us to Caden. I hate thinking about what they're probably doing to him."

Max reached over and ran his knuckles over Justin's cheek. He sighed. "I'm going to be there when you do this, and if I think anything is going wrong, well, I'll ask if you want to stop."

Justin smiled. "Thank you. Carson said to meet him in Medical at nine."

"I'll be there. What're you going to do until then?" Max didn't want him to hang around the apartment alone and think too much.

Max watched as Justin pushed his egg around his plate. "Probably head up to see Ryan."

"Ryan?"

Justin's eyes rounded, and his mouth dropped open. "I forgot to tell you."

"Tell me what?"

Max listened to the far-out story of Doc taking in Tommy's son. Actually paying the mother off. Things never ceased to amaze him. After that he left the apartment and was late to meet Lincoln at seven. He ran from the elevator and slid on the worn soles of his sneakers, nearly missing the door. When he gained traction and entered the room, Lincoln eyed him, pursing his lips and glancing at the clock. He wasn't in uniform but a suit and tie. He generally only did that when he was heading out of the office.

"Fifteen minutes late."

Tia, who sat at the table with him, barked out a laugh. "And who strolled in here just three minutes ago?"

"Shut it, Warez. That's mutiny." Lincoln leaned back in his chair, sipping from a mug and assessing Max thoroughly. "So, how's it going, lover boy?" His grin was obnoxious.

Tia tittered.

Max frowned deeply at them both but didn't answer Lincoln. He walked casually to the table.

"Someone called the switchboard last night, oh, around seven. Reported screaming, possibly coming from your apartment." Lincoln raised a brow.

Steel butterflies beat in Max's stomach and his cheeks heated. Oh gods, someone had heard him and Justin and frickin' reported it. Max hadn't even thought….

"Wait. No one came to the apartment last night about noise." Max waited for Lincoln to crack and spill what he was getting at.

"No? Said they banged on the door for ten minutes and no one answered."

Max's mind raced to remember if he'd heard anything. Justin had been screaming loud. "No one banged on the door. Quit messing with me."

"Then they called me."

If they had called Lincoln, he would have gotten a key and come in without knocking.

Still grinning, Lincoln whispered, "I knew better than to… interrupt."

Tia was staring at Max, and he felt like a bug behind glass. Who had heard them? Who lived around Max that could have….

Lincoln.

"Fuck you. You're the one who heard."

He laughed out loud. "Me and Carson."

"Shit." Max felt his cheeks flush.

"Oh, and Warez here, who was hanging out with us."

Could Max get any more embarrassed? "You can't tell anyone." What if they said something to Justin and he freaked out?

Tia laughed. "Chill, Kincaid. It's just sex, and we aren't going to tell anyone. I say, go you."

Lincoln's grin widened. "Welcome back to the game, buddy. Well, same game, new, well, junk."

"Jeesh, have a party or something." He plopped into a chair, brooding from their fun. He had to change the subject quick. "Did Carson tell you what he and Justin are planning on doing?" Maybe Lincoln had nixed the idea already.

"Yeah." He dropped the front legs of his chair to the floor, setting his cup down. "I think if Carson helps, then Justin will be okay. If we can get anything concrete about people or places, that would be helpful. Our worker elves found nothing last night to back up Sarina's claim that her father is controlled by her stepmother. They did find tons of friends and neighbors to corroborate that this isn't the first time Mr. Nelson has hit his wife. Many describe him as controlling and aloof."

Tia looked to Lincoln. "So you think the daughter is trying to make the parents look bad as payback for something. Poor rich girl who never was loved?"

"I wanted to believe her." Max thought her caring for Caden had been real. And who made up shit about their parents like that?

"Me too. She's a good liar, though. Got past my bullshit meter."

Max cracked up. "Your bullshit meter sucks."

"Better than yours, lover boy."

Max gave the finger to his superior, who pretended to snatch something from the air as if Max had blown a kiss at him.

"Okay, boys." Tia eyed them both. "That leads us back to Gale Nelson, who is possibly hiding out in another country. I have a list of buildings Jenkens Holdings owns in DC and the surrounding area. He has others scattered across the country. This man has got to be loaded. To search them all would take months."

Lincoln stood and straightened his gray suit jacket. He wore matching slacks, a white shirt, and a yellow tie with diagonal blue stripes. A wolf whistle from the door caught their attention.

Taylor walked in with Maggie, Dwayne, and Wes. "I hear every girl's crazy about a sharp-dressed man." Taylor grinned wide and winked.

"Or guy." Maggie approached Lincoln, giving him the once-over. "You do clean up nice, boss. Meeting the bigwigs?"

Lincoln fidgeted with his collar. "First I'm meeting with Director Williams to update her about this case. Then we're meeting with the mayor and the metropolitan police commissioner to try to hammer out details for a possible agreement between the NVJ and the MPD."

"Agreement?" Wes sat next to Max and nodded to him. Max nodded back. Dennison and the new guy, Jordan, who Max had only seen a couple of times, entered the room. He was a quiet guy.

"Aww, Lincoln, you didn't need to dress up on my account." Dennison dropped a box of donuts onto the table. Wes snagged one and ate the entire thing in two bites.

"Yes, I'm in a suit. Not the first time and won't be the last." Lincoln turned his attention back to Wes. "The agreement we're working on with MPD is a pilot agreement to share resources, work cases together, ride-alongs, even employee swaps. Our third hire, Sara Phillips, a vampire, has been training with the MPD. All of this in a bid to create unity and harmony between the Nons and the vampires. There's a consensus that this could be good for tensions in the city. Get us out there more. You know... create a good example."

"Why don't you just make us all go to cultural sensitivity training?" Dennison frowned from behind his coffee cup.

Max snorted. Dennison and sensitivity in the same sentence was an oxymoron.

"Be careful what you wish for," Lincoln warned. "Listen up. Today's assignment is to pair off and check out properties that belong to Jenkens Holdings in the city. Tia will give each team a couple of locations to check. This is strictly surveillance, no entry unless it's a public business. If you see anything suspicious, call it in. No heroics. Gale Nelson is still number one on our list, but we aren't ruling out other possibilities. Max, you have that appointment at nine o'clock, so stick around here. Turner, you're on the phone continuing to track down Mr. Nelson's whereabouts."

Jordan nodded.

Taylor leaned over. "You'd have an easier time finding Hoffa." Max chuckled, but Jordan merely smiled in an almost condescending way.

"Oh, and Sarina Jenkens is still in the building. Turner, you can lean on her a little, see if she gives up her father's location, but make sure you have a couple of rookies around when you do so she can't cry police harassment. We can't keep the daughter if she wants to leave, but if she sticks around, at least we'll know where she is if we need her." Lincoln adjusted his cuffs, then checked his gun in the holster under his jacket. "I'll be back here by two at the latest."

Lincoln left, and the team collected their assignments. It was only a little past eight, giving Max some time to kill before heading up to Medical. Gods, he wasn't anxious much about that or anything, so he decided to distract himself by double-checking the work the rookies had done last night. Maybe they'd missed something. Grabbing an armful of files, he headed to his office, sat on his couch, and got to work.

When his phone rang thirty minutes later, he yanked it out of his pocket. On the screen was a DC number he didn't recognize.

"Lieutenant Kincaid."

"Lieutenant Kincaid, this is Marshall Stone. I need your help." Her voice was low and breathy, little louder than a whisper.

"How can I help you, Ms. Stone?"

He heard the phone rustling and then a gasp. "I need you to come to my condo. It's Gale. He called and said he was coming here. He...." There was a tremble in her voice. "He threatened to hurt me. He thinks I gave you information about what he's doing at the club. Please, I'm really scared."

"I'll call MPD and get a car out there quick. If—"

"No! You don't understand. There are very important people in the police department who are members of my club, and he's bought them. He's made people disappear before, Lieutenant. Please, help me." Her voice was pitched high with terror.

"Where are you located?"

"350 L Street, Southeast. Please hurry. He said he'd be here soon."

Max grabbed his gun and holster and headed out to Jordan's desk. His head went up when he heard Max, but he remained expressionless.

"Leave your house, Ms. Stone. Go to a neighbor's or someplace public. Can you do that? When you get there, call me." Pointing to Jordan, he said, "Come on. We're going out."

Jordan gathered his items and followed Max as he sprinted down the hall.

"Ms. Stone?"

There was more rustling, and then she whispered, "He's in the house. I'm hiding in the upstairs closet. Hurry.... Wait.... No. Gale, please...." Then there was silence.

Max repeated her name several times but got nothing. "Shit. Gale Nelson may have just attacked Marshall Stone." They went down the stairs to the garage, and once in the SUV, they were on the road.

"I need directions here." Max handed Jordan the address, and he typed it into the computer.

Jordan pointed to the right. "Right here. Potomac Avenue, by the stadium."

Max blew past a line of cars at the red light, hitting the siren. Cars parted, and he made the turn. Even though they arrived at the location in under eight minutes, the trip seemed to take longer. Parking a few houses down, they pulled on their bulletproof vests as they exited the SUV. Coming across the lawn of the adjacent house, they checked out the narrow, yellow home in the center of the row of houses. There were no sounds from the house. No screams. Silence was never good.

Max motioned with his hand. "Front door. Watch yourself." They crouched down, made it to the front stoop, and squatted down. The front door was ajar. Again, no sound. Gun drawn, Max pushed open the door slightly. Inside, the light was dim.

"She said she was in an upstairs closet."

"You want to wait for backup?" Jordan peered into the house past Max.

"Let me shoot a text to Lincoln." As Max pulled out his phone, there was a crash from inside.

"Let's go." Max pushed open the door, gun raised. Crouching, they entered, stopping in the entryway. Silence met them. Max cocked his head and looked to the left into a room with two wingback chairs. A man sat in one of the chairs. Max turned and pointed the gun at him.

"NVJ. Don't move."

"Look there." At the top of the stairs, there appeared to be someone lying on the floor. At the same time, there were footsteps and a door slammed near the back of the house.

"Got it." Jordan took off running.

Max moved slowly to the doorway of the room where the man sat in the shadows. His legs were bare… and his feet? Max couldn't see his upper body.

"Show me your hands. Put them out in front of you."

The man complied, his hands coming from the shadows.

"Who are you?"

No answer.

Max's heart pounded in his ears. Any minute someone was going to jump out at him. He stopped. Looked left and then right. He moved closer.

"Answer me!"

The light from the window blinded Max. One more step, and he could see the man. Max adjusted the grip on his gun. He recognized the man with the short red hair.

"Gale Nelson?"

The man nodded. A leather collar circled his neck. Max raised an eyebrow as he spotted blue panties encasing his bulge. Sarina's words ran through his head, but Max wasn't taking any chances.

"On the ground, Mr. Nelson."

He appeared despondent, almost regretful. "I'm sorry."

Before Max could speak, something was pulled over his head. He flailed and dropped his gun. Arms wrapped around Max's chest, and he struggled to break free. Grunting, he bent over and tried to flip the person over him, but they were too big. Snapping his head back, he connected with bone, and there was a crunching sound. The man shouted but didn't let go. Max struggled, but his arms were pinned behind him. His legs were kicked out from under him. He fell to his knees. His wrists were quickly bound, and then he was pushed onto his stomach. All he could think about was Justin.

CHAPTER 24

CARSON SAT before Justin, their eyes locked, their postures mirroring each other. They had waited for Max, but he hadn't shown or called. Doc checked downstairs and told Justin he wasn't sure where he was. Justin couldn't hide his disappointment, truly needing him there, but they couldn't wait.

They sat in one of the interview rooms with Doc on the other side of the mirror. Lincoln was at his meeting; however, Carson would communicate with him through their mind thing so Carson could ask the right questions. The interview room was cold and impersonal, but Justin had wanted to do this outside of Medical where he and Max had… well, he didn't know what to call it. But what Max had done to him in that bed…. Justin closed his eyes, breathing deep until he heard a chuckle.

Opening his eyes, he saw Carson's cheeks had reddened. "Maybe you should refrain from thinking about Max." Carson shifted in his chair. Justin wasn't sure what the issue was until he covertly adjusted his pants. Shit, Lincoln would kill Justin if he thought he'd aroused Carson with his thoughts.

"Sorry."

Carson smiled gently. "I'm really happy for you and Max. He's a great guy. I can tell that he really cares for you."

"Did you read that from him?"

"No. Just saw how much he cares for you, but today was different, less friendship, more intimate. Like I said, I try to stay out of people's heads."

Justin cocked his head. "So you're better, just like that?"

Carson raised his hands and dropped them. "Yeah, ever since I fought back against Miriam. I can enter your mind without feeling like I'm two steps away from dying. I have no clue why, but I'm not complaining."

"Maybe Doc can do whatever he does and figure it out."

"Maybe. We'd better get back to working on your memories."

Justin cringed. He'd been distracting himself from just that. He'd swiftly been kicking out any memories of the time he'd been catatonic, avoiding them by thinking of Max. There was a terrifying uncertainty, a probability that he'd be bombarded with images and sense memories of horrific pain, torture, maybe even rape. So far he hadn't experienced that vulnerability, that helplessness, of being forced to endure someone else's will, of being debased. Violated wasn't something he currently felt, but he knew as he allowed the memories to surface he'd become a larger train wreck than he already was.

Carson leaned forward. "Hey, I get it. If you don't want to—"

"No. I have to do this. I might remember something important. Let's just get it over with." He blew out a breath and clenched his jaw. "I'm ready."

Carson touched his knee, and Justin flinched, the action vibrating over his nerves.

"Sorry." Would he ever get used to other people touching him?

"It's a normal reaction when someone you don't trust has hurt you."

Someone he trusted. Like Max. Was that why wanting the pain from Max was different? Damn, he hadn't thought of that.

"Okay. Just relax and open your mind. I'm going to try to guide your focus on the memories and hopefully take the edge off your emotions. I might not be able to see what you're remembering, so if you need to stop, just tell me, and we'll take a break."

Justin nodded. Relaxing, he pushed Max from his head, closed his eyes, and let the memories come. Within seconds, he was on that table, the one in the Mystique, tied down, unable to move or speak. The man with the leather mask leaned over him, and Justin was hit with another memory. A different room, one like he'd been in during his dream. The chair, the restraints, the same man, same mask. His heart rate increased as he watched the man clamp one nipple, then the other. He remembered how painful that was. The clamp was round and pushed his nipple to a peak above the metal circle. Justin saw the needle coming toward his nipple, closer and closer, and the sight both terrified and excited him.

A nudge in his head, possibly Carson, pushed his focus from what was being done to his body. That's when Justin remembered the man had been speaking. What was he saying?

"The man with the mask, he was talking to me. He said I was doing so well in my training. Something about only having been in the program for... three months?" Justin swallowed hard. "He said I'm a natural."

"Do you recognize him?"

"Yeah. I've dreamed about him a couple of times."

"Do you know where you were?"

Justin kept his eyes closed. A well of panic and anxiety and a crapload of other feelings was just waiting to attack. He clenched his jaw and fought back.

A woman's voice filled his head.

"No, but there's a woman. She sounds really familiar. Maybe I've heard her before…. Yes…." Why couldn't he remember what she looked like? "I remember hearing her voice a lot, but I can't remember what she looked like. I think she's in charge or something because she's giving orders."

"Does she sound like someone you know?"

"I've never heard her anywhere else that I can remember."

The memory ended, and Justin frowned. He was sitting behind metal bars. His mouth was dry. He was thirsty and hungry, and he wasn't alone.

"Are you in a cage?" Carson's voice was strained with his disbelief.

"I think so. It's kind of dark. I can't see much, but…." He heard breathing and whimpers and maybe even crying. He wanted to call out, speak to whoever was there, but it was as if he was locked in his head again. He squirmed in his seat, trying to break away from the memory.

Next he was in a small empty room, his arms stretched above his head. Everything hurt, yet his skin felt alive as if it were buzzing, his head clouded with the pain and high from the adrenaline and endorphins. Looking up, he saw he was hanging from the ceiling.

He gasped in shock, and then another wave of calm raced over him. Justin was grateful for Carson's abilities at that moment. The man stepped before him and smiled through the slit in his mask. His hand ran over Justin's cheek, and Justin shuddered in revulsion. He wasn't Max, and that touch felt dirty and sleazy.

"Good boy. You did really good as usual. You're healing faster, so we can do this more often. Get you ready for your new life. I have to say I'm jealous to know someone else will be hurting you." With that he pinched Justin's nipples and gave them a twist. The pain instantly spun his head. "Time for the resting stage." Another twist and Justin's loud groan masked the words the man was saying. Immediately his thoughts and feelings—the pain—seemed distant.

"He said, 'Time for the resting stage.'"

"Do you know what that is?"

"I don't know. I remember not being able to speak sometimes and not do much of anything. My mind feels fuzzy, very slow, almost like I'm drugged, but I don't think I am. I can see and hear other people." His memory shifted, and he was in the cage again.

The light was brighter this time. "There was a cage next to mine. I remember someone was in there. One time he—or she—was curled up against the bars, trying to get me to talk to them. Wait…." His image was fuzzy. "It's a boy. I remember him saying 'I wish you'd talk to me again.' The voice was small, like a kid."

Carson cleared his throat, and for a moment, Justin felt as if he'd been left alone. He didn't want to open his eyes for fear he might not get back there. "Carson, don't leave me."

Hands were on his knees. "I'm right here. Just talking with Lincoln. Not going anywhere. You're doing great. Max will be proud of you."

Justin didn't want Max in his head when he was in that place.

"Do you know who the kid was?"

Oh gods, Manuel. It had to be him. "Yes." Before he could say anything more the memory changed, and he was in a different room, in a chair, tied down, sitting upright. Still trapped in his head, but he could see and hear. The woman was back, and he could see her this time. She wore what looked to be a ski mask made of black fabric. Only her eyes were visible. They were green. She wore an expensive-looking silky white button-up blouse, gold jewelry. The man fiddled with Justin's inner arm. A pinch and an IV was inserted into a vein. When the man opened the flow, blood ran through the tube and tingled as it entered Justin's body.

"They gave me blood through an IV." His gut churned. Why had he needed blood? "I can't remember why," he said, before Carson asked. The woman said something about healing faster. Her posture was stiff, and her arms were crossed. She didn't look happy. "The woman wants to know why I'm not changing. I'm able to heal faster, but…." Well, that explained why he could heal so quickly. He frowned. "She's mad because my body is resisting something…. I can't remember what she said. I'm not like the others."

"Did she say anything about genes or DNA?"

He recalled faint memories of those words but nothing tangible. "Sounds familiar, but I can't remember."

"It's okay."

"Wait." The man removed the IV. Then he prepped Justin's other arm. A needle went into the crook of his arm, and this time the blood flowed out and was collected in a bag.

"They're taking blood from me now." No one spoke, but the woman watched as the bag filled. She really creeped him out.

"Do you know why?"

He shook his head. None of this was helpful in finding Caden. With that thought, the memories of Caden struggling hit hard, so real and visceral that he sucked in a breath as he watched Caden fight off the vampires. Caden shouted for Justin to run, but that had only increased the severity of his beating until someone intervened. A man Justin didn't recognize spoke.

"At the Mystique there was a man who told them to stop beating on Caden. That he was a valuable catch. They shot something into his arm, and he passed out." Justin's fear from that night was forefront even with Carson helping.

"Newer memories have more emotions attached to them, a greater recollection of everything that happened and more detail. They're stronger."

Justin nodded.

"Do you know who the man is?"

"No."

Justin squeezed his eyes shut tighter, searching, focusing on Caden and where exactly in the Mystique he went. But he was on that table, with the masked man who dared to call him baby. Another nudge in his head, but nothing changed.

"Justin, don't fight me."

"I'm not. I don't want to be there." The man leaned over and whispered in his ear. Justin flinched, turning his head, but his head didn't turn in the memory. The man flicked at his clamped nipples. And the scream filled his head.

"Try to think of something else. Think of Max."

No matter what Justin tried he was stuck where he was, in a body that wouldn't move.

"You need to come out of your memory, Justin. I'm trying to pull you out. Can you feel me?"

Justin felt the tug, but it was if he'd been welded to the memory. He was going to be forced to endure the agony while Carson watched. Since being with Max, being violated by that man and the memories of what he'd done were horrible.

"I'm trying, but I can't." Justin's breaths increased, and his heart raced. His skin flashed hot and cold. He heard Doc speaking and tried to focus on his voice, but the man twisted the nipple clamps. His teeth clenched as the pain built upon itself.

Grunting, he tried not to scream. "Fuck."

The pain was so real, so fucking real that he wasn't entirely sure he hadn't fallen asleep while Carson had been trying to help him. The man shoved that rod into his hole and attached the alligator clips to his genitals. All the while Carson pleaded with him to get out of his head. Justin's entire body tensed as he remembered the jolts of electricity to his cock and balls.

"Justin. It's Doc. I'm going to give you a sedative to relax you. Just a pinch in your arm."

Justin felt his body spasm with the jolt of electricity to his groin as his jaw clenched. He wasn't sleeping if he could hear Doc and Carson, just trapped in the nightmare of his past. A movement to his left caught his eye.

"Wait." Had Doc heard him? He knew he had to see what was coming into his field of vision.

"What is it?" Carson asked.

Another jolt and his eyes closed in his memory. *No! Open!* The noises from outside his head were mixing with those in his memory.

He waved his hand at Doc and Carson. "Shhhh." He needed to concentrate through the fucking pain pushing into his mind, clouding his thoughts.

In his memory, his eyes opened, and he tried to see what had caught his attention. He watched a man as he walked past the end of the table with an unconscious Caden slung over his shoulder. The woman followed close behind.

"Get him next door and prep him for transf—"

Another wave of pain and his eyes closed, a roaring in his ears, and then the flogger. After that it was over for that memory other than the pain and the goggles.

"Justin, talk to me."

But Justin couldn't answer Doc. There was a pinch in his arm. He felt as if he were floating away from the pain. The memory faded from his head.

His body was shuffled about, and he felt thoroughly drugged. His eyes would only partially focus. He was on the floor, looking up at the lights in the interview room.

"Justin. Look at me."

Justin's head lolled, and a blurry Doc was beside him.

"You with us?" Doc studied his eyes.

"Yes."

"Damn, you scared the crap out of me." Carson was on the other side of him. "Couldn't break you out of it."

Justin swallowed, his throat dry. His head started to clear.

"I gave you a low dose of sedative so it'll wear off sooner. When you're ready to get up, let me know."

Justin squeezed his eyes shut and then remembered what he saw. "I remember Caden. They…." What had he heard? "Some guy carried him out and was told to take him next door."

"Anything else?"

"No."

"Okay, let me tell Lincoln. Good job, buddy."

Justin hoped what he'd heard would help. "Where's Max? Did he show up?"

"Not yet," Doc said. "Want to try to sit up?"

"Yeah."

Doc's hand went under his shoulder and pulled him upright. His head swam, and his stomach roiled. He closed his eyes and swallowed hard.

After a few moments, he opened his eyes. "My phone's in my pocket." He worked to get the phone out. "I need to call Max."

As he freed his phone, he heard someone in the hallway speaking with Carson.

"We can't find him," a woman said. "We're checking to see if he left the building."

"When you find him, let me know."

Carson reentered the room as Justin was calling Max. The ringing was relentless, and then he got his voice mail. He hit the End button. He typed out a quick text asking him to call. He added "love you." His ability to say that to Max was an entire world of happiness to him.

Justin stood, wavering, but quickly gained his equilibrium. Carson watched him with a wary eye.

"Did you tell Lincoln about what I remembered?"

Carson pursed his lips. "Yeah. He's on his way back."

Something was up. Justin could feel the unease in the room from both Doc and Carson. "What's wrong?"

Carson looked to Doc, who was silent.

"Don't freak out, but we don't know where Max is."

CHAPTER 25

MAX STRUGGLED against the restraints, the hood still covering his head. He'd been thrown into a vehicle. He'd tried to count in his head how long they'd traveled. Around two thousand seconds, give or take a mistake. After being forced from the car, he was guided by someone holding his arm. He counted fifty-seven steps into a building and then counted ten stairs they descended. At the bottom, he was pushed forward, stumbled, and went down onto his knees. The metal clank behind him sounded like a cell door closing.

The air was damp and cool but not cold. He listened to the noises around him. There were no voices, no sounds of machines or blowing air. He did hear movement and shifting fabric, then a cough.

"Hello?"

No one answered.

He worked to pull the hood off, but it was secured tightly.

"I hear you. Can you answer me?"

A groan was the only answer. Max continued to work on the restraints digging into his wrists. Even if he got his hands free, he knew he was locked in. At least he'd be able to get his hood off. Being blind was a huge disadvantage.

"Hi."

Max froze. The voice had come from behind him and was young. A kid. He tilted his head back. "Hey. Who are you?"

"Number five."

Seriously? "Okay. I'm Max. Where am I?"

"In a cage."

Well, that answered the metal sound question. "Can you let me out?"

"No. I'm in a cage too."

Shit. "Do you know where we're located? Are we in DC?"

He heard more rustling, and when the boy spoke, he was closer. "I don't know. I used to be somewhere else, but then they brought me here."

"How long ago?"

"I don't know. One of the others said it was maybe four months. I don't even know what month it is."

"It's July." Max struggled again to pull off the hood, twisting and turning and pulling his head across the rough concrete.

"What're you trying to do?"

Max collapsed onto the floor and exhaled. The heat from the hood was stifling. "I need to get this hood off."

"I can reach between the bars."

Max rolled onto his back. Using his feet, he pushed himself across the rough floor until the top of his head hit the bars.

"I can't reach. It's tied in the back."

Max maneuvered himself so his back was against the bars. He felt a tug on the hood as the boy worked to free him. Within a minute the hood was worked over his head and cool, fresh air hit his face.

Max took in several deep breaths. "Thanks, kid. Can you free my wrists?"

"No. I can't get those plastic things off." He sounded sad.

"It's okay. At least I can breathe." He was definitely in a large cage, probably three feet square and just as tall. There were a dozen more just like his in the space that looked to be a basement. He rolled over and was met with a familiar face. A little older but the same dark eyes, olive skin, and black hair.

"Manuel?"

Instantly, the kid frowned, and his lips thinned. The rigidity of his body worried Max.

"Hey, are you okay?"

Visibly distressed, the kid hugged his legs to his chest. "No one's called me that for a long time."

Over three years, Max imagined.

"How did you know my name?"

Max pulled his body upright, struggling until he was sitting. He blew out a breath. "I'm an officer with the NVJ. We've been looking for you."

His eyes widened. "Did my mom send you? She's an NVJ officer too."

Max's stomach dropped about ten stories. Shit. How could he tell him that his mother was dead and his father still missing? "Umm, I was brought here against my will. I don't know your mom." Which was true.

He'd never met her. "But we knew you were missing. I'm going to get us out of here. Somehow."

Big promise since there were padlocks on the doors. His cage was empty, but Manuel had a thin pad and a blanket. Max clenched his jaw, knowing he slept there each night. He wore a blue T-shirt and black sweats. He had on black socks. He looked small for eleven, too small. Couldn't be good for anyone to live in those conditions for years.

"Do they always keep you in a cage?"

"Most of the time, but I get to take showers and sometimes the people let me stay out for a while. Some let me watch TV. I usually have books and crayons, some toys, but since I've been here, I don't have them anymore."

"Do you know why you're here? I mean, what do they do to you?" If it was anything like what they'd done to Justin, he'd skin them all alive.

He raised his left arm. Something plastic stuck out from beneath a white bandage wrapped around his biceps. He pointed to the round plastic end. "They take my blood a lot. This thing stays in there."

Max recalled that Manuel was a Sanatore, like Lincoln. Max swallowed hard when he thought of Justin's ability to heal quickly. Had these people done something to give others those healing abilities? Max had never heard that transferring a vampire's abilities to another person was possible.

"Just your blood? Nothing else?"

He nodded and picked at a thread on his sock. Max was more thankful for that than he could say. He looked into the other cages. While Manuel was close to him, the others were over three feet away, some farther. The light wasn't bright in the room. There were no windows, but he could make out people in the other cages, lying on their large square pillows.

"Who are they?" Max gestured with his head to the other cages.

Manuel looked up and gazed around. "People they brought here. Sometimes they talk, but most of the time they just lay there. I like when they talk because I get lonely."

The kid was breaking Max's heart.

"Do you know why they're here, what they do with them?" Max shifted. His shoulders screamed from his wrists being bound. His hands were starting to fall asleep.

Manuel was silent for a minute. "They take them out a lot. When they come back, they are hurt. Some are bleeding, but they don't cry or anything. The people here are mean to them."

"Do you know who those people are?"

He nodded. "Sal is really big and isn't nice at all. He's loud, but he never hurts me. Terry isn't loud. He's nicer. He brings me chocolate and sometimes books and toys. Debbie...." He shuddered and lowered his voice. "I don't like her. She likes to pinch me, but if I don't scream or cry, she gets mad and goes away. There's Mel. She's in charge because she tells everyone what to do. She doesn't pay attention to me." He paused, appearing to think. "Oh, and Gale."

Max raised his brow.

Manuel smiled. He was missing the two teeth beside his two front teeth. All Max could think was the kid missed out on the tooth fairy. "Gale's funny because he crawls around like a dog with Mel."

Mel had to be Yvonne Nelson. And that meant Sarina had been telling the truth about her parents.

"He has a collar and a leash and everything. But he wears...." He covered his mouth, appearing embarrassed.

"He wears what?"

Manuel leaned closer, cupping his mouth as if telling a secret. Damn, even after all he'd been through, the kid appeared so normal. "He wears girl's underwear." He sat back. "But I haven't seen him in a long time." That seemed to sadden Manuel.

"Do you know what happened to him?"

"One day he came in here, but he wasn't crawling. He snuck over to that cage in the corner and took Tara. He's not supposed to do that. I heard someone say he got into trouble."

Gale had been the one to drop Tara at the NVJ. Why the hell hadn't he gotten help for the rest of them?

"He said he was coming back for me, but he didn't." Manuel sighed and looked to the cage door. "I don't want to be here anymore. They keep telling me if I'm good I can go home."

Max knew those were all lies to keep him in line. The poor kid might get out of there, but his life wouldn't be what he remembered.

"Have you seen them bring in anyone new lately?" Max strained to see who was in the other cages, but their faces weren't visible.

When he looked back, Manuel was nodding. "Yeah, Caden. He talked to me for a while, but they took him out of here and didn't bring him back."

"When they take people out of here, are they gone for a long time?" Max hoped he answered yes for Caden's sake.

"Sometimes. But some of them never come back. I've heard some of them say that they were transferred. Whatever that means."

He wondered what else the kid had overheard. "What did you and Caden talk about?"

Again, his eyes lightened. "Lots of stuff. He's a vampire. No one else here is, except for me and Tara, but she used to be human. Caden said that wasn't possible because vampires are born, but they did something to her and her teeth grew longer. Oh, and he knows Justin. He used to be here, and then they took him away too."

The name lanced a sharp pain through his heart. "I know Justin too."

"You do?" Manuel was up on his knees, gripping the bars. "He was there when I first got to the other place. He used to talk to me a lot. It was nice because I wanted my mom." He sat back on his heels. "But then they started hurting him, and he stopped talking so much."

"I saw Justin just this morning. He's...." Should he tell a kid what they were to each other? Why not? "He's my boyfriend."

That brought a frown to his little face, but what he said next wasn't what Max thought he would say. "But he said his boyfriend was Carson."

Max chuckled. "Carson was his boyfriend a long time ago. Now he's my boyfriend so when we get out of here, you're going to get to see him again. He remembers you."

"I'd like that."

"So what about the people who keep you in these cages? Are they humans or vampires?"

"Vampires. I don't think they like humans very much. They're always hurting them."

Damn, the kid was smart.

"Can you tell me what any of those people look like?"

He shrugged a shoulder. "They wear masks all of the time. Debbie wears scary ones and is always trying to make me scream. I hate the clown mask. It gives me nightmares."

Debbie sounded like a real douchebag. Max wished he could reach through the bars and touch Manuel. "I'm sorry she's so mean to you. When I get out of here, I'm going to make sure she can never scare you again."

That didn't appear to excite him or even bring hope to Manuel's face. "A lot of people say they're going to get me out, but they don't." The kid had dealt with more disappointment than most adults.

Max leaned closer. "The thing is, the entire NVJ is going to be looking for me, and I know they'll find me."

They'd taken him to get to Justin. But Lincoln would never let anything happen to Justin. Max would gladly—well, grudgingly—stay in that cage if it meant Justin was safe. He had no clue what their plan for him was past that. He just had to wait for his opportunity to act. Maybe if Gale came back…. But they probably wouldn't let him out of their sight after what he'd done.

He wondered if they'd taken Jordan as well. Maybe he'd chased that person down and hadn't returned in time to encounter the man who'd taken Max. He'd let the NVJ know what had happened. Max needed all the help he could get.

Max was about to ask Manuel about the schedule of their captors when a door opened and footsteps sounded on the stairs. A large man in a white tank top and jeans entered the basement. He wore a black leather mask like those Max had seen in some bad pornos. Eying Max without his hood, he then looked to Manuel. Manuel looked down, rocking nervously, his knees squeezed tight against his chest.

"I see you've made a friend, number five. Don't get too attached." The man cackled in a deep voice. "I've got some nice plans for this one. He's got that twink look to him even if he's a little older."

Max narrowed his eyes. "Fuck you."

The man appeared to be sneering under the mask, but his eyes said different. Nope, he was smirking. "I saw you out with one of my favorite play toys, sitting by the river, throwing that Frisbee he found, living like some normal person."

Max shuddered. The man had been watching them, waiting to get to Justin.

"That one is special. Bet he gave you a real hard-on, didn't he? I can tell you he sure did it for me. Tying him down, hearing him scream and beg for me to stop hurting him, and then begging for the pain, begging me to hurt him more."

Max ground his teeth, the anger rising like a venomous snake from the pit of his stomach.

"Loves the CBT, that one. I'd beat on his cock and balls for hours until he was crying, sobbing for more, doing anything to come." He chuckled. "Got five orgasms out of him in one session, and he was still begging me for more."

Max jumped from the floor, tripping as he lost his balance, but regaining enough to ram into the bars. The man laughed maniacally as Max rammed into the bars over and over.

"You fucking son of a bitch! When I get out of here, I'm going to tie you down, rip you open, and watch you fucking bleed!" Max wavered on his feet, chest heaving, anger lighting a fire in his blood. He'd kill the fucker for touching the person he loved.

"Just try it! I'm the one who's going to be tying you down, and you're going to squeal like the pig that you are. And when I get my pet back, I'm going to make you watch as he begs for me do all kinds of nasty shit to him." The man leaned closer. "Begs me to fuck him."

Max rammed the cage door over and over, his shoulder a fiery mass of pain, knowing the action was useless, but he didn't stop until someone shouted.

"Enough!"

Max dropped to his knees as a woman entered. Her head and face were covered with a black hood, with only her eyes and mouth visible. She wore a silky tank top and short skirt, leopard high heels. Looked like a high-priced call girl.

"Sal! Get number eight like I told you. The boss will be here shortly. Do you want to explain why he's not ready?" Sal shook his head and reluctantly went to one of the cages. She turned her eyes on Max. "I'd save your energy, Lieutenant. You're going to need it."

He furrowed his brow, recognizing the voice. He scowled. "I knew you had something to do with this, Mrs. Nelson. Nice performance at the NVJ, I have to say. Where's your dog?"

She laughed. "Puppy was very, very bad and had to be punished." She exaggerated a pout. "But don't worry, he'll survive. I think."

"Do you seriously think the NVJ isn't looking for you? You're now their prime suspect."

She appeared surprised at that, then smiled graciously. "Now why would I be a suspect? My husband is the one who runs everything at Nelson

Technologies. I've made sure to implicate him in every way. Amazing what people will do for money."

Max clamped his mouth shut, not wanting to associate Sarina with his knowledge. Unfortunately, the rest of the NVJ still assumed Sarina had been lying.

When he was silent, she went to where Sal pulled a young man with deep black hair and bright blue eyes from a cage. Max recognized him as one of the first missing humans. He believed his name was Adam Mitchell. He was nineteen.

Those mesmerizing blue eyes were vacant, much as Justin's had been. Nothing there. Yvonne ran her hand over the kid's bare shoulder, the light skin contrasting with Adam's olive tone. Yvonne stepped behind him, wrapping her arms around the boy's chest. Over his shoulder, Yvonne smiled at Max. With her lips close to the boy's ear, she said, "Whiskey. Alpha. Kilo. Echo. Adam."

Adam blinked rapidly, his eyes focusing. While he appeared lucid, he didn't move or speak. Yvonne grinned. "Adam, tell our visitor what your purpose is."

"To serve and suffer." His monotone response was disturbing.

"Do you like pain, Adam?"

"Yes, Mistress."

"Do wish for me to hurt you?"

Something in the kid's eyes ignited, bringing the dullness to life.

"Yes, please."

Yvonne continued to smile smugly as the man in the mask scowled. Yvonne ran her hand over the boy's bare chest, and Max looked away, sickened by the display.

"Aww, you don't want to watch, Lieutenant? Oh, wait. You like to watch two men. Forgive me."

She stepped from behind Adam but kept her hand on his shoulder. "Adam here is a star just like Justin. A natural at accepting pain. It's quite beautiful. He's going to bring in a handsome price. His time is coming soon."

Adam was Justin. All of the humans they'd taken were Justin. "You're pretty sick, you know that? You're molesting kids, raping them. All for what? Kicks? Money?"

Yvonne didn't appear to be fazed. "I'd think you wouldn't care. Don't vampires hate all humans? They consider you scum, animals. I'd think you'd be glad to see them finally getting what they deserve."

Max snorted. "You're a human. When do you get what you deserve? Compared to a vampire, you're low on the food chain."

Yvonne scowled and pushed Adam toward the large man. "Take him to room one and prep him."

The man nodded and led the overly cooperative kidnapped teen from the room. He had a feeling he wasn't truly in control of himself, still in some kind of a programmed state of consciousness. His robotic manner wasn't like Justin, who had still been Justin even if under the influence of the training.

"Where's Caden? He's a vampire. Why did you take him?"

When she looked to Max, she smiled demurely. "He's the brother of one of the most powerful vampires on earth, of course. Imagine the price he'll fetch when he's trained and ready to obey." Max wasn't sure, but he thought he saw her shudder. "Besides, that filthy animal was sniffing around Sarina. She thinks I don't know, but I keep a close eye on her. It was disgusting how she was flaunting herself in front of him, throwing herself at him. When she wrote to her friend that she was in love with a vampire? Ugh! Can you imagine if anyone found out?"

So much for her support of the vampire community.

"She's an ungrateful bitch. I tried to bring her in, make her part of the business, teach her how to dominate in a male world. She played along for a while but doesn't have the backbone. That girl needs a reality check, and I'm going to give her one. Her vampire is going to be turned into a mindless animal. Gale has completed a program that will essentially block all high-level functioning in the brain, bring out a person's innate, animalistic nature. I have some clients who would appreciate a wilder pet."

"You can't mess with people like that!" Jesus, she couldn't do that to Caden or anyone else. Max didn't think she was as smart as she claimed to be. He'd wait for her to slip up and take her operation down. What choice did he have?

"Sit tight, Lieutenant. Once everyone gets here, we'll be coming for you. See you soon."

With that she left. Max lowered his head and tried to see past his rage. When Manuel sniffed, Max turned to him where he had curled up in the far corner of his cage. He didn't look afraid but appeared to merely be waiting. Max's shoulder was on fire, having ignited the injury from the Mystique. His hands were totally numb, but he shuffled on his knees to the side of the cage where Manuel scooted to meet him, dragging his blanket with him.

Max rested his forehead against the bars. Manuel wrapped himself in the blanket and lay down, facing Max. His small hand reached through the bars and rested on Max's knees.

"Hold tight, kid. We'll get out of here." Manuel didn't respond. Max knew he didn't believe him any more than Max believed himself.

CHAPTER 26

"Why aren't you going to find him?" Justin's voice echoed around Lincoln's office. Carson stood to the side, watching Justin.

Lincoln had just returned from wherever he'd been and wasn't moving fast enough. The other officers were returning as well. The only thing Justin knew was that someone had seen Max and Jordan tear out of the garage in an NVJ vehicle a little before nine. Then nothing.

Officers were on the phone and running around, but weren't going out to find Max.

"Calm down, Justin." Lincoln peeled off his suit jacket and tie and started to unbutton his dress shirt.

"Calm down? No one knows where he is! He's not answering his phone or the radio in the car. Taylor either!"

Justin's breaths were short, and his gut pushed into his throat, but nothing was going to keep him from getting Max back. He wouldn't think otherwise. They'd been through too much shit to have it all end now. When he felt a nudge at his head, he turned to Carson and shot him a warning glance. Carson raised his hands in what appeared to be surrender. He didn't need any help calming down. This was as calm as he was going to get.

Lincoln had just yanked off his dress shirt and pulled on his NVJ T-shirt when Taylor shouted from his desk. "MPD just spotted the NVJ vehicle parked on L Street, SE."

Lincoln went to the doorway, unbuckling his dress pants. "Simpson, Wright, and Dennison, head down there and check it out." Within seconds, they were gone.

"Does anyone know why they went down there?" Lincoln scowled at the room of officers, who all shook their heads.

"Comms has no record of them calling in their intended destination," Tia said.

"What the fuck was he thinking?" Lincoln stalked back into the office, stripping off his pants and tossing them aside. He pulled on his black cargo pants. As he zipped them, he looked to Justin. "Do you remember if they mentioned any locations other than the building next to the Mystique?"

"No."

Lincoln slipped his holster over his shoulders and then pulled on one of his black boots. "Well, I went straight there from my meeting, and the place was vacant. I broke in and checked every floor, and while it appears that someone has been there recently, there wasn't anything left. I've got the MPD and a team of rookies checking the Mystique from top to bottom, but I'm thinking they're going to come up empty-handed."

"I don't think they're far from the Mystique. I don't know why. It's just a feeling I have." *Or wishful thinking.*

Lincoln pulled on this other boot. "I have to agree. Utica NVJ didn't find anything at Oneida Commons. If this operation here in DC was based there, they've vacated the place." Lincoln grimaced and then stalked from the room. "How many Jenkens Holdings buildings did we get to on that list?"

Tia picked up a paper on her desk. "Five. There are six left. One's way up in Forest Hills."

Lincoln rubbed his chin as if he were thinking over some complex problem. Justin just wanted him to do something, anything, to get Max back. In about a minute, he was going out to look himself.

"I've got Dennison on the phone." Wes hit a button on the base of the phone and cradled the handset. "What do you got, Dennison?"

Justin swore his heart stopped beating as he waited to hear John speak.

"We didn't find them so we started knocking on doors. A woman saw them arrive about two hours ago and go into the house next door. She said she heard what she describes as a scuffle and that it's been quiet ever since. No one's left the house or gone in through the front door that she's seen. Guess who the house belongs to? Marshall Stone."

Lincoln braced his hands on the edge of Taylor's desk. "Anything in the house?"

"The house is clear. Hold on." They waited as John spoke to someone. Justin clasped his hands together, his fear ratcheting up by the minute. "It appears that Ms. Stone arrived home just before Max and Jordan. Her car's still parked out front. Maggie's going through it now."

"Do we think she's responsible for what happened there?"

"There appears to have been a struggle in the bedroom. A nightstand is knocked over. Some of the clothes in the closet that were hanging up are on the floor. Some of the shoes look as if they were pulled out of the closet. Not sure what happened because the woman next door says that the noise she heard came from downstairs."

Wes leaned toward the phone. "Do you think Ms. Stone was hiding up there?"

"It's possible. Could be why Max and Jordan were here. Did anyone call in requesting assistance?"

Lincoln looked to his team. Tia frowned. "Nope. Comms said nothing has come through today."

"Hold on," John said. There was a pause. "What've you got?"

Justin could barely hear Maggie speaking in the background.

"I have the registration for Ms. Stone's car, but the address doesn't match her residence. This is on New Hampshire Avenue northwest."

"What address do we have on file for Marshall Stone?" Lincoln asked.

Wes typed on his computer. "350 L Street, SE. That's where they are now."

Tia raised her hand as her eyes scanned the paper she held. "Here. The address matches a building owned by Jenkens Holdings."

"That's where we start. Dennison, keep collecting any info you can. We're heading to the New Hampshire Avenue address. We'll contact you when we get there. If that's a bust, we'll start on the rest of this list."

"You got it, boss."

John hung up, and Lincoln pointed to Tia. "Bring that list. Let's go."

Everyone bolted into action. Lincoln and Carson disappeared into his office, and then Lincoln emerged with his NVJ windbreaker and stopped before Justin. "You hang tight here; you hear me? We'll find Max."

"Please" was all Justin could manage. Lincoln nodded and then went down the hall, followed by the rest of the officers. As Wes walked by Justin, he patted him on the shoulder, then left. It was all Justin could do to stop himself from following them.

Carson stood in the doorway to Lincoln's office. When someone called his name, he looked down the hallway.

Justin looked up to see Graham walking into the office area, looking around. "Where're they heading? I passed Lincoln and everyone else on my way in."

Justin couldn't help but notice how tired the man looked, how sad.

"They're checking out a lead, Uncle Graham."

His eyes lightened. "Caden?"

Carson's brow dipped. "Maybe. Right now we don't know much, but Lincoln will call if he finds anything."

Graham nodded. Carson approached his uncle and wrapped his arm around his shoulder. "Let's get a coffee in the commissary while we wait."

"Sure." Graham looked to Justin. "You want to join us?"

Justin couldn't sit still even if he tried. "No. I'm just going to stay down here and wait."

Carson nodded. "Sure. Can we bring you something?"

"No, thanks." He wasn't about to feed the monster butterflies in his gut. They were large enough.

"Okay, I'll be back in a bit."

Justin waved as they walked away. The area was quiet with everyone gone. He wandered into Max's office. On the sofa was a pile of files, and there were papers on the floor. He didn't touch them but shook his head when he saw the collection of dirty cups on the table next to the desk. The man was a slob. Taking the chance to do something to distract his mind, Justin gathered the mugs and headed for the small kitchen down the hall. As he rounded the corner, he nearly ran into someone. Jumping back, he was surprised to see Caden's friend Sarina standing there.

"Sarina?"

"Hey, Justin. Need a hand?" She pointed to the pile of cups he cradled to his chest. Without waiting for an answer, she took three of the seven cups he carried. "Where you heading?"

"Kitchen."

She followed him. He set the cups in the sink. She added the rest. "You drink a lot of coffee?"

He frowned and looked into the sink. "No. Those were in Max's office. He's miss—" He cut himself off.

"Missing, Yeah, I heard."

He'd only met her once, the night at the Mystique. "What're you doing here?"

She shrugged. "I was worried about Caden when he didn't answer his phone after you guys went to the Mystique. I called here, and Director Samuels had me come in and talk to him. I told him what I knew. Kind of been hanging here ever since. Turns out they're looking for my father."

"Your father?" He wasn't sure why, but she looked scared.

"Yeah, something to do with all of the missing people at the Mystique, but he didn't have anything to do with it. I told them that, but now...." She sniffed. "Now I think something happened to him. It's possible my step-monster is involved."

"Involved in what?"

She waved her hand. "In everything. The missing people, Caden, you.... Your programming."

Justin took a step back, warning bells sounding in his head. "My what?"

She gave him a puzzled look. "You know, your need for pain, need to serve, yada, yada."

His gut twisted. "How'd you know about that?" And was she saying her stepmother was responsible for what happened to him?

"I told you. Director Samuels brought me in to talk to him. He interviewed my step-monster too, and she lied. Tried to make my father seem like some monster when it's all her." Her scowl was deep, and anger flared in her eyes, making her appear more intimidating. "I don't know where my father is, but I'm sure she has him somewhere."

Lincoln told her about him? So much for thinking he was a good guy.

He wasn't sure what to say to her. Until then she'd only been a friend of Caden's, or maybe more than a friend since Caden had alluded to there possibly being something between them. Now she was someone who was in the same boat as he was since someone she cared for was missing too. Actually two people: her father and Caden.

"You don't have any idea where your stepmother is?" Justin needed someone to know something.

She bit her lip and shook her head. "I wish I did. I've been calling my dad and texting him, but I haven't heard from him in days."

Justin felt bad for her. Even though he barely knew her, he touched her shoulder, trying to comfort her. He wasn't good at comforting others, but he tried.

She smiled wanly. "You wanna hang out while we wait for some news? Maybe watch a thoroughly stupid movie?"

Justin exhaled. "Yes. Anything to distract my mind. Follow me."

He led her to a small lounge with a couch, a couple of chairs, and a TV. Sitting, Justin grabbed the remote and began searching the channels. As he did, Sarina turned to him.

"So what was it like? I mean, what happened to you at the Mystique."

Justin froze. Did she know about that too? Did everyone know? He kept his eyes glued to some man on the TV chopping vegetables.

"I… I don't want to talk about it." He blinked hard, then started to surf the channels again, hoping Sarina wouldn't push him.

"To me, it sounds thoroughly awful to be tied to a table and tortured by some large guy. Forced to like the pain so much that you eventually beg for it and can't live without it. And then you start to like it so much you can get pleasure from that pain, actually come from it."

Justin's hand released the remote. He watched as it hit the tiles. The back popped off, and two batteries rolled across the floor.

Justin scooted away from Sarina until his back hit the arm of the couch. "W-what?"

Sarina sat sideways on the couch, leaning against the back. Her blank expression creeped him out. "Even now you still need the pain, don't you, Justin? Still want to be hurt? What about Max? Does he matter to you more than the pain, because I'm thinking, right now, with four little words I can change that. Put you back into that space where only the pain matters."

His breaths barely escaped as he stared at her.

"Do I need to say those words to get you to come with me?"

With her admission, he remembered exactly what those words were and what they would do to him. He shook his head.

"Good, because I'd rather not use that deceptive crap to get you to come with me." She pulled out her phone and texted something. "There. We have a very important date. So let's go. With you, I'll be able to get back what's mine."

Justin wasn't sure if he could move, but then his brain caught up with him. "Max. Do you know where he is?"

She frowned and shrugged. "It's possible that he'll be where we're going."

"I'll go." He knew that his decision wasn't the best, but if he didn't agree, she had a way to make him go anyway. He'd rather go with his wits about him. When she stood, he followed.

"My car's in the visitor parking lot. We need to get out without being seen."

"Follow me," he said and left the room.

He peered around each corner until they reached Max's office. He closed the door and went to the desk. When Sarina looked away, he palmed the small black box, hit the power button, grateful when the green light came on, and stuffed it into his pocket. He prayed it worked. In another drawer, he came across an extra set of key cards and held one up. Thank gods for all of that time he'd spent in Max's office bored out of his head. "This will get us out the back gate."

Within minutes, they were in her car and speeding away from the NVJ and toward Max. He clamped his eyes shut. *I'm coming, Max.* Just what he was going to do when he got to their destination, he hadn't a clue.

MAX HIT the floor hard, the pain crackling through his knees, jostling his shoulders. He spit blood onto the linoleum floor. He'd struggled when Sal dragged him from his cage, which resulted in the man backhanding him and splitting his lip. When Max righted himself, he took in the large room. They were in what looked like a conference room in an office building, but without any office furniture. Instead, a few metal tables and dental chairs were scattered about. Machines of all types sat on different tables. Many implements he knew were meant to cause pain hung on the walls: whips, floggers, crops, metal rods, cuffs. Looked like a medical version of a torturous hell.

Max gasped when he looked behind him. Caden was bound to a table with red rope knotted in an elaborate pattern over his body. He only wore a pair of white underwear, but his erection was highly visible. Goggles covered his eyes, and his body twitched and his muscles spasmed.

"Caden?"

A kick to his back stole Max's breath, and he flopped hard onto his stomach. He fought to catch his breath.

"Shut the fuck up." The masked man grabbed him by the arms and used them to yank him from the floor.

Max couldn't contain the scream as the pain nearly stole his consciousness. He almost fell into the large man. When his eyes focused, Marshall Stone stood before him, her grin as maniacal as any he'd ever seen.

"Hello again, Lieutenant Kincaid. Welcome."

Max tried to push toward her, but Sal held him tight in his grip.

"I want to thank you. I have to say how touched I was by the quickness with which you came to my rescue. Truly touched."

"You won't get away with this. You're already a suspect since your club is involved. We know about Gale and his subservient dog fetish, so Yvonne's claim has already been shot down by the NVJ." Well, only by Max, but she didn't need to know that.

"I know all about our snitch. Not to worry, she'll be taken care of soon enough. That goes for the dead weight of Yvonne and her lapdog. They've outlived their usefulness."

She knew about Sarina giving her stepmother up? Although it sounded as if Sarina wasn't so innocent after all. And she was back at the NVJ where Justin was. Lincoln wouldn't let anything happen to him. They'd all protect Justin.

"The NVJ won't stop until they find you."

"Oh, they'll find me all right. Currently, there's a fire at a building owned by Jenkens Holdings. Huge fire that should draw a lot of attention, including that of the NVJ. I know they've been searching the buildings owned by Jenkens. I'm sure that one is on the list. What they'll find after the fire is put out is the charred remains of a vampire. Her dental records will match mine exactly. I've planned for just this situation. Made sure I could disappear." She flipped her long brown hair over her shoulder.

"You may have me, but you'll never get Justin back."

She cocked her head. "Why, because he's at the NVJ? Like that will stop me. We infiltrated your headquarters once. What's to stop us from doing it again? In fact, I have a feeling your beloved Justin will be here very soon."

"You're lying."

She shrugged. "Doesn't matter what you think. Everything is coming together nicely."

He ground his teeth. "Your fucking human trafficking plan? Turn people into mindless pain slaves and sell them?"

"That's Yvonne's goal. She's the one who struck the deal with Jameson to run the lab for her research."

"Don't you mean Yvonne and Gale's goal?"

"While Gale wrote the software program Yvonne used initially to create her mindless drones, he'd never intended it to be used to take away someone's free will. Five years researching how and where the brain stores behavioral information and attempting to rewrite that info for some military project went down the drain. All five of Gale's test subjects became overly submissive weaklings who couldn't think for themselves. He trashed the program, but Yvonne didn't stop researching and testing. Do you think Gale really enjoys crawling around like a dog or allowing his wife to make every decision regarding his company?

"But who cares about them? They're done." She waved her hands frantically. "Stupid woman thought she could take over my subjects.

Number eight is mine. He's mine…." She shook her head and dramatically calmed herself. "My motivation, my plans haven't changed from the beginning. The entire vampire community is my focus. Jameson Merrick was right, you know? No matter how hard we vampires work for equality, try to become someone in this world of humans, we're never good enough. We're trash to many people, despite being nearly identical in every way to the humans." She looked to her phone and then Sal. "What's the delay? We need to move."

"Don't know. I'll text him." Sal pulled out his phone.

"And where is the brat? She'd better be here soon, or she'll be sorry." Marshall typed on her phone, frowning.

"So you ran the lab at Oneida Commons?"

She was actually surprised by that claim. "Me? No. That would be Yvonne, and maybe Gale. I don't know, maybe before his penchant for doggie play and subservience. While I didn't run the lab, I knew Jameson quite well. Very well. In fact, he was my father."

Max froze. Shit.

"That shut you up really quick, didn't it? He was murdered by his own creation, because he'd lost sight of his original vision. He was a visionary, but he was seduced by the power he gained through other vampires. The more power he had, the more his plan morphed into something too fantastical and impractical. Did he really think the Salutem wouldn't turn on him? I warned him, but he wouldn't listen. Stupid fool."

Max couldn't disagree.

"When he first started his research into vampires and how they differed from humans, the work he was doing was unprecedented. The powers he'd harnessed, the mission he was on to bring vampires to the forefront of the humans, was genius. Truly having the best intentions to raise vampires from their third-class citizenship, and then he fucked it all up. I'm not going to make the same mistake."

"And how in the hell are these humans being turned into pain slaves going to change anything? Planning on turning all humans into pain slaves? I guess it's good to have high goals." Jesus, could she sound any more deluded than her father had been?

She gave him a condescending glare with an added smile. "No, I plan to turn them into vampires."

Shit, he'd forgotten about that. But she couldn't, could she?

"I'm carrying on my father's greatest work, which he abandoned because of his grand delusions." She paced, her heels clacking on the tiles.

"He had the solution in his grasp, and he threw it all away. Then that creation of his killed him."

Max wanted to anger her, throw her off-center. "So this is all a spoiled little girl getting revenge for her father's death?"

That had the intended effect. She grabbed him by the shirt, her sneering mouth inches from his face. "I can assure you my father never spoiled me, Lieutenant. I came last in his world, and I'm glad he's dead. If he had continued with his mad theories, vampires would have been worse off than we are now. If Carson hadn't killed him, I would've done it sooner or later."

She released his shirt and pushed him away. Walking away, she turned, calm and in control once again. "Some of my father's greatest work was on the Human Genome Project. He masked his identity as a vampire, and when he died, I had unlimited access to all of that research and information. Through some business dealings, I was able to obtain the vampire genome. Add in some gene therapy, and I was able to activate the vampire genes in a human."

Tara was that human.

She tapped her chin with a manicured nail. "Need to refine a way to amass those enzymes...." Her words trailed off.

"What enzymes?"

"Doesn't matter, Max. Nothing you need to worry about." She smiled wide as she gazed over Max's shoulder. "Well, it's about time you showed up."

Max followed her excited gaze. "Fuck, no."

Justin was led into the room by Sarina, who clutched his arm.

CHAPTER 27

MAX STRUGGLED to get to Justin as he was held by one of Justin's worst nightmares. Inside, Justin sobbed in relief to see him alive. Outside, he fought to remain neutral. Sarina had warned Justin that if she couldn't control him, she'd shove him back into his head with those four words. Those words that caused him more fear than his masked torturer.

"Justin." Max's expression was pained, no doubt terrified that Justin wasn't responding to him. Justin's throat burned as he fought to hold back his tears, seeing Max bound on his knees. They were so screwed at that moment. Sarina was trading him for Caden—didn't want to, but didn't know another way to save Caden. Of course, she'd mentioned how sorry she was and was nice enough to give him one piece of information that might help him… or might not.

"You sure took your time getting here, Sarina."

"I'm here now, aren't I?" Sarina's hand tightened around Justin's arm. "What the fuck? You aren't supposed to be training him anymore! We had a deal!"

Justin cringed as her screech penetrated his skull. He looked in the direction Sarina had turned. Caden was tied to a table and enduring programming. Somehow, he had to get them out of there. He covertly patted his pocket, praying someone noticed the signal at the NVJ and found them quickly.

"Deals are made to be broken, sweetheart. And you've learned a valuable lesson here. Always to have a backup plan. Too bad you'll never get to use that lesson." She waved a hand to Sal. "Put her in with her doggie and his master."

Sal didn't move, didn't even twitch. Justin watched Max as he looked over his shoulder at the stoic man, expression void from his face.

"Move it!" Marshall shouted. When Sal still didn't move, she reached behind her back and came back clutching a small gun, which she aimed at Sal. Unfortunately, Max was in the way. "Did I not speak clearly enough?"

Behind them a man and two women crowded into the room, decreasing any chances of any of them escaping. Sarina pulled Justin closer to where Caden was lying.

"Stop!" She used Justin to shield herself as she ripped the goggles from Caden's eyes. He blinked rapidly, then absently looked to Sarina.

"Whiskey, alpha, kilo, echo, Caden," Sarina said.

Caden blinked rapidly. He frowned as his gaze darted around. "Sarina?" A deeper frown. "Justin? Where am I?"

"Hey, baby, give me a minute and I'll have you untied, then we're getting out of here."

Marshall snorted. "What makes you think I'm letting you leave?"

"Try me." Sarina's jaw was set, her eyes narrowed. Justin knew she had something to back up that scowl. "Why don't you tell everyone why you've been jonesing to get Justin here back?"

Marshall didn't lower the gun. "You don't have the right to tell me wh—"

"Tell them!"

Marshall lowered her gun, apparently realizing she didn't need it with her group of supporters by the door. "It doesn't matter what you all know. Justin's blood has something I need."

Justin recalled the memory where his blood was taken. "Why?"

She folded her arms and exhaled noisily. "You couldn't be turned into a vampire, but in analyzing your blood, my partner found something interesting."

"That something is what you need. Right, Marshall? To make your humans-into-vampires plan a reality. You see, why Justin here can't be turned into a vampire is because, technically, he already is one. Right?"

Justin frowned. He definitely wasn't a vampire.

"He's not a vampire," Max said. Their eyes connected, and Justin allowed his gaze to reach into his heart. His brow furrowed, and he wanted Max to tell him what to do. Max looked to Marshall with some understanding. "But he has some kind of enzyme you need."

She waved her hand nonchalantly. "Those needed to activate the sleeper genes. We're close but not close enough. The only issue is that some humans have been found to be… resistant to the change. Justin being one of them. But with continued testing on variations of the enzymes, I'm very sure we'll succeed. I've invested too much time and money into his testing to lose him now."

"Makes him kind of indispensable, doesn't it?" Sarina wore a smug grin. Probably glad her hostage trade would still go through.

Marshall grinned. "Well, that's where you're wrong. Turns out what I need to turn those humans into vampires is available out there in other humans. Those whose parents are a mix of humans and vampires."

Justin swallowed. He'd never known his father. He'd left when Justin was born, and that was that. He hadn't given him much thought. Just at those times in a boy's life when a father should have been around. He hadn't missed his actual father, just what he represented.

Sarina laughed. "Don't play me, Marshall. I'm not stupid. There're only around 2 percent of vampire and human offspring that have the enzyme you need. And you've had no luck replicating that enzyme, so you have to get it from the source. How many does that number equate to of available donors in the world? Maybe ten thousand. Can't be easy to locate them all over the world. Admit it. You got lucky with Justin here. Very fucking lucky. Hear that, Justin? You're like the golden key or egg or something."

Justin frowned at her.

"Believe what you want, little girl."

"Maybe I should kill him right here?" Sarina wasn't helping one bit.

Marshall was seething. Justin watched as her gaze landed on him. Her expression was one of ownership, of finality in his future. He was hers, part of her plot from the moment she'd found he could give her what she wanted. He didn't want to be responsible for changing people into vampires, for taking their humanness from them. Who had a right to do that?

"Let Max and Caden go. You've got me, and I'll do what you want. Just let them go, please."

"Justin, stop." Max's words were woven with pain and fear, but Justin didn't see another way out.

"I have all of you, and no one is going anywhere. Could the rest of you get in here and get control of this mess instead of just standing there?" The men and women moved farther into the room.

Justin's mind raced. He was the key that gave Marshall her power. Take away the key, and she couldn't make more vampires.

Take away the key.

As the men and women advanced toward them, there was the pop of a gunshot. Justin jumped back. Everyone in the room jolted.

"Go see what that was!" Marshall raised her gun at Justin and Sarina, her gaze continually shifting to the doorway and back.

All of the guards fled the room. Sal continued to hold Max. Justin took the opportunity and charged Marshall, not giving a shit that she was a woman. His shoulder connected with her hip, his arms wrapping tight around her legs. He took her hard to the ground, and she screeched as he wrestled her for the gun. Her nails dug into his face, the pain distant to the adrenaline pushing him. One of them was going to win, and the victor would be him. He had to hurry before Sal intervened. Justin reached for her outstretched hand as she pushed at his face. Planting his feet, he pushed forward and leaned his forearm down against her neck. As he pushed harder, she gurgled, and her face turned red. Her strength faltered, giving Justin what he needed to grab the gun.

He jumped up and away as she kicked out at him. Backing into the corner, Justin held the gun on Marshall. When he noticed Sal and Sarina hadn't moved to help Marshall, Justin was confused. Despite hacking and trying to catch her breath, Marshall was on her feet and ready to charge him. He'd never held a gun or pointed a weapon at another person. He turned the gun on himself and with a shaky hand placed the barrel to his temple.

"Justin, stop! What're you doing?" Max was still on his knees, trying to move toward Justin. Sal held Max back when more gunshots popped in the distance. Sal sprinted from the room. Sarina worked on untying Caden. Marshall shouted at Justin to stop the drama and give her the gun as she inched closer.

In the chaos, Justin focused on Max. Frantically, his lover struggled to get to his feet, and Justin's heart ached with each beat. Justin wanted to go to him, touch him, hold him, kiss him. He was so important to Justin's world, and Marshall had continually taken that world away from him; so much of his life had been wasted. Then she'd dumped the greatest of all responsibilities onto his shoulders. He was part of her crusade, her weapon against the humans. He was human—or had thought he was. If her scheme continued, he'd be used and tortured endlessly. He was her key, and without the key, she couldn't open that lock until she found another human/vampire hybrid like him. Finding one in the billions of people on earth wasn't an easy task, right? Could he take that chance?

Two of the guards returned, eyes wild. "The NVJ is in the building. We have to get out of here!"

The woman holding the gun looked terrified. "They're being held on the first floor. We have to move fast!"

Justin could have cried tears of relief. He looked to Max, who gazed back intently and appeared to be working to remove the ties on his wrists. They would be saved, and the bad guys arrested, but then what? Justin would still have the enzyme needed to create vampires, and Marshall would still have influence—even from jail—to use him. Others had helped her with her vendetta against the humans, and her minions could continue her work. He'd never be safe.

"Everyone calm down." Marshall turned to Justin, lifted her chin, and with a confident air said, "Romeo, Echo, Sierra, Tango, Justin. Now, put the gun down."

Justin frowned at her. The words were foreign to him. He continued to hold the gun to his temple.

Her confidence wavered. "Romeo, Echo, Sierra, Tango, Justin! Put the gun down, now!"

Sarina cackled. "Sal and I might have changed the programming a tad. Ultimately, we have control over your precious cargo. Maybe you're the one who should have had the backup plan."

Marshall's expression morphed into a spiteful rage. "We have to get out of here and don't have time for this! What did you do?"

No reply from Sarina.

The gunshots sounded closer. Marshall's commanding facade was cracking, her fear showing through. "Tell me the code words! The NVJ is going to bust in here, and we'll all go to jail, Sarina, including your father!"

Sarina narrowed her eyes. "You know my father had nothing to do with this! Let them come, because you really could use the reality check of a jail cell."

"Shoot her!"

Guns pointed at her, but Justin shouted. "Stop! Or I'll pull the trigger!"

His hand shook, the metal of the gun dancing against his skin. He was waiting for the right time, but it was so hard. So hard to just do what needed to be done, to stop everything right there. No more pain and torture. The permanency of the solution, the finality at his hands meant no going back.

Max shuffled forward on his knees. "Justin, please, please, please put the gun down. The NVJ's here, and she won't get away with it."

Justin's lips trembled as the terrified agony on Max's face nearly obliterated his heart. Gods, how he loved that man. "Yes, she will. She's already gotten away with it for too long. If I don't stop th-this… stop this now, someone else will take over even if she's in jail. She has the knowledge. She knows what I can do, the people here know, but she's the one who has the most to gain by continuing. She'll send them after me."

Marshall was tense, her expression showing she was ready to do anything to stop him. In a blink of an eye, he was going to take everything from her. And she was right, but Justin just needed to see that Max would be safe, that someone would get him out of that building and to safety, because once he pulled the trigger, he wouldn't survive.

"It's going to be okay, Max. Really. I love you. You saved me, and without you I wouldn't have the strength to do this."

Max was crying, and Justin couldn't say anything to his lover that would make the moment better. Justin was tired of being a victim. Time to take back his control, even if that moment would be the defining moment of his entire life. He'd sacrifice himself to save Max.

When he caught sight of Lincoln and Wes peering into the room, guns drawn, ready to bust in, Justin exhaled. His time had come. Marshall was only a few feet away, prepared to stop him, but she would be too late.

He mouthed "I love you" to Max, cocked the gun, aimed, and shot Marshall Stone in the head.

MAX HUNCHED over, elbows resting on his thighs, where he sat on the deck of the ambulance. The minutes ticked by as he waited for Justin to emerge safe from the building. Images of him being killed were quickly pushed away. He rubbed his hands together, trying to cease their shaking. The feeling was slowly returning to his arms and fingers. His wrists had been bandaged. His shoulders screamed despite the shot of pain meds the medic had given him. His entire body trembled as the paramedic took his blood pressure.

"You might be going into shock."

Max was past shock. Past anything but the fucking hell playing over and over in his head. Justin had shot Marshall Stone in the head. When Justin pushed that gun against his temple, Max thought he'd lose him forever. The shiny steel glinted in the light as Justin's hand shook, that detached expression of acceptance on his face. Then he pointed the gun at Marshall, and the side of her head exploded, her body crumpling to the ground.

Max had fallen back on his ass, unable to look away from Justin, waiting for someone to shoot him for his actions. He shouted for him to get down as Justin's face twisted with an expression of self-satisfaction and horror. Then the horror took over. He stumbled back, hand over his gaping mouth, eyes pinned to the bloody mess before him. Then he fell to his knees and threw up.

Before Max could get to him, the female guard fired shots. Wes took her out, a clean shot to the neck, then snagged Max from the floor and hauled his ass out of there as he screamed for Justin. Outside, Wes sat his ass down, told him not to move, and then raced back into the building. That had been nine minutes ago, and in one minute, Max was going in. He'd go to hell and back to get the man he loved.

When that minute passed, he stood at the protest of the paramedic and dropped the blanket off his shoulders. As he passed Warez, he shrugged her off, determined to get to Justin. A sea of cop cars blocked his path. Keeping his eyes on the front door, he wove through the cars. His guts twisted as he fought the reality that Justin could be dead. What if Lincoln didn't make it out with him? He couldn't breathe with that thought, couldn't fathom losing him.

Feet from the door, Lincoln emerged, his arms supporting Justin, who looked ready to drop but was alive. Max's breath caught, tears burned his eyes, and his chin quivered at seeing his Justin alive. Justin raised his arm, reaching for him. Max slid over the hoods of the remaining cars until he broke free and finally swept Justin into his arms.

Justin sobbed, trying to catch his breath. "Max, don't hate me, please. I'm so sorry." Justin clutched to him for dear life.

Max couldn't speak as he buried his face into Justin's neck, thanking every god for Justin's safety. The idea of ever letting him go was absurd. The idea of hating him even more so.

"I killed her. Oh gods, I shot her." Justin whispered the words over and over. Max took his face in his hands as tears coursed over his cheeks.

Fuck. "You didn't have a choice. She didn't give you one."

"But I wanted to kill her. I didn't want her coming back for me. I didn't care if I went to jail. I just needed everything to stop. She didn't have a gun, and I shot her." His whispered confession damned near broke Max's heart.

"No, sweetie, listen to me. You're not going to jail. She wasn't ever going to let you go. Once she had hold of you, she would have used you to get away. You didn't have a choice."

But Max could tell Justin didn't believe him.

"It's true." Lincoln stood beside them. "She had Gale Nelson's plane ready for takeoff. We intercepted three of her people trying to sneak the other kidnapped humans out of the building. A little persuasion and they fessed up about the plane. By the way, smart thinking grabbing that GPS. We never would have found you without that signal. Luckily, Comms picked it up. This location isn't owned by Jenkens. You saved the day." Lincoln patted Justin's shoulder as he walked away.

If they had reached that plane, Justin would have disappeared forever. "You hear that, sweetie? You saved us all. You did, Justin. And she can't ever hurt you again."

Justin's chin trembled, and he nodded. "I love you so much."

Max smiled despite a tear escaping over his cheek. "I love you, more than anything in this world."

Max squeezed Justin, running his hands over his back, soothing and caressing and thanking the universe for bringing Justin to him safely.

CHAPTER 28

JUSTIN PEERED out the window of Medical. A sea of news vans lined the street in front of the NVJ. They'd been there for two solid days and weren't showing any sign of leaving.

"Still there?"

Justin turned to see Max carrying a box into the break room.

"Yeah. They aren't budging."

Max set the box down on the table. "They won't until they get their story. Lincoln's setting up a press conference for later today. Until then they're just going to have to wait with their hands on their asses."

Justin chewed on his lip. Three days and he was still with Max. He'd been terrified he was going to jail the moment he'd decided to shoot Marshall. He'd actually aimed for her chest but hit the side of her head instead. He shuddered, his stomach roiling each time he remembered the side of her head exploding. He'd taken a life. And even if she was the vilest person on earth, he'd still killed someone. And of everyone, including Max, who tried to assure him he hadn't had any other option, it was John Dennison who said something that had made a difference: *"Marshall Stone made her choices when she kidnapped and tortured humans. She took their free will, their freedom, robbed them of being human, all without their consent. She may have even killed since we've been unable to locate one of the humans taken. She treated you like animals and in the end was shot. You can't do all of that and expect someone isn't going to come after you. In that moment, that second, when your life and the lives of others are at stake, you make the best decision you can with the resources you have. And that's what you did."*

Later, Max told him how John had shot someone in the line of duty when the man drew a gun on Taylor. Taking a life was nothing Justin would get over anytime soon, but he had to try for both himself and Max.

Max wrapped his arms around Justin's chest. "You okay, sweetie?"

Justin leaned back against him. Damn, the man felt so right.

"I'm good. It's just going to take some time."

Max kissed the nape of his neck, and Justin shuddered. Justin turned in his arms and brought their lips together. Nothing compared to when Max held him, kissed him. Justin deepened the kiss, their connection reaching into his heart. He wanted to move forward and put all the last seven years behind him, but the memories he'd worked so hard to avoid had been coming in regular intervals since he'd killed Marshall Stone. Doc, Carson, and Walt had all been helpful. Doc with meds. Carson influencing his mind. And Walt allowing him to ramble through the memories. Max was there when the nightmares woke him in a cold sweat.

Max pulled back, his eyes soft and comforting. "I love you, sweetie, with all my heart. You're the love of my life. The minute I saw you in that building, I was drawn to you even though I denied my feelings for you ever since. I'm so happy you're mine. I can't wait to settle down with you and do everything."

Justin grinned wide as he rubbed their foreheads together. "That sounds like heaven. I love you too. And to quote Doc, 'It was about time you got your head out of your ass.'"

Max tilted his head back and laughed. Justin had never heard anything sound so sweet.

"I totally agree."

Justin kissed his lips, his cheeks, his brow, his nose. "Thanks for taking a chance on us."

Max attacked his lips, pushing him back against the counter, hands running over Justin's back. He groaned as their groins pressed together, his cock hard and wanting. When someone coughed, Justin sighed and parted their lips.

Wes and Maggie stood in the doorway, holding trays of food. The adoring expressions on their faces were a little too much.

"Don't let us interrupt." Maggie waggled her eyebrows. "I mean, really, you don't have to stop on my account."

Justin's cheeks heated.

"Jealous, Wright?" Max asked.

Maggie snorted. "As the day is long." She set her tray down. When Justin reached for a piece of pepperoni, she smacked his hand.

He snatched it back. "Ow!"

"It's for the party. Hands off, lover boy."

Wes leaned against the counter next to them, a wide grin splitting his face. He nodded, his gaze moving between them.

"What?" Max pulled Justin against his side. With a covert move, he put a piece of pepperoni into Justin's hand. Quickly, he popped it into his mouth, then pecked Max on the lips.

"I saw that," Maggie called out from where she was arranging cups.

"I did nothing," Justin declared.

Wes shook his head. And was about to grab a piece of pepperoni when his hand was slapped as well. He pulled back. Smirking, he turned his chin up to Maggie, and his eyes softened. The coy smile she returned had Justin raising an eyebrow.

Max brought his mouth close to Justin's ear. "Hey, did we just share their moment?"

Justin beamed. "I think we did."

"What're you two whispering about over there?" Maggie had her hands on her hips and her eyes narrowed.

"Justin wanted me to steal him another piece of pepperoni, but I said I liked my fingers on my hands." Max's expression was totally sincere.

"I did not!" Justin poked Max in the ribs, and he yelped.

"Hey!" Justin jumped at the loud voice. Lincoln stood in the doorway. "Let's go. Short meeting, then we party."

Max took Justin's hand and led him down the hall to the conference room in Medical. Inside, some of the team members already sat around the table while others stood around and talked.

"Okay, everyone. Listen up." Lincoln joined Carson at the end of the table. The room quieted. "First off, I want to thank all of you for your hard work. As usual, you went above and beyond. And I'm proud of each of you for your role in stopping Marshall Stone and Yvonne Nelson. The places this case went were... well, out there."

There was a round of applause and cheers. Max hugged Justin to his side and kissed his temple.

"A quick update. Yes, the news vans are still outside, and a reminder, if they shove a microphone into your face, you can't shove it back."

All eyes went to John, whose petulant stare didn't falter. He shrugged.

"Just avoid them and they'll go away when something shiny catches their eye. We've recovered all but one of the kidnapped humans and one vampire who can't stay out of trouble."

"I'm pretty sure he's learned his lesson." While Carson smiled, Justin could see the cloud of concern in his eyes. Caden was lucky to have come out of the ordeal unscathed except for some mental scars.

Lincoln raked his hands through his hair. "Marshall Stone was Jameson Merrick's daughter, a fact unknown to most everyone. Taylor and Tia found out that Merrick divorced Marshall's mother when Marshall was young and she spent little time with her father."

"Enough to influence her career path." John narrowed his eyes. "Are there any more of Merrick's spawn running around out there that we need to worry about?"

"She appears to be his only child, but Tia and I are still looking into it," Taylor said.

"The biggest problem? She created a fucking vampire. Out of all the humans recovered, it appears that Adam Mitchell is the only one showing signs of transforming. Doc's best guess is that the transformation takes between three to six months. He's doing genetic testing to determine if any of the other humans will turn. All of the humans missing from the Mystique were located except for Devon Hastings, abducted last. None of the information retrieved from Marshall Stone's records lists his name. The records recovered from the trafficking operation are being analyzed now. They were encrypted by software developed by Gale Nelson, and he's directed the programmers at his company to fully cooperate with us in this investigation. Sarina, Yvonne Nelson, and the others who worked for her have lawyered up. Possibly someone will talk if offered a plea deal. Since Devon Hastings was sponsored by Gale Nelson, we've requested to interview him, but he's undergoing psychiatric care. His lawyer is slowly feeding us information as Gale gives it to him. His lawyer did tell us that Gale was the person who left Tara at the gate."

"Did he say why?" Max asked.

Lincoln shook his head. "He didn't, but I'm sure as he releases more information, many of our questions will be answered. His lawyer is working on getting anything that might lead us to Devon Hastings."

Justin's gut twisted as he thought of the missing human, possibly sold to some sadist or dead. He'd been close to being a prisoner of Marshall Stone until she no longer needed him. After that he probably would have been disposed of quietly.

Max squeezed Justin's shoulder and gave him a grateful smile. They were coming off the high of defeating those out to hurt them all.

The aftermath was just as scary for Justin with the flashbacks, moments of confusion, and dissociation when he tried to fight off the automatic responses and behavior. Sometimes he wondered if he was any better off than he'd been during the three months after he first woke up. At least then he couldn't remember, wasn't subjected to flashbacks and nightmares. The only thing that was the same was the anxiety. At least now he knew why.

"Doc is sifting through mountains of medical information. He did find the name of a researcher located in London who discovered the enzymes and the process to evoke the change. London police have confirmed his death in a fire in his lab almost a month ago. The cause of death and the fire is still being investigated, but they suspect foul play."

"Was he working with Marshall Stone?" Dwayne asked.

"That's not clear at this time. They are looking into any connection between the two. Doc has confirmed this researcher was part of the Human Genome Project team. It's possible he worked with Merrick or that they stole his research and he had nothing to do with any of this."

"Possibly."

"So that information dies with both of them? No more vampires from humans?" Justin needed him to say yes.

Lincoln furrowed his brow. "We can't say for sure."

Justin closed his eyes, praying that was the end. If only two vampires were the result instead of billions, that was a win in his book.

Lincoln rubbed the back of his neck. "We still have a load of information to sort through and interviews to conduct. There'll be trials for Yvonne Nelson and those who helped her and those who aided Marshall Stone as well. Sarina Jenkens is cooperating by providing access to their homes. Director Williams and the DA are working closely to assure a smooth transition of evidence between the Nons court and the NVJ. Let's keep it tight and make sure every T is crossed and every loophole closed. Let's make this a slam dunk."

Everyone around the room nodded. Across the room Justin spotted Jordan, who had a bandage covering his forehead. The person he'd chased from Marshall's house had jumped him and hit him hard in the head. He'd needed ten stitches. Sitting by Dwayne, he appeared sullen and withdrawn, even more than usual. Justin wasn't sure what the stolid man's issues were. He'd never been social since he'd arrived.

"Okay." Carson slapped his hands together. "We have a party to attend. We could all use some fun, so everyone out into the lobby."

Officers filtered out of the room, and Justin followed Max. The lobby was decorated with streamers and balloons. A sign on the wall declared, "Happy Birthday, Tommy." Another "Welcome, Ryan." Doc had arranged sort of a birthday for Tommy slash welcome to the world party for Ryan. Tommy's bed had been arranged in the center of the room. He'd been dressed in a T-shirt and sweats, and his hair had been cut. If he wasn't so pale and thin, he'd be close to his old self.

Music started playing, and Doc entered the lobby carrying Ryan, and his beaming smile was indicative of a proud father. The women immediately swarmed him, oohing and aahing. Doc was in his glory.

Justin hung back near the sides of the room, a little overwhelmed. When Max touched his arm, he jumped. "You want a soda?" Max asked.

"Sure. Anything is fine."

Max kissed him and went to the cooler across the room. The noise instantly increased as John's wife and his brood of kids entered. Most of the NVJ officers were single, so it was nice to have a family around. In fact, they were all family, and Justin was finally beginning to feel at home.

Caden entered the room holding Manuel's hand, along with Graham. The kid looked terrified, however when Manuel spotted Justin, he ran over and hugged him around the waist.

Justin accepted his hug gratefully. "Hey, buddy. Glad you came."

Over the past few days, Justin had spent time helping Manuel adjust to freedom and the fact that his mother had truly died. Manuel admitted Yvonne had told him his mother was dead, however he'd held on to some hope. Justin's heart had broken for his tears. He spent time with Walt, and even if Justin hadn't trusted the man at first, he saw how he could help Manuel. Justin was sure eventually he'd be okay.

"I wasn't gonna come, but Caden wanted to but was too scared. He needed someone to come with him."

"You're a good friend, Manuel." Justin looked to Caden, who appeared innocent. "Nice one."

Caden ruffled Manuel's hair. "Hey. It's okay to be scared. Right, Manuel?"

"Right." Manuel's gaze darted around, and when he saw Graham at the snack table, his eyes widened.

"You want some snacks?" Caden asked.

Manuel nodded shyly.

"Okay. But remember, don't eat everything and get sick like yesterday. I swear the kid ate every snack in Lincoln's apartment. Then he puked."

Poor kid had missed a lot.

They walked to the snack table, and Manuel immediately started eating until Caden handed him a plate.

"Animal, I tell you." Caden snickered.

Justin looked across the room and found Max speaking with Casey. Not a twinge of jealousy. Max raised a finger when he noticed Justin and went back to talking.

When Manuel moved down the table with Graham, Justin asked Caden if they'd found any of his family.

"Not yet. For now, he's going to stay with Lincoln and Carson. I swear Lincoln won't let the kid out of his sight. I took him to the commissary yesterday, and he called out a manhunt. Thought he was going to rip my head off when he found us. Nearly floored me when he asked me to watch the kid this morning. And Carson is mothering all over the kid. It's quite disgusting."

Justin thought the kid was very lucky to have them. Caden helped Manuel to sit at one of the tables, and he immediately started to stuff his face.

Caden looked past tired and sad. Justin didn't want to ask, but he did. "Have you seen Sarina?"

Yeah, that flinch was the reason he hadn't wanted to say anything.

"No. She's a bit psycho. I think she thought there was more between us than there was. I liked her as a friend. She was fun, but she wasn't my type. I came back from her beach house because she was getting pushy. Then she showed up at Skylar's that night and tagged along. Then I find out everything…." He snorted. "That she knew what they were doing and may have helped? Yeah. I have enough crazy in my life, thank you very much."

"But she was your friend, so that's gotta hurt."

He shrugged but didn't say anything, and Justin wasn't sure what he was thinking.

"Here." Max handed Justin his soda. "Sorry, just talking to Casey."

"Thanks." After taking a drink, Justin set the can on the table, his arm back around Max.

Lincoln and Carson came to the table, and Manuel looked up at Lincoln with what looked to be a questioning expression. Lincoln grinned and pulled his iPhone from his pocket. "Can I play Minecraft?"

"Play on my phone?"

Manuel rolled his eyes. "Yeah, on your phone."

"Well I guess you can play if you can get it away from me." Lincoln took off across the room.

"Lincoln!" Manuel chased after Lincoln, trying to tackle him around the waist, but he merely dragged the underweight kid. Lincoln bent and grabbed Manuel and threw him over his shoulder. The kid squealed, begging to be put down, laughing raucously as Lincoln galloped around the room.

"Say Lincoln is the king of the universe!"

"Never in a million years!"

Carson shook his head, but Justin could see the love in his expression. "I live with two kids now." Carson growled like a monster and chased after them.

"Yeah, there's only two kids in that apartment." Caden crossed his arms, rolling his eyes.

They chuckled, and Justin took in everyone in the room, talking—in fact, celebrating—for so many reasons. Across the room, Doc had broken free of everyone and placed a sleeping Ryan in the crook of his father's arm, surrounding him with pillows. Doc ran his hand over Tommy's cheek and whispered something in his ear. The sight of Doc, Tommy, and his baby caused a flutter in Justin's stomach.

"I'll be right back," Justin told Max, who smiled and nodded.

Justin made his way to Tommy's bed, gazing on the sleeping angel beside him. He tried to imagine a little Max in their lives and found that he liked the idea. Someday, he and Max could have a family. Nothing could stop them from having whatever they decided.

"B-baby."

The word had been whispered, but when Justin looked up, no one was near them.

Tommy shifted, his head turning slightly. "Baby." The word was long, drawn out, but Justin had understood. He gasped, stepping back, unsure what to do.

He searched the room for Doc and yelled to him. "Doc, could you come here?"

Doc came to the bed, his eyes on the baby, who still slept. "What's wrong?"

Justin pointed to Tommy. "He said 'baby' twice. I swear."

The astonished look on Doc's face as he turned to Tommy was priceless. "Hey, Tommy Boy, did you say something?" He rubbed his thumb over Tommy's forehead. "Something you want to say?"

Tommy blinked rapidly, his eyes appearing to go in and out of focus on Doc's face. His legs moved in a jerky fashion. His mouth opened and closed without sound, and his arms twitched. Ryan snuffled in his sleep, then quieted.

"It's okay, honey. Just relax. You don't have to talk if you don't want to."

Tommy's agitation lowered, and his eyes remained on Doc's face. His cheeks twitched, and his lips moved in an exaggerated fashion. "H-hold... baby."

Doc smiled wide, his lips trembling. "Yeah, you're holding your son. You're holding Ryan."

The glassiness in Doc's eyes told Justin something amazing had just happened. He went to Max to tell him what he'd seen when the music abruptly stopped. Max smiled and pulled Justin close as Lincoln pointed a remote at the TV.

"Director Williams just called me. We need to watch this."

The room was quiet as the TV showed a man and a woman standing at a podium with a cluster of microphones on the front. The man had his arm around the woman. Both were clearly distraught.

"Oh, fuck me." Lincoln glared at the TV.

"What is it?" Justin tried to read the words on the screen.

Max wiped at his mouth. "Those are Tara Collette's parents. What the...." Max trailed off as the man began to speak.

"We're here to warn the public of a great danger to all humans, to our families, our children. Our daughter Tara was kidnapped by vampires. She was held captive in a cage and tortured." The man frowned, his lips quivering as his wife cried silently beside him. Justin wanted to puke right there, because he knew what that man was going to say and was horrified by the scene before him.

"Don't do it," Max muttered. "You son of a bitch, don't do it."

Justin's heart pounded in his ears. He'd been the one responsible for turning their daughter into a vampire. He was still the key. What if people found out about him? What if...? Suddenly, any semblance of safety he'd acquired fled.

The camera closed in on their faces, their anguish and pain. Their fucking human privilege about to declare war on vampires.

"She was turned into a vampire. Our baby girl is a now a dirty, disgusting vampire. We are all in danger. Every single one of us. The vampires must be stopped."

The silence in the room was loud. Justin turned helplessly to Max and saw the terror on his lover's face. All they could do was wrap around each other as the room exploded into chaos.

JAKE C. WALLACE started writing from a young age, but took a break for marriage, kids, and college (in that order). A few years ago, he rediscovered his passion for writing stories and ventured out into the brave new world of publishing. He has published several novels and short stories. Recently, his novel *Jerricho's Freedom* was a finalist in the Rainbow Book Awards.

At night and on the weekends, Jake writes about all things men, believing there is nothing hotter than two men finding and loving one another, whether for a night or forever. An avid reader of M/M romance, Jake loves a good twist of a plot, HEA, HFN, or tragic ending, and has over two thousand books in his library. He also writes what his best friend calls HUNKs (Happy Until the Next Kidnapping). In his daytime hours, Jake works with individuals with autism and behavior issues. He is owned by a beautiful partner, three kids, and two grandchildren. He lives in northern Vermont.

Website: www.jcwallacebooks.com
Facebook: www.facebook.com/jcwallacebooks
Twitter: @jcwallacebooks.com
E-mail: jcwallacebooks@gmail.com

JAKE C. WALLACE

NEW VAMPIRE JUSTICE: BOOK ONE

DARE
TO LOVE
FOREVER

New Vampire Justice: Book One

With pain and loss in their pasts and evil threatening their futures, two vampires will find a love that lasts forever… if they dare.

Carson Locke is dangerous, even by vampire standards. A rare Tabula Rasa vampire, he can wipe the mind of those he bites—human or vampire. Because of this, he's lived his entire life in isolation. When his family is murdered, Carson runs from those who want him dead. Injured, starving, and about to be executed, he meets Commander Lincoln Samuels, an officer in the New Vampire Justice police force.

Lincoln, a Sanatore vampire, possesses the gift of healing. The moment he encounters Carson, broken and terrified, trying to steal blood to survive, he is compelled to help the other man—despite the risk to himself. Their bond creates something the world has never seen, but others have plans for Carson and his destiny was written long before he was born. He'll either become a tool to control the vampire world or, with Lincoln by his side, find the courage to fight and become its savior.

www.dreamspinnerpress.com

FOR **MORE** OF THE **BEST GAY ROMANCE**

www.ingramcontent.com/pod-product-compliance
Lightning Source LLC
Chambersburg PA
CBHW051541260626
47170CB00003B/1042